Inbound to Earth

1st Edition printed 2009: ISBN 978-0-9781357-8-2

Note for Librarians: a catalog record for this book that includes Dewey Decimal Classification and U.S. Library of Congress numbers is available from the Library and Archives of Canada. The complete catalog record can be obtained from their online database at:
www.collectionscanada.ca/amicus/index-e.html

ISBN 978-1-927438-29-9

Powell River Books
Powell River BC, Canada
Book sales online at:
www.powellriverbooks.com
phone: 604-483-1704
email: wlutz@mtsac.edu

10 9 8 7 6 5 4 3 2 1

Inbound to Earth

Wayne J. Lutz

2018
Powell River Books

Science Fiction by Wayne J. Lutz

Echo of a Distant Planet
Inbound to Earth
Anomaly at Fortune Lake
When Galaxies Collide
Across the Galactic Sea

Other Books by Wayne J. Lutz
in the series *Coastal British Columbia Stories*

Up the Lake
Up the Main
Up the Winter Trail
Up the Strait
Up the Airway
Farther Up the Lake
Farther Up the Main
Farther Up the Strait
Cabin Number 5
Off the Grid
Up the Inlet
Powell Lake by Barge and Quad
Off the Grid – Getting Started

Cover Photos:
Front Cover – M31, Andromeda Galaxy, with satellite galaxy
(M32) at lower left; Hubble Space Telescope
Back Cover – M57, Ring Nebula in Lyra, with 15th-magnitude
central star that created the nebula; Hubble Space Telescope

Chapter 1

Home Planet

MQ was fully reclined in the blockhouse, looking through the digital displays covering the glass wall. Beyond the transparent panels, the powerful transmission tower dominated the landscape. Easily the largest structure on the planet, the edifice was even taller than the lofty structures needed for scrubbing the atmosphere.

MQ's body was stretched full-length on the chair-like device that allowed him to arch his back as much as possible into an upright position. It was more like lying down than sitting. But his head was high enough to simultaneously watch the projected displays and the scene outside, all the way down to the horizon.

Cool drops of salt water seeped from the life-support machine, landing just below his eyes, sliding slowly down his skin – a gentle cascade of water to keep him wet while he worked.

He felt a voice. Surely it was SJ, so he changed his concentration to receive the full message. He liked the feel of her soft tone.

"Our opportunity is approaching. Are all power sources reasonable? Sources reasonable?"

"Power is reasonable," said MQ. He paused to give SJ a chance to feel his confirming message. "But is it really worth it? Worth it?"

Someone else might be listening. This was taking a chance. Although the Great Minds encouraged discussion, this wasn't the place for it. Caution was prudent.

"We must try," said SJ. "Our vehicle is approaching the target, and will begin decelerating soon. Our module will be prepared to receive us. Receive us."

"The tower is ready to transmit. Too bad it won't be on our shift. Our shift."

He waited for a reply from SJ, but he might have missed it. The digital displays were requiring more of his attention now. He felt her voice, but he missed the first few words.

". . . get back to the water soon. Next shift gets the glory. The glory."

The next shift would transmit the data. But no one was making claims for success quite yet. It was an untested procedure. Plans for engineering changes to the receiver module aboard the spacecraft were complex. And without those critical modifications, the vehicle couldn't complete its mission. This signal would send the data, but the likelihood of the signal getting through was minimal. Yet they had to try.

Outside the window, the tower was tilted slightly away from the zenith, aligned with the target star and precisely focused on the soon-arriving vehicle. The majestic structure represented the first major phase of new technology developed since the launch of the spacecraft over a decade ago.

For MQ to remain out of the water this long was difficult. His species was much better at thinking in the sea than working on the land. It took thousands of them, operating in seamless teamwork, to accomplish a task like this. It seemed you no more than sat down than it was time to relinquish your position to the next shift. Then it was back to the sea. But if you wanted something bad enough, it was possible. They wanted this bad enough.

"That's about all we can do. Can do," said SJ.

To MQ, the feel of her voice was worth all of the effort.

"It's time," replied MQ. "The transmitter is ready. And we did it. It won't be instantaneous, but it's a lot faster than the speed of light. Of light."

"Yes, it's time to go," said SJ. "The next shift will send the message. And the vehicle's machines will have to make their own decisions. Own decisions."

MQ stretched back even farther. That put him in a near-horizontal position, looking straight up. The digital displays extended to the top of the rounded dome that formed the ceiling.

"See you again. You again." Said MQ.

He hoped it was true.

"Yes, maybe. Yes, maybe."

Chapter 2

Inbound

Darkness and absolute cold. Computers lived their sterile existence without even the blink of subdued panel lights. Within the hollow sphere hurtling toward the target star, communication was alive in the dark.

There was no sound – not even the hum of these machines. When sound did try to propagate, it evaporated into the vacuum of space. Within this vehicle, no hint of atmosphere had existed for more than a decade. Nor was breathing necessary for these mechanisms. Analyze and report – that was their only functions for the present, and reporting had meant little in the most recent portion of this journey. Information transmitted now would be received back at the home planet long after the spacecraft arrived at its target.

The target was a nondescript yellow star, and a decision was imminent. As the star revealed details of its planetary system, the final route continued to be debated. At time of launch, only four planets were known to surround this star, all of them gas-giants. The gravitational pull of giant planets promotes the development of smaller planets and supports life throughout the galaxy. Moons around gas-giants like these are common, and such moons are sometimes covered with ice. Beneath that ice, oceans may be found. And in those oceans, heated by the giant planet's tidal force, life may abound. Such may be the case within the extensive satellite system around the largest planet within this solar system. One of these icy moons is a prime candidate for life.

Four more rocky planets and numerous outlying objects were detected during the voyage. Two of these planets were being analyzed regularly, their moons long ago removed from consideration. The largest gas-giant remained the prime target. But recently, the third planet from the star was overshadowing that candidate, especially after detection of sporadic electromagnetic emissions. Radio transmissions, including video and audio data, were detected and translated. The first signal received was in the VHF band – a strange video transmission featuring a resilient creature called David Letterman. More unique signals had been detected since then, translated through a variety of fuzzy-logic conversions.

The new candidate was a rocky world, covered by liquid water, so exceptional in the universe. It displayed moist shores – opportune for life. Creatures had been able to transition from the sea, a process demanding an extended period of adaptation, along with a bit of luck. Back on the home planet, life had been held almost perpetually hostage to the sea.

Two encouraging planets, significantly dissimilar and offering distinctly different life sources. The gas-giant possessed an additional advantage as a fuel source for the spacecraft, if it was ever to return home.

The interior of the vehicle was dark and smooth. The panel displays on the flat wall were visible only in the infrared. No known form of intelligent life could see anything in that darkness, unless aided by artificial optics.

Absolute cold sunk into every surface. Yet, on the other side of the flat wall, there was heat. Some of the heat was derived from the continuous energy of the computer bay itself. Most, however, was residual energy from the fusion of atoms, standing ready for the tremendous deceleration. This spacecraft had floated ballistically for the last portion of its journey; initially accelerated to a tremendous velocity and then allowed to hurtle through space unpowered for nearly the entire voyage. No similar engine had remained idle in the cold of space for so long. But the Great Minds at home were confident the powerplant would respond again when needed.

The first deceleration burn would begin soon, but it would be merely a prelude to the powerful fires still to come. The selection of the target world was imminent, followed by additional deceleration burns and then orbital insertion. But the Great Minds would have no say in those decisions, for the communication delay now far exceeded the value of any otherwise constructive inputs. So the final selection of a destination would be made within this spacecraft by intelligence evolved during the flight between the stars.

Darkness and cold within. But soon there would be heat – tremendous heat. And there would also be light – brilliant light visible to an entire solar system.

Chapter 3

Sunday, January 10, 2016

Mercurial Flare

Kelly's feet were curled beneath herself on the sofa. Within the darkness of the living room, she spoke into the telephone. The muted television was the only source of light.

"Hi, Christine. Sorry I'm so late."

"No problem. Where've you been?"

"Oh, I've been around. Right now I'm getting ready to go outside with Tannon. He's chasing some stars."

"Figures."

Kelly waited for more, but apparently Christine had made her point. Kelly broke the silence.

"I won't be able to make it tonight. It's getting late, and we haven't had dinner yet. How's your schedule next week?"

"Same old thing," said Christine. "I work every night through Thursday, but Friday is open."

"Friday it is. Shall I bring Tannon?"

"Very cute. Why don't you bring him, and we'll barbecue him for dinner."

"Nice talk, friend. He likes you, whether you believe it or not."

"I know," said Christine in a more conciliatory tone. "But he really doesn't get the big picture."

"He's pretty understanding. You just have to break things to him gently. Brothers are like that, I guess."

"Okay, I'm sure you're right. But he's still a guy. Not his best trait."

Kelly laughed. Christine was always quick to criticize her brother, but it was Christine who was the most unwilling to compromise.

"How are you feeling, Kell?"

"Better. Lots better. It was just one of those things. Not your fault."

"I know that. Try getting some sleep."

"I will. See you Friday."

* * * * *

It was cold by Southern California standards, even for January. The clearness of the night added to the penetrating chill, as Tannon Bessimer waited impatiently. His lanky body was encased in a ski parka that could take care of winter in Alaska. The jacket was zipped to the top, creating an annoying rub against his throat. His toes, bundled in thick hiking boots and two pairs of socks, wiggled with anticipation.

"Sis, I may have launched us on another wild goose chase. What time is it?"

Kelly slid the cuff of her oversized windbreaker above her watch and brought her thin wrist toward her face. In the dim evening light, she could barely see the watch's unlit digital display. It seemed her vision was deteriorating lately – not really alarming, but certainly noticeable. Her body released a shiver, and her throat faintly echoed it.

"Fourteen minutes before six. Pretty soon?"

"A few minutes now, but it won't take much to miss it in these crappy sky conditions. Clear, but way too much light." In the cold air, Tannon's voice sounded even rougher than his normal raspy tone.

How often had Tannon dragged Kelly out of the house to view some promised astronomical phenomenon? Their standing joke was that most of these events were missed in their obscurity. Once in a while though, they hit something remarkable.

Tannon, college teacher, age 39, soon to turn 40. But his younger sister knew better than to have anything planned for his birthday, except maybe a private dinner together. For the last 30 of his years, Tannon had kept his head pointed skyward. Most of the time, he concealed his interest in astronomy from those around him. In his youth, stargazing wasn't considered macho. Astronomy was no longer his career ambition – that had been squelched almost twenty years ago. But now he enjoyed being a devoted amateur astronomer.

"Mercurial satellite flares are quite predictable, except for brightness," noted Tannon. "This one is supposed to be magnitude minus three, which is brighter than any star, so it should be spectacular, even if it's way off in magnitude."

Kelly obediently kept her neck craned upward. Her tall, thin stature was enhanced by her oversized windbreaker. She looked southward, halfway up the sky. Her interest in astronomy was all but nonexistent. Her only consolation in this cold event was that it excited her brother.

"So, will it light up suddenly?" she asked.

"Well, if you're staring at the right spot when it catches the sun, it'll seem to grow from nothing. The satellite's antenna array is what catches the sunlight. The solar panels are silver-coated Teflon for thermal control – makes them perfect mirrors."

"Antenna array with thermal control. That sounds like you. Lay off the tech talk, Brother."

"Hey, you're about to witness a celestial phenomenon."

Tannon had observed older-generation communication satellites as they flared through their brief dab of sunlight. But he had never treated Kelly to their short-lived brilliance, and this was the more-reflective Mercury constellation of telephone satellites. There wasn't much he didn't share with his sister – thus, this evening's venture in the twilight and cold behind their house. The backyard was neither large nor very dark tonight. The patio's small size confined the astronomical view, with many of the constellations out of sight behind the nearby trees to the east or behind the house itself to the south. In the center of the patio was a picnic table, leaving enough room for several chairs and a small hot tub.

The western sky was still orange from the departing sun. The glow of the small city of San Dimas merged with nearby Los Angeles to make the stars barely visible. It wasn't the ideal spot for astronomical observations.

On the picnic table sat Tannon's trusty old Astroscan telescope, an ancient piece of equipment from his first astronomical observations when he was only 10 years old. But, for now, watching a Mercury satellite flaring to brilliance was best seen with the naked eye.

"There!" yelled Tannon.

He felt that same youthful stab of excitement as the satellite flared from nothing. The bright light moved quickly downward toward the southern horizon, passing behind a high cirrus cloud. The cloud dimmed the flare only a little, like a bright aircraft landing light pealing through the overcast. The satellite swooped toward the horizon, quickly dimmed, and was gone behind the roof of the house – five seconds, at the most.

"Wow," said Kelly, with honest enthusiasm. "That's really incredible."

She regretted her enthusiasm immediately, as Tannon went into a three-minute dissertation about the Mercury satellites, including their launch history, orbital parameters, and the usual technical stuff.

"Uh huh," said Kelly.

She really did appreciate Tannon's attempts to share his interests with her. But the technical details weren't important.

"Maybe you should get back inside?" prompted Tannon, knowing Kelly's light jacket wasn't very warm for the conditions.

"Yeah, I should. Are you going to stay out awhile?"

"I'll only be a few minutes. There's a star on my viewing list called Tau Ceti. Then how about Burger King?"

"Okay. Let me know when."

As Kelly carefully stepped toward the French doors in the darkness, she pondered Tannon. She appreciated all of her older brother's attention. There was very little not shared between them. Tau Ceti and Burger King were a strange combination, but it worked for them.

Chapter 4

Kelly

Tannon is my brother. I find it necessary to remind myself of that quite often.

He saved me from myself five years ago. Upstate New York, after Dad died, wasn't the place for me. But I didn't know that. I got into trouble by hanging out with the wrong people. Nothing big, but any record of drugs could've killed my flying career.

Then Tannon insisted I come live with him in California. He wouldn't take "No" for an answer. After we discussed things for months, he finally showed up on my doorstep in Syracuse, and moved in. Eventually, he simply hauled me away. I didn't leave kicking and screaming, but I certainly didn't make up my own mind to go. If he hadn't handed me that airline ticket, I'd probably still be thinking about it.

We've shared a lot, particularly in the past few years. Before then, we hardly knew each other. He was just my nerdy older brother, and he embarrassed me a bit. I knew he was smart, but he really didn't seem to be headed much of anywhere. He knew how to handle school, but the universities and the military didn't equate to a real job, at least in my convoluted mind. It just seemed to me that he was where he was because he couldn't handle anything else.

Of course, my family treated me like I was precious. But I resented the fact it was mostly because I was a girl. I didn't believe it in the least. Nor did most of the people who really knew me.

I had no real goals, except my passion for flying. I can't live without it. Everybody, especially Tannon, told me I needed to finish college, if I was going to make a career out of flying. I'm still working on it, but not very hard.

When Dad died, Mom saw no need to hoard the insurance money. She's pretty well set for life, and she asked us what we wanted. Tannon was on his way to a successful career in science, such as it was. And he wanted to do it on his own. I asked for money to fly. It's the best investment anybody ever made in me, although far from inexpensive. Someday I may be able to pay Mom back, if I get an airline job. But I'd just as soon delay that for a while.

I really thought I was going to blow the money with only a fly-to-brunch pilot's license to show for it. But pretty soon it was clear I could be a flight instructor, if that's what I wanted. The question was whether or not I really wanted it.

There wasn't anybody willing to hire an inexperienced female flight instructor in Syracuse, but Tannon made a great student in the meantime. When he moved in with me that summer, I almost had to trap him into learning to fly. He had just finished playing junior physicist in the Air Force and needed to wait for the next semester of graduate school to begin at USC, so he gave in. I had a full summer to get him hooked on flying, and it gave Mom a use for the rest of her loose money. Of course, Tannon insisted on paying Mom back for his flying lessons, and I think he eventually did.

It was a summer to remember. Just fly and be with Tannon. Nearly every morning, we'd head out to the practice area from Hancock Field, Tannon in the left seat and me in the right. He was the perfect student. And the perfect brother. As my flight student, he asked some tough questions, but together we worked them all out. For the first time in our lives, I was in charge.

I loved the challenge of teaching my brother to fly. We spent most evenings pouring over the books and charts, getting Tannon ready for his private pilot flight test. We really got to know each other. You could almost say we were two distant relatives who finally began to like each other and then ran off to live our lives together.

Tannon got his private pilot license and eventually his instrument rating. That's the first real role I played in his life, and it became an important accomplishment for both of us. That instrument rating made me especially proud, since it proved Tannon was really serious about flying. I know it didn't start out that way. I'd like to think my brother learned something from me that he couldn't have found anywhere else. And I gave it to him. Two years ago, he even bought an airplane, a Piper Arrow. And now flying is an even bigger part of his life. So am I.

After we moved to California and Tannon settled into graduate school, I didn't have many constructive uses for my abundant free time. And that caused some problems. I finally got a job as a flight instructor, but it only got me further into trouble. I did the things girls my age were supposed to do, and that was the real source of the disaster. Men aren't my cup of tea. Nor is growing up.

I went downhill fast. On my worst days, I blamed it on Tannon for leaving me at home while he made a routine of going to school during the day and studying endlessly in his room at night. On my better days, I blamed others for taking Tannon away. In an attempt to punish somebody, I moved out, renting a small apartment a few miles away. I was really only punishing myself. I somehow thought it would make me feel better, but it didn't.

I knew Tannon didn't have any real friends other than me. He has always been a loner. Within Tannon is a bit of a recluse. I worry about it because it reminds me of myself.

When Tannon decided to stay in California after graduate school and take a teaching job, I refused to talk to him for months. I felt I had lost him forever. If Tannon weren't so forgiving, I certainly would have.

But he came back for me, asking me to move in with him again. Just like coming for me in Syracuse. He saved me from where I'd been. He may have even saved me from where I'm still headed. Who knows for sure?

Chapter 5

Tau Ceti

Kelly entered the living room, passing through the tall French doors from the backyard, careful not to turn on any lights that would disrupt Tannon's stargazing outside on the patio. She took care of her brother these days the best she could. And he took care of her, beyond what any sister should expect or even desire. Within both of them was a private pledge of protection.

She paused in the darkness just inside the house to let her eyes adjust. The warmth of their home replaced the evening cold. She peeled off her windbreaker, flinging it onto the back of the sofa directly ahead of her. She could find her way from here in the dim light. It would be quite awhile before her brother returned from the patio, because that was always the way it was. Tannon loved his stars, and Kelly understood. You didn't have to share the same interests to share your lives.

* * * * *

Out on the patio, Tannon surveyed the southern horizon. It still wasn't fully dark, but the viewing conditions in this brightly-lit town were so poor that the visibility of stars wouldn't get much better. Besides, for Tannon, it was the perception of what he was viewing that really mattered. A small aperture Astroscan wasn't going to let him see anything particularly astounding, even in totally dark conditions. But he knew enough about astronomy to let his mind fill in the gaps.

Leisurely, Tannon surveyed the sky. His ears were a bit cold, but his hands were comfortably sunk into his lined jacket pockets. Out of the corner of his eye, he watched Kelly moving farther into the living room. He knew she would be careful not to turn on lights that would disturb his night vision. No matter how hard she tried to act disruptive with the rest of the world, Kelly couldn't refrain from being his caring sister. In Tannon's eyes, she could do no wrong. Tannon and Kelly possessed powers over each other neither of them fully understood, nor try to analyze.

He focused on Kelly now and watched her thin silhouette, barely visible against the dark background. In profile, her boyish figure was that of a tall child. She stood motionless for a few moments and then stepped farther into the darkness of the living room.

Tannon returned his attention to the glories of the night sky. His target tonight, now that he had seen the Mercurial Flare, was low in the southern sky. Tannon's telescope was somewhat of a joke to both professional and serious amateur astronomers. His father had purchased it for him in preparation for what was to become the astronomical flop of the 1980s – Halley's Comet. That decade prompted the sale of a lot of Astroscans, since it was an ideal scope for wide-field observing. As the Volkswagen of telescopes, it was inexpensive, rugged, and available in a single color – red. Amateur telescopes had transitioned to high-tech instruments, and this relic wasn't even close. For the same 1980s price as the Astroscan, even considering inflation, you could now buy a computer-driven scope of gee-whiz proportions.

Tannon kept the telescope as a prized possession. It reminded him of his father's love for science, and his desire to see Tannon conquer things he himself had been unable to tread. These days, Tannon was pretty much there, although still only an amateur astronomer. His dad hadn't lived to see his academic achievements, but the Astroscan served as a reminder that his father would have been very proud.

The unusual telescope sat on the table, looking like the collision of a stubby plastic tube with a bowling ball. Overall, it was less than two feet high with a reflecting mirror in the spherical base. Rather than a tripod, a curved tan metal cradle held the telescope. The eyepiece was focused through a less than precise gear-knob arrangement. But the Astroscan was rugged and traveled well. With a comfortable field diameter of three degrees, six times the size of the full moon, the Astroscan was a gem for wide-field viewing. It wasn't a high-magnification instrument, with an eyepiece of only 56-power, but the lights of Los Angeles didn't allow serious astronomical observing anyway. The chubby Astroscan, after all these years, was still the perfect set-it-up-quick telescope for Tannon.

Most amateur astronomers liked the Astroscan's rock-solid design, but hated the contortions needed to align an object for viewing. The flimsy sighting rack was simple but problematic, consisting of a piece of flat-black metal with a hole in each end. When trying to sight up the tube to find a star, the bowling ball got in the way. But Tannon put up with these flaws – his red telescope's quirky personality was worth the tradeoff for optical simplicity and a rugged design.

Like all astronomical telescopes, the Astroscan's mirror projected an inverted image, so every movement had to be managed in reverse. Up was down. Right was left. But with a little experience, movement came naturally.

Before trying to find Tau Ceti, tonight's primary target, Tannon selected a familiar friend in the sky to test-focus his Astroscan. This bright star, Vega, was easy to find – low in the northwestern sky, and stunningly brilliant.

Using the metal sighting rack, Tannon aligned the red tube of the bowling ball on Vega. When he looked in the eyepiece, a slight nudge to the right brought the star into the center of the field of view. Shining bright, with optical diffraction spikes extending outward, there really wasn't much to see except one very bright white star. But concept was everything to Tannon. His mind drifted to the oblong dust patch extending outward from Vega with dimensions similar to our own solar system, and possibly even its own set of planets. Of course, in Tannon's Astroscan, none of this was visible – just brilliant Vega shining in the eyepiece. Twenty years ago, the 15-meter mirror at the Keck Observatory in Hawaii had identified a huge dust disk around Vega. Using infrared technology, the Keck telescope had detected an infant solar system. At least that's what astronomers believed they were seeing. The tiny Astroscan was neither large enough nor infrared in its capabilities. So Tannon gazed at the dazzling star and thought about the concept. As usual when observing objects with a possible tie to alien life, it made him feel very small and comfortably lonely.

He picked up a circular plastic sky chart from the picnic table and beamed his red-lens flashlight on it. To get a rough placement of the constellations, he rotated the 6:00 pm mark on the chart to the date, January 10th. He faced south and held the chart at full-arm's length, aiming about 45 degrees above the horizon. From this vantagepoint, Tannon could scan the low constellations and still see the chart with his flashlight. He rotated the chart so "North" pointed upward and behind him toward Polaris. By matching up a few of the brighter stars with those on the sky chart, he found his target – the constellation of Cetus.

The overhanging roof, only 30 feet away, was too close to permit low telescopic views to the south, so Tannon carefully slid the Astroscan to the northernmost edge of the picnic table. From there, the view would just clear the eaves so he could inspect the proper region of the sky, about forty degrees above the horizon. Tau Ceti, his focus of attention tonight, was in the lower part of the constellation, placing it uncomfortably close to the roof. Now both the city skyglow and the heat waves rising from the roof interrupted his view. But the conditions should be adequate enough for observing this naked-eye star in the telescope.

Tannon was getting colder, especially his hands. He had removed his gloves, since they didn't work well on the focus knob. His fingertips throbbed a bit, so he kept his hands in his jacket pockets as much as possible.

"Great – there goes Kelly!" grumbled Tannon to himself.

She extinguished the living room light almost as quickly as she turned it on, realizing the havoc she had just played on Tannon's night-adapted eyes. It was too late, but at least her action to quickly douse the light was considerate. It was hard to keep up with Tannon's quirky needs, so Kelly simply did her best.

Tannon paused a moment, took a few steps back from the table, and stretched his neck towards the sky's zenith, allowing his eyes to again adapt to the darkness. He crunched his head backward to take advantage of the stretch and felt his neck crack. Cranking his head left and right, the crunching sound repeated itself.

As he walked back to the telescope in the dark, he whacked his shin on the picnic table's bench seat.

"Ouch!" he said to no one but himself. "That'll hurt tomorrow."

He turned back to the Astroscan, lowered his head to the sighting rack, and gazed with both eyes open at the constellation of Cetus. It wasn't a remarkable formation of stars, but the compact tail of the celestial whale (it sure looked like a head) was evident. Just below and to the right of the tail was Mira, a reddish variable star of some fame. Glancing back at his circular sky chart, he compared the constellation's structure, looking for Tau Ceti, supposedly at the corner of the whale's mouth. He was hunting for a 3.5 magnitude star, barely visible to the naked eye in the city's glow.

There it was, shining dimly near the bottom of Cetus. With his right eye open, left eye closed, he tried to align the star with the metal sighting rack. It was an inexact science.

When Tau Ceti seemed to be properly aligned, Tannon raised his head to the telescope's eyepiece. Slightly off-center was Tau Ceti, pale yellow and nondescript. A slight nudge down and to the left brought the image into the middle of the field of view. Similar to Vega, there wasn't much to see except an average yellow star.

But Tau Ceti was only twelve light-years away, and that placed it among the twenty nearest stars. For the past few months, Tannon had been going down a list of the closest stars, viewing as many as possible. Considering the brief period of the hunt, he was pleased to have already viewed five of the nearby stars. Tau Ceti was one of the brightest.

Many of the nearest stars were below the limiting magnitude of his telescope. The brightest stars were generally huge but far away. Even those that were both nearby and bright weren't of much interest. Sirius, for example, was a binary star, each of a spectral type vastly different from our sun, and it was impossible to see the dimmer star in a small telescope. To expect Sirius to harbor a life-bearing planet was almost unthinkable, considering the disruptive gravitational effects of a binary system. The probability of life elsewhere in the universe was part of Tannon's conceptual challenge. Maybe someday we could communicate with beings on planets of nearby stars. Tannon often peered at these glowing balls of gas and imagined other living creatures looking back at him. It wasn't a difficult idea to accept. But it was impossible to prove. So as Tannon Bessimer gazed at Tau Ceti, he considered his hypothesis. There it was again – a comfortable, lonely feeling that often inspired him. It was proof positive that concept was everything.

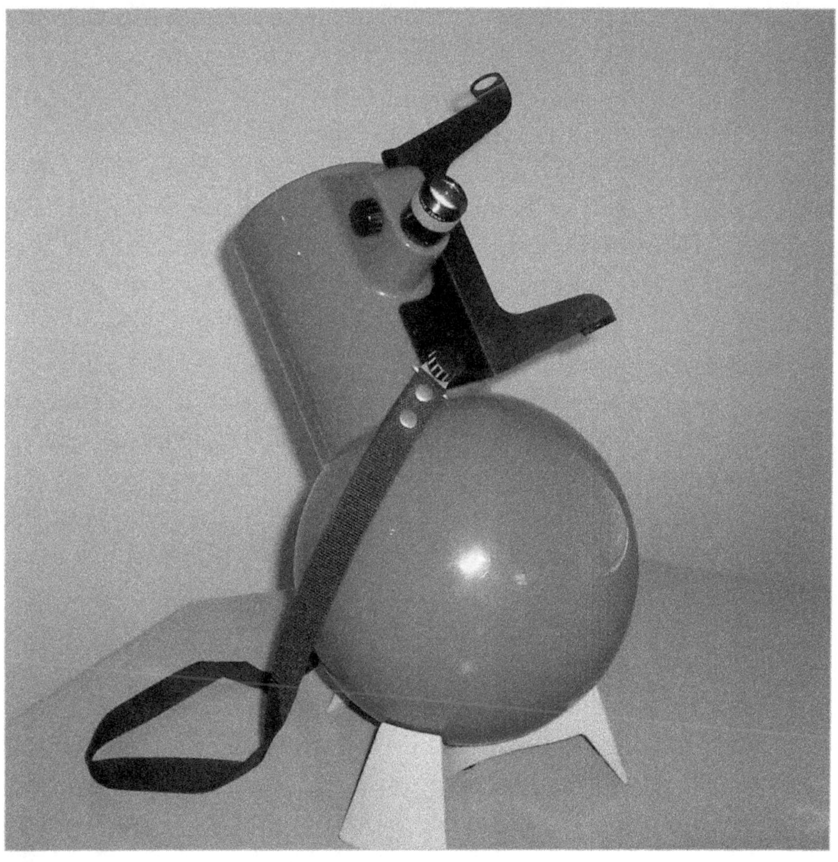

* * * * *

Tau Ceti hovered in the Astroscan, ripples of roof heat disrupting the image. This star wasn't out of the question as a haven for life-bearing planets. It was cooler than the sun, with a spectral class of G8, but any G-star could be in the proper size and temperature range ideal for life-zone planets like our earth. At least that was Tannon's optimistic viewpoint.

As he studied the yellow star, Tannon noted the surrounding field of view in the eyepiece. After crouching low over the Astroscan for a few minutes, he stretched his body up and away from the telescope for some relief. From his pocket, he removed a folded note, transcribed from his star atlas. It was a rough pencil drawing of the star field surrounding Tau Ceti. He turned the diagram upside down to match the telescope's inverted view. In the red light of the filtered flashlight he studied the drawing for a few seconds. Then, returning to the eyepiece, he nudged the telescope a bit toward the west to match the movement of the rotating earth, and centered Tau Ceti again.

Just to the left of Tau Ceti was a fainter star. It shimmered only a few arc minutes away, with a magnitude of about seven or eight. The dim star was barely visible in the roof's shimmering heat. In fact, was it there at all? It flickered in and out of view, holding steady for a moment as the roof's rampage of rising heat steadied. Then the dim star was gone.

Located so close to Tau Ceti, why had his star atlas not shown this object? Or maybe he had missed it on his rough pencil drawing. There was supposed to be a magnitude 8.4 star farther to the right, and Tannon verified this star was in its proper place. It seemed about the same brightness as the unidentified point of light, but was much more prominent because of its position farther away from Tau Ceti's glare.

Tannon pulled away from the red telescope, rubbed his eyes with his cold hands, and rechecked the drawing. What he was seeing in the eyepiece definitely didn't match the pencil sketch. Probably there was an error in his drawing or maybe even in the star atlas itself. Or, on a more exotic level, maybe Tannon had hit on something new in the universe. If so, he wasn't sure what to do about it.

Chapter 6

Siblings

The darkness and cold were easy to abandon. Tannon stepped through the French doors into the living room. The blaring sound of old punk rock immediately surrounded him. A music video station on the television belted out a song that was rough and too loud for Tannon's taste. Nor were the pulsating camera scenes within Tannon's sense of order.

Kelly was nowhere in sight.

Tannon turned on the tall, brass floor lamp and unzipped his jacket. He consciously paused and tried to absorb the warmth of the living room. He attempted to ignore the music, concentrating instead on the reassuring heat of the furnace and the smell from the kitchen that wafted past his cold nose.

He walked to the kitchen and found a pan of clam chowder boiling high and wild. He turned the burner to "Warm." Fortunately, Kelly hadn't waited for a trip to Burger King. Right now, any food sounded great, as long as it was immediate. They lived and ate simply, and at the moment, that was a blessing.

He picked up the large wooden spoon next to the pot, and stirred the chowder, attempting to scrape the congealed liquid from the bottom of the pan. He was still stirring the chowder to smoothness when Kelly came out of her bedroom. She was dressed in a maroon sweatshirt and her favorite olive drab khakis – pants you seldom saw these days, particularly on women. Her black hair was perfectly straight, cut short at the jawline with long bangs. Her hair was perfectly straight, reminding Tannon of an ancient Egyptian priestess. She wore thick white socks and no shoes. Her turquoise reading glasses draped from a blue neck strap. These eyeglasses were her biggest fashion statement, and few people got to see them except Tannon.

Those who met Kelly were usually surprised to learn she was a flight instructor. Everyone was usually surprised such a thin body could yank around a high-performance airplane. But she did just that, and quite comfortably.

"Find anything special out there?" asked Kelly.

"Not much, except a star that's not in the atlas. And a banged shin from the picnic table."

Tannon stripped off his jacket and walked back into the living room, while Kelly followed. He draped his jacket over the back of the rocking chair and sat down to untie his hiking boots.

"Would you mind turning that down a little?" asked Tannon in a slightly irritated tone.

"Sorry. I got carried away."

Kelly picked up the remote control from sofa and ran the volume down to a moderate level.

"Another supernova discovery?" asked Kelly.

She had a grasp on the terminology. Hovering around Tannon all of these years required it.

"Probably more like a star I've misidentified. This astronomy is no kid's game, you know."

Kelly turned her attention to the TV, absorbed by the punk tune. These siblings had very different tastes, but their intertwined lives kept gliding along in tight formation.

"Now what do I do?" asked Tannon.

"Why don't you report it and get famous?" snickered Kelly. "Could it be an error in the star chart?"

"Maybe. But I've never found an error like this before. I'll need to take a look at another atlas."

Kelly plopped down on the sofa, drawing her legs underneath her bony body. She was half watching the gyrating girl on the television, her 32-year old frame gently rocking back and forth on her folded legs. Swaying to the beat, she tilted her small head slightly to the side, remaining focused on the television as she spoke.

"Maybe you've really discovered something. Hey, maybe you'll be rich and buy a Learjet. Okay, okay, I'll fly it for you."

"Thanks," said Tannon. "But first how about some of that soup?"

"Got it," replied Kelly, jumping up abruptly. "But I'm available for that Learjet, if you insist."

Kelly headed for the kitchen. As she pulled the bowls out of the cupboard, EZ perked his golden ears from his sleeping pose on the far end of the L-shaped sofa. This cat would miss no food activity. He listened for a moment to verify the clattering of dishes, hunched his back as he rose, and jumped determinedly to the floor. EZ strutted to the kitchen to check out the action.

As the thick-haired cat passed by, Tannon reached down and grabbed EZ's long puffy tail. The cat stopped intentionally, letting Tannon give its tail a tug that lifted the cat's hind paws a few inches off the rug. As Tannon let go, the contented cat let out his distinctive, brief trill that said *Thank you!*

In the rocking chair, Tannon stretched his body to its full 6-foot-2 length. The back of his neck pushed hard against the wooden back of the rocker, in an attempt to ease his just-recognized headache. The change in temperature when he came inside often seemed to do that, or maybe it was the sudden dryness of the heated living room. He raised his index fingers and rubbed both sides of his head, just forward of his ears. His fingertips still seemed cold to the touch, and they felt good on his temples.

As Kelly continued with the dishes and spoons, Tannon pushed himself from the chair and knelt in front of the basket of magazines. It was filled to the brim with recently read gems of the Bessimer household -- *Newsweek*, *Flying*, *Astronomy*.

Wasn't there a recent article about how to report the discovery of a new comet? He flipped open the only issue of *Astronomy* in the stack and scanned the table of contents. Nothing here.

"Do you remember seeing a pile of astronomy magazines?"

"Try the garage, over behind the ladder," yelled Kelly. "But dinner's almost ready."

Tannon went to the garage, found the half-foot-high pile of magazines, and brought them with him to the kitchen. As he plopped them down on the table, Kelly eyed him suspiciously.

"Do you really think you've found something?"

"Could be. It isn't in the star atlas, unless I made a mistake with my diagram. And the atlas takes things down to eleventh magnitude, well below the capabilities of my puny telescope."

"Could you be seeing a variable star that's flared up or maybe an old comet?"

Kelly had learned a lot about astronomy from Tannon, but she seldom showed it.

Tannon spooned his first mouthful of soup from the bowl. Blowing on the hot chowder, he paused, slid the spoon into his mouth, and looked squarely at Kelly. Then he made a contorted smile, spoon still in his mouth. He placed the spoon back in his bowl and spoke with conservative determination.

"A comet or an asteroid is the best bet. They're not in the atlas at all due to their movement. So it's probably one of those, already reported by someone."

"There must be a way to verify things like that," responded Kelly.

"I'm sure there is. But wouldn't it be nice to have a comet named Bessimer?"

"Sounds good to me. It would be pretty wild to simply stumble across a new comet on a cold San Dimas night."

"True. There are lots of comet hunters out there, and some of them scan forever without finding anything," noted Tannon. "This thing is very star-like, no fuzziness like your standard comet. Still, it's too small to tell."

Tannon's voice was nearly as deep and raspy as it had been out in the cold night. He continued.

"I suppose it could be an asteroid. In that case, the discoverer gets to name it anything they desire."

"How about calling it EZ?"

Kelly raised her eyebrows, as she peeked at the cat crouched on the windowsill in ready-position for any stray food morsels.

"He's a cat who deserves to go down in posterity. But what's he done for the world lately?" Tannon paused and then continued.

"This thing is about magnitude eight. It didn't just pop into the sky tonight, so probably somebody has reported it already, if it's there at all. It kept flickering in and out of view, right at the limit of the telescope. Of course, you know me. I can make a supernova out of a bonfire."

"Hey, not everybody has that knack."

Tannon reached for the pile of magazines, all still ordered chronologically as he had left them. Kelly never messed with Tannon's sense of order, but sometimes it was necessary to clear away the piles before they took over the house.

Tannon and Kelly formed a unique pair. Their lifestyle together generated a few stares and often didn't compute in the minds of those who barely knew them. That very morning, Tannon had gone out to retrieve the newspaper from the driveway. Like many Southern California residents, Tannon didn't even know the names of people living next door. He liked it that way. One of his neighbors, only two houses away, yelled a greeting, as she too headed towards her morning newspaper.

"Hi, neighbor!" she waved. "Tell your wife I love her yellow convertible."

Tannon waved back, smiling outwardly and laughing inside. It was a reasonable mistake. Kelly might as well be his wife. They were that close. And they were always together, so what's the surprise? On the other hand, it was a bit remarkable a neighbor wouldn't know a sister from a wife.

As he thumbed through the magazines, starting with the most recent issues, Tannon looked for the article he remembered. By the third magazine, he had it in front of him. "Report that Comet" – with the byline of Stewart Heneise, famous comet chaser. Here it was, in the *Sky Trails* section – how to report a comet to the International Astronomical Union. Dr. Heneise was calling for avoidance of Internet announcements of new discoveries until the IAU verified the object. Verification implied confirmation by an independent observer. So right there in front of him was the reporting process, even the email address. But where could he turn for an independent confirmation of his discovery?

Independence had two sides. Both Bessimers certainly understood that. Their relationship was a close one, but they experienced little social contact outside of their household of two people and one cat. They were downright reclusive in many ways. Tannon especially. He refused to participate in social activities unless it was professional required. Even then, with extraordinary thoroughness, he avoided people. For many years he had feared his antisocial behavior. It seemed people like him were destined to strike out in life. But in time, Tannon became comfortable with his private nature. He learned to live with it, and as he grew older, he even relished it.

Although he loved astronomy, Tannon knew absolutely no one in the field, professional or amateur. So where would he find an independent observer? Yet astronomy had been his love for decades. Originally, he had intended to work professionally in the field, but his bachelor's degree in physics took care of that. Tannon quickly learned that those who worked full-time in astronomy were much more serious about academics than he was. A summer astronomy internship after his senior year in college closed the door. He was fortunate enough to get an appointment to the U.S. Naval Observatory in Washington, DC. Tannon spent a wonderful summer exploring the nation's capitol on his motorbike, while working with professional astronomers. But those scientists didn't do the things he expected. In fact, most of the work was pure boredom. The data crunching certainly didn't strike his heartstrings, and it was hard to believe astronomers actually punched a time clock! The evening assignments at the Photographic Zenith Tube were enchanting, but far from the cutting edge, having long since been replaced by newer technology. In fact, the PZT film plates were used to update the Naval Observatory's ancient pendulum clocks. There didn't seem to be much real science in that.

The Naval Observatory was his last contact with astronomers, either professional or amateur. He couldn't even recall the names of the astronomers from that period of his life. There was one classmate at the University of Buffalo he did remember well. She was probably now a professional astronomer somewhere -- Lori Talcott. If he could find her, she might be the independent observer he needed.

Lori had been the skinniest girl imaginable. Why she dressed as she did was beyond Tannon's comprehension. You'd think anyone so skinny would wear pants, but Lori always wore a skirt, and her bones showed. They also showed in her face. Coupled with acne worse than severe at the age of 20, she wasn't a pretty woman – except to Tannon. He found her enchanting. When his college roommate kidded him about the skinny female physics major, they both laughed. But that was only because it allowed Tannon to talk to somebody about Lori. She was the only other physics major he really knew, male or female, and that was the extent of his social life. He had watched her studying in the physics library nearly every night. But he never felt comfortable enough to talk to her, except for a quick "Hello." Anything more would've been too bold for college-age Tannon.

There was little doubt Lori wouldn't remember him after all of these years. But she might be an astronomer, and that was what he needed right now. Where she lived was anyone's guess. But at least her name was unique. Maybe there was a way to find her.

* * * * *

Tannon clicked on the bookmark for "World Email Directory." The Web page loaded quickly. At the top was an advertisement: "Pretty Women – Meet Girls from Eastern Europe." A photo of two typical Eastern European beauties bordered the framed advertisement. Well, maybe not so typical.

He entered her last name: TALCOTT. Then her first name: LORI. He selected only one "limiting keyword," – "astro" – then clicked the button marked "Search World Email Directory."

"Host contacted. Waiting for reply. . ." The "Results" window popped up quickly. Best of all, only one name appeared, and it had to be the right Lori. The name was listed with a University of Arizona address, and it included an email address, phone number, and a residence listed in Tucson. So much for privacy.

Tannon wrote down the phone number and email address and placed the small slip of paper on his desk under his "Tomorrow Rock," a handsome specimen of quartz. As a geology teacher, he had rocks stashed all over the house, to say nothing of his office. They served little purpose except as paperweights to enhance his sense of organization.

If he was going to contact Lori, it had better be good. He needed a night to sleep on it. Tau Ceti wasn't going anywhere. And the odds were substantial that its tucked-in-close companion wasn't moving very far either.

Chapter 7

Home Planet

MQ thought he felt a voice. At first he wasn't sure, but he wanted to believe. Yes, it was certainly SJ, but he couldn't discern the words. "SJ? SJ?"

He thrust his tail with all of his might, executing a tight turn in the warm water, pivoting his body and scanning the area. There she was, approaching rapidly from below.

"Yes, MQ. I'm glad to find you. Find you."

The feel of her voice was always enough to bring MQ out of his self-inflicted discouragement. With SJ nearby, his mood could change in an instant.

"Have you heard anything about the signal? No one here seems to know. To know," said MQ.

"The signal has been sent. Been sent," said SJ.

In her voice there was excitement and pride.

"Of course," said MQ. "I knew it would work, and it will be received by our vehicle. Our vehicle."

"I hope you're right, but I have my doubts. It was such an effort for all of us. I've been looking for you. For you."

"I'm glad. I've had my beacon set for you. Did you hear it? Hear it?"

MQ was sometimes overwhelmed by the enormity of the sea, but life concentrated in certain pockets. Those lost could be found again.

"I heard it many times, but there is so much confusion," said SJ. "The water is crowded. Maybe there is too much thought. On land we could handle much more. Much more."

She possessed intelligence just short of the Great Minds. They were no different from her, or from MQ for that matter. It was all a matter of definition. But to be a Great Mind would leave no time for living. SJ enjoyed living, and she enjoyed being with MQ, however briefly.

"Someday we'll go to the land," said SJ. "For more than a moment, for more than the time it takes to launch a vehicle or send a signal. But for now, our place is here. Is here."

"Yes, SJ, it is true. But I wish it were otherwise. We need to know so much more. It is our way to survive. To survive."

SJ and MQ were headed for the surface, swimming in close formation, nearly touching. Darkness had fallen in the atmosphere above, and it was time to enjoy their cherished sea. And their cherished air. As they approached the surface, MQ flexed his tail, although there was little noticeable movement. As he swerved to the right, SJ followed precisely. They were speeding upward now at their very best momentum.

MQ was growing excited in anticipation of the feel of the waves above. He felt SJ trying to talk to him, but it wasn't easy to concentrate on her voice. Just above them was the surface, the tumbling waves, and the night air. That boundary between sea and sky was their playground, and for the moment sensations of high-spirited harmony took priority over everything else. It even took priority over thinking.

And so, as MQ broke the surface of the sea, he knew SJ was talking to him. He didn't feel her voice directly, but he was sure it was there. Her presence and the darkness of the night was enough for him to feel total unity with his emerging world. MQ had the sea and the air and the night.

They broke through the surface together, in perfect formation, right near the top of a breaking wave. They burst out of the side of the wave into the night. For one passing moment, they pivoted near the crest of the wave. MQ's huge eyes peered at a world that seemed frozen in time. His gaping stare was through eyes of intelligence; eyes of need; eyes of hope.

Chapter 8

Inbound

Within the spacecraft, the level of activity was ever increasing. These were entirely invisible events. There was no movement, no sound, and no indication of increased activity. But information was being compiled and evaluated at an ever-increasing rate. From this distance, even if the earth's best optical telescopes were aboard, the details of the solar system would be totally undetected. The planets were still too dim and too close to the bright yellow star, lost in its glare. But the alien spacecraft had advanced telescopic instruments – all automatic, of course.

This star had been the focus of close study since well before the journey began. As the spacecraft progressed, onboard instruments detected more details. The initial discoveries increased the number of candidate planets requiring analysis. And so, there was a significant escalation in observations, most in the non-optical portion of the spectrum. There was a corresponding peak in communication with the home planet. But since then, communication delays had increased to a point where decisions from home were useless. Well before the mid-point in the journey, any message transmitted at the speed of light wouldn't receive a response until after the spacecraft had arrived in the distant solar system.

As a result, external transmissions from the spacecraft decreased during the final portion of the flight. But onboard communications didn't dwindle. At first there was a lull, as the initial data about the target solar system was digested. Now, as the journey neared its end, there was quickening pressure to select a destination world. Currently, two objects of interest absorbed over 90 percents of the spacecraft's computational activity. The information about these two candidates was cascading into the spacecraft's sensors in nearly overwhelming quantities. Onboard electronic terminals were busier than during any previous segment of the journey. Analyzing and comparing – communication between computers.

Over the long period of this flight between the stars, a new means of decision-making had developed. It wasn't the same process as in the beginning. These computers were designed to evolve, and it was a different spacecraft now than at its time of launch. And with the ever-multiplying influx of new data, this evolution was still far from complete. The pace of development was approaching a crescendo.

The cold, dark interior was physically unchanged. The first deceleration burn was nearly complete. It had gone flawlessly. Onboard computers acknowledged this preliminary rocket firing as nominal in all respects. The burn was fully automated, with no intervention required. In a way, it was merely a test of the long idle motors. The spacecraft was slowing gently, but that would soon be replaced by significant deceleration and a change in trajectory.

No light had entered this spacecraft since its departure from home. The constant activity of the tiny circuits and the rare firing of the powerplant contributed little measurable heat. Visibly, this ship was inactive and dead. But within this chamber, there was change and growth, hovering on the boundary marking the definition of life.

Chapter 9

Monday, January 11, 2016

EZ

Tannon awoke at six am. His sinuses felt both stuffy and puffy, and the fog outside was the likely cause. He liked his bedroom cold and fresh, so the door to the patio was cracked open, protected by the screen. He loved the cold morning air, but his sinuses hated it. Tannon lay half-asleep and too tired to get up to attend to his stuffy nose. It probably was an indication his 39-year old body was lacking care, but his morning congestion was so routine it had become ignored long ago. It was just one of those things he expected when he woke up. After a few minutes, Tannon pulled back the covers and swung his feet to the floor. He sat there for a moment, and then pushed himself up and shuffled to the bathroom.

EZ detected the rustling noise. The cat was on his early morning vigil outside the closed bedroom door, seldom missing a chance to remind Tannon of his presence. He was already clawing the carpet. Tannon yelled at him through the door. Lots of good that would do.

Tau Ceti was on Tannon's mind immediately, and his plan was clearer now. He needed another look at the star tonight. No one was going to beat him to the discovery of a new object in such a short time. How often do folks stare at Tau Ceti through a telescope? And when they do, are they really paying attention to the surrounding stars? So the real verification would be a second view tonight. Then he would call Lori. She might be able to help with confirmation as an independent observer. But his expectation was there would be no need for such a telephone call after another observation. Even if he had found something new, it might have already moved away from Tau Ceti, especially if it was a comet or asteroid. So there went his fleeting claim to fame.

As he scuffled back to bed for some extra morning moments, he clicked on the bedroom television, and watched the morning news. In another half hour, he opened the door to reveal EZ huddled under the tall-legged hallway chair. The cat was pretending to hide, ready for the day to begin. After all, it was his house.

The television in the living room echoed the sound of his bedroom TV, the same morning news channel. It seemed unusually early for that. He stood in the doorway, trying to decide whether to go back to bed again.

"Kelly, are you up?" he yelled from the doorway.

"Sure am. Do you see that fog? It looks like I get the morning off. Nothing like a nice case of dreary fog to make my day."

Kelly didn't like to rise early, but when she did, it was always with a purpose. She was scheduled to fly with a student this morning, and the weather had changed that. Kelly was a full-time certified flight instructor, a rarity in the field – most CFIs worked part-time, needing another job to support themselves. But full-time, in Kelly's case, didn't mean fully employed. She was a free-lance instructor who eked out her income from a profession briefly visited by those on the way to airline careers. Few learned to fly for recreation these days – airplanes and avgas were simply too expensive. However, a high-time flight instructor like Kelly, female and licensed through multi-engine aircraft, was in high demand by the airlines. But she didn't seem to be seriously interested in an airline career. As Tannon always told her, she was sure working hard to make certain she didn't become a millionaire. But it wasn't entirely true, and they both knew it. Her muddied background was a significant obstacle in the way of an airline job. She had a tendency to ignore obstacles rather than attack them face-on.

Flying was everything to Kelly. Judging by the progress of her life so far, flying seemed to mean more to her than the pursuit of men. Age 32, never married, she had few close male friends, although her boyish figure had its share of admirers. She didn't have a lot of female friends either, since her occupation didn't bring her into contact with many co-workers of the same sex. The female friends she did have were cherished. Tannon knew most of these women rather well, since he and his sister shared this house. They also shared a lot of effort to keep their home theirs and theirs alone. They liked it that way. Of course, there was EZ. He had been part of the deal when Kelly moved from Syracuse five years ago. Although the cat really belonged to Kelly, both she and Tannon often referred to EZ as "your cat" when he got into trouble, which was a regular occurrence.

Rather than go back to bed, Tannon slid into baggy shorts and his favorite tan hiking boots, unlaced, and strode into the living room. As he passed EZ, the cat clamored at his feet for attention, scratching the rug again.

"How about breakfast?" suggested Tannon.

Although he wasn't talking to EZ, the cat immediately jumped up and headed towards the kitchen, as if he understood.

"You and your breakfast," said Kelly. "Don't you pay any attention to those articles about cholesterol"

"I personally prefer the ads touting the protein benefits of eggs. What do you say? Think you can fly that yellow convertible to breakfast in the fog?"

"I say, let's go. But let me call my student first. You're Mr. Leisure this week, aren't you?"

"Yes, on recess all week. And I'll be Mr. Leisure in San Francisco, beginning tomorrow. No partying with the guys while I'm gone. . . or the girls."

"Fat chance, brother. You wish, don't you?"

Tannon's smile was artificially wide. He headed to the kitchen, and Kelly and EZ followed. While Tannon gathered up EZ's dish and stepped towards the refrigerator to fill it with what remained of the can of cat food, Kelly made her phone call.

It didn't take a special invitation for EZ. The cat was at the refrigerator door as soon as it opened. As Tannon prepared the yellow plastic bowl, EZ leaned with all of his weight against his master's calves – *rub, rub* – feed me, feed me.

Kelly's phone call was short, and when she completed it, she grabbed the keys to her car, her gaudy yellow windbreaker, and off they went. Like the married couple their neighbor envisioned, they picked up the newspaper in the driveway on the way to the car. They usually read the paper over coffee at breakfast. Tannon always read the world news first, and Kelly always read the sports section. Their routine was standard, as were most aspects of their lives. And this morning, like most others, it was just fine for both of them.

* * * * *

After the eggs, toast, and bacon were delivered to their table and the newspaper was temporarily put away, Kelly asked: "What have you decided about Comet Bessimer?"

"Do you mean Asteroid EZ?"

"Oh, yeah, I forgot. So what do you think?"

"I think I need to take a better look at it again before making a fool of myself. This low layer of coastal clouds doesn't make it look very promising for tonight. So how about a trip to the desert for a better view?"

"I've got a night cross-country lesson scheduled. It's the ol' Santa Barbara route, pretty standard for a flight review. But if the flying weather doesn't improve, I'll be grounded. That creepy fog might slip right back in tonight and put me out of business. Out of money, too."

Kelly continued: "What's the next step, if you verify Supernova Tannon tonight?"

"Next on the list is a call to an old college friend. I located her last night on the Internet. It looks like she's an astronomer at the University of Arizona, so I assume she has contacts at Kitt Peak."

"I thought telescope time was at a premium," noted Kelly. "How do you plan to entice her to drop everything for an amateur's supposed discovery?"

"Well, either I'll have to convince her it's the discovery of the decade, or I'll have to remind her of our private days in the rooftop observatory at Buffalo."

"Yes, Tannon. I bet that was a really big deal," Kelly smirked.

Tannon smiled and emitted a quiet laugh. His sister understood what made him tick. No one else ever came close.

Chapter 10

Cajon Pass

Kelly drove that evening. The low clouds had broken at midday, but were back before sunset. Her night flight was canceled, and she was eager to accompany Tannon on this trip to the high desert. It gave her a chance to play with the new-to-her yellow Mustang. This was a model that had dominated American automotive history for over fifty years. No longer produced, this car was seen on the road less often these days. While hybrids and electric cars now ruled the highways, Kelly trimmed her meager personal budget wherever necessary to keep her yellow convertible filled with gas. Her Mustang, although mechanically derated in horsepower to meet California's emission standards, was still spunky. Many considered such a vehicle a rude extravagance, but the vehicle fit Kelly's personality perfectly.

As they climbed the Cajon grade, east of Los Angeles, the convertible top was down. But even in the cold evening air, the car's robust heater made it cozy, especially with the windows rolled up. For Tannon, it was much too windy and noisy. And what good were these high-quality radio speakers when you couldn't understand the words to the music over the noise of the wind?

Trucks segregated themselves in the far right lane, struggling up the incline. Near a green sign marking the road's 2000-foot elevation, the gutsy little convertible broke through the top of the clouds, with the dusk sky glowing blue-violet above. To the west, orange shades of sunset reached upward between divides in the San Gabriel Mountains.

The yellow Mustang was Kelly Bessimer's child, protected from the world by its doting mother. The car was an indication of her character, but like a lot of things in her life, the message was mixed. Music blared loud but indistinct in the open convertible, and this time it wasn't punk rock. Kelly's taste for music was varied, and one of her favorite singers was Frank Sinatra. She was more than a little bit behind her time.

As 1950s music blasted from the speakers, her closest friend and brother accompanied her up the mountain pass. In the back seat sat the red Astroscan, propped up carefully against the side, surrounded by a towel and wedged erect with Kelly's heavy-with-charts flight bag. She sang to the Sinatra tune as they thundered up the steep grade of Interstate 15 in the fading light, passing every electric car in sight.

* * * * *

As they approached their turnoff, a large neon sign proclaimed "EAT." This was Tannon's clue to the location of the upcoming exit. He had been here many times, but he closely inspected the sign for the hundredth time – it certainly looked like old-fashioned neon, a marvelous relic of the past.

For dark sky exploring, this was one of the closest spots to the eastern Los Angeles Basin, although it still had its share of traffic and the accompanying interference of car lights. Near the Silverwood Lake exit, a green sign indicated "Elevation 3000 Feet." As they pulled off to the right, McDonald's displayed its tall arches. Just down Frontage Road, back past the neon "EAT" sign, was a small country cafe. Judging from the parking lot, McDonald's wasn't interfering with their business.

A large sign marked Tiffany's Restaurant, a name that didn't fit. Kelly parked in an outlying spot, least likely to induce damage to her Mustang.

In the chilly January air of Southern California, they walked up to the entrance. The restaurant was double-doored for the winter season, and a sign beckoned "Best Burgers in the West." It was that kind of a place.

Tannon noted the lack of an "A" sign in the window. He was accustomed to paying attention to the Health Department's grading system. After all, why eat at a "B" restaurant? But there was no sign, and that disturbed Tannon. Maybe this wasn't the kind of place that paid a lot of attention to administrative details. Then again, this might be San Bernardino County, and maybe that meant they didn't need a sign.

They seated themselves in a booth by the window. Small jukebox machines were mounted on the wall near each table. And they still worked! Of course, it now took four quarters to spool up a song.

Kelly's short hair was pulled back in a ponytail, with a narrow red tie holding the excess. There was hardly enough hair to clamp it back. Her shirt was long-sleeved plaid flannel, fully unbuttoned to reveal a dark blue T-shirt. Her small breasts didn't need the restriction of a bra. Kelly looked like she belonged in this restaurant.

"You couldn't resist the chicken-fried steak, could you?" noted Kelly.

"Look, wife, knock it off."

"Sorry. But I'm concerned about your diet. I'm even more concerned about your lack of it. Dad didn't die just to make our life miserable."

"He also didn't die of heart disease," replied Tannon.

"Well, it was close. Dying of old age at 61 isn't exactly living up to our country's life expectancies. It's all related."

"Right."

Kelly changed the subject: "Isn't this where we first saw Hale-Bopp?"

"We've seen at least two comets here, Hale-Bopp and Hyakutake. Hyakutake – now there was a comet."

"Long time ago," said Kelly. "But you can't forget comets like those. We were just kids, even you. Mom brought us here in her car, but you had the same old red telescope."

"Hyakutake was so big, you couldn't even use a telescope. And don't talk about my trusty telescope like that."

"Sorry, I forgot he's out there in the back seat listening."

They talked for a few minutes about some of their shared astronomical adventures, many of them on dark nights with nothing to show for the observing sessions except cold fingers and toes. Kelly would do anything, absolutely anything, to be with Tannon. And her brother had the same mutual respect, tempered by the knowledge that all brothers and sisters went through troubling periods at times.

Kelly had the knack of finding enjoyment in any adventure, even those well outside her area of expertise. But sports were her passion. And she tried to involve Tannon in that passion, at least as an observer. Once in a while Tannon would give in, but usually he refused. Just last weekend, however, he had accompanied Kelly on a skiing trip – their New Year's celebration. Of course, for Tannon it meant sitting in the lodge reading a geology book, while Kelly braved the cold slopes. She was physically tough and free spirited. He was mentally rigid and disciplined. Together, their differences contributed to each other and made them a formidable team.

"This is a nice spot," said Tannon.

"For food or astronomy?" asked Kelly.

"Both. Maybe we should try the apple cobbler."

Tannon looked across the table at Kelly. Her sparkle, almost always present, inspired him. She drove him in ways neither of them fully understood. Tannon and Kelly were more than brother and sister. But how could you define it?

Recently, on some days, Kelly looked frail, almost ill. But not tonight. They were both feeling wonderfully comfortable, relaxed and in-tune with each other. When Tannon was with Kelly, he was a different person – a better person. When Kelly was with Tannon, she was both supercharged and simultaneously overwhelmed. Within both of them were many words that remained unsaid regarding their relationship. They worked hard to keep it that way.

* * * * *

The road to Lake Silverwood spanned four lanes for only the first few hundred feet. Then it changed into a two-lane winding road that alternately climbed and dipped for the next mile. Kelly drove slowly as they neared their intended turnoff, looking for a poorly defined road to the left. In the darkness, they sought the outline of a dirt driveway with a white fence and large side posts designating the entrance.

They passed the entrance just as Tannon saw it, but Kelly stopped in time to require only a short backup exercise for the Mustang. They made the turn through the unmarked entrance that had probably once boasted a ranch's top identifying bar between the tall posts. Kelly navigated the darkness in first gear. This decade-old car was one of the few on the road with a floor-mounted stick shift, and this was a place where it was in its element.

A washboard of hard dirt met them immediately. Kelly slowed further and crept past a "No Shooting" sign. In a short distance, the road smoothed a bit, but the overwhelming darkness, mixed with substantial-size rocks along both sides of the road, kept her speed slow. They passed some spired Yuccas and a large Manzanita bush on the left. Then the one lane path opened into a broad "Y" intersection. Kelly navigated around a car-eating rut and a puddle remaining from a recent rainshower. She wasn't going to put mud on her Mustang.

Kelly carefully maneuvered the car within the confines of the "Y." They would park here, of to the side the intersection, not expecting any other traffic tonight. Once they were in proper position, she turned off the ignition. The car pointed east, and the headlights of the Interstate were now slightly above them, about a mile to the left.

Tannon spoke: "Let's sit here for a few minutes to get our eyes night-adapted."

Kelly engaged the ignition switch again, far enough to allow the radio to play and the heater to gasp its final warmth from the cooling engine. She pushed in her favorite old Frank Sinatra CD. They said nothing to each other. As the first song ended and transitioned to the next, Kelly began to sing. In her deepest voice, she belted out the first line of "Strangers in the Night," perfectly in concert with Frank, but Tannon interrupted.

"Nice thought, but the only romance tonight is in Cetus the Whale."

As they sat motionless in the convertible, the heater no longer protected them. Cold and darkness began to engulf their topless cocoon. Tannon spoke over the ending of the next song.

"Time to put the top up?"

"Sure. I'll take care of it."

He pulled open the door latch, and then remembered to zip his jacket the rest of the way.

"It's a lot colder up here than in San Dimas," he noted.

"Just like upstate New York in winter," Kelly kidded.

"Well, it isn't exactly Snow Ridge. I'll take California any day," replied Tannon.

When he stepped out of the car, Tannon surveyed the scene. To the east, Orion was battling upward, just skimming the bushes. On the left side of Orion, the dim Milky Way poured upward and to the right. It was a very dark night.

Tannon's toes felt toasty in his thick hiking boots. He was gloveless, but his fingers weren't yet assaulted by the cold. Kelly quickly finished raising the Mustang's convertible cover. She stood next to him now, bundled in her maroon and blue ski jacket, zipped to the top with the black cloth inner lining protruding at her exposed skinny wrists. Although tall and thin, she wasn't a delicate woman.

Their eyes continued to adjust, steadily seeing increased detail. Tannon turned to the south and noticed the broad line of hills. They were probably patched with snow, but there was nothing to illuminate the white. The towers of electrical powerlines poked above the hills, barely visible in the darkness. To the right, the ridgeline of the tall San Gabriel Mountains blocked the lights of Los Angeles.

Tannon now turned to face north, where he had a good view of the Interstate highway well above them. But he protected his night vision, using care not to stare at the car headlights moving down Cajon Pass. Below the highway was a terraced ledge where a long freight train maneuvered down through the pass. He could barely see the train in the distance, but he could easily hear it. There was the faint sound of metal wheels scraping on cold rails. *Squeak, squeak*, and then a continuous and louder squeal. *Squeak, squeak, squeak.* Then the power of a throttling-up pusher engine at the rear, humming at idle and clearing its throat as it used its energy as a brake. The train glided noisily down the incline.

Tannon set the Astroscan on the car trunk, using a towel to prevent scratching Kelly's pride-and-joy. The metal base mount rested in the narrow space between the rear window and the spoiler. He lowered the red telescope tube to the south and sighted through the metal viewfinder rack. A small cedar tree just off the "Y" intersection nearly interrupted his view of the constellation of Cetus. But this was an acceptable location.

Tannon pulled back from the telescope and stood straight. Cetus was directly to the south, hovering about twenty degrees above the hills and powerlines.

"The air smells like sage," said Kelly. "I bet it's struggling for survival this time of year."

She was a bit of a plant buff. As in a lot of other areas, she always stopped her knowledge short before she became a true expert.

Tannon stood erect, with his hands warming in the pockets of his jacket. The train was gone now, and there was only silence. His raspy voice spoke slowly and softly in the quiet air.

"Now, if you've got a real active imagination, there's the whale. The tail is quite evident in the upper left of the constellation."

He walked closer to Kelly and stood immediately behind her. Their fat nylon jackets rubbed quietly. He reached over her left shoulder and pointed to the south. His tall frame required him to lower his torso in a slight slouch in order to align his arm properly with her shoulder. That should give her a fairly accurate indication of where he was pointing. He swung his arm towards the group of stars that marked the tail of Cetus.

"To me, it looks more like it's the head," said Tannon. "Because it's such a circular formation. But the ancients thought it was the tail."

"Got it," said Kelly. "So if that's the tail, where is the head?"

"It's supposed to look more like a large mouth of a whale, but to me it's just that mess of stars to the right. Now go back to the tail, and follow the line of stars down and to the right. The first star is Mira, very reddish. Then continue down two more stars, and that's Tau Ceti."

"I've got it, I think. Not very spectacular, if you ask me."

"Nope. Just your typical fourth magnitude star, but it's pretty close to us by celestial standards, only twelve light-years away. It was the first star Frank Drake studied with a radio telescope in the 1960s. He was listening for people but didn't find anybody home."

"Frank Drake, huh? Never heard of him. Why did he think there might be life there?" replied Kelly.

"Tau Ceti isn't really a great candidate, but it's nearby and has a spectral class similar to the sun. So it was a good target for Drake. And in recent years, the nearest stars are the best targets for detecting planets, so it's been studied quite a bit. But astronomers haven't found any planets there, although they've found lots of Jupiter-size planets orbiting other stars."

"Jupiter-size doesn't sound promising to me. Too much gravity for life, don't you think?"

"True. But big planets should have big moons. Some of Jupiter's moons are almost as large as the earth. Besides, earth-like planets are still awfully difficult to detect, so planet hunters spend most of their time looking for the gas-giants."

Tannon bent over the trunk of the car to guide the telescope onto its target. He moved from the sighting rack to the eyepiece, centered the image, and carefully focused it. He made sure the pinpoint of light was as small and as distinct as possible.

"There's Tau Ceti. Just like last night. And there's her faint companion, tucked in close to the left. More prominent tonight, with this darker sky."

He drew his head away from the scope, motioning to Kelly with a downward nod. She took her place at the eyepiece, needing a few seconds to find a comfortable viewing position. She fine-tuned the focusing knob for her eye. Then she stared silently for almost a full minute.

"Does it look like this?" asked Tannon.

Kelly drew away from the eyepiece and focused on the star atlas, illuminated by Tannon's red-lens flashlight. He held the atlas upside-down in front of her, to provide the view she would see in the telescope.

She silently studied the page, and then she moved back to the eyepiece, staring again for only a few seconds. When she pulled away, she said nothing at first, but nodded her head as if saying "Yes."

"It looks just like the chart," she stated, slowly spacing each word. "Except there's one tiny star that's not supposed to be there."

* * * * *

It was a long night for Tannon. When they got home, he dug out his old astronomy books, none of which had the detail needed to verify any stars below the seventh magnitude.

That night, he spent a lot of time on the Internet, viewing images from the Palomar Digitized Sky Survey. These professional photos provided much more detail than his star atlas. And despite the disparities caused by the smaller fields of view in the Sky Survey, the brightest stars surrounding Tau Ceti lined up just as expected. But one star was missing.

Chapter 11

Tuesday, January 12, 2016

Lori T

Tannon slept fitfully and awoke with a dull headache. Taking a shower helped a lot. After feeding EZ, he dialed the number he had found for Lori and waited through four rings.

"Astrophysics," answered the young female voice on the other end of the phone.

"Hello, I'm looking for Lori Talcott."

Tannon used his most determined voice, although it wasn't much of a tone. His dislike of telephones was sometimes almost debilitating. It was tough to avoid telephones, when most professions required it.

"Just a moment please," said the young voice.

Tannon waited while another connection rang.

"Jason here," said a gruff male voice.

"Is Dr. Talcott there?"

"Dr. Talcott? You mean Lori T?" The voice sounded interrupted and grumpy.

"Yes, Lori Talcott."

Click. Was that a "Hold" button or simply an angry astronomer hanging up? There was no dial tone, so probably he was on hold. Apparently, this fellow didn't have any more telephone charm than Tannon.

Tannon imagined that astronomers didn't work for anybody in particular, because their far-removed bosses probably understood little regarding the scientific details. If astronomers were just "out there" doing university research, they probably felt immune to the normal pressures of business. That could lead to disinterest in callers like him. Maybe it was just this guy who answered the phone, or maybe it was a mark of the profession.

After a lengthy pause, a soft female voice: "This is Lori Talcott."

"Lori, this is a friend of yours from the University of Buffalo." Tannon's heart was pounding like mad. "Actually, I'm a former classmate. My name is Tannon Bessimer."

There was a pause, long enough to convince Tannon she had forgotten him.

"Tannon! Now I remember. Sorry, it's been a while."

"Twenty years ago, Lori. Do you really remember me?"

"Sure! Not at first, but now I recall you very clearly – tall, rather lanky, with the curliest blond hair. You were in that terrible thermodynamics class we endured with Doctor Herman."

"You've got it. I had forgotten about Herman. That's the only class I ever failed. And I still remember him tossing those pieces of chalk to keep everybody awake."

"Well, thermodynamics isn't exactly the garden spot of science for most people." Lori was bubbling now. She really did remember him!

"Where are you?" she continued.

"Near Los Angeles, in a town called San Dimas," replied Tannon. "And my hair is still blond, but it has a touch of gray these days."

"Oh, I do remember you," she said. "Do you still keep your books piled at attention wherever you sit? I remember you in the physics library."

"Thanks for the memories," he kidded.

He paused, waiting for a reply, which was a simple laugh from Lori.

"I got your phone number off the Internet. What are you doing at the University of Arizona?"

"I'm in the theoretical research group – cosmology, to be specific."

"Cosmology. I remember you were always studying that on your own at Buffalo. Does it involve any telescope time?"

"Not really. I get some occasional sessions on the consortium's radio telescopes, including the Very Large Array in New Mexico. But that's only because I assist a colleague in his studies in the 21-centimeter band."

That should mean something. Tannon remembered the 21-centimeter band of radiation as having something to do with the glow of the universe's hydrogen gas. But there was no sense demonstrating his ignorance now.

Lori paused, in case Tannon wanted to intervene, but he didn't. She continued with a sparkle in her voice.

"How about you? Are you in astronomy these days."

"No, I'm teaching geology at a community college near Los Angeles, Mount San Antonio College. It doesn't involve any research, but it's fun."

"Hey, you community college guys get to teach a lot. I try to, but this research thing has a mind of its own. I never would've guessed geology for you."

"I wouldn't have guessed that either, Lori. I was headed towards astronomy when I last saw you, but then I did a brief stint at the Naval Observatory right after graduation. That scared me off."

"Hey, that's a different kind of astronomy," said Lori. "Did you work for Nicole Scott?"

"Now there's a name I had forgotten. But, yes, she was in charge. As I recall, her specialty was parallax measurements of stars."

"Still is," noted Lori. "She's right here in Arizona, and distance measurements are still her baby. We're pretty close friends."

Lori probably still had a bit of that Buffalo appearance. But by now the acne must be under control. He wanted this to continue. He was actually comfortable on the phone with her. But there was the matter of Tau Ceti.

"Lori, let me tell you why I called. I've never lost my love for astronomy, and I'm still an amateur observer. The emphasis is on the word 'amateur.'"

"Sure, sure. Aren't we all?" It was almost a giggle.

"For the last two nights I've been looking at something that puzzles me, and I thought you might be able to help."

Tannon outlined his observations of Tau Ceti. He was surprised when Lori admitted she wasn't familiar with the star. In fact, she had to inquire regarding the location of the constellation of Cetus. She did remember, when reminded, that Tau Ceti was a nearby star, but that was about it. Tannon listened as she explained how most professional astronomers pay little attention to the constellations.

"Just right ascension and declination will do for me," she remarked. "Heck, I never do any visual observations anymore. But I do have some friends at Kitt Peak. The team on the 1.8-meter telescope might be willing to investigate your mystery star. They enjoy an occasional change in their observing schedule. They're using the scope to search for near-earth asteroids anyway, and this might be one of them."

"I'd guess it isn't an asteroid," replied Tannon. "I haven't noticed any change of position, although I've only been watching it for two nights."

"Still, I bet they'd be interested," said Lori.

Tannon gave Lori the right ascension and declination coordinates for the star near Tau Ceti, as best as he had been able to estimate them. He also provided his home telephone number and the phone number for the Parc 55 hotel in San Francisco.

"What's going on in San Francisco, business or pleasure?"

"Pleasure, at least for me. Surely you didn't think it was a geology conference. I'm not a real geologist, you know. Us community college guys are just amateur scientists."

"Not so," intervened Lori. "I bet you're every bit the expert. What's to see in San Francisco?"

"There's a computer conference there every January. I'm a bit of a wirehead."

"Sounds like fun," said Lori. "I won't have anything to report until at least tomorrow morning, so I'll call you in San Francisco, say about 9 am… uh, 8 o'clock Pacific time. Is that too early?"

"No, sounds fine. It was great talking to you, Lori."

"Same here. What a surprise – a real nice surprise."

* * * * *

Christine Todd grinned as she spoke into the telephone. Christine was a caring friend, and she understood why Kelly hadn't called until now.

"I worked last night," said Christine. "So I slept it off this morning. But it wouldn't have bothered me if you called and woke me up. In fact, I dream about it."

"Your dreams are scary," said Kelly.

"Not as scary as yours. I bet you dream about spinning those baby Cessnas and watching your male students puke. Miss Tough Guy."

"Not today. In fact I could use some tender loving care."

"I'm listening."

"Tannon's headed for San Francisco. Just overnight, but could we arrange some time together before you go to work tonight?"

"Sure, what do you have in mind, Miss Sensitive?"

"You know – spend the day together. We could have a late lunch at your place or just order a pizza. I've got a video I'd like you to see."

"Another one of those dialog films or a real shoot-em-up?"

Kelly's taste in movies was varied, and Christine liked to tease her about the dichotomy between love and violence.

"Neither. It's a DVD of a program I copied on TV last night. I haven't seen it yet, but it's supposed to be pretty interesting. Now don't laugh – it's a biography of Dean Martin."

"Dean Martin? The old, dead singer? Some kind of joke, I hope."

"No, as a matter of fact. Dean Martin was a pretty unique fellow. The program was on late, so I didn't watch it, but I bet we'd both like it."

"Well, you'd like it because you're you," replied Christine. "And I'd like it because I like you."

"Good enough for me," laughed Kelly. "So is it a date?"

"Oh, a date. Dates with you I just love. Bring Dean Martin, and I'll take a bath. Heck, I'll just prepare the bath for the two of us."

"Let's just start with Dean Martin."

"Dean it is. How about noon?"
"I'll be there. Love ya', Christine."
"Hope so. See you then."

* * * * *

Tannon approached the hotel lobby with a sense of nervousness. He knew his reservation over the Internet was confirmed, but now he had to talk with real people. He was turning forty and still felt uncomfortable facing routine conversation.

It was different in the classroom. He was clearly in charge there, and there was no need to communicate without a course outline. He could handle students in their varied temperaments, but real adults were different. This was uncontrolled ad lib.

The desk clerk seemed to be waiting for his shift to end. His smile looked artificial, but Tannon suffered through the brief check-in. The clerk handed him a large white envelope marked "Parc 55 Fax Service." It was thin enough for a single page, and it was undoubtedly Kelly. She did it just to put him on the spot. Usually she waited until he was checked in. Then she would transmit a fax from her computer with enough simplicity and mystery in the short paragraph to get the attention of the receiving clerk. She wasn't averse to adding some artificial spice, knowing Tannon would have to show up at the front desk to claim it. He sort of liked it, sort of didn't.

On the elevator ride to the eleventh floor, he opened the envelope. Inside was a computer stick figure with the words "Take me to your leader" in large print. He was still laughing when the elevator doors opened. Kelly worked hard at reminding him there was humor in life. And Tannon was a person who needed such reminders.

Chapter 12

Wednesday, January 13, 2016

Kitt Peak

The phone rang, and it took a few moments for Tannon to realize where he was. Subdued morning light slipped through the curtains. He didn't allow a telephone in his bedroom at home. But the ringing was coming from the nightstand. This was a hotel.

He tried to sound wide-awake: "Hello."

"Hi, Tannon. This is Lori. Hope I didn't wake you."

"No problem. I've been awake awhile," he lied. "Is this the astronomer's obligatory 'Sorry about your object' call?"

"Not exactly. Stewart Observatory has confirmed your object. And it doesn't conform to the location of any other reported comet or asteroid." Lori sounded excited.

Tannon pushed his lanky body up against the headboard of the bed. He purposefully paused long enough for some dramatic effect.

"Okay, you tell me. What does it all mean?"

Lori's reply was so immediate that Tannon missed a few of the first words: ". . . something new. Something that simply wasn't there before."

Tannon's heart thumped hard, and it wasn't for Lori.

"A comet or what?"

"Not in this universe, Mister Geologist. This baby is pretty strange, and it's certainly new."

Tannon said absolutely nothing. If this were a joke, it wouldn't last long. But finally Lori interrupted the silence.

"Yes, my fellow physicist, you've gotten hold of something here. But I'm afraid we don't have much to put our fingers on yet. Kitt Peak got a spectrogram, but it looks a bit messy. So they set it aside for computer analysis today."

Tannon waited for something further, but apparently Lori was waiting for his response.

"Messy spectrum, you say?"

"Yes, but displaced emission lines can do that. And later in the night the 1.8-meter Stewart scope returned to the same spot to see if any movement could be detected. They haven't found any velocity indications yet."

Lori explained the rest of the details that had been relayed to her. Professional observers don't normally do courtesy calls for amateur astronomers, but with Lori in the loop, they made an exception. The night hadn't been exceptionally clear, with a high cirrus layer of clouds blanketing the Tucson area. But gaps in the cirrus allowed clear identification of the object near Tau Ceti early in the evening. The lack of a coma didn't necessarily eliminate it as a comet, since it could be a long distance from the sun. But a spectrogram should give a hint. What they had found was a point of light with a jumbled spectrum.

Lori gave Tannon her home phone number and asked that he call her when he returned to Los Angeles. She offered to assist with the reporting of the object to the International Astronomical Union, but she recommended he email the Central Bureau for Astronomical Telegrams at Harvard University as soon as he could. There wasn't a big rush, since his discovery was safe, and it would be in his name. Professional astronomers, she noted, have no desire to steal discoveries from amateurs. But a confirmation email would prevent any confusion. Meanwhile, Kitt Peak had allocated more observing time for the new object. Even the 8-meter telescope might be interrupted for the event, and Lori asked permission to tip off her contacts at Mauna Kea in Hawaii.

"Oh, if you insist," kidded Tannon.

As he put the phone down, a strange sense of calm swept through Tannon. Here he was, feeling more excited than he ever dreamed possible; yet he felt totally relaxed, almost sedated. He stretched back down on the firm mattress, and tried to stop thinking about the new object. His thoughts drifted to Lori, picturing her scurrying from her desk to get her day started. He concentrated on the image. What would she look like after all these years? And then he promptly fell asleep.

* * * * *

He awakened an hour later, bright sunshine pouring in between the layers of curtains. The window was cracked open far enough that he felt the cool morning air. He heard the street below, mostly heavy vehicles accelerating and braking, and a trash truck lifting dumpsters, clanking the bins metal-upon-metal, and then the tumbling rush and crash of falling trash.

Within Tannon was a feeling of peace. How could this be? He had made what could be a major astronomical discovery, pretty much by accident, and he felt perfectly calm. Even a bit calm was an improvement for Tannon. He felt somehow different today, unusually confident. This was a characteristic that seldom invaded him. His celestial discovery brought with it a tranquility he had never expected.

He took the time to call Kelly, reporting first on his reaction in the elevator to her stick figure. Then he told her about his conversation with Lori. She didn't say much, but she obviously understood the importance of the discovery. In her reaction, he sensed even more excitement than he felt himself, which was a relief from his normally over-anxious outlook on life.

He would still go to the computer conference today, a decision that surprised him. There didn't seem to be anything to do except complete the email report to Harvard. He could do it from his mini-laptop during a break in the conference – there would be wireless connections everywhere. For now, his stomach was rumbling with even higher priorities –- breakfast.

* * * * *

Tannon strolled down Market Street, arms swinging briskly. The warm sunshine permeated the sidewalk, the sun blocked occasionally by the high buildings and leafless trees straddling the street. This was one of his favorite places. He found himself here every January, same time, same computer conference. Same hotel, same restaurants, same schedule. But within Tannon Bessimer today was a sense of calm that couldn't be explained. This was different. He just wanted to absorb the feeling of composure. And he hoped it wasn't simply passing through.

As he walked, he closely watched those who approached him, except for the poor street people. He couldn't make eye contact with them. As he inspected the passer-bys, Tannon looked particularly close at the women. He played his little game. Who is she? Why is she here? Is she a tourist or a regular shopper? He liked imagining that the most attractive women were regulars here. He wasn't shopping for a companion. Yet it was only the women who interested him.

Across the street at the next corner was one of his favorite restaurants, or maybe you should call it a deli. In any case, the food was great. He could still make the first seminar session, but it would be tight. He hated being late for anything, but breakfast would be worth it today. Why wasn't he in his normal hurry?

Tannon prepared himself for the restaurant's expected delays, but it was a short line. The customers all looked like locals. The line formed just inside the door, between gold posts with thick black sagging ropes outlining the queue. The velvet swags seemed out of place in this inexpensive restaurant, making it appear more like a funeral parlor. The line of customers was moving nicely, and the woman in front of him gave him a chance to play his little game.

The woman carried a dull orange shopping bag, nearly empty. Her back was all he could see at first, except for the edges of her face as she looked around. Her tightly curled dark hair looked natural, and she wore a black silk loose-fitting blouse with huge white polka dots. Smooth black silk pants and shoes with fat wide heels revealed skinny ankles and no nylons. She looked comfortable being by herself. Tannon could easily identify with that. But still he looked closely at this woman. An invasion of privacy perhaps, but it was Tannon's innocent little game.

Her upper body was soft, somehow intriguing. She had dark skin, and Tannon guessed she was Hispanic. She turned, noticing Tannon behind her – just noticing him, not staring. Her face now revealed narrow lines around her mouth. She was probably a bit older than Tannon. In that brief glimpse, he saw her downturned mouth, looking cynical rather than sad.

The hostess-on-duty this morning appeared to be about sixty, but she moved quickly and efficiently, and now it was almost Tannon's turn. He always found moments like this rather nerve wracking. He would have to speak to the hostess, and he hadn't rehearsed his exact words. That was unusual for him. He always wanted to simply get it over with, but today Tannon hadn't even prepared for the moment. As the hostess returned to the black ropes and their gold posts after leading a couple to their table, Tannon was now second in line. And his speech was still not prepared.

The hostess reached for a menu in the wooden rack, as she turned to the woman in front of Tannon. The woman was ready to open her mouth when Tannon spurted: "I'm with her."

The woman in front of him turned slowly – no smile, no frown, just that downturned cynical expression.

"No he's not."

She stared through Tannon as she spoke, without a hint of emotion. Tannon smiled broadly. The hostess grimaced.

"One?" the hostess smirked.

"One," the woman replied without any additional emotion.

Off they went, leaving Tannon at the gold posts. Now both women were bobbing and laughing as they disappeared around the corner.

When the hostess returned, she was still grinning. She pushed her lips forward.

"One?"

"Looks like it."

The hostess led him in a direction opposite from the route of the polka dot woman. Maybe she had been asked to take him to a different location. Or maybe the hostess simply understood his needs at the moment. But Tannon wasn't embarrassed, and he was inwardly surprised at that fact.

"Nice line," teased the hostess, as she seated him and handed over the menu.

"Yeah, it worked great."

Tannon relaxed, menu unopened. Here he was at a time that dictated "rush," and he was relaxed and flirting more openly than ever before. He had never been so bold with a woman he didn't know. Never!

He sat smiling, not feeling the least bit defeated. Nor did he feel humiliated, and embarrassment was his specialty. Within Tannon at this moment was a feeling of comfort from this minor incident. And to consider it minor was an accomplishment in itself. Something within him had changed. This morning hadn't been prodded by a need for love or even attention. He would never see this woman again. And it was just fine with him.

* * * * *

A dry wind from the north pummeled the airliner as is began its descent into the Los Angeles Basin. Tannon was trying to pick out landmarks as the jet approached the last line of mountains. This mountain pass could be either Cajon or Newhall. Things sure looked different at night. And his geographic perspective from the window seat was limited. Then came the biggest bumps, but the airplane took them as a series of quick jolts. He snugged up his seat belt, and peered westward through the dusk at the orange horizon. He imagined the giant telescopes of Hawaii awaiting the setting sun and making plans to zero in on Tau Ceti.

* * * * *

The observatory dome of the 8-meter telescope was already rotating towards the south at Kitt Peak in Arizona. The sky was completely dark to the east, and the western glow was almost gone. The cold metal structure of the dome enhanced the feeling of winter, but at least there wasn't a hint of wind. The largest of the jutting rocks along the walkway were so tall they remained uncovered by the high snow banks. The view of the desert below from this perch on the edge of the mountain was spectacular, but the astronomers and their assistants weren't impressed. Instead, they were mentally preparing themselves for the first images from the stars.

It was unusual to interrupt the schedule of this important telescope. Generally, only weather altered an agenda planned in detail, hour-by-hour, for months in advance. But Lori Talcott was a friend of Rita Pemberton, and she could spare a few minutes to get some data from a newly discovered object. Especially intriguing was its unique spectrum, as indicated by observers using the 1.8-meter Stewart Observatory Spacewatch telescope the previous night. Something was probably in error, but it was still intriguing.

* * * * *

Tannon cautiously pushed open the extra-wide door to the house. EZ would be there, waiting for the opportunity.

No EZ. Then a trilling sound from the living room, as the golden cat appeared from behind the sofa. He bounded towards Tannon, not seeming to slow until he slid to a stop on the wooden entryway floor. He immediately thrust his puffy tail against Tannon's leg.

Tannon tugged EZ's tail, and then turned and walked to the den, deposited his briefcase in the corner, and stripped off his jacket. A pile of mail was stacked neatly on his desk, mostly advertisements, and a properly folded *USA Today* next to the stack. How could anyone, even Kelly, resist the news? Also in the pile of mail was an envelope for Kelly. She wouldn't even open her own mail unless he placed it in front of her. Another sign of defiance, thought Tannon.

Mingled with the mail was a formal small envelope, probably an invitation for something horrible, like a wedding. Tannon would use his standard: "I'll be out of town that weekend. I wish you the best of everything." He wasn't a sociable person, to say the least. But he could always be relied upon for a prompt regrets reply.

Tannon walked down the hallway to Kelly's room. Her door was cracked open, so he knocked once and simultaneously pushed the door open a bit farther.

"Hello there. You wouldn't have liked those bumps over the San Gabriel Mountains," said Tannon.

Kelly was sitting at her desk with her back to the door. Tannon pushed the door fully open now and stood in the doorway. Kelly pivoted in her chair, turning towards him.

"Hey, I was there," said Kelly. "Not tonight, but it's been blowing pretty hard all day. It was a good day to practice cross-wind landings."

"Sounds like fun, but not for me. Did you feed your cat?" he asked.

"Oh, he lies a lot. He's just looking for another handout."

Kelly was sitting with her elbow draped over the arm of the wooden chair. Her bedroom television was tuned to a sitcom – she probably wasn't watching it. Her buff-color T-shirt was loose on her thin body, and she wore her favorite pair of olive drab khakis with thick white socks and no shoes. The front of her T-shirt was emblazoned with "Will Fly for Food."

"The freeway is a mess," said Tannon. "The construction on I-10 is taking forever. Add to that a bunch of jerks on the road, and you've got a real mess in Montclair."

"Nice way to end a trip," remarked Kelly. "There's a message for you on the voicemail that sounds important. Something about little green men."

Tannon chuckled, but he went immediately to the kitchen to check the telephone. He and Kelly shared the home phone and voicemail, keeping what little privacy they needed on their cell phones, which they also used in "satellite mode" in remote areas. In 2016, there was almost no place in the world out of communication reach.

The voice was Lori's, asking him to call her as soon as he arrived home. She left her home phone number again.

Tannon dialed the number, trying to forget his unreasonable fear of telephones. A male voice answered. *That's the end of that*, thought Tannon.

When Lori came on the line, she sounded strangely formal.

"Hi, Tannon. Have you sent an email notification to the IAU yet?"

"I sent it from San Francisco. Should I be concerned?"

"Oh, not at all. They've got the data they need to make an announcement, especially with Kitt Peak's confirmation. But it would be helpful to get the bulletin out right away, considering the nature of the beast?"

"So what kind of beast do you think it is?"

"Well, I've already heard from Kitt Peak tonight. They pointed the 8-meter scope at your object right after dark. They got a solid spectrogram to compare to the one from last night."

"Anything further regarding last night's spectrum?"

"No, I think the analysis team has been waiting for the 8-meter results. The first spectrogram was pretty jumbled, not unusual for complex stars. The emission lines are way out of whack. And it gets worse."

"How so?" asked Tannon.

"Well, the big mystery is that asteroids and comets don't produce emission lines. So the new spectrum tonight should help clear things up. The initial indications from last night suggest hydrogen emission lines showing a rather extreme Doppler shift. In fact, that's what's messing up the spectral analysis. It looks like it might be a shift towards the blue end of the spectrum."

"You mean it's coming toward us?"

"Looks like it is." replied Lori. "Determining exactly how fast will need some more work."

"Thanks, Lori. I really appreciate your keeping me posted. I'm sure you've got other more important projects."

"Well, I don't get to see much of this kind of astronomy in my research group. It's a pretty interesting object."

"Did they check for sideways movement tonight?"

"There's still no tangential velocity at all, which means one of two things."

"It might be too far away to detect sideways velocity, I imagine," guessed Tannon.

"Yes, that's one possibility."

"So what's the other?" asked Tannon.

Lori brought her voice up an octave as she replied.

"Maybe it's coming straight at us."

Chapter 13

Mauna Kea

Later that night, while Tannon slept, darkness arrived on the top of Mauna Kea. Ten telescopes watched the last glimmer of Hawaiian sunlight, as astronomer Blayne Kaler stepped into the observatory. He had arrived early in the afternoon, after a grueling ride up the washboard road to the summit of the 14,000-foot dormant volcano. He had to pull over to the side of the road twice, as his car hood popped loose from the jolting ride. And his engine was visibly steaming after climbing the steep grade. Blayne's Toyota wasn't worth a service call at this altitude, particularly when a tow to sea level was advertised as an even five hundred dollars, Auto Club insurance not accepted.

Few astronomers drove up mountains these days, although earth-based astronomy was still holding its ground in the face of the elaborate space telescopes that had revolutionized the science. Computer technology and advanced imaging systems had made an even greater impact. Giant scopes still did their work on top of the highest peaks. What had changed was where astronomers did his work. These days, you could sit in a comfortable air-conditioned office miles away from your telescope, robotically driving the optical equipment to any desired coordinates in the sky. The images appeared on computer screens rather than in eyepieces, so physical location wasn't that important anymore. But some astronomers still preferred the old-fashioned way of touching the metal of the equipment on a cold night, and experiencing the long drive up a mountain road.

Tonight, Blayne Kaler had been assigned to the 2.2-meter instrument. Other telescopes on this mountain, four times larger, humbled this one. But with nearly ideal observing conditions above almost half of the earth's atmosphere, even a small telescope could do some remarkable work. Earlier in the evening, the telescope operator had prepared the 2.2-meter telescope for the observing schedule. Much of the time had been used to set up the software and calibrate the charge-coupled device that was the heart of the image detection system.

* * * * *

Inside the observatory, smooth-sounding motors slued the 2.2-meter telescope and its dome slowly, keeping pace with the rotation of the earth. A gentle hum marked the movement of huge structures on precise bearings.

Below the telescope, in a detached control room dubbed the House of Stone, Blayne Kaler sat before his computer console. The well-lit room looked like the working end of any other high-tech industry. It could have been an air traffic control center or even a modern newsroom – banks of computerized workstations, desks and cushy chairs, and a trusty 10-cup coffee maker.

From the House of Stone, Blayne entered the initial celestial coordinates into the computer that drove the telescope. The first target to be observed was allocated only 30 minutes observing time and was the lowest on the night's priority list. This object near Tau Ceti would receive the disadvantage of the still darkening sky, allowing the real night's work on other objects to be accomplished under more favorable viewing conditions.

Blayne Kaler tugged on his thick beard, while directing the capture of the image with only a few keystrokes. He launched a computer program that snapped a brief exposure. Within the telescope dome above him, individual pixels were activated on the charge-coupled device. With another single tap on the keyboard ("Send"), the stored image was transmitted to the House of Stone.

Inside the House, which served as a combined warm room and astronomers' dormitory, a post-doc named Kai got his first look at the stream of data. The fiber optic computer line to the House would be busy all night, and this image certainly wasn't the most important photo scheduled. The first batch of computer data for Tau Ceti streamed in over the computer cable. It was a simple visual image, designed to resolve intricate details of the stellar background.

Kai noted the point-of-light image on his monitor. It was yellow-white and star-like with no unusual defining qualities. The spectrum of this object with its newly reported mysterious emission lines was next on the viewing list. It would take only a few more seconds for the data to appear on his monitor.

Until recent years, it took a lot of artistic talent to match spectral lines with their atomic reality. Fast-moving objects cause these lines to shift quite dramatically, obliterating the scheme of things. But tonight the powerful software handled the task automatically, as the bright lines were shifted back to their true resting-place.

Kai's computer cycled automatically to receive the incoming data. The emission spectrum began to appear gradually, spreading in jerks and spurts across his monitor, until the download was complete. Then the computer-enhanced spectrum sat centered and steady in the middle of his screen.

The Doppler shift in front of Kai was like that of a distant galaxy. Far-away galaxies move outward from the earth at speeds approaching that of light itself, as space-time grows. They mark the universe's relentless expansion, and provide astronomers with the expected shift of lines towards the red end of the spectrum. But this spectrum was shifted in a different direction. Its emission lines were shifted towards the opposite side, the blue end. It was speeding toward the earth rather than away. In the upper right corner of Kai's monitor, a digitized counter spun, slowed, and then stopped. It read 0.57. This thing was moving inbound at a velocity of 57 percent the speed of light.

* * * * *

The turn of the century had been a time of hype regarding asteroids colliding with the earth. Several high-drama movies and one embarrassingly incorrect prediction had highlighted the period. The International Astronomical Union had gone through upheaval after the incident. Revised calculations placed the closest approach of the errant asteroid at 600,000 miles, far outside the orbit of the moon – not exactly a near-miss, except by astronomical standards. The excitement had passed rapidly, but the IAU became more conservative in issuing predictions from their Central Bureau for Astronomical Telegrams.

However, this week's new sighting received the IAU's immediate attention. It was simply too important for astronomers to ignore. Tannon Bessimer's discovery proceeded rapidly through the reporting system. Kitt Peak's assistance, as a credible verification source, didn't hurt the cause.

The object needed a name, and it received one in IAU Circular 8523. It was initially designated 9840 Bessimer, since it appeared to be an asteroid rather than a comet. No coma was visible, as expected with a comet. Although an emission spectrum was evident – not at all asteroid-like – both the spectrum and the speed were still considered observational errors that would be resolved through further observation. It didn't fit into the categories astronomers found so familiar, but it appeared to be more like an asteroid than a comet. Yet, no asteroid moved with such speed. In fact, no object larger than an atomic particle moved toward the earth at this velocity. Observational data from around the world should resolve the dilemma quickly.

A distance measurement for the object was needed, but so far none was available. The only clear fact was it was outside the solar system, since no parallax over the breadth of the rotating earth had been detected. A close object would appear to shift against the background stars as viewed from distant geographic locations. Observations compared between Arizona and Hawaii hadn't detected the slightest parallax shift.

The International Astronomical Union was very guarded in its first news release. It was a straightforward announcement of a mysterious object with some very unusual properties, still pending speed and distance verification. But the Associated Press and United Press International picked up the news. The AP name for this new object was the name that stuck. The designation "9840 Bessimer" was simply too scientific for such a mysterious object. The Associated Press immediately christened it "The Bessimer Object."

Chapter 14

Kelly

We're together again, Tannon and me. Now we have each other. For him, it might be all he ever needs. Unfortunately, it's not true for me. Living with Tannon is just too easy. He takes care of things so thoroughly that I get sloppy. Sloppy in every way. I'll suffocate if it continues much longer. I love it, and I hate it. I know this won't last, and I'll have to get out of here soon. I look forward to it, and I dread it.

Sometimes I feel bad about the house. I don't keep my part of the deal. We haven't talked about it much, and it doesn't seem to bother Tannon at all. The house is his, but I don't even pay rent. He says he enjoys my help with the little things. I usually buy the groceries, but we don't eat at home very often. And I try to buy my own clothes and personal stuff. But I know I'm not pulling my weight. It's really his home.

My name is even on the FAA registration certificate for his Piper Arrow as a co-owner. But that's just so Tannon can feel comfortable about sharing. He bought the Arrow, and he lets me use it whenever I desire. Your own retractable-gear airplane comes in handy for a flight instructor. He calls it "our" airplane. I call it "his."

EZ belongs to me though. That's something important I've given to Tannon. He certainly wasn't a cat person before EZ. Now that cat is a big part of both of us. Heck, I'd let Tannon have EZ, even if he wants to take him on a trip to the stars. Who knows, he just might.

Despite living together, Tannon gives me lots of space. He seldom asks anything about my life. He sees what he sees, and that isn't much. He never asks if I'm a lesbian or bisexual. It's not important to him, I guess. It's not important to me. I'd like to think I'm just a bit of both.

Right now, it feels like I'm finally going somewhere, but not very fast. I'm still not close to a college degree. But I do love to fly, and that's enough for now. At least it's almost enough.

This whole Bessimer Object thing hasn't gotten out of hand – yet. Tannon is taking it remarkably well. He's much more comfortable with things than I can ever remember. Which seems a bit backwards. He must see the public pressures building, but it doesn't seem to bother him right now. For the first time I can remember, he even seems to be rather sociable. He's been attending to the details of his sudden fame quite well. In fact, the more famous he becomes, the more relaxed he seems. That's a big improvement over the Tannon I grew up with. It's also an improvement over the Tannon I've lived with in recent years.

But still, I worry about him. Most of all I worry about his health. You couldn't find a stronger person, if determination counts. But he's fragile in a physical sense. You can't see it, but he is. I worry about the way he eats, the way he sleeps, his headaches, and the many ways he could be taken away from me.

The recent change within Tannon is hard to explain. I like it. He's better when he's more relaxed with life. But wait until Monday. Today I saw the pending news release from the University of Arizona. Tomorrow should be a hell of a new semester at Mount SAC.

Chapter 15

Inbound

The original target, the largest gas-giant planet in the solar system, became more inviting as the spacecraft's journey drew to a close. Early in the journey, four large moons of this big planet had been identified. And recently, the bright icy surface of one moon further encouraged the targeting sequence. As the spacecraft approached the solar system, the surface of that promising moon became even more interesting. Few major craters appeared in the icy crust, and calderas were detected, lacking central peaks and high rims. The tidal heat from the pull of the gas-giant liquefied the ocean below the surface ice, and appeared to be recycling it. Disrupted icy plates floated in the surface matrix. Tilted ice sheets and chaotic surface features verified the existence of heat from below and the probability of deep subsurface water.

At a closer distance, a microwave transmitter would map the thickness of the ice crust. But all evidence pointed towards a tidally heated ocean. Elsewhere in the universe, other home planet spacecraft had found similar subsurface seas with the chemicals needed for life, prolific environments even without sunlight or oxygen.

On this moon, seafloor spreading was evident in ridgelines with distinct central troughs. Flow-like features disrupted the ridges. Although plate tectonics didn't seem to fit here, the mechanisms for heat and abundant sea life appeared everywhere the spacecraft sensors concentrated their attention.

For the balance of the inbound journey, data would continue to accumulate. The full definition of this solar system was becoming evident. One of the rocky planets was receiving increased analysis – the third planet from the star. The planet's liquid water surface came as a surprise. Life could develop abundantly in such an environment.

There was only a short time remaining to select the final destination. The spacecraft was fully autonomous now; time delays for outside decision-making were far too excessive. It wasn't yet too late to change the target from the icy moon of the giant planet, but soon the interstellar motors would fire in their final arrival sequence. Once the fusion drives roared to full life, the deceleration trajectory into this solar system would be set. A final decision couldn't wait much longer.

Within the cold darkness, machines talked to machines, working continually to assure all possible information was taken into account. What was to be decided would occur right here within this ship.

One of these worlds was a likely environment for life hidden under an icy sea, as proven elsewhere in the universe. The other tempting planet was overflowing with rare liquid water and intelligent electromagnetic emissions. Which form of life was most valuable to explore? It was a question that couldn't be debated much longer.

There was already some initial heating of the fusion engines in preparation for the major deceleration, including relay circuits beginning their confirmation tests. Residual heat from the preliminary firing of these motors hadn't yet cooled. And heat was pouring out from these powerful thinking machines. But none of this made even a dent in the cold of space.

Darkness prevailed. There was no atmosphere in this spacecraft, so there was no sound. Infrared indicators blinked inside electronic modules, as communications within the spacecraft thrived. Information about the rapidly approaching solar system was being processed by the spacecraft's sensors at a rate that made it difficult to fully handle all of the incoming data. Information analyzed by computers, discussions between machines.

Deceleration parameters were now being uploaded into the computers in favor of the gas-giant planet and its icy moon. The recent firing of these nuclear engines was nothing in comparison to what was to come. Cold was soon to be replaced with incomparable heat. Darkness was about to become light of overwhelming brightness.

Chapter 16

Monday, January 18, 2016

First Day

Front Page
Los Angeles Times

Mysterious Object Headed Toward Earth

Astronomers announced yesterday the discovery of a mysterious object closely aligned with Tau Ceti, a star only twelve light years away. Tannon Bessimer, a geology professor at Mount San Antonio College in Walnut, discovered the object with an amateur-size telescope, and reported his finding to the University of Arizona. Kitt Peak National Observatory (Arizona) and Mauna Kea Observatory (Hawaii) verified the object.

Details of the discovery are still sketchy. However, astronomers worldwide have launched an investigation into the nature of this star-like object. It doesn't appear to be either a comet or an asteroid, and it's moving straight towards our sun at an incredible speed. If initial reports from Hawaii are correct, the inbound velocity is in excess of half the speed of light.

"This object doesn't follow the parameters of any currently known astronomical object," says Dr. Vernon Franklin of the University of Arizona. Dr. Franklin, an astrophysicist at Kitt Peak, noted this object isn't on a collision course with the earth, but it does appear to be headed directly for the sun. "It will enter our solar system well below the plane of the earth's orbit, so it doesn't constitute a hazard to our planet," says Dr. Franklin. He noted the current trajectory places the object no closer to the earth than 50 million miles during its approach to the sun.

The distance of the new object is still undetermined, so there are no current estimates regarding its arrival date. Astronomers hope to have distance and revised speed estimates available within a few days. Its size is also currently undetermined.

One area of concern, according to an astronomer from the California Institute Of Technology who asked to remain anonymous, involves the effect of a collision between this mysterious object and the sun. If it is large enough, presumably planet-size or larger, a collision with the sun could have effects on the earth. However, University of Arizona astronomers have been quick to point out that this scenario is extremely remote. According to Dr. Franklin, no object larger than an atomic nucleus has ever been detected at these high speeds within our portion of the Milky Way. "None of this fits with our current level of knowledge about high speed objects, so we're learning as we go along," says Dr. Franklin.

The Cal Tech astronomer who declined to be identified has noted the initial trajectory doesn't necessarily aim the object directly at the sun or earth. Instead, according to this Cal Tech source, the object most likely will pass "close to" the sun and no closer than 100 million miles from earth, with the expected trajectory continuing past our solar system and then back out into interstellar space. "The object will accelerate tremendously under the influence of the sun's gravitation pull," he says. "But then the sun will act like a sling shot, hurling the object off into space at a weird angle still impossible to determine."

* * * * *

As he customarily did on the first day of classes, Tannon arrived at school well before anyone else. The faculty parking lot was empty except for his dark green Jeep Wrangler and the night custodian's brown Chevy truck. Neither vehicle resembled 2016. Trucks these day were normally small hybrid vehicles, but not this one. It was an old-fashioned personal cargo hauler, including a pickup bed full of old boards, colorful cargo straps, and a sprinkling of gravel and decayed leaves. Tannon's Jeep was no longer in production either, but it fit

Tannon's go-hiking personality as well as Kelly's Mustang fit her go-fast image.

Tannon preferred being firmly in place before the first day of confusion began. The beginning of the January semester wasn't nearly as stressful as the August start, but it was still worth handling with care. He unloaded two 3-ring notebooks from the front seat of the Jeep, checked the pockets of his pants for school keys, and headed towards the almost-windowless brick building. This was his third year of teaching, and it was a job that suited him just fine. He had avoided the responsibilities taken on so willingly by many other professors. Tannon was careful to avoid assignment to committees involving controversial issues, and he never volunteered for any extra duties. His small department rotated leadership responsibilities regularly, but so far he had avoided the prospect of being the department chairman. Others seemed to enjoy the responsibility, so why should he stress himself? Most professors wouldn't feel the sense of anxiety Tannon felt when faced by such responsibilities. And teaching had enough demanding routines of its own.

The glass entry door was still locked, but he managed his key and the security latch while simultaneously balancing his notebooks on his forearms. He pulled the door open awkwardly, the notebooks wedged against the glass. The hallway floor caught his eye, shining as it always did on the first day of classes. He smelled the wax and noticed the quiet. The air conditioner wasn't on yet, so the building was completely quiet. The hallway had a different feel from its regular busy mood. Glancing left, then right, Tannon noticed the wooden fire doors were all closed, making the hallway appear short and confined.

He unlocked his office door and pushed it open. The telephone message light flashed in the darkness. The illumination from the hallway was just enough to see his office chair on top of the desk, a reminder from the custodian that his office had also been attended to during the winter recess. The office floor glistened, and the wax smell was even more intense in this small room.

He reached around the doorjamb for the light switch. The fluorescent overhead lamps winked briefly, buzzed in the stillness, and then burned bright. Tannon dropped his notebooks onto the yellow upholstered chair by the door, reached for the telephone, and punched in his voicemail security code. The division secretary's voice came through in faster cadence than he ever remembered:

"Tannon, this is Laura." She barely paused between sentences. "I just saw the *Los Angeles Times*. Your name is right there on the front page."

Laura went on to explain she would be on campus early to show him the article, in case he hadn't seen it yet. Early to Laura wasn't Tannon's idea of early.

He smiled to himself and purposefully held the pose, feeling strangely calm. He hadn't seen the *Times* article and was a bit surprised to learn he had made the front page. He composed himself, pushed his mouth purposefully outward and spoke out loud to himself.

"So here's your fifteen minutes of fame."

While driving to school that morning, he had listened to the news on the radio, thinking this might be the day for the first news release. But he warned himself to be careful. First, he didn't handle society very well. Second, he was only the discoverer of the object, so he was finished with this whole thing, except for the expected questions by friends and maybe the news media. The truth was he had looked up, saw something unexpected, and that was that. He wasn't a professional astronomer, so he didn't have an opportunity to learn more, except through others. His fame would be brief. Very soon everyone would realize he had merely found this object rather than invented it. It was too bad he couldn't be more involved in the adventure that would follow, reserved for the professional astronomers. The excitement was just now beginning. But it wasn't necessarily a bad thought that he would soon be forgotten.

Tannon walked down the hallway to the Division Office, unlocked the glass door to retrieve his mail, and then relocked the door behind him. Back in his office, he reviewed his small pile of first-day announcements, and then he walked to his nearby classroom. He was busy setting up the multimedia projector while the rest of the campus was just coming to life.

Laura burst into the classroom, holding the newspaper high in her outstretched arm.

"Professor Tannon, astro-geologist!" she proclaimed.

"I'm definitely an amateur astronomer, and most would say I'm an amateur geologist."

"So have you seen this yet?" she asked.

"No. I'm glad you brought it."

She extended the article forward to him, and he took the folded newspaper without expression.

"So this is what you call the front page. I guess the lower right corner counts."

Laura planted both of her hands firmly on her waist in her most motherly pose.

"I'll tell you what. The front page of the *Times* is the front page. It's rather tough to compete with the big stuff about China."

"I suppose you're right. Will you help me with any incoming calls on this? They'll probably hit your office when my phone goes unanswered."

"Of course, Mister Astro-geologist. I'll invite everybody right into your classroom."

"Thanks. I'm sure I'd like that."

As if on cue, the classroom door swung open, and a serious-looking fellow strutted inside, with his tie swinging in front of a short-sleeved white shirt.

"Professor Bessimer?" His raised eyebrows echoed his question.

"Yes." Tannon answered hesitantly as he and Laura studied this early arrival on the first day of classes.

"I'm from the *Valley Tribune.* Can I have a few moments of your time?"

* * * * *

Tannon's classes went rather routinely that day. Not a single student mentioned anything about the discovery. Either they hadn't heard the morning news or they hadn't noticed his name. Maybe the *Los Angeles Times* was the only local news source that had picked up the story. In any case, Tannon was grateful for oblivious students who seldom read newspapers.

He had three voicemail messages waiting for him when he returned to his office at noon, but none of them were from reporters. Even the morning's early visitor hadn't probed very much, as soon as he learned Tannon didn't know any more than the major news wires had already announced. It seemed the reporter planned to divert the thrust of the story toward the hometown aspect of the discovery. After that, there wasn't much to say.

One of Tannon's messages was from the division dean, asking him to visit his office as soon as possible to formulate a plan in case things got a bit wild. The other message was from Kelly, offering: "Good luck with the paparazzi." Other than the interruption of the Tribune reporter, there was little to deflect Tannon's routine. His fifteen minutes of fame looked like it would last cumulatively less than ten minutes.

* * * * *

Kelly pushed herself up further in her seat, her routine action before entering a stall. It wasn't that she feared stalls as much as she wanted the added visibility to all sides. There were a lot of planes in this part of the Los Angeles Basin, many of them piloted by students practicing airwork. Kelly's student, Robert, sat fully upright next to her. His position of attention was dictated more by outright fear than by a concern for visibility.

"Let's clear the area, and then try a departure stall straight ahead."

"Okay," said the young clean-cut looking youth.

Robert's sunglasses gave him the desired fighter pilot look, but right now he was as meek as a kitten. He hadn't experienced much luck with yesterday's first series of stalls. Today wasn't something he looked forward to.

Robert obligingly maneuvered the airplane to the left, craning his neck far out towards the windshield of the Cessna 172, looking for conflicting traffic. Then he repeated the maneuver to the right. Nobody was in this chunk of airspace at the moment.

"Now watch your rudder control closely this time," said Kelly. "That was the only real problem yesterday. Keep an eye on the ball as you approach the stall, and that should help."

The future fighter pilot flexed his left hand on the control wheel, trying to relax a bit. He slowly pulled the yoke toward his stomach. Full power was how this tiny airplane flew in cruise, so there was no need to add power during a departure stall. Up came the nose, as the Cessna slipped into an aggravated climb. The airspeed dropped rapidly, and Robert maintained wings-level with the control wheel. The back-pressure required to hold this steep attitude wasn't a problem, but it certainly was noticeable to anyone handling the controls. Control of the ailerons and elevator began to mush as the airspeed dropped, as if the flight control cables had turned into rubber bands. Robert grimaced and worked the control wheel rapidly. His relaxed hand on the yoke became a death grip.

The Cessna 172 slowed further, the engine noise seeming even louder as the slipstream noise abated. The airspeed indicator dropped below 50 knots and then below the green arc itself, the needle notoriously inaccurate at this slow velocity. The small airplane started to turn to the left, pulled by the combined torque effect of the high power setting and unusually low airspeed. Robert gritted his teeth, not from the force required on the control wheel but from anticipation of what awaited him on the other side of the green arc.

"Torque is pulling you to the left," noted Kelly calmly. "Check the ball."

Kelly's feet were flat on the floor, and her hands were firmly in her lap. It was important for Robert to know he had full control of the airplane.

Robert glanced down at the ball. It was half-scale to the right as the Cessna skidded leftward from the torque of the engine.

"Step on the ball," reminded Kelly, still taking no action to correct the slow speed skid.

Robert pushed down tentatively with his right foot, but it wasn't nearly enough, and the airplane was hanging on the edge. The departure stall was imminent.

Whoosh! The nose of the aircraft fell suddenly as the wings stopped flying. But now Robert's increased right rudder pressure caused the Cessna to drop off suddenly to the right. And he didn't counter with immediate left rudder. They were headed into a spin.

"Oh!" was all Robert could exclaim as the airplane's nose pointed itself nearly straight down, the rotation to the right winding up into a fully developed spin. Kelly purposely tried not to overreact. These little Cessnas could spin quite safely. Maybe a little crisis would go a long way here.

Robert had instinctively pulled the throttle back to idle, so that was a step in the right direction. But the control wheel was still firmly in his lap, a natural reaction, but certainly not the right one.

"Okay, Robert. You've got us in a spin, but think it through, and get going with the recovery."

She spoke as if the engine of her Mustang was hesitating a bit as it climbed a steep grade. No big deal for Kelly. Robert was nearly panicked.

Robert said nothing and did nothing. The control wheel was still full aft. The world was spinning by, the earth coming rapidly closer, and Kelly was watching it, counting the rotations. As the altimeter unwound through 4000 feet, altitude was beginning to become a factor.

"Yoke forward to break the stall!" said Kelly in a slightly higher pitch, but still showing little tension.

Robert did nothing except continue to clutch the wheel in his left hand. His right hand was firmly glued to the idle throttle.

"I've got it," said Kelly distinctly but as calmly as possible.

Robert released his death-grip with a groan, and Kelly immediately pushed the control wheel full forward and kicked hard on the left rudder pedal. At first the nose of the little Cessna was pointed even further earthward, and Kelly and Robert were staring at nothing but the roof of a large building. But then the aircraft regained its flying speed and came smartly out of the spin. Almost simultaneously the rotation stopped and the airspeed smoothly increased. Kelly began slowly pulling back on the control wheel to regain cruise configuration, being careful of a secondary stall by a too rapid increase in pitch. Robert reached up and pressed both of his hands firmly against the sides of his headset. He held onto his head as if it was about to depart his body.

Kelly said nothing for the next few minutes, giving her student some time to calm down. When she spoke, she simply explained what had happened and how it could have been prevented. She asked Robert if he wanted the landing. He didn't.

Within Kelly, the world spun a lot, and it wasn't a problem. Recovery also came natural, a routine part of life. Sometimes those around her, like Robert, just didn't understand how regimented spinning could be. They also didn't understand how commonplace recovery could be for a frail little flight instructor.

Chapter 17

Tuesday, January 19, 2016

Millennium Fever

The new semester had started without additional fanfare. However, by Tuesday, everyone on campus had heard of Tannon's discovery, and students started asking questions. Tannon had none of the answers. It seemed evident no one from the scientific community, except Lori, was going to contact him. Lori called once on the second day of classes to tell him astronomers at Kitt Peak were studying the object further, but there was little new information. Their telescopes, even in tandem with other instruments around the world, still hadn't detected any parallax shift. Before a distance estimate could be determined, the earth itself would have to move. Eventually, as the earth progressed further in its orbit, the shift in the position of the object relative to the background stars should become noticeable. It was evident from the initial lack of parallax movement that this object was a long distance away. Maybe it was well beyond Tau Ceti – maybe even beyond our galaxy.

* * * * *

Tannon pulled his Jeep into the driveway, punched the garage door opener, and immediately regretted it. As the door swung upward, he envisioned EZ awakening from his nap, perking his ears upward, and leaping for freedom. To avoid jamming the garage door mechanism, he decided to wait for the door to fully open before hitting the "Close" button. In the meantime, he took advantage of his error and pulled the Jeep into the garage as soon as the door was high enough. Kelly's Mustang was already there.

Sure enough, EZ ran through the kitty door linking the garage and the house. He had selected his explorer's trot and was headed out the inviting exit. There was no stopping him now, so Tannon left the garage door open and walked to the mailbox at the driveway entrance. At the side of the driveway, the golden cat was using a small birch tree as a scratching post. Tannon considered leaping for EZ, but knew it would be an exercise in futility. Once this cat was outside, there was no catching him.

"Okay, EZ, enjoy your adventure. But don't forget to come home for dinner."

EZ gave Tannon his "catch me if you can" look, and Tannon was wise enough to ignore it. EZ would return home when he was ready, and not a moment sooner.

Tannon emptied the mailbox and picked up the driveway copy of *USA Today*, which had arrived after he left for school, an unusually late delivery that distressed him. He tended to worry about events well beyond his control, one of his personal quirks unchanged by the discovery of an astronomical object.

Tannon scanned the headlines as he walked into the house, leaving the garage door open for the return of EZ. There was nothing on the front page of the newspaper regarding the new object.

All of the news sources had picked up the story by now, but there was nothing more to report. At first the story had been treated as another millennium omen, more of the same from the previous two decades. Throughout the early years of the century, Millennium talk had continued, especially with the natural disasters that had absorbed 2015. A deadly earthquake in Alaska, followed almost immediately by the Swamp Flu pandemic that began in China, had marked the previous year as a deadly chunk of history. The stock markets of the world were only now slowly recovering from the impacts of the pandemic on the world's economy. Now in January of 2016, the world still looked for omens. At first, Tannon Bessimer's new object was called the "Discovery of the Millennium." Most aspects of "Millennium Fever" came and went quickly. In 2016, it was in its third or fourth pass, dependent upon how you counted. This discovery had already become a non-story, but probably there would be something in the next issues of the scientific journals.

As Tannon stepped into the hallway leading to the living room, an afternoon talk show hostess was yelling about something, but there was no one in sight to hear. He went directly to the TV remote control and held it steady for a moment, trying to determine what the controversial topic was. Unsuccessful and impatient, he clicked off the television. Now he could hear music coming from Kelly's bedroom. As he approached her room, he tried unsuccessfully to identify the singer.

Kelly's door was wide open, and she was propped up on her bed, reading a copy of *Pacific Flyer*.

"Is that Dean Martin?" he asked.

She lowered the newspaper.

"Not bad. You're getting better."

"What's new in the news?" He knew her only kind of news was aviation-related or sports.

"Oh, those new avgas fees look like they're going to happen. Things aren't looking very good for us fly-girls. And now they're talking about insisting on lead-free avgas, a bullet we've dodged for a long time. That'll kill us."

Tannon wasn't pleased with the trend either. He spoke with a note of sarcasm.

"As little as we fly our Arrow, I wonder if it's worth keeping."

"I'm standing by for another 'Let's sell that thing' spiel."

She waited, but she didn't get the expected lecture, so she continued.

"You always talk that way when you're frustrated about your flying. The problem is. . . you haven't been doing any. How about a flight to catch up with those instrument approaches you need?"

Kelly was referring to the instrument currency regulations that temporarily kept Tannon grounded.

"You're right. And I'd like to get away this weekend. Maybe you could sign me off during a flight to Kern Valley."

"It's a bit cold for camping, even for me," she remarked.

Tannon paused to consider that.

"We'd have to bundle up," he said. "But it'd be a great spot to get a clear look at our object."

"Our object? Now it's _our_ object. So we'll fly up to Kern in _our_ airplane to see _our_ object."

"Okay, let me rephrase it. Let's spend a night under the stars watching the EZ Object."

Tannon understood Kelly's resistance to accepting joint ownership of everything. But he knew their lives were shared, even if she didn't always accept it.

"Speaking of your cat," continued Tannon. "He escaped on me. Right out the 'ol garage door. What a pain."

"He'll be back. It isn't a bad time for him to take an excursion – almost kitty dinnertime."

"So what do you think?" asked Tannon. "We could leave for Kern Valley Saturday morning, get some hiking in before dark, and come home early on Sunday."

"Sounds fine to me," Kelly agreed. "But keep those pesky reporters away from me."

Tannon smiled. "Wait until they find out this thing is bigger than a galaxy. Then you'll wish we had joint custody of it."

Chapter 17

Cerro Paranal

Northern Chile was basking in the summer heat, but the top of the mountain was far from balmy. High-altitude observatories, particularly on clear nights, were well known for their numbing cold.

The European Southern Observatory at Cerro Paranal housed the largest optical telescope in the world. Such a claim was easy to dispute, since the structure of telescopes varied. But if you were talking about optical instruments and total light-gathering power, this was the world's largest. The VLT or Very Large Telescope consisted of four giant reflectors working in parallel. When linked together they gathered as much light as a single instrument with a 16-meter aperture. It placed this telescope in a category three times the diameter of Palomar Mountain's 200-inch telescope, for decades the world's largest. From a light-gathering perspective, the VLT, with all of its mirrors coupled together, was ten times as effective as the Palomar classic.

The VLT and other large earth-based telescopes had become increasing important in recent years. The Hubble Space Telescope's multiple gyroscope failure had caught astronomers off guard. The HST had performed nearly flawlessly for years, but its age was showing. Now well beyond it's originally anticipated lifetime, a NASA maintenance mission to the HST was needed. But the Space Shuttle had finally been decommissioned, and the new Orion was still in its test phase. The European Herschel space telescope was operating fine, and it boasted an even bigger primary mirror than Hubble, but it functioned in infrared wavelengths, which limited its competition with earth-based observatories. And the Webb space telescope was still floundering on earth, now several years behind schedule because of NASA's backlog of launch delays.

NASA had hit a series of setbacks in the last two years, including the financial problems involving repairs to the International Space Station, to say nothing of the psychological burden of trying to recover from 2015's ISS accident. It all seemed another spinoff of millennium omens.

Tonight, Vincent Leeming of Cal Tech had the helm of the European Southern Observatory's VLT. He was neither very European nor at all South American. The telescope was available for use by a number of universities and scientific consortiums around the world. If you had a plan, the ESO would listen. But plans had to be approved many months in advance. Vince Leeming's luck occurred when the quartet of telescopes was taken out of service, one-by-one, during 2015, receiving needed upgrades to their already-aging mechanical bearings, optical coatings, and software. The overhaul of the 16-meter array was completed earlier than projected, unexpected in a time of constrained science budgets. On unusually short notice, Vince Leeming's proposal for observation of planetary nebulae was suddenly approved. He was more than happy to adjust his plans for early 2016.

This was his first working night on the mountain. It was already a big disappointment, as clouds obscured northern Chile, and the forecast for the rest of the night looked poor. Tomorrow evening would be his second and final night on the observing schedule. After that, other projects would bump him. Movement of this weather system out of the area was unlikely, but the forecast indicated some improvement was expected. He prayed the forecast would hold. Otherwise, he would be headed home without a single observation of planetary nebulae. His year would be off to a very bad start.

* * * * *

That same night, under clear Arizona skies, the Kitt Peak 8-meter reflector detected a small parallax shift in the Bessimer Object. It wasn't much movement, since the earth had traveled a mere 11 million miles in its orbit since the first photos of the object were taken the previous week. But it was enough orbital change to detect movement in the position of the Bessimer Object against the distant stellar background. The parallax shift was still an imprecise measurement that would be improved over time. For now, the estimates of the astronomers would have to be considered tentative.

Initial calculations revealed that the object currently resided at a distance of 2150 astronomical units, approximately 200 billion miles. It was a stone's throw by interstellar standards, a mere three-hundredths of a light year. Then again, that placed it a long way outside all of the orbits of the planets. Astronomers argued about the outer boundary of the solar system. Beyond Neptune's orbit, the Oort Cloud of comets formed a distant border, and the nearer heliopause marked the merger of the solar wind's flowing particles with the interstellar medium. This new object was outside the heliopause but well within the outer boundary of the Oort Cloud. At its present disputed velocity of 57 percent the speed of light, the object would be in the vicinity of the sun by early February.

* * * * *

The news from Kitt Peak reached Cerro Paranal the next morning. It was the primary topic of discussion over breakfast. As Vince Leeming entered the cafeteria, he was weary from a night of waiting for clear skies that never came. He would have to determine his new observing priorities and reprogram his objects for this evening, since there wasn't enough time to hit all of the intended targets. But breakfast and sleep would come first on his list of priorities.

As he picked out pancakes and sausage in the cafeteria line, Vince pondered the upcoming evening's observing schedule. He was running out of observing time. Twilight lasted over an hour in Chile during the summer, so it would be a short night. Time was quickly slipping away.

He chose a table near the window, joining James La Point, one of the doctoral candidates from Cal Tech. Across the table from James was Geoff Randazzo from one of the European institutes.

"How's everybody this morning?" Vince asked, as if more than one answer was expected.

"Not bad," said James. "We were just marveling at the ugly morning. It must have been a fun night."

"Fun isn't the word for it. I couldn't coax a change in the forecast, so I read a good book. The rest wasn't so good."

"The weather's a bummer," replied James. "Did you hear the latest from Kitt Peak?"

Vince was tired. He had hoped for a quiet breakfast before a nice long nap and then reprogramming of the VLT. His brain wasn't prepared for additional input.

"What's happening there?" asked Vince, hoping the answer was simple.

"It looks like that Bessimer Object is going to be here sooner than we thought," said James, pausing to pry some suspense from the situation.

But Vince just stared back at him, so James continued.

"Kitt Peak found a parallax shift last night. It's only 2150 AUs out."

Vince Leeming didn't know what to say, so he said nothing. It all sank into his numb brain. James continued with additional information, but Vince's mind was ignoring it. As the young astronomer continued to talk, Vince's tired brain ran a few mental calculations, using the disputed Doppler shift of point-five-seven 'C' reported by Mauna Kea. If the numbers and his tired brain were right, the new object would be here in two weeks. He needed a calculator right away. His brain was awakening from its slumber, sleep or no sleep.

* * * * *

Vince Leeming didn't sleep that day, not even a nap. He would be a vegetable for the night's observations, but his graduate student assistant and the telescope operator would take care of the details. Once an observing plan was formulated, there really wasn't much to do except watch it fall into place. So in his small motel-like room on top of the Andes, he pondered his calculations.

If something was bright enough to be seen from over 2000 astronomical units, it had to be large. But it wasn't at intergalactic distances or even interstellar ones. Instead, it was just outside the solar system. It was between the sun and the nearest stars. Yet it was moving at nearly the speed of light. How could any object, other than a microscopic elementary particle, establish such a pace? Sure, the distant galaxies traveled near the speed of light, but they were expanding with space-time. In a relativistic sense, they weren't really moving at all. This new object was a lot closer than the galaxies. And it had significant size, as evidenced by merely being viewed at a distance of several thousand astronomical units. Yet it was careening toward the sun at a speed unheard of for large physical objects near the solar system. Even in astronomical circles, such high speeds didn't make sense.

An even bigger question involved the emission spectrum that had allowed detection of the unexpected inward velocity. This couldn't be a star – it was right on the solar system's doorstep. But it had emission lines, the normal property of nuclear processes in stars. What was emitting all of that energy?

Vince talked out loud to convince himself a change in tonight's observing plan was warranted. He had spent months of preparation for these two nights of research on his beloved planetary nebulae. He was about to squander all of his planning on a target of opportunity that was probably an observational error from Kitt Peak or Mauna Kea. But that's what the profession of astronomy was all about.

* * * * *

As the astronomers in northern Chile were settling down at lunch, Tannon was playing with his morning bowl of cereal, pondering the fate of EZ. He couldn't eat much. EZ still wasn't home.

San Dimas wasn't untamed wilderness, although its residents liked to claim they lived in an authentic western town. It was hard to be rural when the Los Angeles Basin spread uninterrupted for more than 50 miles inland. But there was enough open space for coyotes to roam, and Tannon awoke many nights to the rolling howl of a pack on the hunt. Cats weren't on their main menu, but coyotes never passed up a free meal.

Tannon's general optimism toward most things didn't extend to EZ this morning. His best friend, if you didn't count his sister, was probably dead. Just like that, he was gone. EZ was always looking for a quick exit, often found one, and always came home after a few hours of adventure. But not this time.

Tannon had killed him. How could he be so negligent to pop open the garage door without thinking? He had personally left the kitty door to the garage unlocked when he left for work, to provide EZ access to his favorite hiding place, the garage loft. Tannon was the classic absent-minded professor. Now he was being repaid, and he felt both remorse and regret. Even his discovery of a new astronomical object didn't seem very important this morning.

It was time to leave for school. He couldn't delay it any longer. There was one more trip around the neighborhood and a few more rounds of dish banging. Maybe EZ was trapped in somebody else's garage, a victim of too much exploring. Maybe he'd come home when released from a temporary prison when a neighbor opened his garage door. And maybe EZ would be sleeping on the sofa when Tannon returned home today, a night-creeping cat catching up on his sleep.

Tannon made one last series of dish banging and verified the patio door was cracked open for the cat's return. He headed for his Jeep, checking his pocket for the set of keys needed for school.

There in the garage sat EZ, perched on the hood of Tannon's Jeep, washing himself without concern for the world. Tannon felt a rush of relief and a moment of anger.

"Where have you been!" scolded Tannon.

EZ stopped his washing in mid-lick, arched his back in a slow stretch, and stared at Tannon. He issued a soft trill, reminding him it was time for breakfast.

* * * * *

In the mountains of Chile, the evening was perfectly clear. The meteorologists were flat-out wrong. Even the high clouds dissolved before sunset. The clear twilight would lead to insistent cold, but it was a wonderful tradeoff.

Vince Leeming's observing plan had been revised to concentrate on the Bessimer Object. The abundance of observations of the object from around the world hadn't led to anything new in recent nights until Kitt Peak's news of the parallax shift and the outrageously close distance. Worldwide, astronomical observatories would now go into high gear. Vince had one of the largest telescopes in the world at his fingertips at the perfect time. He wouldn't squander the opportunity.

Spectroscopic measurements of the new object had been cursory until now. No one had delegated the time necessary to get a detailed breakdown of the object's composition. The approximate speed and distance were now available. But how big was this thing, and what was it made of? Maybe those answers could be determined tonight.

As soon as darkness allowed, the first order of business was obtaining spectral data. The VLT had been converted into a flux detector for the initial round of observations. VLT astronomers referred to such a configuration as a "light bucket," both as a descriptor for what was really happening and as an insult to the quality of telescope needed for the task. To use the VLT as a light bucket wasn't a typical observing mode for this precision instrument. Any crudely figured reflecting surface could carry out spectral analysis, since no image would be formed. But such a large light bucket could measure the object's intensity and spectrum precisely.

In the House of Stone, four stories below the telescope, Vince typed in the right ascension and declination for the Bessimer Object. Right after twilight, Tau Ceti was posed nearly overhead, as viewed from this mountaintop in Chile, thus reducing the thickness of the earth's atmosphere and making observing conditions ideal. The observatory's high altitude cut down further on the atmosphere's slice. The night was crystal clear, and local skies had settled to atmospheric stability after passage of the storm. The astronomers atop Cerro Paranal rated the night's seeing conditions as "outstanding."

After the spectral data was recorded, the next instrumentation package was rotated into position. It was rare to change equipment in the middle of an observation run, since time was too precious. But tonight there was a single object of attention, and everything was being thrown at it. The visual package wasn't the most common configuration, but it was next. A large portion of current astronomical research was in the realm of spectroscopy and infrared imaging, and these technologies didn't produce true visual pictures. But tonight the VLT would be used like a giant eye, with photographic images just like the old days. Charge-coupled devices were the modern replacement for sensitive film.

By now, several hours of data collection had taken their toll. Vince was getting weary, his lack of sleep creeping up on him. A second wind from his busy preparation during the day had kept him running until now. He had placed an order for a night lunch before going on-duty, and he was looking forward to the break. Maybe the lunch would perk him up a bit. His adrenaline level was plenty high, but the altitude and lack of sleep depleted his physical energy.

He leaned against the table that held the image monitor and his lunch, stretching to flex his body and clear his brain. When he stood upright once again, Vince Leeming watched the pixels fill from the accumulation of exposure time. By astronomical standards, this was a bright image, and a filter was needed to attenuate the light. The cryogenic attachment for the charge-coupled device could sometimes produce erratic results. Some nights, it seemed to reduce CCD images to a near-meaningless blur.

Tonight, either the optics package was experiencing some kind of anomaly, or Vince Leeming had hit it just right. The image building before his eyes wasn't a point of starlight. It was a distinct tiny spherical disk.

Chapter 19

Thursday, January 21, 2016

Texas-Size

The report from Cerro Paranal, along with further data from Kitt Peak and Mauna Kea, was transmitted to astronomers around the world via the Internet. There was no attempt to protect these discoveries. History had shown that the real discovers of scientific information almost always received recognition for their findings. The sharing of information was critical when data accumulated so fast. Visual observations scheduled in places where it was cloudy could be replaced by locations where it was clear. Of course, the visual spectrum produced only a small part of the information. Radio telescopes would reveal an abundance of data, even under cloudy skies.

Still, Vince Leeming worried about the news of the spherical shape getting out so soon. For now, there was an attempt to confine the flow of information to the astronomical world. Before contacting the news media, solid verification was always preferred, but increasingly difficult in an intricately wired world. Discoveries announced before verification often proved erroneous, and it was the kiss of death for future research funding. In consolation, Vince was assigned an unprecedented additional night on the VLT, accompanied by astronomical experts from the Harvard-Smithsonian Center for Astrophysics who owned the next night's observing slot.

By the end of the next night of observations, the results were verified right at Cerro Paranal, and the data was enhanced even further by additional computer analysis. The object was definitely a spherical disk, though only resolved with advanced cryogenic equipment on a huge telescope. This equipment operated at unbelievably cold temperatures, near absolute zero, and reliability was part of the sacrifice. Most observatories had decommissioned cryogenic CCDs in recent years, in favor of simpler and more reliable designs. Still, it was this super-cold technology that provided the most detailed images – when it functioned properly. The VLT was thus the first observatory to determine the object was much smaller than a star or a planet and was producing energy on an unheard-of scale. It wouldn't be easy for the rest of the world to comprehend the meaning.

* * * * *

By the end of the week, Tannon felt frustrated. Scientists studying the object had plenty of time to analyze their observations. Surely there was more information available by now. Yet he received no phone calls, no email, nothing. He understood he didn't own the object. But he had a special interest in knowing what the experts discovered.

Newspapers and television were no help. The lack of updates from astronomers had led to a complete disappearance of the topic from the news wires. He decided to call Lori.

Of course, he also felt disillusioned by her. When he had first contacted Lori, he assumed she was still single and unattached. But even a skinny acne-covered face could find love in this world. He hadn't thought about Lori, except fleetingly, in two decades. But he was still disappointed.

He dialed the number for her office, but Lori wasn't there. A dubious messenger promised to relay his request for her to return his call. Tannon was turning into the worst kind of pessimist, not believing anyone about anything.

As he sulked on the patio, Kelly came home from her latest aerial venture at nearby Brackett Airport. Tannon heard her pull into the garage, drop her backpack in the living room, talk to EZ, and then make her way to the patio.

"He tried to kill me again," said Kelly.

"Who did?"

"Robert, my notorious student. He's a hazard to himself. I should tell him to give up."

Tannon searched her face for a hint of sarcasm. He saw none.

"There goes your gas money," said Tannon. "Maybe you should just charge him for a pilot license, send him for a flight test, and hope for the best. You could use the money for a trip to Vegas."

"Oh, sure, that's a brilliant idea," replied Kelly. "But the Feds might have something to say about my instructor's license."

After Kelly's latest bout with her student, her hair was still pressed down on top of her head, pasted flat. She called it "headset hair," the mark of an active flight instructor. Her bangs were jagged, and she looked typically casual in her man's blue denim shirt and tan khakis. Black high-top sneakers rounded out the ensemble.

Tannon studied her face. She was thin featured, with soft round cheeks. There was a slight frown today no one else might detect. It wasn't the killer student that was bothering her.

"What's on your mind?" he asked.

She flinched, and her shoulders twitched a bit, as if caught trying to hide something.

"Nothing really. But I did want to tell you about a job interview."

"Whoa. Now that's news."

She paused before continuing. "It's in Houston next Tuesday. National Express is building up their Regional Jet routes, and they're hiring like crazy. Maybe even me."

Tannon was devastated, but he refused to show it.

"That's wonderful. You're a shoo-in."

"Well, let's see what happens. The pay isn't so hot, and most of the new-hires are assigned to Cleveland."

"Hey, they have a great baseball team," joked Tannon.

He was hurting inside.

"And wonderful thunderstorms in the summer and nice ice in the winter – a regular pilot's paradise," joked Kelly.

She understood he was hurting. And, in her own way, she was hurting too.

"What an opportunity," Tannon said. "Going straight to jets sure beats those old turboprops."

"Yeah, I never would've guessed I could skip that step. Times are booming for the regional carriers. I guess my low multi-engine hours didn't deter them much."

"When they're in a hiring mode, don't question it, Sis. The new RJ is a real gee-whiz machine."

"True enough. Not exactly state-of-the-art, but those babies come equipped with autopilots and white sidewall tires. But it's just an interview."

Tannon refused to show his concern at losing Kelly – again.

"The interview will go fine. And you're going to be a tremendous jet jock."

Tannon smiled at his sister, and she crunched her mouth into a twisted grin that could be registering frustration. Within Tannon Bessimer was a desperate feeling, and Kelly saw right through it.

* * * * *

As Tannon sat on the sofa skimming through *Scientific American* and stretching EZ's tail, the phone rang. This was a two-ring burst, meaning it was someone who knew his secret number.

He picked up the phone cautiously, and was pleased to find Lori on the other end.

"I got your message," said Lori. "Sorry I didn't call earlier. I just got back from a conference in Chicago, and this place is going bananas."

"I thought all astronomers were bananas most of the time."

Tannon tried to change his own sour mood, and this phone call might help.

"The bananas are because of the your famous object, my friend. In fact, you can expect to see some news from Katie Couric real soon."

Lori sounded stunning. Tannon wondered what she looked like these days. He provided Lori a simple "Hmm" in reply. It was an invitation for her to continue.

She explained the latest observations from Kitt Peak and Cerro Paranal, with the latest distance estimate of less than 2000 astronomical units.

"That's still a long way out," noted Lori, "And the distance is giving us fits. There's nothing there to illuminate it, so it must be radiating like crazy on its own. But it's definitely not a star."

"How about a rogue dwarf? Or something smaller than a star but bigger than a planet?"

Tannon had followed the two-decade controversy regarding dark matter in the universe. There was a lot of missing mass that might be Jupiter-size.

"Well, that's not impossible, but the European Southern Observatory has put the VLT on it. They've got some detailed spectral data and what looks like a resolved image. At least it's right on the edge of being something other than a point-source. If their reports are correct, this thing is about the diameter of Texas."

"Sounds like an asteroid to me."

"Yes, but to be observed at that distance, shining by its own light, doesn't make any sense. The whole concept of an emission spectrum from something this small is outrageous. The parameters simply don't fit. It's way too small to burn by nuclear processes on its own. And even if it did, it would've burned itself out in a matter of minutes. And then there's the matter of its shape."

She paused for affect, and Tannon immediately took the cue.

"So what's its shape?"

"If the ESO is right, it's a perfect sphere. Which seems impossible for something the size of Texas, based on the resolving power of the VLT at 2000 AU. Must have been one crazy night of perfect seeing in the Andes."

"Actually, I don't get it," said Tannon. "It doesn't add up, does it? So what are you telling me?"

Tannon's mood was escalating.

"What I'm telling you," she continued, "is this spherical thing is lit up like a Christmas tree, but it isn't powered by any energy source we understand. Stars burn by nuclear processes. This thing is simply lit up."

* * * * *

Their conversation continued for another ten minutes. Lori took the time to explain many of the details. The spectrum from Cerro Paranal was a problem. It possessed strong spectral emission lines, indicating the object was transmitting energy in huge amounts. The spectrum possessed a strong hydrogen line, along with distinct metallic signatures. Some of the spectral lines seemed to be high atomic numbers, those not found abundantly in nature. One particularly unexpected line appeared to be molybdenum or a similar metal. The weird alchemy of this object had the astrophysicists perplexed.

Before she hung up, Lori offered one more thought.

"You know, Tannon, this has raised some major questions around here. We've been in constant contact with Cerro Paranal for the past two nights, and they're hesitant to release their findings to the public. I bet you can guess why."

"I'm not good at guessing," replied Tannon as calmly as possible.

"Well, neither am I," said Lori. "But the emission lines in this spectrum are a problem for everybody. The only source of hydrogen lines we can come up with is either a star or a giant fusion power source with lots of escaping energy."

Tannon thought he understood. But the conclusion was mind-boggling.

"You mean like a rocket."

"One heck of a big rocket," replied Lori. "This object may have some man-made properties. . ."

Tannon interrupted.

"Don't you mean alien-made?"

Lori didn't laugh.

Chapter 20

Friday, January 22, 2016

Blue Shift

After studying the object for two nights at Cerro Paranal, astronomers had lots of facts to talk about. Add to that the results pouring in from other observatories around the world, and there was more than the normal amount of speculation. Not surprisingly, the news media was now involved. How the information had leaked was of no importance – it was inevitable.

The story was the lead item on the eleven o'clock TV local news on Friday, and it made headlines in the *Los Angeles Times* the next morning. This time it wasn't in the lower right corner.

The details were comprehensive, although they stopped short of spectroscopic speculation. There was no mention of artificial illumination of the object or the unusual metals in the spectrum. And no rocket sources were suggested. However, the distance of the Bessimer Object and its scheduled arrival in early February was more than enough to generate excitement.

An interview with the Director of the Griffith Park Observatory by the *Times* calmed the issue a bit. His composed appearance was evident in a photo on the observatory's outside patio, overlooking downtown Los Angeles. His long muttonchop whiskers provided a retro look that seemed appropriate for an astronomer. He didn't waiver under the reporter's questions, reiterating that the object wasn't going to hit the earth. And probably it would miss the sun as well, scooting by in a bright display, to continue onward into the blackness of space. But this same Griffith Park astronomer expressed concern with the unusual nature of the object. His interview included the contradiction between the size of the object and its tremendous speed.

"I'm just not sure what kind of object could travel this fast," said the observatory director.

* * * * *

There was no reason to delay their trip to Kern Valley, although further Astroscan observations of the new object under high-desert dark skies wouldn't prove a thing. But Tannon wanted to try to see it again before Cetus became too low in its seasonal journey toward the western horizon, and he simply wanted to get away with Kelly. They always enjoyed flying together. Tannon, who seldom flew solo, felt confident with Kelly beside him in the cockpit. And Kelly enjoyed the relaxation of not having to watch an inexperienced student's every move. When they flew in their Arrow, they were different people in the same world. Better people.

Immediately after gear-up, Tannon maneuvered the aircraft in a climbing left turn to intercept the departure airway. He always flew left seat when he was with Kelly. As much as Kelly loved flying, she was more comfortable on the flight instructor's side of the aircraft. Besides, she enjoyed navigating and communicating with ATC more than flying. She got plenty of hands-on flight proficiency practice with her students.

The maroon and white aircraft was ordinary from the outside. But inside it had an instrument panel rivaling bigger aircraft, including an airline-style flight director system. One of the most valuable black boxes was the satellite navigation system, the Polaris R2 GPS. But it took both Tannon and Kelly to keep track of everything – comfortably. This was an airplane that was a joy to fly, but it kept a pilot plenty busy simply monitoring the onboard equipment.

Tannon completed the first climbing turn, rolling out on a heading of 130, the direction prescribed for airway interception. Passing through two thousand feet, they found themselves engulfed in coastal stratus clouds. Tannon increased the rate of his instrument scan, more of a mental process than physical movement of his eyes. Peripheral vision could keep track of nearly the whole instrument panel at one time. He checked and rechecked the horizontal situation indicator, awaiting verification that the navigation needle was starting to swing. Nothing yet.

"Forgetting something?" Kelly asked in her best nonchalant voice.

"Probably, but I'm darned if I know what it is. The needle should be moving by now."

"Seems that way to me," noted Kelly with no sign of concern.

Tannon reached up and flipped the switch to receive the Morse code identification for the VOR. The code was beeping, as expected. He rechecked the setting on the HSI pointer. It looked perfect, 164 degrees.

Tannon knew Kelly was aware of what he was doing wrong. But she wasn't going to tell him until he was in over his head.

"Garbage in, garbage out," she said calmly.

"Yikes!" exclaimed Tannon, just as he recognized the problem.

He gave the navaid selection button a quick glance, hit the button squarely with his finger, and the HSI needle came back to life. The selection button had been in the GPS position, and he was trying to navigate using a VOR signal. He had already swung through the airway but caught it quickly and turned back to the right to intercept properly. Air Traffic Control never questioned the errant radar blip that momentarily signaled his error.

"It's not like those baby Cessnas," Kelly noted. "This bird will keep you on your toes all the time."

"You've got that right, Kell. That's not the first time I've missed the selection button, checklist or no checklist."

Tannon was glad Kelly was as much of a sister as a flight instructor today. She knew how to make her point, and it was with gentleness, at least in an airplane. Instead of intervening when he made the mistake, she let him work it through – a good instructional technique. And safe enough, under the circumstances.

Things settled down after that. Passing through four thousand feet, they broke out of the clouds, climbing in the bright blue sky. Leaving six thousand feet, Tannon clicked on the autopilot, instructing it to level the Arrow at eight thousand.

On the way to the mountain valley 100 miles north of Los Angeles, they discussed the latest Bessimer Object news. Kelly listened intently as Tannon explained the details provided by Lori, noting her concern regarding the emission spectral lines.

"Do you think astronomers are withholding information from the public?" asked Kelly.

"I don't see why they would. The fusion rocket stuff is nothing but a wild possibility, so it shouldn't be released unless it's verified. I bet they're letting most of the information out as soon as they receive it. And that's probably best. Besides, it's hard to limit information these days."

Kelly thought about it for a moment.

"Yes, but when the public finally absorbs the concept," Kelly said, "I wonder how they'll handle it."

* * * * *

In the late afternoon, after the local mountain downflow wind died down, Tannon and Kelly set up their tents. Camping was second nature to them, and there were camping places you could only visit by airplane. In the case of Kern Valley, the airport had its own campground right on the field. It was one of their favorite destinations.

"It's gonna' be cold tonight," noted Tannon, his voice already raspier in the cool, dry air.

"We're tough," stated Kelly. "Or at least I am."

"Those mountains will make for an early sunset," said Tannon. "So it'll get chilly fast. But it won't be fully dark until after 6 o'clock."

"I'm not sure how much astronomy I have in me tonight," said Kelly. "I hope you don't go and discover another super-star."

"One is plenty for this lifetime. But Cetus is moving west, and we won't be able to see it much longer in the western sky after sunset. Of course, if my super-star gets bright enough, we can just watch it in the daytime."

* * * * *

As they sat in their cloth camping chairs near their tents, Kelly and Tannon waited for the sky to darken. They talked about the obvious changes in the world since the discovery of the object.

"Wall Street will get a chance to react on Monday," said Tannon. "I hope I'm not blamed for the results. Most pundits are expecting a rather bad reaction."

"Don't give yourself so much credit," said Kelly. "The market has been in the tank lately, anyway. And I bet the world reacts better than you expect. There's nothing that indicates any danger to the earth. Well, almost nothing, except the possibility of blowing us all to bits."

Tannon knew Kelly had a firm grip on the big picture most of the time, and she could always couple it with a sense of humor. Yet she consciously avoided the national and international news. Within Kelly resided an innate understanding of the processes of life others usually missed. But she often tried to hide it.

They bantered over the disappearance of international issues from the front page. Major world situations like the China crisis seemed subdued by news of the inbound object. It wasn't merely a bigger story overshadowing lesser news. It seemed more like a readjustment of priorities on a global scale. Maybe some lasting value would come from this temporary interruption of mankind's war-focused routines.

When it was finally dark enough to capture Tau Ceti in the Astroscan, Tannon centered the star in the eyepiece and focused carefully. The dim companion point-of-light blazed in the same position as when he first viewed it from San Dimas.

"You'll have to change the focus a bit for your eye," Tannon reminded Kelly, as he turned the telescope over to her.

Tannon was concerned with the change in Kelly's vision lately. Her eyes had been notoriously better-than-perfect for most of her life, but seemed to have deteriorated rapidly since she moved from Syracuse to California. Her outpatient eye surgery six months ago didn't seem to change anything, except for inconveniencing her flying schedule during the month-long recovery. Tannon noticed her deteriorating acuity as she scanned for other aircraft when flying the Arrow. She used to always be the first to find conflicting traffic – "Miss Eagle Eye," he called her, but not any more.

"It's in pretty sharp focus just the way it is," replied Kelly.

Tannon knew she was lying, but she refused to move the focus knob.

"It looks brighter than last week," added Kelly.

"Well, I doubt it's noticeably brighter quite yet. As it gets closer, its magnitude will increase, but nobody seems willing to guess how bright it'll become. Everything about this object has got real astronomers squirming."

"You're a real astronomer, as far as I'm concerned," said Kelly. "Besides, you're practically famous."

She was bundled up for the cold, looking plump tonight in her maroon ski jacket with a heavy sweater underneath. Her tan wool ski cap was pulled down over her ears. She wore bulky mittens that made it difficult to adjust the focusing knob, so maybe that was the reason she had insisted the image was clear.

"I'm serious," she said. "If it's not brighter, maybe it's a slightly different color or something. It sure looks dazzling tonight."

Kelly pulled away from the eyepiece, waving her arm towards Tannon, inviting him to take another look.

Tannon approached the red bowling ball, bent his tall frame to the eyepiece, and said nothing. He looked at the object in a different way now. Yes, now that Kelly mentioned it, it did seem brighter, and it also seemed whiter than its previous whitish-yellow color. As he watched, he thought he saw it pulsating slowly, but it was undoubtedly the unstable atmosphere. The winds above this mountain valley were almost always blowing, even when it was calm at the surface.

"What do you think?" inquired Kelly.

"I think it might be changing. But if it is, this time there's no rush to report it. Because at this very moment, there's a whole bunch of really smart folks looking at this very same tiny ball of light."

Chapter 21

Saturday, January 23, 2016

Change of Name

The night was cold and dark. Bundled in his sleeping bag, Tannon got his first adequate sleep in nearly a week. He awoke without a headache, even though the air was downright chilly. The sun was barely above the horizon, breaking through a saddle in the mountains to the southeast. The piercing sunlight cut through the thin fabric of the tent, and Tannon felt a hint of its early warmth.

His voice cracked in the cold morning air: "Hey, over there! Have you seen any bears around here?"

He spoke loud enough to awaken Kelly but not to scare her.

Kelly grunted. She wasn't an early riser. Nor was she afraid of bears in this campground.

When Kelly finally stumbled from her tent, Tannon already had the fire-ring aglow. As she approached the campfire, she squinted as if she had a hangover. She wore a heavy black sweatsuit and unlaced, low-cut hiking boots. Her sweatshirt boasted: "Woman Power – Get with

It!" Her ski jacket was unzipped with its neck crooked and partially tucked in on one side.

"I guess the honeymoon is over," Tannon kidded her. "You never dress for breakfast anymore."

After warming themselves by the fire, it was time to eat. For Tannon, it was always time for breakfast. He cooked, while Kelly gratefully sat by the warm coals. The small ice chest and the two-burner Coleman stove produced a miraculous mix of scrambled eggs, bacon, toast, and coffee.

After breakfast, they walked to the airport office at the far end of the long taxiway that angled away from the runway. By the time they reached the halfway point, the sun was already generating sweaty warmth, so they unzipped their jackets. Kelly removed her coat as she walked, sliding her finger through the neck-loop and swinging it over her shoulder. Tannon felt this was as appropriate a time as any to probe a bit.

"Are you concerned about the airline's medical exam?"

"Not a problem. They'll notice the decline in my vision, but they won't be concerned, as long as I can read those approach charts with my glasses. My distance vision is fine."

"Not perfect though."

"No, but still within Class One limits."

"Yes, but you never reported your eye surgery, did you?" inquired Tannon.

He knew the answer.

"No, but it depends on their hiring mood. If they need pilots, they won't look for any evidence of an eye operation. They wouldn't have called me for an interview if they weren't hiring."

Tannon removed his jacket now and threw it over his shoulder, holding it by the collar.

"But not reporting the surgery is chancy," criticized Tannon.

"It's a tough one for both the Feds and the airlines. There's nothing illegal about the eye operation, and it did the trick for me. Except for the near vision."

"Doesn't seem like it changed much."

Kelly seemed ready to change the subject, but Tannon took his chances and pushed the final step.

"What about the drug test?"

"What about it?"

"They can only detect recent stuff, I assume. And you've never declared anything to the FAA."

"Of course not. It's not a problem. You're not hinting there might be something still in my system, I hope."

"No, no," Tannon quickly tried to recover from any hint of an accusation. "I know you're clean, but I was just wondering if you're concerned with the test."

"What, me worry?"

Kelly was an emblem of another era. It showed in her dress and in her attitudes. Tannon considered it both good and bad. One thing for sure, it kept him on his toes.

Kelly purposefully jogged over to a shrub at the side of the runway and examined the bush like she was interested. They both knew otherwise. The conversation about Kelly's FAA medical exam was obviously over.

"The lake has been high this winter," said Kelly. "Look at this bush. It looks like the beavers have been busy."

"Yup, looks like they have," said Tannon.

"And, Tannon, knock off the medical stuff. I'm fine. There's no problem. So just forget it."

"Okay, it's forgotten, Sis. But just keep me posted. I do care, you know."

* * * * *

After they paid their overnight camping fee, the lineboy gave them a ride back to the campground. They spread their collapsed still-moist tents on the aircraft parking ramp and let them dry in the sun. There was no reason to rush, since they had all day to get home.

While they waited, Kelly sat on the curb of the aircraft ramp, legs spread, bouncing a flourescent green tennis ball between her feet. Tannon paced the pavement, inspecting the surrounding terrain. He looked back at Kelly from across the ramp and noticed her tall boyish figure, bouncing the tennis ball. Why did she always bring the ball along with her? She was a lot smarter than she looked. But not as smart as she pretended to be.

As Tannon watched her, Kelly sneaked a peak back at him. She knew he wanted to talk further about her airline opportunity and her medical situation. But she wouldn't put up with it. She peeled off her sweatshirt, mussing her uncombed hair even further. She preferred to leave it that way. Her now exposed and faded T-shirt looked like it was a victim of too many rounds with bleach. It was dull lavender, with white letters reading "Pilots Have Attitude."

While the tents continued to dry in the sun, Tannon preflighted the Arrow. A few minutes later, they packed up their tents and the rest of the gear, and took their seats in the airplane.

Soon they were airborne, climbing above Lake Isabella as they headed out the Kern River Valley towards Bakersfield. Tannon flew, while Kelly played with the radios. She tuned the ADF navigation receiver to an AM station and turned up the volume. A last-decade tune blared through their headsets. ADF was no longer used anywhere in air navigation, but the old radio still served a purpose.

While they climbed out of the valley, Tannon thought about Kelly winging her way to Houston, leaving him far behind. He consciously broke his train of thought and concentrated on the cockpit gauges. This was no time for day-dreaming.

He gazed over at his sister. She was slumped comfortably in the right seat, eyes nearly closed and at peace with the world. She too appeared lost in thought, but her thoughts probably involved flying jets and finally breaking free.

* * * * *

Monday came and went. Tannon had only two classes that day and was finished by two o'clock. When he arrived home, there was a voicemail from Kelly, announcing she had arrived in Houston safely. She promised to call as soon as the interview was over on Tuesday. She sounded like she wasn't concerned about the job, one way or the other. Probably she was pretending.

Tannon spent most of the evening just sitting on the sofa, reading a cosmology book and thinking about Kelly. But the cosmology book proved he also had Lori on his mind.

He was very proud of Kelly tonight. She would ace the interview, despite her straightforward critical manner. And the simulator ride would be a breeze – barely a challenge for her. The medical exam was the part he worried about the most.

And then she would be gone. He would be alone. He reminded himself that Kelly wasn't his wife. She was his sister. Both of them knew it. Tannon, however, knew it a bit less than Kelly.

He hadn't been really alone in quite a while. Yet Tannon Bessimer was the epitome of a loner. There was a big difference between being alone and being lonely. He always enjoyed his time alone. But now he wasn't so sure.

EZ decided Tannon needed some attention, or maybe the cat decided he needed it himself. EZ pushed at Tannon's ankles with his nose, jostling with the laces on Tannon's sneakers. The golden cat repeatedly shoved and retreated, catching the laces in his claws, then shaking them loose. Tannon pulled EZ's tail as repayment for the attention. As the cat's tail took EZ's full weight, his rear paws came completely off the floor. When Tannon lowered him back down, EZ slipped away. Then, with a trill that was more like a chirp, EZ come back for more.

As he played with EZ, Tannon watched the news on TV. After a commercial break, the screen filled with the station's logo, and then the word "Bessimer" spread itself across the TV at a forty-five-degree angle.

Tannon laughed out loud. First it had been "9840 Bessimer." Then it was the "Bessimer Object." And now it was merely "Bessimer." Tannon wondered if anyone watching the channel knew who Bessimer was.

The news anchor used the last five minutes of the program for a solo commentary, with the word "Bessimer" now inside a rectangle in the upper right corner of the screen. In his editorial, he talked about how the world was being affected by the new object. In the small rectangle, a chaotic scene from the New York Stock Exchange appeared. Tannon knew that in recent months, it was always chaotic there.

The newscaster provided some final comments about the brightening detected by astronomers over the last three nights, an increase from magnitude 7.6 to 5.5. It was a substantial change in brightness on the visual magnitude scale. TV viewers were reminded of the Texas-size analogy. The object could now be seen without binoculars on a dark night, if you knew where to look.

As the news anchor signed off, he raised the question: "Are Homo sapiens ready to match wits with an alien spacecraft?" It was the first time Tannon heard anyone in the news media use the word "spacecraft."

Chapter 22

Kelly

I'm worried about Tannon. I'm worried about me. I'm worried about us.

They offered me the job. It was pretty obvious early in the interview that they wanted me. Things are booming with the regional airlines. The pay is terrible, but it's the best avenue to those big-buck jobs with the majors. You've got to pay your dues.

They want me to start next Monday with Regional Jet training. I could stay right here in Houston until the class begins. Just a few days for preliminary ground school, then on to my real training at my assigned base in Cleveland, which isn't the best place to for winter flying. Jets can top most of the bad storms, but the short routes I'd be flying require climbing up and down through a lot of messy weather.

I've been protected too long, and that makes me nervous about moving on. Life with Tannon has been too simple. As far as he's concerned, I could stay in San Dimas with him for the rest of my life. Sometimes I think he expects it.

But now I've found my big break. I can fly these jets. In many ways they're easier to fly than Cessna trainers. The simulator ride today was a snap. They teamed me up me with another pilot to see if we could work together efficiently. They call it cockpit resources management. I call it common sense. Having another professional pilot to share the workload is like flying with Tannon. It's easier than riding with student pilots, doing practice stalls and touch-and-goes all day long. It's a lot safer, too.

I haven't given them my decision yet, but it's pretty obvious. What's to hold me back? I could move to Cleveland tomorrow, if I had to. No husband, no kids, no family to worry about. And I'm not leaving a real job. One-day's notice wouldn't choke anybody up. Except Tannon.

This airline doesn't care about my past. They only care about my ability to handle the right seat in one of their jets. They've decided I can do it. And I've decided I can do it.

But what about Tannon? He's been enjoying life more than ever before, even with the pressure of his instant fame. His notoriety is dwindling now, and soon everything will be back to normal. But I hope he doesn't lose what he has gained. He's found confidence, a slower pace, and less fretting over everything. Heck, he's even eating better. But he still thinks he needs me. He doesn't. Maybe I need him more than he needs me. In fact, I'm sure of it.

Mom will be pleased. Now she'll have a daughter flying with the airlines. Well, it's not a major air carrier, but the word "jet" helps a lot. And she has a famous son —famous for a discovery she doesn't understand. It's a discovery even I don't understand. In fact, most of the world doesn't understand.

This thing is hurtling toward us, and I think it was constructed by alien creatures — sort of unnerving, to say the least. Already the world has started to react. It might be the end of the world. Or the beginning of it. Either possibility is scary to most of us.

Maybe this is an appropriate time for me to leave. Tannon has gone through a lot in the past two weeks. For him, even eating at a new restaurant is traumatic. Now he's world-famous for finding a mysterious object. If this spaceship is full of little green men, maybe none of this matters. I bet they're big purple women.

I haven't told Tannon about my decision yet. It won't be easy. I'd be pleased if he would cry or at least act sad. But he won't. He'll just tell me how proud he is of his little sister. I'm grateful for what he has given me. But now it's time to move on. Time to escape. It seems like it's my last chance.

Chapter 23

Inbound

The deceleration burn was nominal. Everything went exactly as programmed. After a brief but powerful burn, the nuclear engines were throttled back, nearly to idle. In this short period, the speed of the spacecraft had slowed by almost half. None of the trajectory parameters had yet changed. This was merely a preliminary reduction in velocity. If the previous pace had continued, the spacecraft would have sped past the target star and off into interstellar space again.

Intelligent life on these planets probably witnessed the burn. If their vision spread broadly from the infrared through the ultraviolet, they would have detected the increase in brightness during the burn. If they hadn't seen us before, they saw us then.

When the brief burn ended, Newton's gravitational laws ruled the inward plunge towards the solar system. The heat of the fusion reaction was dwindling rapidly, with some residual energy remaining. The heat was confined to the other side of the almost-perfectly insulated wall.

Intelligent beings on these planets would be asking lots of questions now. Onboard the spacecraft, a variety of scenarios were being considered. Machines asked the questions. And the answers came from the same machines in a series of comparative actions. Which of the two prime targets should be selected? There still was time. The decision could be delayed until the spacecraft entered the heart of the stellar system. But that moment was approaching fast.

Chapter 24

Thursday, January 28, 2016

Waiting

Just as suddenly as the brightening began, it ended. After four nights, the object abruptly decayed to magnitude 7.1. At first, the overall increase in magnitude was cautiously (and incorrectly) explained as the result of the rapid approach of the object to our solar system. Some scientists argued otherwise, particularly when the magnitude suddenly dropped.

Most astrophysicists and other self-proclaimed experts agreed a nuclear burn could account for such a brightening, but the length and magnitude of the burn indicated a powerplant far superior to anything on earth's immediate technological horizon. By now, the Bessimer Object was universally referred to as a spacecraft, although there was no real justification for the term. The lack of natural explanations from scientists had precipitated acceptance of its artificial nature, and certainly, this object hadn't come from earth.

Radio astronomers held a continuous vigil. In New Mexico at the Very Large Array, radio antennas were electronically coupled together, gathering data whenever Cetus was above the horizon – day and night, under clear and cloudy skies. When the object was on the other side of the earth, radio telescopes in Russia and elsewhere took up the vigil. These observations confirmed the spectrum data of the optical telescopes. But there were no transmissions from the object in the bands of most interest, those frequencies used for radio communication on the earth. All reasonable frequencies were scanned, including AM and the higher frequencies. Attempts for contact at 1420 megahertz, the universal hydrogen emission frequency, were closely monitored, but no coded information was detected.

The visual magnitude of the object was of concern to scientific investigators. The brightness, considering its relatively small size, was beyond that of a perfect reflecting sphere or any object with familiar sources of illumination. News reports concentrated on the mystery, comparing the spacecraft to a Texas-size object, fully lit by laser-like beams exceeding the highest intensity known on earth. Lab demonstrations and mathematical calculations simply couldn't explain the intense emission properties.

The sudden four-day increase in magnitude could be a pure fusion reaction. A variety of Doppler shift measurements determined the spacecraft had slowed to approximately 30 percent the speed of light, a two-fold decrease in velocity. But the energy detected was larger than could be mathematically justified by the deceleration of an object the size of Texas. So none of the numbers matched.

It was believed, almost universally, that a fusion reaction couldn't have propelled the spacecraft to its original velocity of 57 percent the speed of light, especially for an object this big. In even the most optimistic calculations, another source of thrust was necessary. Or maybe the original Texas-size estimate by the VLT's experimental optics was wrong. Other scientific contradictions also raised their ugly heads. Except for the spherical disk image resolved by the VLT at Cerro Paranal, the object's shape hadn't yet been confirmed elsewhere, even though it was now 60 billion miles closer to earth. Not even the astronomers at Cerro Paranal were able to repeat the task. It was assumed that the seeing conditions in Chile were so perfect on that remarkable night that the reduction in distance hadn't made up the difference yet. There were still a number of skeptics who questioned the results from Chile. But most accepted the Texas-size sphere analogy.

* * * * *

Kelly didn't call after the interview. Tannon had the phone number of her hotel, but he refused to give in. If Kelly preferred to wait, so could he. Finally, the day after the interview, Kelly phoned. She said she had been thinking things over. So had Tannon. She wanted to talk to him in person, rather than over the telephone, and she would be home tomorrow. Tannon was elated that she was coming home at all. He told her so.

By now, Tannon's fingernails were back to normal – that is, thoroughly chewed and hurting. How many times had he told himself to stop? His cuticles looked ugly, and some were torn to the point of bleeding. The headway he had made in calming his body and soul was gone. But with regard to the spacecraft, he still retained a sense of serenity. The rest of the world didn't universally share the feeling.

* * * * *

There were many changes in the world since the spacecraft's discovery. The financial impact was probably the most prominent, and it was entirely psychological. At first, on the Monday after the brightening of the object, the stock market tumbled out of control. Trading was temporarily halted on the New York Stock Exchange for two days in a row when declines hit the 400-point mark. In both cases, after the required 45-minute pause in trading, stocks continued their decline, closing down nearly 500 points each day.

After two days of financial madness, stability returned. The *Wall Street Journal* attributed this to the "Why not?" attitude of many investors. The market climbed back to near-normal. Tech stocks, by comparison, didn't level off, but instead zoomed further upward. Everyone assumed these high-tech companies and their expertise might soon be needed for important new challenges involving the spacecraft.

Governments worldwide met in a variety of summits and videoconferences. Most preached a wait-and-see attitude, since there weren't a lot of other options. The Big Five formed a consortium to discuss what to do about the inbound spacecraft. The political leaders of the Big Five met via video-link several times each day. After a few days, there was little left to discuss.

Everyone considered the eventual involvement of the military as an obvious recourse. Weapons research, especially nuclear studies, climbed in a revived frenzy. The START 4 nuclear disarmament treaty was suspended to allow research on new devices that could defend against an inbound spacecraft, but there simply wasn't enough time to make any real progress. And there wasn't much new, since most of the scenarios had been previously considered in computer simulations many years ago. The threat of near-earth asteroids had been discussed in research circles for several decades, and think-tank studies had been in progress for the past few years. There were no real answers.

People changed. Humanity changed. Many of the smaller issues of society disappeared, and some of the bigger social issues received renewed emphasis. A judgment day, of sorts, was created. It didn't matter whether the spacecraft stopped or passed on through the solar system. Its mere existence had already changed the world.

Probably the most noticeable change was in communication between people at all levels. They talked mostly to those they knew best – farmer to farmer, poet to poet – but they all talked.

* * * * *

Tannon was waiting for Kelly. Tomorrow was Friday, and he had no classes, so it was his excuse for staying up late. The reality was he couldn't wait to see his sister.

Kelly arrived soon after Tannon dozed off. He was asleep on the floor in front of the living room TV. The *Midnight Show* was blaring, and a book entitled *California Geology* was spread open on his chest. He was startled when Kelly plopped down on the sofa next to him, but he immediately tried to act relaxed.

"Welcome home, Sis," he said, trying not to sound drowsy.

Kelly gave him a simple "Hi." She sounded strained. He didn't think it would be that hard for her to tell him she was leaving. He had already figured it out, and she must know that.

Their usual banter was gone, partly because of the late hour. They talked about her trip, about the interview, and about the spacecraft, but not about her decision.

The *Midnight Show* was over, and a series of middle-of-the-night infomercials went unwatched. Tannon turned the television off, and Kelly used it as an opportunity to slip away to bed.

Tannon followed her to the bedroom, standing at her door, acting as nonchalant as possible under the circumstances.

"Do you want to go flying tomorrow?" he asked.

"Not sure. Can we talk about it in the morning?"

"Okay."

She sounded torn between flying and the topics still not addressed. Maybe they could take care of both tomorrow.

While Tannon stood in the doorway of Kelly's room, she dropped her suitcase on the bed and began unpacking. Tannon's tall body leaned against the doorframe, and he told her the story of an unusual man who had come to the house earlier in the evening. Tannon was worried their address had been compromised, and he explained how this fellow had talked of redemption. It wasn't pure religious fervor, but a social one instead. Tannon tried to explain to Kelly how uncomfortable he felt regarding the confrontation, although the stranger departed as soon as Tannon asked him to leave. There was no worry in Kelly's face, only feigned interest.

Kelly silently finished unpacking, listening to Tannon. It wasn't often he talked without obvious purpose. As he continued with an update on their mother's newest real estate venture, Kelly plopped down on the bed with a thump. Her hands went under the back of her head, elbows straight out. She listened without speaking.

She pulled her knees upward and tugged on her shoelaces. She pulled off her black sneakers and then her socks. Without getting up, she struggled with her sweatshirt, pulling it over her head. Her hair went every which way. She lay there in her tan oversized T-shirt and faded black jeans, just listening. She didn't say a word, except for an occasional "Uh-huh" or a simple nod in acknowledgement of her brother's ramblings.

To Tannon, it didn't seem she was disinterested. Instead, she appeared to be committed to taking care of unfinished business tomorrow rather than tonight. Finally, Tannon said a simple "Goodnight" and left.

Kelly rolled over to reach the bed-stand light switch, clicked it off, and then scooted back into the center of the bed. In a few minutes she was sound asleep.

* * * * *

It was typically in the pre-dawn hours that Tannon did his best thinking.

He clicked on the web link for University of Arizona's Department of Astrophysics. The home page built quickly, a simple layout with only one image at the top – M31, the Andromeda Galaxy, with its satellite galaxy, M32, tucked in close.

It took him two more links to find the faculty page. He clicked on "Dr. Lori Talcott." He was prepared for the surprise, but he still uttered a "Hmm" as the image popped into view. Lori had grown up. Her acne was gone, and her face had filled out. She had chubby cheeks! Pretty cheeks. The photo was cut off at the shoulders, but it was evident Lori wasn't the skinny, bare-boned girl he remembered from Buffalo.

He read her brief bio, including the part about her home in Tucson with her two dogs. There was no mention of a husband.

He switched to the word processor and tried to spend a few minutes with a curriculum report due next week. But he was just killing time, waiting for the world to wake up and bring him his morning newspaper.

As he worked, his mind drifted. He wondered if Lori had done similar research regarding his photo? Probably not. It was available on the Mount SAC web page, but Lori was interested only in science. He remembered that from the University of Buffalo – a characteristic that Tannon considered all the more alluring.

* * * * *

They sat facing each other across the weathered picnic table at Oceano Airport near Pismo Beach, their Piper Arrow only a few feet away. The plan had been to visit the beach, but neither of them had left the picnic area. On this January afternoon, the air was cool and this little spot was comfortable. Wind and cold would batter the nearby beach, but the sun was warm and inviting here.

They waited while a Bonanza taxied by. The air reverberated for a few minutes and then slid back into quiet. There was only the sound of sparrows chirping in the nearby trees and the now-distant sound of the Bonanza performing its engine runup in preparation for takeoff.

Kelly spoke, getting immediately to the point.

"They offered me the job."

"Congratulations. I knew they would."

"I'm going to put them off."

"You're going to do what?"

Tannon heard, understood, and was surprised. His brow scrunched up.

"Well, they made it clear I've got the job, but I told them I need some time to think about it. So I'm thinking."

"How long do you have?" asked Tannon.

"If they really want me, they'll be there when I'm ready. I've got some flight students here who are real close to their licenses. I really should finish them up first. That'll take another month, except for Robert. I'll just kill him instead. In the meantime, I won't take on any new students."

Tannon never thought of Kelly as dedicated to her students training schedules. She was an excellent flight instructor. He was certain of that. But what happened to her students was up to them. She always made that clear.

"Great," said Tannon. "Those jets will wait for you. But I hope this isn't because of me."

"Right!" Kelly nearly yelled, her face in a concerted scowl.

She was seldom riled by anybody or anything, but now her irritation showed.

"Tannon, you're a real problem!"

"Sorry, Sis. I'm trying to be supportive. I really want you to get the things you want."

"I know." She calmed a bit.

Her voice was low now. They paused to watch the throaty Bonanza climb out to the west, finally reducing its propeller RPM over the beach. The sound of chirping birds returned.

Kelly looked into Tannon's eyes. She didn't look there often. Within those eyes were questions that were sometimes frightening. When she spoke, it was with resolve.

"Yes, you're supportive. That's part of the problem. It's real hard to leave you. You're the fuckin' problem, Tannon, not those students."

"Oh," he said.

He paused, popped the lid of a can of Pepsi, and slid it towards her.

"Try this. Caffeine is good for the heart."

Chapter 25

Wednesday, February 10, 2016

Artificial Intelligence

Front Page
Los Angeles Times

Alien Spacecraft May Orbit the Sun

The mysterious object, detected four weeks ago, is headed directly towards the sun, say officials at Spacewatch, an Arizona-based asteroid search project. Most astronomers now believe the object is an alien spaceship. The Texas-size spherical object has already performed at least one deceleration maneuver, to slow it from its nearly light-speed pace and allow entry to our sun's system of planets. Because of its recent speed reduction, it is now expected to reach the boundary of our solar system on March 1st. At its present speed of 30 percent the speed of light, it will cover the distance from Neptune, the farthest planet, to the sun in less than a day.

Spacewatch officials noted the arrival could be delayed due to another expected deceleration. Spacewatch astronomer Dr. Ted Lunde says: "If the spacecraft doesn't decelerate again before entering our solar system, it's likely to crash into the sun or pass very close and speed off into space on the other side." The sun's gravitational pull is insufficient to capture this spaceship unless it slows considerably from its current velocity. If it reduces speed, time estimates for its arrival will again be affected. "There are a variety of possibilities," says Dr. Lunde. "It would be logical for a spacecraft to begin deceleration well before entry to the solar system, resulting in a gradual speed reduction and its capture in an orbit of the sun."

Astronomers are still groping for answers. Most experts accept the fact the spaceship will decelerate again, rather than simply pass on through our solar system or be burned up by the sun. "Why would anyone or anything come this far, slow down a bit, and then charge off into oblivion?" noted another Spacewatch official who asked to remain anonymous. "This object is almost certainly going to go into orbit around the sun, but where it goes from there is anybody's guess."

The origin is unknown, but Dr. Lunde notes: "The object is too closely aligned with Tau Ceti, one of the closest stars, to tie it to any other source. At first we were concerned it was displaced too far from the star, but now it appears that a gravitational 'slingshot' launch around a massive planet within the Tau Ceti system could have caused the offset." However, no planets have been detected orbiting Tau Ceti, regardless of increased research on the star in recent weeks.

Astronomers at radio telescope sites in New Mexico and other locations have maintained a continuous watch on a variety of radio frequencies for any transmissions that might indicate an attempt by the spacecraft to communicate with the earth. Astronomers have also transmitted powerful coded radio beams to the spaceship, attempting to get a response. There have been no reports of success, even on the standard frequency of 1420 megahertz, where natural emissions are concentrated.

* * * * *

Worldwide, most scientists had deviated from their personal research projects to concentrate on the remarkable discovery. Chemists and astrophysicists had a field day with speculation about the spectroscopic results and the unexplained intense brightness of an object this small. The hydrogen emission lines seemed to be the classic signature of a fusion reaction. The variation in intensity of these lines since discovery of the object indicated periodic deceleration thrust.

Engineers and physicists worked on propulsion possibilities involving proton rockets that might convert mass to energy with near-perfect efficiency. They determined that acceleration to 50 percent the speed of light would be possible for an object the size of a Texas, if 75 percent of the mass of the vehicle was proton fuel. Some scientists theorized the spacecraft might have scooped up protons for fuel along the way during its long voyage through space. The interstellar medium isn't completely empty, and at high velocities it would be a credible source of available matter.

Nuclear fusion technology, still not harnessed as an energy source on earth, could account for the initial deceleration that had been observed. But no one could adequately correlate these energy requirements with a spacecraft the size of Texas.

Biologists discussed the deceleration effects on beings similar to those found on earth. Therein, rested a major problem. Life on board, if it were at all similar to moderate-size animal life on earth, couldn't withstand such rapid deceleration from 57 percent the speed of light, to say nothing of the technology required to sustain life for a journey of over 20 years.

Assuming Tau Ceti was the launch source, the star did have a lot going for it. Tau Ceti resides on the main sequence of stellar evolution, giving it a long period of stability, a factor assumed necessary for the development of intelligent life. And it's the proper spectral type, a G-class star similar to our sun, although somewhat cooler.

But Tau Ceti had several negative properties that concerned astrophysicists, including the lack of any detectable planets. Planet detection technology had increased rapidly in recent years, but Jupiter-size planets around Tau Ceti seemed to be lacking. Current technology couldn't detect worlds much smaller than earth, but many astronomers believed you couldn't have a planetary system unless at least one gas-giant planet dominated as a gravitational shepherd for the smaller worlds. These huge planets were the only obvious method of keeping perpetual asteroid bombardments away from small, rocky worlds, by attracting asteroid impacts to their larger masses. Stability factors in solar systems were far from understood, but the fact remained that Tau Ceti had been studied for many years without the detection of a single planet, large or small.

Lori Talcott was one of the many scientists who temporarily cast aside her research specialty to engage in new fields of study. In Lori's case, she returned to spectroscopic studies that had enthralled her during graduate school. To delve into such an area, she had to bone up on principles of astrophysics untouched for years and somewhat removed from her beloved cosmology. But now she had lots of reasons to head in a new direction, not the least of which was an amateur astronomer named Tannon Bessimer.

* * * * *

During mid-February, Tannon had a four-day weekend, Presidents Day recess. He reserved the days to spend some secluded time in Death Valley, one of his favorite geological haunts. Although he took along some of his class course material, including two exams for the upcoming week, he isolated himself from his normal routine. His Jeep was loaded with camping equipment, a few geology field manuals, and his trusty rock hammer and magnifying glass. His Astroscan was included, with some dark nights expected in the remote desert valley. Tannon looked forward to the weekend as a time to get away from everybody and everything. But he would keep in contact with Kelly – his cell phone's satellite mode should work fine, even in the remotest reaches of Death Valley.

Kelly was busy with her remaining flight students that weekend, and Tannon noticed she held to her promise not to start any new ones. He wasn't sure whether she was really leaving, but he held firm to his commitment to avoid bringing the subject up. He had noticed some mail from National Express Airline, and one day he saw a copy of the *Cleveland Plain Dealer* on the coffee table. The classified ads were on top of the pile, and there were several apartment rentals circled with a red pen.

The Death Valley trip proved valuable, primarily due to the satisfying boredom that set in after the first day. Tannon always found it refreshing to realize he wasn't really enthralled with being completely alone. It was valuable mental ammunition when he became flustered with the pressures of people and society. And being away from Kelly was never pleasant.

He decided to camp in the same remote location he found on a geology field trip for one of his classes several years ago. It wasn't a formal campsite, but the flat area adjacent to a small dry lake was perfect for his tent, and it was nestled in a picturesque nook surrounded by several large boulders. It was far enough off the main road that traffic was nonexistent. The narrow gravel road leading to the site was seldom traveled by anyone, except those like Tannon who sought seclusion and temporary removal from society. But it didn't seem so remote on this visit, since he knew every corner of the area from his previous trips. By the second day, he was ready to come home.

He found a nearby rocky peak he had never climbed, and planned a hike to the top. It took him most of the morning, although the total elevation gain was less than 500 feet. He paused repeatedly along the way to inspect the rocks. His trusty hammer blasted geological samples, and his magnifying glass checked the fractures, finding no surprises. As he climbed higher in his comfortable, tan hiking boots, the warm February sun penetrated his almost-white skin. He wore shorts and a T-shirt with the arms rolled up fully to catch the sun's rays. Climbing to the top of the small peak, he kicked up a lot of surface dust composed of finely weathered volcanic lava. It wasn't an easy climb, but he wasn't in a hurry. Finally reaching the top of the hill, he stretched out on an almost-flat boulder, nearly falling asleep in the warm sun.

Tannon convinced himself to stay at least another day, recognizing his need for a change of pace, and the second night offered a relaxing view of the universe. As soon as the sun set, the temperature dropped quickly in the dry February air, and he was engulfed by the darkness and cold. Tannon felt little need for a lengthy sky session, so he probed lightly with his Astroscan, picking some of his favorite Messier objects, dim galaxies too far away to appear as anything but faint smudges in his telescope. But within Tannon, concept was everything.

He also turned his telescope to Tau Ceti, now low in the west. He checked his discovery every clear night from San Dimas, and there wasn't anything more to see from this remote desert site. By now the new object had brightened to nearly the magnitude of Tau Ceti itself, forming an ominous-looking double star. As he gazed through the Astroscan's eyepiece, isolated from the rest of the world, there were a few moments of stark fear. Later that night, alone in the dark desert, Tannon tossed and turned in his sleeping bag. He pondered an alien spacecraft hurtling toward the solar system at 60,000 miles per second.

* * * * *

Returning from Death Valley on Sunday, Tannon found the house quiet. Kelly had left a note:

> *I'm at Christine's. Call when you get home.*
> *How about a belated birthday dinner tonight?*

* * * * *

To Kelly, dinner meant a trip to BJ's Restaurant, where they could order from the counter or chose a more formal table in a booth. Tannon's 40th birthday had come and gone without any fanfare, but he did appreciate Kelly's attempt to celebrate at BJ's with him tonight. After getting their drinks and settling into their favorite booth, they awaited delivery of their food. Their talk soon turned to the spacecraft.

"I called Lori when I got home for an update," said Tannon.

"The same Lori you romped with in the back room at Buffalo?" she kidded.

"You remember all of the secret stuff," replied Tannon. "She's been keeping me posted on the developments from her perspective."

"So what's the latest that the government is covering up?" she asked matter-of-factly.

"I don't think they're covering up anything. It looks like the government is getting the same information as the news media. Lori says she heard there's a secret military weapon that could be activated quickly, but there isn't any indication of a plan to use it."

The waitress brought their plates, and Tannon began to eat as Kelly spoke.

"Those little green men are being awfully quiet. Maybe they're little green robots instead."

Tannon took a moment to swallow and then replied.

"I wouldn't be surprised if it's a robotic spacecraft. By now we should've heard something resembling an attempt at communication. I would think alien intelligence capable of building a spacecraft would be able to broadcast in any portion of the electromagnetic spectrum."

"Unless they don't want us to know what they're thinking," replied Kelly.

"Oh, that's the ol' 'bad alien' mindset, don't you think? Who's to say aliens would have any reason to seek us out for harm? Sounds like a waste of intelligence and time to me."

"I agree," said Kelly. "But look what everyone is saying about the horrors that could be in store for us."

"Too many sci-fi movies. Not exactly realistic. Anybody capable of traveling this far must have endured for a long time. And it's hard to do that unless you survive in peace."

"Good point, and I sure hope you're right. Maybe their silence is an attempt to prevent us from getting too excited."

"Maybe," said Tannon. "But if they're trying to sneak up on us, they blew it with those rocket blasts."

Kelly had been picking at her plate. Now she stopped eating and pointed a fork at her brother.

"Why can't robots be alien intelligence?"

"Another valid point," said Tannon. "Robots would be built by living beings, but there is such a thing as artificial intelligence. It doesn't necessarily mean robots."

Kelly tipped her neck and squinted. "But artificial intelligence is still computers, or live-action robots at best."

"Not really," said Tannon. "To me, artificial intelligence implies some learning is going on. Maybe the artificial intelligence aboard this ship is autonomous. Living beings might have originally programmed it, but now the spacecraft could be thinking on its own. For a trip this far, machines would be better passengers if they could make some decisions along the way."

"Such as what planet to visit," said Kelly as she resumed eating.

"You bet. It's hard to imagine an intelligence that would know what's the best planet in our solar system to visit. If this object came from

Tau Ceti, that's still 12 light years away, and I can't imagine technology that could detect enough planetary details from that distance to make a sure decision."

Tannon paused with fork-in-hand, and then continued.

"Heck, maybe they're just passing through, using the sun as a sling shot to shoot somewhere else or right back home."

Kelly was obviously thinking, so Tannon waited for her to respond. When she spoke, she sounded a bit combative.

"But who's to say how advanced their tools might be. We may be only immature Homo sapiens, but we can already detect planets around other stars, and we're pretty new at science."

"True. But I can't imagine a technology that would base their final decision on observations of a distant solar system before they launched their spacecraft. Why not take advantage of the trip to learn more as the spaceship gets closer? Then decide where to land."

"Talk about jumping to conclusions," replied Kelly. "Who says they're going to land. I bet they could get a lot of information from low-earth orbit, if they're coming here at all."

"Can't argue with that. In fact, unless they're coming to blast us to bits, why not enter an orbit around earth and wait for us to visit them?"

"Blast us to bits, of course," said Kelly. She was sounding a bit irritated now. "Why else would any aliens or their artificial brains care to visit us? It would make a terrible movie if they just arrived to exchange theories of science and the secrets for everlasting peace. Laser blasters are what everybody thinks of first."

"Agreed. Look at what's in the newspapers and all over the TV."

"TV. Now there's a reliable source. Maybe we should just blow them up before they get here. It would make great video for television."

Tannon paused, hoping Kelly's voice would come down an octave. No one in the restaurant seemed to be listening, but Kelly could get quite vocal. Tannon never liked the attention it sometimes caused.

They both returned to eating. Kelly then craned her neck, and Tannon knew she was about to get needlessly vocal. He just knew it, and he didn't like it. They agreed on almost everything they had been discussing, but Kelly wasn't about to be stopped. She spoke loud and distinct.

"Piss on 'em!"

Tannon knew she was kidding, but she looked at least half-serious.

"Blast those aliens out of the sky!" she exclaimed. "And the spaceship they came in on."

Tannon guessed no one else in the restaurant was brave enough to look their way. Probably everybody except Kelly was embarrassed. Tannon certainly was.

Tannon's meat loaf and mashed potatoes, sitting half-eaten in front of him, looked awful. After enough time had passed, he spoke in a low raspy voice.

"You act like you're thirteen."

There was no humor in his voice.

"Thank you. I'm flattered."

Neither spoke for several minutes. But Tannon knew they both would cool off quickly. They always did.

When the silence ended, it was Kelly who spoke.

"I'm leaving for Houston next week for training, then to Cleveland."

Tannon looked directly at her, not replying. Then he returned to his meat loaf, looking unaffected by her statement.

He didn't say anything more until he was finished with his meal. Nor did Kelly. Then, as he pushed away his now-empty plate, Tannon looked Kelly straight in the eyes. She returned his gaze, as if it was a contest. His raspy voice provided a note of seriousness:

"Gonna' miss you."

* * * * *

On the way home in the Mustang, they discussed some of the necessary details. Tannon offered to bring Kelly's things to Cleveland over his spring recess. He'd rent a trailer and take most of her belongings, if she could do without them until then.

"Thanks, Tannon. But I'd rather do the move myself. And I'd rather do it now. I'll take my stuff to Houston with me for training, then to Cleveland."

"I can help."

"Of course. But there's really not that much stuff. I'll take what I need for now, and later I can come back for the rest. Besides, I don't have many winter clothes, so I'll wait until I get to Cleveland to buy them there."

"Better buy some long johns."

"Yeah. Especially for those cold morning preflight inspections. That's what they need co-pilots for."

Kelly ended their conversation with a simple: "I've already rented a trailer."

That was the way it would be.

When they turned off the freeway, Kelly ran a yellow light that was turning red. Tannon kidded her about how much he was going to miss her driving and these elaborate birthday parties. They laughed their way back to Tannon's house in San Dimas.

They said goodnight in the hall, before they had a chance to get sentimental about anything. There was an unspoken agreement that they shouldn't talk about the details any more for now. Tannon headed for his bedroom, clicked on his television and undressed for bed. He crawled under the covers, lying on his back. He reminded himself there were no surprises tonight. This was an important career opportunity for his sister. He tried to put the whole thing out of his mind. The TV weather map illuminated the screen. It looked cold and snowy in Cleveland.

As he lay in bed thinking about losing her, Kelly knocked on his bedroom door. She almost never came to his room. She didn't wait for him to acknowledge the knock, but simply came through the door and closed it behind her to prevent EZ from accepting an invitation for nighttime terrorism in the bedroom. On most mornings, the living room where EZ slept looked like the aftermath of a minor earthquake.

Kelly stood just inside the door without any emotional expression, wearing an oversized pink T-shirt she used as a nightgown.

"Are you going to let me go to Cleveland?" she said.

"I'll think about it. Do you promise me free airline tickets?"

"Free tickets apply only to parents. But you can afford to come visit me."

"Might. Just might."

"Well, I hope you decide to visit me in Cleveland."

"You can visit me here, too," said Tannon.

"Sure. You know I will."

She walked directly to the foot of the bed and then crawled forward on her hands-and-knees, her legs spread around Tannon. She stopped when her head was just above his chest. He lay motionless under the covers, and for a moment their eyes met. Her eyes were moist, the stare of a caring sister. She lowered herself flat on his body, her head on his chest and her hands on his shoulders.

Kelly wasn't a tiny woman, but neither was she heavy on his body. He felt the full extent of her weight and clasped his arms around her shoulders. They both held on, motionless. Neither spoke. They just breathed and held on tight for a few minutes.

And then, with the television still in the background, Tannon felt Kelly's deep breaths as she contentedly fell asleep. Tannon felt his own tears welling up, blinked several times to push them aside, and then consciously relaxed. He drifted into sleep a few minutes later.

Tannon awoke a half-hour later, when Kelly moved to get up. He felt her lifting her body from his and then rolling off the bed. She clicked off the TV, and then she was gone.

Tannon rolled over on his side and stretched his long body to its full length. Then he drew his legs to his chest in the fetal position and fell back into a fitful sleep.

Chapter 26

Wednesday, February 24, 2016

Skyscraper

"You must be Kelly."

Kelly stared at the woman standing before her. She held the door partially open, trying to prevent EZ from escaping from the house. She thought she should know this woman, but it was a complete mystery. She was very attractive and was dressed in a dark blue business suit.

"Yes, I'm Kelly. Please come in. Sorry. There's a cat just waiting to spring loose."

"EZ," said the well-dressed woman.

As she crossed the threshold, Kelly surveyed the woman closely. Her legs were finely sculptured, and Kelly was immediately attracted to her features.

Kelly closed the door quickly and then stepped back a few feet to get a better look. The woman was carrying a soft brown briefcase. She looked professional and very pretty.

"You're just like I imagined," said the woman. "Tannon described you well."

Kelly felt flushed. She stood there in her oversized T-shirt and khaki pants, and that was it. No shoes or even socks. No way to cover her casual appearance. And this woman was a knockout.

"Excuse me," said the woman. "I'd hoped you would guess. One more chance."

She wanted to guess. She desperately wanted to know. But she hadn't a clue.

"Got me," said Kelly.

"I'm Lori."

Kelly threw her chin downward and swung her head sideways and back upwards again. What a dope. Of course, Lori. So this was the pimply creature.

"Uh, okay. Now I get it."

Kelly was regaining her composure. Expect one thing and get another.

Lori briskly extended her hand to Kelly, and Kelly grasped it. Soft hand, gentle hand, beautiful hand. The touch of this woman was from a dream.

"Sorry, you really threw me there. I wasn't expecting you."

"Heck, I wasn't expecting me either," said Lori. "I'm not sure how Tannon will react, but I was sort of in the neighborhood."

"San Dimas?" laughed Kelly.

"Not exactly." Lori was smiling. Beautiful smile. "I'm on my way home from Seattle, and it didn't take much to get routed through Los Angeles. Well, not exactly true. It took a bit, but I thought it would be fun to surprise Tannon."

"Oh, he'll be surprised," said Kelly.

Tannon hated surprises. Usually. Maybe not this time.

"So I hear you're a flight instructor, maybe soon an airline pilot," said Lori.

"Yes, it's a living. Sometimes."

Lori laughed. "I took a few lessons once. But I never did fly solo. I really respect what you do."

"And I respect what you do," Kelly replied immediately.

There was this feeling – a feeling of intimacy with someone at first sight that didn't come along very often. Lori seemed sincere, and she was undoubtedly right – this was going to be quite a surprise for Tannon.

* * * * *

"**W**ho? Don't kid with me, Kell. I've got to get to class."

"I'm serious. She's standing right here. Want to talk to her?"

"Uh, okay."

"Hello, Tannon," Lori spoke into the phone. "Hope I didn't interrupt things too much here. I'm on my way home, and I thought I'd try to surprise you."

"You did. Uh, let me think a minute."

"Okay, what are you thinking about?" There was a laugh in Lori's tone.

"Well, I'm just trying to think about my schedule. You sort of caught me by surprise."

"So I gather. Would you prefer that I come to campus to say hello, or is there a chance for dinner."

Tannon stretched his tall, lanky body straight upward in his office chair and consciously tried to relax before replying as nonchalantly as possible under the conditions.

"Dinner? Of course. I've only got one more class, followed by a meeting I can skip. In fact, I need an excuse to avoid the meeting. I'll be home by 4 o'clock. Kelly will be glad to cook dinner for us. What a surprise."

* * * * *

"**C**ook? Surely you jest," said Kelly. "That's what he said? I never cook, and he knows it. But I order a mean pizza."

"That suits me. But Tannon sounded rather concerned or something."

"You bet he's concerned. He's been talking about you for a month. And he's probably as nervous as you can imagine. I bet he's got that geology class of his tearing their hair out right now."

"Oh, he's not that bad. You exaggerate."

"Maybe a little. But you can bet this has thrown his schedule for a tizzy. Missing a meeting is a big deal for Tannon. You must be important."

Lori looked across the backyard picnic table at Kelly. Lori had removed her suit jacket on the patio, to reveal a formal looking short-sleeve white blouse. Her trim-looking body overwhelmed Kelly.

The patio was shaded and pleasantly cool in the late afternoon air of February. Kelly and Lori hit it off well. This would be a great woman for Tannon. This would be a great woman for anyone.

"Can you stay with us tonight?" asked Kelly. "The sofa spreads out into a bed, but I'd really prefer you use my room. I sleep nice and sound on the sofa."

"Thanks. It does sound better than a hotel. But the sofa will be just fine for me. My flight goes out at 7:40 in the morning. But let's see how Tannon feels first. Maybe this wasn't such a good idea."

"It was a wonderful idea. Otherwise, how would I have met you?"

Kelly was sincere, and Lori seemed to know it.

"Beautiful house," said Lori.

"This is one of the best parts – the back yard. It's shaded most of the year, but during summer its simply too hot out here during the day, so we just hibernate inside."

"Tell me about it. I'm from Tucson."

"The house belongs to Tannon, but he shares it with me. I'm very lucky."

"Yes, you are."

"I'm really glad you decided to surprise Tannon. It'll do him good."

"Listening to you, I just hope it doesn't do him in."

* * * * *

The pizza was tasty, and their conversation was mostly small-talk. It was an awkward evening from the moment Tannon arrived home. He was pleasantly shocked by Lori's visit, but he couldn't seem to relax with the situation. To make matters worse, Kelly and Lori were interacting like giggling sisters who hadn't seen each other in years.

Tannon tried to steer the conversation to the spacecraft, but both of the women seemed intent on avoiding the subject.

"What more is there to say about it," said Lori. "I suppose I could pull out a pad of paper and give you a few lessons in orbital mechanics."

Tannon stared at her. He couldn't figure out whether she was kidding or actually ready to give him a lesson. He was, in a word, "overwhelmed" and unable to think in this demanding social situation.

"Oh, let's do that," said Kelly. "I do so love those elliptical orbits."

Both women laughed, so Tannon attempted a subdued laugh himself.

"Even my colleagues in Arizona are pretty well talked-out on this one," noted Lori. "They can drive almost any topic into the ground. We can talk about it, if you want, but personally I'd rather hear EZ's life story."

When it sunk in that the spacecraft wasn't on the list of acceptable topics, Tannon started to panic. He kept insisting they "do something," but both woman insisted that just talking was plenty. Tannon wasn't much for small-talk, and soon he began to feel he was more in the way than a part of Lori's visit. Kelly detected his concern, and tried to come to his rescue.

"Why don't you two get away for a while. I really didn't mean to interrupt this long overdue reunion. I bet Lori would like to see the campus."

"Not much to see," responded Tannon.

Kelly gave him a knowing stare that indicated he was blowing it.

The drift of the conversation left that topic, and with it Tannon lost his opportunity to interact with Lori in private. Kelly looked like she was going to try again. But she didn't. Finally, Tannon intervened with an attempt at being a caring host.

"Can you stay with us tonight?"

"Kelly has already offered. I'll take you up on it as long as I get the sofa."

Tannon felt offended. His sister had already offered their home before he did? What was the problem here? Was he afraid of Lori or Kelly? Maybe he was afraid of both of them.

"Who's the guy I talked to when I called you at home?" stammered Tannon.

It was an abrupt question, and Lori looked a bit insulted. Kelly turned her head as if her brother embarrassed her.

"That's Tom. He's a guy I see a lot. We don't live together, but we're close friends. We even talked about a serious relationship once. Now it's mostly occasional dates. He's a biochemist and a great friend."

Now it was Tannon's turn to be embarrassed. Why had he asked such a question? And he certainly hadn't expected such a candid answer. Lori merely smiled and changed the subject.

"What about your family. Besides Kelly and EZ, where are the rest of your relatives?"

Tannon remained silent, confused by his feeling of frustration. He was making a fool out of himself, and he felt very uncomfortable. This woman was beautiful, and she had caught him by surprise. He should be thrilled with the visit. But he was uncomfortable instead. Surely Lori must sense it, and he didn't know how to remedy the deteriorating situation.

Kelly waited for Tannon to speak, but when he didn't, she took charge of the question.

"It's really just us out here in California," said Kelly. "Mom has a nice condo in Florida, though we all used to live in Los Angeles together. She's retired and dabbling in real estate these days. Dad died over ten years ago, and Mom is just now learning how to enjoy life on her own."

"Well, you two have got it made here in California. I love your house, and it's really nice of you to share it with me."

Kelly cracked a genuine smile, and Tannon cringed uncomfortably. From there it turned to girl-talk, one of Tannon's least favorite things. He was squirming in his seat. Finally, he excused himself.

"It's getting late, and I've got early classes tomorrow. See you in the morning."

Lori reached out for his hand as he arose, and he reluctantly took it in his. Her hand was soft. His hand was sweating, and it was too late to recover from his feeling of stupidity.

Tannon didn't ask what time Lori would be getting up or how she was getting to the airport. He'd let Kelly take care of it, and he knew she would. He had to get out of this room right now.

Through his closed bedroom door, he could hear the two woman talking and laughing. Kelly was speaking in an excited pitch, almost yelling. Both seemed to be enjoying themselves immensely. And Tannon was jealous. He was jealous of Lori, and he was jealous of Kelly. And he hated himself. It was one hell of a first date.

* * * * *

Late on March 1st, three days before Kelly departed for Houston, the spacecraft entered the solar system. It crossed the heliopause, the boundary between interstellar space and the region of the solar wind's influence. Its inbound trajectory was inclined radically below the orbits of the planets.

The brightness of the spacecraft had increased steadily in recent weeks until it now burned at first magnitude as it passed below the orbit of Neptune. It was an object as bright as the brightest stars, but now the spacecraft's dimensions had been radically downsized by observations at a closer distance – it was only a little more than 1000 feet in diameter. That made its brilliance even more of an enigma.

As it dropped inward toward the solar system, a new fire erupted from the sunward side of the spacecraft. It was another major deceleration burn, a fire unmatched by anything from the weeks before. When the fire exploded, the magnitude of the spacecraft, as viewed from earth, erupted to minus 11 in less than a second and then immediately dropped back down to magnitude minus 7. If you knew where to look, it was bright enough to be seen from the earth in the daytime. And it would become even brighter as it crossed the orbits of the outer planets and headed toward the sun.

As the spacecraft decelerated, its trajectory simultaneously changed, and astronomers on earth quickly determined the new course. Computations confirmed it would barely miss the sun on the south side, grazing the inner portion of its tenuous corona. Astronomers could now resolve the object in their telescopes for the first time with conventional optics. The true volume was estimated as equivalent to a skyscraper, so it could no longer be referred to as Texas-size. But it was perfectly circular, just as Vince Leeming had determined, though it was inexplicable how the VLT could have resolved the object's shape so far from earth. One prominent newscaster deviated from the norm and called it a supertanker-size object, but the skyscraper analogy prevailed in most news reports.

The spacecraft's deceleration continued for three full days, with the fire pointed straight at the sun and nearly directly at the inner planets. It grew even brighter as it continued closer, until it equaled that of the full moon concentrated into a single white point. It blazed particularly bright when low in the western sky right after sunset. It set less than an hour after the sun and rose again shortly after sunrise. It was now visible throughout the day and attracted the attention of all on earth, even those who didn't know where to look. It was now called the Bessimer Flare.

Chapter 27

Monday, March 7, 2016

Perihelion

A week later, the brilliance of the Bessimer Flare stopped. The spacecraft had now radically slowed from 30 percent the speed of light to a mere two million miles per hour. It would still race past the sun and outward into space, uncaptured, unless another deceleration maneuver occurred. The spacecraft was approaching perihelion, the point of closest approach to the sun.

From the perspective of the spacecraft, the growing sun loomed straight ahead in the constellation of Virgo. Screaming past the outer planets, the object entered the solar system slightly below the orbital plane of the planets. From the spacecraft's viewpoint, a crescent Jupiter loomed well to the right and slightly above the brilliant sun. From the spacecraft's location, Jupiter's brightness was equivalent to a nondescript distant star. The sun ahead now blazed at a magnitude of minus 20.

As it sped past Jupiter, there was enough time for the spacecraft to download some additional bits of close-range data. But most of the memory cells of the ship were busy with perihelion maneuvering updates and one last decision.

Earth now appeared off to the right and slightly above the sun, tucked in close to its parent star. The water-covered rocky planet, as viewed from the spacecraft, was nearly lost in the sun's glare, as was its sister planet, Venus, which hovered above the earth and slightly to its left.

The earth and Venus planet moved farther off to the right and then behind the spacecraft as it quickly crossed their orbits. But in this brief period, the spacecraft downloaded one final data series that would be a major part of the final decision. For this spacecraft, much could be learned in one close look.

As it careened past, the almost fully-lit earth was glowing far off to the right at magnitude minus 2.5, with Venus brighter still at magnitude minus 4. The sun, of course, outshone everything in the darkness of space. The sun and the spacecraft would merge at perihelion on the seventh day of March, 2016.

* * * * *

Since the sun is a gas, its visible yellow surface merely marks the end of the thicker inner atmosphere. The yellow gaseous ball defines where the thicker inner atmosphere ends and the tenuous outer atmosphere begins. It was later widely reported that the spacecraft passed through the outer portion of the sun's visible "surface," the photosphere, as it rounded the star, and that wasn't totally inaccurate. Classified military imaging systems, as announced weeks later, observed the spacecraft as it merged with the sun from below, passed behind the star, and reappeared out the top. The final deceleration burn occurred behind the sun, with the spacecraft's powerplant pointed away from earth. This final burn was so close to the sun and at such a difficult observing angle it wasn't detected from earth.

* * * * *

Tannon returned Lori's phone call within minutes of receiving her voicemail message. She answered her office phone on the first ring and seemed pleased to have located him so soon. He had worried about talking to Lori ever since the awkward night of her visit, but her voice immediately put him at ease. She greeted him warmly, but he sensed she was all-business today.

"There are new orbital parameters," she reported.

"I heard that on TV. The press is talking about an outward swing to Jupiter or Saturn, but it would be elongated and above the plane of the planets."

Tannon had been paying close attention to the news reports, and was spending a lot of time on the Internet chasing the scientific details.

"Everybody here is in agreement with that, but we think there'll be another major deceleration burn near perihelion that will set things back into the orbital plane. And it could be a burn that would completely change the trajectory. For now, it looks like they're headed towards one of the outer planets."

"They?" kidded Tannon.

"Whoever," responded Lori.

She continued, without losing her professional tone.

"This could take months or even years. It's a long way back to Jupiter at this reduced velocity, and the spacecraft could slow even more. The last check show it traveling about 5000 kilometers per second. That's about. . ." She paused as she calculated. ". . . one point one million miles per hour. It's still a lot faster than we're used to in our space program, but its approaching velocities in NASA's ballpark."

"NASA's funding is probably not as large as theirs," joked Tannon.

"Tannon, look. I know you're having fun with this, and so am I. But it's also a job for me."

"So that means you have to take it serious?" He almost sounded like he was scolding.

"It just means our department needs to be accurate in everything we announce. Speculation is one thing, and so is humor, but they're best left for the news media."

"Agreed. I do appreciate your updates. I wish I could be there with you guys to see how astronomers really have fun in times like these."

He was braver now. He had half-expected she would never want to talk to him again. But now he was fishing.

She bit. Maybe she was simply a glutton for punishment.

"Well, why don't you come out here. Spring recess is coming up, isn't it? And I've been looking for a ride in that Cherokee of yours."

Now that she bit, Tannon didn't know how to handle it.

"I prefer to call it an Arrow. But you're right. It's in Piper's family of Cherokees."

"So what do you say?"

She pressed him and seemed to be enjoying it. Her business-like approach began to disappear. Maybe having him in a corner was her idea of fun.

For Tannon, it seemed that seeing Lori without Kelly looking over his shoulder might actually work. So he told her he'd like to see the lab and make a visit to Kitt Peak. It would be a great time to see the action. Imagine, being with real astronomers. And being with Lori, alone, without Kelly. In Tannon's viewpoint, that would take some guts. But wasn't it worth a try?

He told her he would do it. But he knew he wouldn't.

* * * * *

Kelly was settling down in Cleveland for the final portion of her jet training before the spacecraft passed perihelion. It was the only news she followed. These days, she watched the first five minutes of the national news on television almost every evening. That's when she saw the newest information on the spacecraft. Everyone else paid attention, too, but Kelly watched for an additional reason – she knew how much it meant to Tannon.

The name Bessimer didn't appear in the news even once after the flare died out. The object was now universally called "the Spacecraft," with a capital "S." The news focused on orbital estimates, broken down so laymen could understand it. The hard data was interspersed with widely varied predictions regarding the trajectory of the Spacecraft, covering the extremes and everything in between. It wasn't a lack of technology that affected the wide variety of predictions. The uncertainty sprang from other unknowns, including how many additional deceleration maneuvers would occur and when. Most of the scientific experts agreed that the orbital position at perihelion indicated the destination was an outer planet, almost definitely Jupiter.

* * * * *

Looking down on Lake Erie from 35,000 feet, Kelly observed a placid world. The lake divided Canada from the United States, but in most other places the boundary remained invisible. The land spilled from one place to another, and from the right seat Kelly wasn't sure whether she was looking ahead at Pennsylvania or Ohio. No boundary existed there either. Clarion VOR – 43 miles ahead.

A layer of broken cumulus clouds spread below the small jet as it pushed forward at eight miles per minute. In five minutes they would be over Clarion. Their descent into Allentown would begin in a few minutes. Things happened fast in a jet. You had to think ahead, and simultaneously going down and slowing down were the hardest part.

The aircraft functioned flawlessly on autopilot. Kelly monitored the air traffic control frequency, while the captain verified the navigation management system's output, backed up by his trusty paper charts. Most pilots used only electronic charts, but this captain was old school. In cruise configuration, there wasn't a lot for either pilot to do.

This was a training flight on a revenue route, a process considered perfectly safe. But the paying passengers would be hard pressed to accept a female pilot learning to fly a jet while they tried to relax in their seats. If only they knew.

Kelly reached down to disengage her seat lock, and slid the high-back seat to its full aft position.

"Back in a minute."

"Again?" the captain chided.

"Must be the coffee," said Kelly.

"What coffee?"

"Precisely."

Closing the cockpit door, Kelly saw the passengers looking up at her – all of them. At least it seemed that way.

The only lavatory in the small jet was in the rear. She walked past all thirty-seven passenger seats, smiling and exchanging a brief "Hello" every other step. As she approached the lavatory door, an "Unoccupied" green tag encouraged her. But she didn't want to go inside. That might make it worse. Kelly didn't need any chemical smells to edge-on her already revolting stomach, so she stopped at the door.

Just stretching her legs seemed to help. She paused and turned back toward the front of the aircraft. Relaxing with this brief walk might even solve it, except for those staring eyes from the little girl in the right window seat two rows forward of the lavatory.

Before starting back to the front of the airplane, Kelly stretched both arms overhead, clasping her fingers backward in an elongated reach, nearly touching the ceiling of the small jet. The young girl nearly climbed over her seat, focusing on her.

"Wanna' be a pilot?" Kelly half-yelled to be heard over the muted scream of the jet engines.

"Sure! Are you a pilot?"

Kelly got it. The little girl didn't know whether she was flight attendant or a pilot. Confusing to a ten-year-old.

"I'm a pilot. Girls can be pilots, if they want to be."

"Cool," replied the little girl.

Cool? When's the last time she'd heard that from a child? Kelly laughed, flashed a broad smile at the girl, and thrust both thumbs up in acknowledgement. The little girl giggled and just kept staring.

Kelly exhaled and started back to the cockpit. No one else seemed to be looking at her now, but she knew the whole cabin watched as she passed. She used her key to unlock the cockpit door.

"Okay, now?" said the captain.

"Did I say I wasn't okay," replied Kelly tersely.

She slipped into the right seat, brought it forward to her favorite slot, and noted the slowly unwinding altimeter. It was the first instrument that caught her eye – they were descending through twenty-six thousand feet.

"Starting us down early?"

"Pilot's discretion to seventeen thousand on heading one two zero. They're using the visual approach to Runway Two-Four at Allentown. Your landing."

"Thanks, Andy. I didn't mean to sound so secretive."

"I didn't mean to pry, but it's obvious something's not right. I'll have to report it, you know."

"Report what?"

"I'll have to report something, unless you agree to see a doctor first or decide to talk to me about it."

He clicked off the autopilot, leaving the flight director engaged as a visual aid during the descent.

"We've been through this before, Andy. I don't need a doctor, and you don't need to report anything. I do have a life, you know."

"That's obvious, Kelly. But as long as you're in the front seat, there are other lives more important to this airline."

"Oh, cute. And Captain America is going to save all of these passengers teetering dangerously near the brink of death."

"Look, Kelly, if you don't want to live by the rules, you'd better go fly somewhere else."

"Precisely," said Kelly.

* * * * *

"**Y**ou rang?" Kelly answered frivolously, figuring a phone call at this time of night had to be a friend.

"Hey, jet jock," said the raspy voice.

"Tannon! What are you doing awake in the middle of the night?"

"It's only the middle of the night if you live in Cleveland. It's time for the *11 O'clock News* here."

"Well, 'scuse me. I'm glad this phone call didn't wake you up."

She was sitting up in her bed now.

"Sorry, Sis. You know I wouldn't normally do it, but my calendar says you go out on a flight in a few hours, and I didn't want to miss you."

"You're right. It's almost time to get up. Now I won't have to."

They always communicated well – not just talked, but also communicated. In fact, they talked very little. There was a lot of communication, by a variety of means, and the unsaid things meant the most. Just like those cartoons, where characters bounced quick words off each other.

Kelly wondered if Tannon phoned because he knew. There was no way he could know.

"Tannon?" She waited.

"Yes, kid."

Kelly paused before continuing. In slow motion, she slipped out of bed and carried the phone to the plush chair in the corner of the bedroom, sat down, and spoke.

"I'm glad you called. I miss you."

Now it was Tannon's chance to pause for effect.

"Now how'd I know that?"

* * * * *

Tannon left the office of the division dean in shock. He loved his job and his working hours calculated out nicely – fifteen hours per week in the classroom plus four office hours. Theoretically, that was full-time for nineteen hours on campus. Most instructors spent a lot more time at home with lesson plans. Tannon was no exception to that. But most instructors also spent considerable time on-campus with students, committees, and a variety of campus activities. Tannon didn't bother with such extras.

He did a fine job in the classroom, as evidenced by his student evaluations and the lack of student visits to the dean's office. A student complaint or even a compliment hadn't precipitated today's visit to the dean. His boss had just told him he expected more.

More committee work, more involvement with the Faculty Senate, even becoming an advisor for a student club. He was expected to do more.

The problem, as Tannon saw it, wasn't the extra time or effort it would take. It was the people. He felt uncomfortable around nearly everybody. So far with this job, he had successfully avoided the added social responsibilities.

The dean also told him he expected Tannon to answer his telephone. He always answered his phone during his office hours. But the rest of the time Tannon let it ring, whether he was in his office or not. Voicemail was a great invention.

This visit was prompted by a complaint from one of his fellow faculty members. He didn't know who it was, but he could guess -- probably Dennis, right there in his own department. Dennis, a campus activist, was involved with the faculty union. Unlike Tannon, he attended meetings, social functions, and was faculty advisor for the Geology Club. Good for Dennis. Bad for Tannon.

For the first time in his pleasant years at this college, Tannon felt anger toward the system. That same system had protected him until now. Tenure, scheduling seniority, and union contracts were his protection. Most days he felt this was the best job in the world. But not today.

Chapter 28

Tuesday, March 8, 2016

Slingshot

Heat from the sun was now pushing the metals and composite materials of the Spacecraft to their design limits. Adding to the intense heat, the deceleration drive activated once again. The vehicle had now passed the sun, where small maneuvering rockets fired to veer the sphere to the left. The Spacecraft plowed upward behind the sun toward the star's north pole and was flung over the top, looping backward towards the planets it had just passed. It plunged out and away from the sun, back into the blackness of space, thrown by a giant gravitational slingshot. The Spacecraft was now headed directly towards its final target.

* * * * *

Most of the earth's television programs were preempted by the news that day. The food and music channels were among the few spared interruption. Many of the live images finding their way into homes throughout the world were of an artificially eclipsed sun, beamed from a solar telescope in California. There was nothing to see except a black disk surrounded by a bright, glowing corona. The corona was nearly circular, with a few outward spikes. At the edge of the black disk, two solar prominences could be seen, evidence of the receding eleven-year peak of solar activity.

Astronomers awaited the reappearance of the Spacecraft near the sun's north pole. It was expected that new orbital data would be available soon after telescopes reacquired the object.

Since there was nothing to see during perihelion, reporters interviewed scientists, most of their voices in the background while the sun's blocked-out image took center stage. One of the astronomers reminded the audience there could be a long wait before more information was available. The Spacecraft would be too close to the sun to be viewed for several hours, and no telemetry was being received from the quiet object. Nor could radar detect such a small object at the distance of the sun.

Several news reporters focused on details regarding Jupiter and its unique moons. One of those moons, Europa, was suspected as having an ocean under its surface ice. At the Spacecraft's current speed, it would take at least two days to cross the orbit of the earth and another ten days to reach Jupiter. And the Spacecraft was expected to slow down further, so it might be a long voyage.

By 5 pm California time, television transmissions beaming the sun's image to the public were transferred to Hawaii, as the earth's terminator of darkness moved westward. At 9 pm Pacific time, live TV coverage from the observatory ceased. Most of the world behind the earth's moving terminator went to sleep. In some locations, all-night Spacecraft parties prepared the earth's inhabitants for the morning news.

* * * * *

Tannon watched the television coverage that evening, switching off the TV when the local station returned to normal programming at 9 pm. He had a headache that demanded some caffeine, but it would delay his sleep. He tried two aspirin tablets instead.

By 10 o'clock he was in bed, but his head was still pounding. He finally fell asleep listening to music on his favorite classical station. That station never worried about the world news.

When he awoke, his headache was gone, but it was only 3 am, and he was wide-awake. He tried to sneak to the kitchen, but night-creeper EZ caught him as soon as the bedroom door creaked open. The cat seemed to be staring right through Tannon, seeking an explanation for the absence of Kelly. This creature wouldn't understand the realities of apartments with "no pets allowed." Nor would he adjust to hectic airline schedules. In repayment for Tannon's lack of explanations, there would be no people snacks without a kitty snack tonight.

"Okay, EZ, I guess we both need some middle-of-the-night attention."

Tannon ripped the top off a bag of cat treats, and poured them into EZ's yellow bowl. The cat attacked the snack with a rough chomping sound that accompanied the crunch of Tannon's pretzels.

The flashing light on the kitchen phone indicated "Message Waiting," so Tannon punched the speaker button and hit autodial for the voicemail. How could he have missed the incoming call, or had he set the ringer to mute? His love-hate relationship with phones was a constant struggle.

"Hi, Tannon. This is Lori. Please call me at my office as soon as you get this. I'll be here most of the night."

He dialed the number, memorized by now. Lori answered on the second ring.

"I see you stargazers are up late tonight," quipped Tannon.

Lori sounded wide-awake: "Not much else to do. The news media left hours ago, but some new information is starting to come in from Europe. They've had the sun for several hours."

She filled him in on the information from her astronomical sources. Most of the newest data was relayed from the military, while still protecting the secrecy of the equipment they were using to extract details from the sun.

"The Air Force has some gadgetry that's beyond me," said Lori. "It must be a powerful radar-like transmitter that can detect passive objects at huge distances. But I don't think they use it regularly to detect bad guys on the sun."

"It figures. I bet they're not too happy about revealing the technology," said Tannon.

"No, they're not, but they've given us some preliminary celestial coordinates that have helped forecast the trajectory parameters. The Spacecraft came out from behind the sun just fine, and now it's sling-shotting back into the orbital plane of the solar system."

Lori paused to let Tannon ask the inevitable question.

"So where's it headed?"

"Well, it sure isn't going to Jupiter on this trajectory. Best guesses now say it's headed toward earth."

* * * * *

The Spacecraft was stable in velocity now, having slowed to 400,000 miles per hour during the perihelion sling shot. The sphere would take nine more days to reach the earth, coming downward from above the orbital plane. Bearing down on its target like a marksman leading its kill, the Spacecraft was headed towards the North Pole.

As the earth grew in front of the Spacecraft, the earth's moon moved slowly inward toward the planet from the right. Halfway between the sun and the earth, the moon nearly merged with the blue planet. The full moon passed just above and behind the disk of the earth in near-eclipse. And now, viewers on earth were treated to an extraordinary sight.

* * * * *

For the past few days, the Spacecraft was visible only in the daytime sky, perched just above the sun. With its still unexplained brightness, it was easily visible in daylight at this close distance. Most inhabitants of earth saw it but were smart enough not to stare. Hospital emergency rooms recorded thousands of cases of sun blindness.

The headlines involving the Spacecraft were matched by no other story. A mass suicide at a cult village in South America received a lot of attention, since it was generally concluded that the arriving Spacecraft had indirectly taken the lives of 280 individuals, many of them women and children. With the focus of everyone's attention on an object headed straight for earth, everything else seemed somehow related.

Then, on March 12, with the Spacecraft now past the halfway point between the sun and the earth, an even more unusual brightening occurred. Exceedingly intense strobe-like lights suddenly flashed into view. The strobe flashes were so brilliant they cast reflections on the earth in full sunlight. The strobes flashed at intervals of 4.7 seconds, an event observed by all human beings on earth, except for hospitalized patients, prisoners, and others confined to buildings. Most animals, too, seemed to notice the extraordinary bright flashes.

* * * * *

"So what do your experts say about the lights?" asked Kelly.

Tannon shifted the phone to his left ear, as he tried to butter his toast.

"The experts know no more than we do at this point. It certainly seems to be some kind of signal."

"Like, here we come," noted Kelly.

"Could be. I would think any intelligent creatures would avoid just sneaking in. They probably know most of the beings in the universe would be tempted to blast them to bits, if they could."

"Haven't we been through this before?" asked Kelly. "In all of the movies."

Tannon laughed and replied: "Seems like we have. But strobe lights are a nice touch, don't you think?"

"It does sound like a 'We come in peace' kind of thing," said Kelly. "Or may its just 'Get the hell out of our way!' I personally prefer the peace thing."

Kelly figured out a lot of things on her own. She probably hadn't heard these opposing views in the news, although they were the two leading theories.

"Meanwhile we're not doing so well with peace down here, to say nothing about keeping peace with an inbound spacecraft," said Tannon. "Those riots yesterday were enough to make you wonder."

"Well, I do wonder. But maybe it's just Chicago, waiting to erupt on any excuse. Nobody was killed."

"If you measure things that way, I guess it was a minor blip on the radar, but those fires were mighty scary," said Tannon.

"Well, it won't happen here. There's nothing worth burning down."

"You're a regular walking advertisement for the Cleveland Chamber of Commerce."

"Actually it's a nice city. My bad attitude might have something to do with all the ice and turbulence inside the local clouds. This flying weather is a real challenge, even for an aircraft like the RJ. We did an ILS into Runway 5 yesterday that made my hair stand on end. Talk about turbulence. That approach was a black hole with boulders inside."

"Careful, Sis."

"Always."

Tannon changed the subject.

"EZ wants to say hello."

The cat was trying to lick the butter off Tannon's toast.

"Well, hello, EZ. Are you getting lots of attention without me there to beat on Tannon?"

"He's got me under control," said Tannon. "Are you sure you couldn't use a cat in Cleveland?"

"I'd certainly like him here. But I don't think he'd like waiting for food while I'm out on my trips. Besides, the landlord won't allow it."

"Since when did you start paying attention to rules?" kidded Tannon.

"Since I got flung out into this boring, cruel world without you to protect me," said Kelly.

"So why don't you come on home?"

"I just might."

Chapter 29

Tuesday, March 15, 2016

Aphelion

The Spacecraft bore down on the earth, coming over the North Pole and plunging downward into the shadow behind the planet. It decelerated one more time, fusion rockets exploding on the dark side of the earth. During the long ballistic journey from Tau Ceti, energy-rich particles of hydrogen fuel had been scooped up by a huge containment tube, long since retracted, and some of the fuel was held for this moment. Ignition led to a self-sustaining fusion plasma that converted some of the particle-mass to energy. The rest of the mass was ejected as a high-energy reaction – a fusion torch.

The torch, coupled with the flashing strobes, entered the earth's shadow, to be viewed by billions of eyes turned to the sky. It burned brightly across the dark side of the earth on the night of March 15. The Americas, Japan, and eastern Australia were treated to a display of energy that cast daytime light across the nighttime half of the globe. Birds woke up and started to sing. Interspersed with the energy display of the fusion torch, the strobe flashes were even brighter now, reminding everyone of the power of the visitors from space.

At this point in its journey, the Spacecraft was in a highly-elliptical orbit around the sun, with perihelion only a few million miles on the other side of the star. Aphelion, the point farthest outward in the orbit, was only two hundred miles beyond the earth.

Under the deceleration forces of the torch, the orbit was changing fast. The Spacecraft emerged into sunlight below the earth as it transitioned from solar orbit to a new set of celestial dynamics. It came up under the earth, crossing over Antarctica and reaching northward as it approached South Africa in its first south-to-north path in low-earth orbit.

Chapter 30

Wednesday, March 16, 2016

Silence

The Spacecraft entered an elliptical polar orbit with a low-point of 140 miles and a maximum altitude of 560 miles. Near the end of the first orbit, the light of the fusion torch and the flashing strobes simultaneously ceased. The brightness of the sphere dimmed to that of a huge artificial satellite of the earth, making it visible only in the reflected light near sunset and sunrise.

Within the next two circuits, the elongated orbit became circular at an altitude of 150 miles. No maneuvering rockets were detected during this adjustment of the orbit, and that fact remained unexplained. The overall magnitude of the object was now minus 2.5, but was blacked out by the earth's shadow during most of the night. When it was visible during twilight on the fringes of the earth's shadow, it was still one of the brightest objects in the sky. Now without self-illumination, it could be mistaken for the International Space Station or the flare of a Mercury satellite.

Radar and visual measurements of the object placed its size at a diameter of 1100 feet. Reflectivity was unusually high, indicating a smooth, steel-like reflective surface. Other than the earth's moon and the Space Station, to which it compared in size, it was the largest object in orbit around the planet.

The Spacecraft sat silently in orbit. No radio emissions were detected. It just sat there in a 90-minute polar orbit while the earth waited.

* * * * *

The world soon returned to normal, or as normal as could be expected while being watched. There were no more riots in the cities, no more mass suicides, and no breakdown in the world economy. Everyone seemed to be focused on who or what had come to visit. The intrigue of the arriving Spacecraft seemed, for the moment, more powerful than all of the negative forces combined. The public generally assumed the Spacecraft was compiling information about the earth and its inhabitants, but few felt threatened. The inbound journey had been so dramatic and so closely observed that there was no major surprise in finding the object orbiting overhead. World governments – at least all that publicly commented – called for avoidance of any hostile action. The Spacecraft had made its point regarding its superior technology by simply arriving in orbit around the earth in a blaze of light.

* * * * *

Lori's voice on the telephone seemed remote and uninterested: "Most of the talk here involves social and political topics, rather than real science. The prolonged warning during the inbound flight, especially the flashing strobe lights, seems to have had a calming effect on everyone. Its as if astrophysics is dead, with nothing important left to discover."

"Maybe we had too much time to think about the here-we-come attitude," said Tannon.

He wondered if Lori was disturbed by his decision to stay home for spring recess. He had expected her to be relieved, but she had said nothing more than a condescending: "If that's what you want." Did it mean she was disappointed or merely disinterested.

She seemed annoyed by today's conversation: "I've got to go," she said. "I'm assisting a colleague who has been allotted some time on the big radio array in New Mexico next week, so I'm supposed to be working on an observing schedule with him."

"So you plan to listen-in on our friends?" asked Tannon, recognizing their conversation had ended.

"That's not quite the plan. In fact, my cosmology research needs to get back on track. Our department chair has been asking us to settle back into our assigned research topics. Money is tight, and who knows when things will return to normal. Those research grants are the pulse of life around here."

"I bet they are," said Tannon.

* * * * *

Articles about the Spacecraft appeared on the front page daily, but they merely confirmed the object was still in its silent orbit. Editorials abounded, but hard facts were lacking.

After a full week in polar orbit, the Spacecraft transitioned to an equatorial-inclined orbit, nearly circular at a distance of 310 miles. How this was accomplished remained the subject of speculation by scientists for months afterwards, and was never fully resolved. Some astrophysicists claimed such a change in orbital dynamics was, in fact, impossible without completely rocketing away from the earth, then reentering the orbit. Yet it happened, again without any detectable firing of maneuvering rockets. The polar orbit first stretched into a highly-elongated path, and then flipped nearly 90 degrees. Within two days, the Spacecraft had slid into an orbit resembling a standard earth-launched Orion mission.

* * * * *

Tannon felt increasingly frustrated by the lack of information he was able to receive. Scientists were learning bits and pieces by studying the history of the object since its first sighting. During the inbound journey, there was little time to intensely study the accumulating data. Events were simply happening too fast. But now there was time to scrutinize more closely and draw some conclusions. Astrophysicists could even reach back to the time before the Spacecraft's first sighting, since historical images of Tau Ceti showed the incoming spacecraft before it was discovered by Tannon. Like replaying an old video in slow motion, astronomers could reconstruct a bit of the past. But Tannon had only one contact in professional science to keep him abreast of these processes, and now she was nearly as silent as the Spacecraft.

He was an outsider on the real issues. His fame from the discovery of the object had nothing to do with real science, and now his notoriety had dropped to zero. His name wasn't mentioned in any of the recent news features, and Tannon was grateful for the improvement in his feeling of privacy. But without the fame, he lacked the tools needed to push his way into the science. He wanted to be a part of the research rather than just an outsider looking in. But nobody involved in this research needed a community college geologist.

In his frustration, Tannon thought through his list of scientific contacts. He had few, even in geology. One geologist he had encountered recently was a geophysicist at Cal Tech named Samuel Jakes. He had watched Jakes lecture on plate tectonics during a public session, asked him a few questions during the after-lecture question session, and that was about it. But Dr. Jakes' specialty was planetary geology, and Tannon wondered if it might be a window he could open.

The telephone operator at Cal Tech gave Tannon the extension for Samuel Jakes and offered to ring it for him. The voicemail greeting didn't sound appealing:

"Hi, this is Samuel Jakes. My office hours are Monday and Wednesday from two to four o'clock. If you'd like to leave a message, I'll call you back."

Tannon thought briefly before deciding. Voicemail was easier than real life. He spoke at the beep:

"Dr. Jakes, this is Tannon Bessimer. I'm the guy who discovered the Spacecraft, and I'm also a geology professor at Mount San Antonio College. I have an interest in learning more about current research on this Spacecraft, and I'm hoping you can give me some thoughts on who I might talk to in pursuit of more information."

Enough – and Tannon was sure he sounded way too formal. He added his phone number, a brief statement of thanks, and hung up. At least he didn't have to introduce himself to the real Samuel Jakes.

* * * * *

"**H**i, I'm Samuel Jakes," said the bearded gray suit. He looked like a businessman dressed for a day in the boardroom. Even before he spoke, he projected a formal and conservative image. His face implied he was in his sixties, and way too busy to waste time on small-talk. He sat behind a desk stacked so high with books and papers that Tannon could barely see the professor over the top.

"Dr. Jakes, thanks for the invitation. I'm glad you were able to see me."

"Sure thing. I visited Mount SAC once. It's been years, but Bob Ballard gave a talk there in the 80s, before he became famous with the first underwater pictures of the Titanic."

"Well, we're no Cal Tech, but we have fun," said Tannon.

"Fun, yes. Especially if you like teaching. Sometimes I wish I had hooked up with a junior college."

Well, the concept of junior colleges had long ago given way to community colleges, but Tannon got Jakes' drift. Mt SAC was a good place to teach, and it was nice to know this scientist respected the concept. Meeting a prominent geophysicist in his office at Cal Tech was an ordeal for Tannon – a social ordeal – so he needed every bit of encouragement.

"So you want to become more involved with your discovery," Jakes continued. "I'm not sure I can be of much help. Some of Cal Tech's astronomers have been watching the Tau Ceti region closely since your finding, using the Palomar telescope, but that's about it."

"That sounds like a lot," replied Tannon.

"Well, all I hear is that they're concerned with Tau Ceti as a source of intelligent life, since no planets have been detected. The lack of Jupiter-size planets might imply no planets at all. And, besides, the star itself has a metal-poor spectrum."

"But the Spacecraft appears to be made out of steel or something similar," replied Tannon.

"Well, as I understand it, that's not a proven fact. And a metal-rich planet could form out of a metal-poor star. It just seems less likely, which has our folks concerned."

"Who's doing the research?" asked Tannon.

"Ben Muther and Regina Ramos," said Jakes.

"I see. Any recommendations."

"Not really. Both Regina and Ben keep pretty much to themselves, but I can promise to keep you posted on what I hear. And we're always looking for an interesting speaker."

Tannon was simultaneously flattered and perplexed.

"Are you serious? What could I say to Cal Tech that would be of any interest."

"Not Cal Tech," said Jakes. "Have you heard of the Planetary Society?"

Tannon knew about the Planetary Society, but he wasn't sure he had anything to say to them either. Besides, would addressing a scientific group really improve his situation? But he felt honored by the offer and told Dr. Jakes he would consider it.

They talked for another ten minutes, discussing geophysical properties of planets and the difficulties of analyzing spectral data. Jakes promised to call Tannon as soon the Planetary Society's April schedule was established. And he'd see what he could do about a contact source at Palomar Mountain. It seemed there was nothing more to discuss, so Tannon prompted the end of the conversation. Unlike talking to Lori, when the science ran out, Tannon was the first to recognize closure.

* * * * *

"Can I come home?" asked Kelly.

Tannon had just said "Hello," and Kelly blurted it out. She spoke with calmness. It wasn't a voice of desperation.

"You can always come home," replied Tannon. "What brought this on?"

"Nothing brought it on, except me. This pace isn't what I want. Oh, the jets are fine, but the schedule sucks."

"Most people don't abandon their life-long ambition because the schedule sucks," laughed Tannon.

"Well, maybe this isn't my life-long ambition."

"You know, Sis, if it's the salary. . ."

Kelly cut him off.

"It's not the money, and it's not Cleveland either. Well, maybe it's Cleveland just a little bit."

Tannon hadn't been expecting this. It had been such a short time.

"Sis, you know you're welcome back anytime. But I wish I could help make this job work out for you."

"It just hasn't worked out, Tannon. This isn't me."

"It's only been a month."

"That's exactly the point. In a mere month, I'm in way over my head. I guess I need things my way, at my pace."

"So you've just figured that out? Look, California has lots of student pilots hunting for instructors to scare."

"That's not my pace either. Maybe it'll be okay for now, but I've been thinking about opening my own flight school."

Kelly sounded half-serious.

"Now there's a great way to lose some money fast. Oh, heck, if it's what you want."

Kelly sounded less than enthusiastic.

"I could do it. I'd run it a lot different than the flight schools I've seen."

"Yeah, I bet it would be one tight ship," said Tannon sarcastically.

Kelly was reaching her limit.

"Do you want me there or don't you?"

"Sorry. Of course I want you. I already told you that."

"So stop throwing barbs," said Kelly. "I'll be home by the end of next week."

"Nothing like giving your company lots of notice," he kidded.

He wasn't easing up.

"The way I look at it, I got to fly jets for a month. I know that burning bridges isn't wise in this business," said Kelly. "Unless, of course, you're never coming back."

Chapter 31

Kelly

It can never be the same. Thank God!

Even though I'll be with Tannon again, I doubt we'll ever be the same. Tannon must know I can't be satisfied in his home. That's not why I'm going back. There just isn't anywhere else to go.

Tannon probably knows that leaving Cleveland wasn't entirely up to me. Those airline folks have their ways. They preach that a pilot's private life is none of their business. But let them catch you doing something they don't like. Then watch them scream.

In some ways, it was a lesson for both of us. For me, it's a reminder I'm not cut out for this world. How can anybody be unhappy flying jets? And for Tannon, I hope it's a reminder our relationship isn't a necessity. He got along well without me. It was probably a surprise to him. And to me.

My critical side says I should keep more distance between Tannon and me. It's probably best for both of us. My other side says: "What the hell!" Tannon doesn't mind it, even when I step on him. And to be close to him is to step on him.

As for my brother, he's become as much of a problem as me these days. It's obvious he needs to let go of his teaching job. What good is it? His boss criticizes him, even though he's one of the school's best teachers. And he really wants to spend his time chasing that Spacecraft. So why doesn't he just quit? It would solve everything, but probably not for Tannon. He forgets Mom is ready to help financially. It's a strange feeling, knowing you don't have to do a thing, because ol' Mom will always bail us out.

What worries me the most is that things are starting to get to Tannon. He has always been the foundation, the bedrock. But now he thinks the world is out to get him. He thinks everybody is trying to beat him up. Why would they bother?

Chapter 32

In Orbit

Maybe this was a mistake.

Questioning decisions that have already been made – it's not how machines are supposed to react. Decisions are based on the best available facts, and this commitment should be no different. The world below is an obvious haven for life. But it isn't the same kind of life as on the icy moon of the gas-giant planet. And fuel is a problem here. Fuel is critical.

VHF television broadcasts were the deciding factor. Generally, such capabilities appear when advanced species fully develop. But these beings have adopted it as their foundation. Their sounds are remarkable, even pleasant at times. But the lack of seriousness on these emission frequencies was a surprise. Maybe the decision to visit this planet was the right one for the study of intelligence, but not for an understanding of individual reasoning.

Contact could take time. In similar situations, it extended over prolonged periods. But the orbit will remain stable, and there is no hurry. Many unknowns exist, including the status of technological developments at home. When the ship departed, remarkable changes were on the horizon. The problem of faster-than-light communication was already solved. Tachyons had taken care of that, but contact wasn't instantaneous, nor was it flawless. As a means of communication, it was far removed from the normal flow of information, providing only a method of basic conveyance. Small-scale transmission of matter was also perfected before the ship departed. That process, too, exceeds the once-worshipped speed of light, but the transmission of complex beings is an entirely different issue.

When the ship departed the second planet of Tau Ceti, there had been talk of a breakthrough in the transmission of beings. It was known that a complex receiver module would be required. You couldn't transmit through wormholes without regard for the destination. The primitive receiver module in the adjacent instrument bay was the best that could be built at the time, but it was far from adequate. Reliable tachyon communication wasn't at hand, so the design of the receiver module couldn't be altered, unless on-board machines themselves initiated the modifications.

The home planet's only attempt at a complex tachyon exchange had been aborted. The results were nearly disastrous, an explosion within the ship that was barely contained. None of the transmitted data could be salvaged. So the spacecraft awaited another attempt. If a wormhole transfer was still contemplated, it was a risk beyond calculation. The machines hoped their vehicle could survive it.

For the first half of the journey, routine communication had been possible. Those transmissions were delayed by the speed of light, but were fast enough to allow for some hardware adjustments. Still, most of the technology was untested.

After the huge expenditure of time and talent, the Great Minds couldn't face a wasted mission. There were alternatives. Adequate fuel was available in the solar system for the trip home. But it wouldn't be found on this watery planet. Was the decision wrong?

* * * * *

After the long interstellar journey, darkness abated for the first time. A highly reflective planet on one side of the spacecraft filled nearly half of the sky. On the other side was an even brighter star. But within the ship itself, cold and darkness still ran deep.

Chapter 33

Friday, April 1, 2016

Me

Kelly arrived home in the middle of the night. She unloaded the essential items from her car, which didn't include much. The rest of her belongings would sit in the small U-Haul trailer she'd pulled behind the Mustang. Maybe she'd feel good enough tomorrow to unload it.

She reestablished herself in her bedroom without awakening Tannon. Her bedroom hadn't been touched since she left, so she just popped open a suitcase and resumed life in San Dimas.

When Tannon awoke on Friday morning, he knew Kelly was home. In the entry hallway was a small cardboard box strapped with tape. If he hadn't noticed it, he would've observed the light left on in the garage hallway. Tannon never missed the details, but he often missed the big picture.

He let Kelly sleep. She didn't appear in her nightshirt and bare feet until 11 am.

She never missed a beat: "Hi, Brother. Guess who?"

"You look like someone I know."

"I inherited a lot of stuff while I was gone. I've got a trailer full of clothes. Wonder where I'll put them?"

"If it's clothes for the new you, put them in your closet," replied Tannon.

"Unfortunately, it's clothes for the temporary me from Cleveland – mostly winter stuff that'll take care of the next ten ski seasons."

"Sounds like nice sleeping blankets for EZ," noted Tannon.

"Where is the lad? He didn't even come down from the garage loft when I slipped in last night."

"He knew you didn't want to make a big deal about coming home," said Tannon.

"He's right about that. I hope the rest of my tiny world doesn't make it into a big deal."

Tannon gave Kelly some verbal space. She looked tired and not happy. Her face seemed drawn and a bit too white. Tannon wondered if things could ever be the same. And he hoped things might be a little bit different.

* * * * *

Tannon Bessimer checked his email every day, even on weekends. When he was out of town, he carried his mini-laptop computer to retrieve his messages. And he always replied to email promptly. As far as Tannon was concerned, email was one of the big improvements in life. It allowed him to avoid face-to-face contact.

The first evening after Kelly arrived home, Tannon sat at his home computer to retrieve his email, while Kelly listened to music in her room and read the latest copy of *Flying* magazine. As Tannon surveyed his in-box, there were eight messages waiting for action. Six were part of his class discussion groups. It was tough to keep these students enthusiastic about geology, but they seemed to enjoy the chance to chat with their classmates.

The message that caught his eye was from Samuel Jakes. He opened it first. Jakes confirmed he had spoken with the president of Pasadena's Planetary Society, and there was a definite interest in finding a spot for Tannon on the schedule. He also gave Tannon an email address for Ben Muther, the astrophysicist working on the Tau Ceti project at Palomar. Samuel Jakes had secured the scientist's permission to release his address, which was a hopeful sign.

Tannon broke his message-checking routine to compose an email to Ben Muther before even opening his other messages. He used it as an opportunity to introduce himself, mentioning his meeting with Samuel Jakes, and wishing Muther success in his study of Tau Ceti. In his last sentence, he asked if he could contact him at a later date with some questions about the Mount Palomar Tau Ceti project. Keep it short for now, Tannon reminded himself. Most scientists don't like distractions.

After he sent the message, Tannon went through his remaining email. He decided to try the student discussion group before facing the junk-mail message flagging itself so readily by its address: "Me@ cyberberth.com"

One of his students was attempting to start a discussion thread on the San Andreas Fault, but the sentence structure made for slow reading. Tannon scanned most of the message and then skipped through the other five student messages, promising himself he'd read them in detail later. He filed the class messages in a folder he used to determine grades for the Internet portion of his classes. Tannon kidded his students about his grading criteria. He hinted he merely tallied up the number of messages at the end of the semester and graded accordingly. In reality, it was the prime factor in his grading system, but this joking admittance probably led his students to believe otherwise. Tannon preferred to think he also evaluated the quality of the messages, but it was difficult with over 100 students gabbing about things typically not geological in nature.

Finally, he clicked on the junk-mail message, entitled "No Subject." Usually these messages didn't make it through the college's email filter, turned back by the blocking codes. But this one had made it through, and Tannon silently congratulated the originator on the uniqueness of the address. The sender obviously had been around CyberBerth for a long time. The screen name of *Me* would have been grabbed a long time ago.

The message was short, only two lines, and more than the normal waste of time. It was completely unreadable, apparently transmitted in the wrong compression format. Tannon's email program didn't react well to unusual email formats, producing a hodge-podge of characters that frustrated the eye. He deleted the message, and closed his mailbox.

He had hoped for a message from the Planetary Society with a specific offer to speak to the organization, but Dr. Jake's message was as close as it got. And what would he do if the Planetary Society invited him to speak?

"I found this thing in a telescope." Period.

* * * * *

The next morning, Kelly left for Brackett Airport before Tannon woke up. Apparently she was determined to get back into flight instructor mode as quickly as possible, even at the sacrifice of her cherished Saturday morning sleep. When Tannon sat down for a bowl of cereal and some toast, he noticed how nice it felt to be alone. He had actually grown used to his increased privacy in recent weeks. But it was far outweighed by the pleasure of having Kelly with him again. The past month could equate to a marital separation, with feelings of regret, frustration, and also relief. But unlike a marital separation, the reconciliation was easy. Kelly simply moved back into their home. And neither of them asked any hard questions or expected any answers.

* * * * *

Later on Saturday afternoon, Tannon dropped by campus to pick up a textbook and class DVD from his office. While he was there, Tannon spent some time catching up on a required faculty report and editing a multimedia presentation for one of his classes. He liked working in his office on weekends when the building was empty. The lack of interruptions allowed him to complete more in an hour than he would normally accomplish between classes on a weekday.

Since he hadn't yet completed his daily ritual of checking email, he used his office computer to connect directly to the Mount SAC mainframe. He watched five messages download. Three were from class discussion group members, but one was from the Planetary Society. The remaining message, once again with "No Subject," was from Me@cyberberth.com.

Tannon turned immediately to the Planetary Society message, finding an invitation from the president to address the group at the Pasadena Public Library on April 28th. That was still over three weeks away, and Tannon had until Friday to confirm acceptance of the invitation. The Society president admitted he had another speaker standing by, just in case, due to the short notice. He promised to arrange a date later in the summer, if April 28th was too soon.

Too soon? It wasn't the timing that was the problem. What would he have to offer the audience? He had seen comet discoverers rise to quick fame, only to find themselves in situations over their heads. If you discovered an object, you were expected to be an inside expert on the celestial body. Usually that wasn't the case. All Tannon could offer was his thrill of discovery and regurgitation of information from credible scientists. Maybe it was all the Planetary Society expected.

He posted the date on his mobile-calendar, but decided to delay his decision. He really should use a few of the allotted days to think this through. He saved the message in his "To Do" folder and then opened the message from CyberBerth. It looked just like the last one, same kind of gibberish. At least it was short – only two sentences, if you could call them sentences. That made it particularly suspect.

Tannon clicked the "Reply" button and typed the word "Remove" on the subject line. In the text window, he wrote: "Remove me from this mailing list." He selected "Send Now" and watched the return message disappear from his screen. This was a procedure that almost never worked for junk mail. Probably "Me@cyberberth.com" was just an alias, but he didn't know how to interpret the message's header return-path to determine if it was a valid address. Nor did he care.

As Tannon dug into the remaining class discussion group messages, the reply message to *Me* zipped out into cyberspace.

* * * * *

"**A**nother one of your societies, Tannon?" joked Kelly.

No one was less sociable than her brother, but the word "Society" fit into a lot of his activities. He was a great listener, and scientific societies need such people.

"Yeah, that's me. Next it will be the Astronomical Society of the Pacific and then the Inland Valley Humane Society. A regular social guy."

Kelly tried to speak in a serious tone.

"Well, I think you should accept. I bet they would like to hear the discoverer's view. Besides, you're quite famous."

"The article in *Newsweek* was pretty remarkable," said Tannon. "It caught me by surprise, just when I thought there was no more interest."

"Your fame will be fleeting," replied Kelly. "But almost all of the television news channels did a repeat of the discovery story, after *Newsweek* blessed the topic."

"It's proof the media will do anything to make news about the Spacecraft. If the scientists could provide any new information, the Planetary Society would bump me out of the spotlight without a second glance."

Kelly seemed pleading when she said: "Well, for now, you're news again. So I say you should give the Spaceship Society your best speech, and enjoy the limelight."

"It's the Planetary Society," corrected Tannon. "And I've already told them I'll do it."

* * * * *

Tannon couldn't sleep. He seldom slept well, and tonight was another example. Fortunately, he didn't have anything important on Sunday's schedule. That was fortunate, since here he was, wide-awake at 3 am. The only way to fight it was to get up and do something. He had a headache, so that eliminated reading. He walked to the den, not finding EZ waiting at his door – probably sleeping in the garage loft tonight.

He flicked on the lamp, then turned on his computer. The monitor would also take its toll in eyestrain, but it seemed to have less impact on his headaches than reading.

His email program launched automatically, but Tannon still had to click the icon to download his messages. The middle of the night was a near-guarantee for a fast connection, even when hefty attachments were involved. But he seldom sent email during the midnight hours. He was afraid somebody would note the time stamp. Tannon didn't like drawing attention to himself. But he would often compose email messages in the darkness of the night, leaving them unsent until normal daylight hours. He got a lot accomplished on this unusual schedule. In return, his body absorbed the punishment.

There were three messages ready for viewing. He wasn't surprised to see that the junk-mail address had reappeared. So much for "Remove" as a way off this mailing list.

Rather than discard the message, Tannon opened it:

Subject: Re: No Subject
Date: 4/02/2016 9:51 pm
From: Me@cyberberth.com
To: tbessimer@mtsac.edu

Reply received now. and continue soon.

- Me

* * * * *

It was evident he was still on the mailing list. This questionable entrepreneur needed some serious help with grammar. Tannon had complained, mostly to himself, regarding the lack of writing skills among his students. He'd seen worse than this from his own geology classes.

But there was something else about this message that drew his attention. Since he couldn't sleep anyway, he opened his Deleted Messages folder and scrolled back, looking for the past two messages from "Me@cyberberth.com." He only found one of them, and then he realized the other had been received on his school computer and wasn't yet synchronized to his mini-laptop. He opened the original message and studied it:

Subject: No Subject
Date: 4/01/2016 4:03 am
From: Me@cyberberth.com
To: tbessimer@mtsac.edu

.noitacinummoc eriuqer.dne-pot,tfel-thgir daer uoy od

.tcatnoc gnidnep,tibro elbats

* * * * *

Tannon sat there in the middle of the night, trying to find some meaning to this gibberish. The assumption that it was a computer-kid didn't make him feel any more secure. Hackers could cause computer viruses and other devastating havoc. If this was supposed to be a coded message, it wouldn't be worth his time to try to crack it. On the other hand, maybe it wasn't as complexly coded as it looked, although that violated the goals of the typical hacker. Could it be a simple palindrome? No. Could it be written backward? A period started each line.

The last word, "stable," jumped out at him! He read the last line backward, slowly spelling the letters out loud:

"stable orbit, pending contact."

And then the first line:

"do you read right-left, top-end. require communication."

Tannon turned to EZ, now sitting in his Sphinx pose in the den's only other chair. Obviously, the cat had heard Tannon in the den, and was ready to night creep. EZ loved these middle-of-the-night sojourns.

"So, what we have here is a wise guy," he said to EZ.

EZ perked his ears, but kept his head down and refused to fully open his eyes.

Tannon felt violated. Although his voicemail at school had received a few crank calls lately, they had been rare. And his email hadn't been breeched even once since his discovery. College email addresses were pretty standard, so it didn't take a lot of effort to figure out an employee's address. In fact, his was posted on the college's faculty web page. But he didn't like the feeling of this prank.

Yet, in a way, Tannon was flattered. Someone had at least taken the time to locate the Spacecraft's discoverer. But he didn't appreciate games. He hit the "Reply" button:

> Subject: Re: Remove
> Date: 4/03/2016 3:32 am
> From: tbessimer@mtsac.edu
> To: Me@cyberberth.com
>
> Very cute. But please do not send any more messages to this address. If you persist, I'll report you to the authorities.

* * * * *

What authorities? He wouldn't even know how to report such a thing. But that should be the end of it. It wasn't.

Chapter 34

Monday, April 4, 2016

Contact

> Subject: No Subject
> Date: 4/04/2016 2:10 am
> From: Me@cyberberth.com
> To: tbessimer@mtsac.edu
>
> Ask. Speak small then.
>
> - Me

* * * * *

When Tannon ran into dead ends with the college email system, he never hesitated to call Lisa. He'd never met her in person, but she sounded very competent over the telephone. Lisa knew the intricacies of the college's computer system, but certainly wasn't hired to respond to every individual email problem encountered by the staff. But she always did.

"I'm getting a rash of junk mail from someone at CyberBerth," said Tannon over the phone. "Is there a way to block an individual email address from sending junk to me?"

"Heck, we'll cut him off from even getting aboard our mainframe. What's the address?"

Tannon provided her the email address, and he imagined Lisa smiling.

"Some address," said Lisa without emotion. "Might be an original CyberBerth member, or more likely a fake address. How about forwarding me a copy of the entire message, including the header with the return-path information? I'll make sure that address gets blocked."

"Thanks, Lisa. I owe you again."

* * * * *

"Ask. Speak small then."
Okay, suppose this wasn't a fake. Why not play with this a bit before Lisa cuts things off? There was always the outside chance this was really the Spacecraft. ET, phone home.

Tannon visualized his reply and echoed it on the keyboard:

> Subject: Re: No Subject
> Date: 4/04/2016 2:42 pm
> From: tbessimer@mtsac.edu
> To: Me@cyberberth.com
>
> Why are you contacting me?
>
> Tannon Bessimer
> Professor of Geology
> Mt San Antonio College
> Walnut CA

* * * * *

Tannon half-expected an instantaneous reply, but there was none. Maybe Lisa had already blocked the email address He checked again before turning off his computer two hours later; and there was no new CyberBerth email.

Chapter 35

Tuesday, April 5, 2016

Little Green Men

On Tuesday, after his early morning jog, Tannon turned on his computer, and as the machine warmed up, he enjoyed a warm shower. When he finally sat down at the keyboard, it only took a few moments to get things rolling. His message box had a single waiting message:

> Subject: Re: No Subject
> Date: 4/05/2016 4:47 am
> From: Me@cyberberth.com
> To: tbessimer@mtsac.edu
>
> >> Why are you contacting me?
>
> You are prominent. Our names together when your news reports appear. No trust or time for waste with others. Efficiency drives calendar. What meaning 'cute?'
>
> - Me

* * * * *

This wasn't what it appeared to be. The hacker was playing with him. Tannon formatted a message to Lisa. He wasn't sure why she hadn't cut off the offending email yet, but he knew she wouldn't let him down. For now, he decided to ask her to hold off on his request. He would advise her later if he still wanted the address blocked.

Tannon studied the message from "Me@cyberberth.com." It sounded like a young child or someone new to the English language. But this message seemed clearer than the last, and it certainly was better than the first message with the reversed words. His imagination began to take hold. He composed a reply:

> Subject: Cute
> Date: 4/05/2016 8:55 am
> From: tbessimer@mtsac.edu
> To: Me@cyberberth.com
>
> >> What 'cute'?
>
> I was accusing you of doing something as a joke. I'm not convinced you're a valid contact. Answer this:
>
> Where did the Spacecraft's first deceleration thrust occur, in astronomical units and miles from the earth? Be specific.

* * * * *

It wasn't a particularly articulate question, considering the availability of online data defining the astronomical unit. But a novice would have to do some research to determine the distance of the Spacecraft from earth during its deceleration burns. A library would have back copies of the newspapers and scientific journals, and most were available on the Internet, but it would take a while for anyone to find the data. A quick response, if it contained the correct information, might mean something.

As Tannon waited, he was surprised to see an email message arrive almost instantly. But it wasn't from "Me@cyberberth.com."

Subject: Re: Blocked Address
Date: 4/05/2016 8:58 am
From: lkernen@mtsac.edu
To: tbessimer@mtsac.edu

Sorry, Tannon, but it's too late. I blocked that email address before I went home yesterday. You won't have any more trouble from that guy, but I can unblock the address again if you want me to. Please advise.

Lisa Kernen
Systems Programmer
Mt San Antonio College

* * * * *

While he was reading Lisa's message, another message arrived:

Subject: Re: Cute
Date: 4/05/2016 9:01 am
From: Me@cyberberth.com
To: tbessimer@mtsac.edu

>> Where did the Spacecraft's first deceleration
>> thrust occur, in astronomical units and miles
>> from the earth? Be specific.

Measure system confuses. Assumed astronomical units measured from your planet to your star. Do not know if you detected first fire, which began at 3683.457 au. Second fire at 28.453 au. Third deceleration was oriented away from your planet and near your star. Probably not observable from your planet.

First fire equates to 342.562 billion statute(?) miles (zeros confuse). Second was at a distance of 2.646 billion miles.

- Me

* * * * *

That was fast and convincing. Tannon had estimated the distances himself, using the data from Lori. No hack would have ready access to that information. "Me@cyberberth.com" seemed real.

Tannon reached over to EZ's chair. The cat had been sitting patiently, now fully awake and waiting for attention. Tannon gave him a few rough, appreciated strokes, and the cat responded with a throaty trill.

"Now what, EZ? Another discovery, and another reporting problem I'm not even sure I should tell anyone. After all, these messages came to me rather than NASA for a reason."

EZ purred as Tannon gave him more strokes. The cat stared back at Tannon and said nothing. Tannon spoke again.

"Maybe the aliens simply like my outgoing personality."

* * * * *

Tannon sat across the booth from Kelly at BJ's Restaurant. He was dressed in black shorts, a tan T-shirt, and brown sneakers with shoelaces recently shredded by EZ.

Kelly looked ill. Her face was peaked and drawn thin. She looked uncomfortably older and visibly exhausted.

"Are you okay?"

"Forget it. Please."

Tannon thought he had a topic that would enliven her.

"I don't think you're gonna' believe this."

"Try me," said Kelly.

"Well, let's just say I'm getting email from the little green men," stated Tannon in a serious face.

"Let's just say you've always been a bit coo-coo. Now you're a lot coo-coo," replied Kelly, without missing a beat.

"Somehow I knew you'd be supportive."

Tannon stopped, and Kelly waited. Then Tannon spoke slowly.

"I'm perfectly serious."

"You're perfectly crazy. Aren't you the guy who always wonders if I'm on drugs?"

"Never said that."

Tannon was quick with his reply. Kelly looked like the aftermath of drugs this morning. And, yes, Tannon did wonder.

Tannon talked rapidly, trying to control his excitement.

"Look, I've received multiple messages, and I was extremely skeptical at first. But now I'm convinced this is for real."

He tried to establish eye contact with Kelly, but she wouldn't let him.

"Tannon, I don't mean to pull your chain, but you're easy to play with, even when I'm sick. Okay, so the Martians have infiltrated your computer. Why did they choose email for their first contact? You'd think they'd have a bit better technology after taking a nice long trip between the stars."

"You'd think that," agreed Tannon. "But email is simple text format, and it's worldwide. I can't explain it, but they're sending me email."

"Doesn't make sense. Not email."

"But it's not subject to confrontational anxiety," said Tannon.

"Confrontational anxiety. Now where'd you dig that one up."

"Well, what I mean is there is little fear associated with this method of communication. The stress of contact could be overwhelming to either side. This way is more relaxed."

Kelly stirred her hot chocolate, staring at the melting whipped cream. She looked up with penetrating eyes. Even when ill, she could have a commanding look.

"Okay, so maybe I buy it. At least I'll consider buying it. But it's only because I'm your sister."

He further explained the messages, and Kelly listened. She didn't respond to any of it until Tannon's voice rose in concern.

"What in the world is going on, Kell?"

"What's going on is mostly in that strange little mind of yours. I'd say your brain is smoked by all of this alien talk.

He knew Kelly was concentrating more than she pretended. He continued.

"You do see a little hint of reality here, don't you? Do you think I should tell someone, maybe NASA?"

Kelly replied with a hint of a smile.

"Why don't you ask the little green men?"

* * * * *

Tannon asked. And *Me* promptly responded with a "suggestion" to withhold the details of this first contact from others for now. *Me* added: "You decide when and how to announce." The wording of the message seemed significantly clearer in vocabulary and sentence structure. *Me's* knowledge of the English language was growing.

Tannon spent part of Wednesday afternoon carefully composing a message to *Me* that expressed his primary concerns. Messages from *Me* had been kept simple so far. It seemed only fair to Tannon that he did the same.

> Subject: Contact
> Date: 4/06/2016 5:07 pm
> From: tbessimer@mtsac.edu
> To: Me@cyberberth.com
>
> 1 - Why did you come to earth?
> 2 - Will there be any harm to those on earth?
> 3 - Are there any living beings aboard your spacecraft?
> 4 - Can you monitor our activities by listening and viewing us?
> 5 – Will you leave this orbit?

* * * * *

The reply was almost immediate:

> Subject: Re: Contact
> Date: 4/06/2016 5:22 pm
> From: Me@cyberberth.com
> To: tbessimer@mtsac.edu
>
> 1 - We are here to study you. Your planet was second choice (no insults). We desired to study life on one of the moons around your star's largest planet. But yours is a more unusual world. There is more for us to learn from you than you can learn from us. But we will both learn.
> 2 - We come without harm in our minds or machines.
> 3 - There is no biological life aboard our vehicle at this time.
> 4 - We monitor your planet as part of our study of your species. Our power to view and listen is primitive, especially from this distance.
> 5 – When we leave orbit, it will be to leave your star. Schedule not decided.
>
> - Me

* * * * *

Tannon studied the message, rereading it carefully. "There is no biological life aboard our vehicle at this time." That caught his eye, and Tannon wanted to know more. Another spaceship could be on its way right now. It was the only part of *Me's* reply where he saw any hint of twisted meaning in the words.

Tannon stretched in his chair and laughed. A week ago he was feeling neglected by the scientists of the world, pleading to be a part of the information gathering process. Now he was in charge of it.

* * * * *

Kelly and Tannon sat behind Christine, watching her CyberBerth welcome screen change into a highlighted connection box, begging for attention.

Kelly had asked Christine if she and Tannon could make a business visit. Her wire-head brother needed some help with a project, and it would take a CyberBerth subscriber.

Christine looked uncomfortable. Tannon obviously knew a lot more about computers than she did, and Kelly was a very private friend. The three of them in this little room was difficult for Christine, and Tannon knew it.

The computer monitor settled at the "Welcome, GottaDance" screen. Under Tannon's instructions, Christine selected the menu labeled: "Get a Member's Profile." Then she typed in "Me." The search took only a few seconds: "There is no profile for [Me]."

"Try this, Christine," said Tannon. "Compose a message. Anything will do. Address it to the screen name *Me,* and let's see what happens."

Now Christine looked even more uncomfortable. But Tannon talked her through the message. In the content box, he told her to type: "Test message. Call home." Kelly laughed, and Christine looked a bit more nervous.

As soon as the message was sent, there was an immediate beep, with a warning message: "[Me] – this is not a known CyberBerth member."

Just as Tannon thought. *Me* hadn't paid his Internet bill.

* * * * *

For the balance of April, military efforts in the United States and other advanced nations were centered on monitoring the Spacecraft. On April 22nd, the U.S. Air Force, utilizing listening techniques designed in conjunction with the Defense Intelligence Agency, detected low volume machine-noise emanating from the Spacecraft. The noise couldn't be deciphered, nor was it at a level that would rule out simple refracted background static. On April 23rd, the Air Force reported this news to the press. At least it was news. This was the first new information about the Spacecraft in over a month.

On April 27th, using the same Air Force classified equipment, a narrow-beam signal of low intensity was detected propagating from the Spacecraft. It was initially reported as oriented towards the Galaxy III communication satellite. These transmissions were intermittent and lasted only a few microseconds. There didn't seem to be any pattern to the timing of the transmissions, but they were detected several times each day.

Lori called Tannon on the evening of April 27th to relay some details reported to her regarding these new transmissions. She had little to add that wasn't already in the newspapers. Tannon told her that he was addressing the Planetary Society the next evening, and she seemed pleased. He didn't tell her about the messages from *Me.*

Chapter 36

Thursday, April 28, 2016

Guest Speaker

On the day of his presentation to the Planetary Society, Tannon awoke to the sound of a plastic dish clanging against concrete. Kelly was on the patio, hollering for EZ.

Tannon slipped on his sweatpants, a sweatshirt, and socks. Then he joined her on the already sunny back porch.

"Got away again?" Tannon asked rhetorically.

"He'll be back. He hasn't had breakfast yet. I was late for a flight lesson, as usual, and he sneaked past me at the door."

Tannon always worried when EZ entered "coyote world," but he remained poised.

"You get going. He's probably hiding over there behind the bushes, laughing at us."

Kelly left for her appointment, now even more rushed. Tannon pounded the plastic dish on the pavement a few more time, then gave up and went back to bed. He crawled under the covers with his clothes on, leaving the sliding patio door open for EZ. He could rest for an hour before it was time to get ready for school.

* * * * *

Subject: Data Upload
Date: 4/28/2016 04:12 am
From: Me@cyberberth.com
To: tbessimer@mtsac.edu

Tannon,

Please transmit word definitions (dictionary?) and encyclopedia data. You can upload as email attachments, but break into segments so not to exceed 1 megabyte per transmission. No graphics.

- Me

* * * * *

This was the first time *Me* had used Tannon's first name. It pleased him. And he found the upload limitation amusing.

A variety of messages would be exchanged in the days ahead. *Me* explained the desire to keep the quantity and size of the messages small. The Galaxy III satellite was relaying data, and *Me* wanted to "avoid upsetting the authorities." Besides, the Spacecraft had more important things to do – email wasn't a top priority.

Me's mastery of the English language mushroomed, with subsequent messages exhibiting increased wit and understanding. Although the messages remained brief, *Me* seemed interested in learning more about Tannon. Sometimes *Me* would indicate knowledge that could only be obtained through an ability to monitor Tannon's activities remotely, but in other instances *Me* seemed to lack a lot of the details. Tannon flattered himself by assuming he was being used as a human example for his species. And he felt increasingly free to express his human concerns to *Me*.

When Tannon explained some of the details about his life with Kelly and EZ, the usually astute *Me* seemed to draw a blank. Kelly didn't require a lot of explaining, although the notion of "sister" seemed unique to *Me*. EZ was entirely another situation. There seemed to be nothing in the Spacecraft's databanks regarding "pets," and it took Tannon several messages to convince *Me* the concept wasn't related to "slaves," a word *Me* seemed to fully understand. Why would humans devote so much time to creatures with so little purpose?

But similar to other topics, *Me* was a fast learner when it came to cats. Soon he was asking about EZ's activities as if he were speaking more of a god than a slave. Maybe he was merely echoing Tannon's opinion on the subject.

* * * * *

"**Y**ou sure don't look like yourself in that thing," said Kelly.

"You're right. A suit and tie isn't my idea of fun. But at least no one who knows me will see this outfit, except Dr. Jakes."

"I prefer you in shorts and T-shirt," noted Kelly. "And your hiking boots wouldn't go well with that color."

"Hey, it's my big night out. Maybe I'll start wearing suits more often."

"You're going to look funny at BJ's."

But Kelly looked at Tannon with visible pride.

"Promise to keep calling for EZ," said Tannon. "He may be your cat, but I'm awfully worried."

Kelly grimaced. "I sure hope he's vacationing in somebody's garage. It's going to be dark soon."

* * * * *

Samuel Jakes met Tannon on the front steps of the Pasadena Public Library. It was a cold evening for April. Jakes looked at home in his dark gray suit. Tannon felt uncomfortable in his. If he was going to wear a suit again, it was time to get a bigger size. This jacket made his armpits sweat. It wasn't entirely the suit's fault.

It was almost dark as they walked into the quadrangle foyer leading to the library's entrance. Before proceeding, Tannon excused himself to use his cell phone. It was now prime coyote time, and he needed assurance EZ was home. Kelly told him the cat hadn't yet returned, but she didn't sound worried. She wished him luck with the speech. "Give 'em hell" were her exact words.

Tannon and Jakes continued into the old library and then to the left, past huge wooden reading tables covered with glass guards. Each table was a duplicate of the next, all with matching old-style small lamps with green glass lampshades, and not a computer in sight. This wonderful room was a throwback to the past, when libraries were still places to read books and research topics by turning paper pages.

A varied group of library patrons were scattered at the tables and standing at the nearby reference shelves. Some of these visitors looked at home with Shakespeare, and some looked like they had simply sought refuge from the streets. One woman was frantically checking a thick reference volume as if it were her ordained duty.

They continued to the Wright Auditorium, an old lecture hall. The room smelled musty and looked plenty historic. There was a podium and microphone on the raised stage, with a small overhead screen extending downward from the ceiling. Between the second and third row of red padded theater-like seats, a computer projector tilted up precariously. It seemed hot in the room. Inside his tight jacket, Tannon was already sweating profusely.

Samuel Jakes led Tannon to the rear of the small auditorium, where the room's only other occupants were sorting Planetary Society handouts. He introduced him to the society's two officers, and Tannon wondered if they called Jakes by the name "Sam." In his flawless beard and fitted suit, he certainly didn't look like a "Sam." The treasurer called him "Doctor Jakes" and the president called him "Samuel."

Jakes asked if he could assist by operating the projector, and Tannon was grateful for the offer. Tannon hooked up his mini-laptop and tested the remote clicker at the podium. Jakes explained the projector was known to die in mid-presentation, but he knew how to reboot it. As they tested an image, a telescopic view of Tau Ceti appeared on the screen – a distorted polygon-shaped image beaming from an ancient projector. The text below the photo was readable but fuzzy.

Tannon and Jakes sat alone in the front row. Tannon removed his suit jacket to cool his armpits, but it didn't seem to help.

The guests straggled in – individuals dressed in everything from suits to T-shirts. It looked like it would be a small crowd. The room's seven rows couldn't handle over 120 people, and it appeared tonight's audience would be well under that.

Promptly at 7:30 pm, the Planetary Society's president climbed the steps to the stage and took his place at the podium. He welcomed the small crowd filling less than half the seats, talked about some upcoming society events, and then introduced Tannon. It was an impressive series of credentials for the guest speaker, unless you listened closely. Tannon wondered if everyone noticed he was really an unknown geologist by the Planetary Society's standards. The punch line, of course, was his fame as discoverer of the Spacecraft.

"And now Professor Bessimer will tell us about his discovery and bring us up to date on the latest information regarding the Spacecraft. Welcome Professor Bessimer."

There was strong applause from such a small group. Tannon approached the podium with tentative confidence.

He started his presentation by relaying some of the routine details of the discovery. The audience seemed to like the personal items he had originally planned to leave out of his presentation. That took only ten minutes, and it was time to ask Dr. Jakes to turn on the projector. The first slide was a Schmidt photo of Tau Ceti taken atop Palomar Mountain. Tannon talked about the star's characteristics for about five minutes, using some of the information supplied to him by Lori. He was repeating information readily available in science periodicals. To illustrate the stellar main sequence classification system, he punched the remote control for the next slide. The slide projector made a popping noise and the screen went black.

Jakes fumbled with the projector as Tannon tried to talk about Tau Ceti's place on the main sequence, comparing the star to the earth's sun. Just as Tannon finished his explanation of the invisible diagram, the diagram itself appeared on the screen. He pushed the slide-advance button, and nothing happened. Samuel Jakes would be his remote control for the rest of the evening.

Tannon continued with his presentation, reviewing the calendar of events as the Spacecraft approached earth. Samuel Jakes advanced through the slides. The textual data was intermixed with some standard astrophotos. Tannon had spent a lot of time preparing for this evening.

As the lecture progressed, he was still sweating, but he felt a bit more relaxed. Now he had time to take a look at his audience, and he didn't like what he saw. Most of the guests were watching the screen rather than him, and they didn't seem enthusiastic about the presentation. These were educated professional and amateur scientists who had kept up with the news regarding the Spacecraft. There was nothing new from the guest speaker. One young man in the audience, probably a graduate student, was thumbing through a copy of *Astrophysics Journal*, oblivious to the presentation. A squinty-eyed woman in the back row was looking over one of the Planetary Society handouts.

Tannon was down to his last ten minutes of prepared text. He watched the audience carefully as he asked Dr. Jakes to turn off the projector. Everyone prepared for the anticipated ending and looked relieved. Tannon took a brief mental break to worry about EZ in the dark of San Dimas. Then he spoke.

"The question of 'What Next?' is, of course, on everyone's mind," said Tannon. "Will communication with the Spacecraft be established, and how will it occur? As you know, an Orion mission is being discussed for August. But that's a long time to wait. The pressures on our country, our economy, our government, and our people are taking their toll. And those pressures are repeated throughout the world."

The woman in the back row looked up briefly and then went back to the handout.

"Will communication be established?"

He paused for several seconds for effect.

"I'm here tonight to tell you it already has."

The young man reading the *Astrophysics Journal* peered over the magazine and stared at Tannon. He looked like a student who had been caught sleeping in class.

"Since the first day of April, I've been receiving personal email from the Spacecraft. Tonight I can reveal some of the characteristics of the artificial intelligence aboard the vehicle. First, let me assure you this Spacecraft has arrived in peace."

No one moved. No one knew how to handle this strange outpouring. Then a few members of the audience started snickering and talking among themselves. But most were riveted on the podium.

* * * * *

The presentation went 15 minutes overtime, and the question and answer session finally had to be terminated after another 20 minutes. Most of the audience refused to leave, besieging Tannon at the podium with further questions. Jakes suggested to the Planetary Society's president that the room be cleared so the Society's officers could talk with Tannon in private. The president seemed grateful for the suggestion.

"Well, my friend, you've certainly dropped a bombshell tonight," said Samuel Jakes, as the two Planetary Society officers listened, all now seated in the front row with Tannon.

"I wonder how many of them caught the date of the first email contact?" smirked Tannon.

"I for one," said the president. "April first is an interesting date."

"Somehow, I don't think that's my biggest problem," said Tannon.

"Well, the whole thing does put us in a bit of a dilemma," said Jakes.

He was stroking his beard as he talked, and seemed to be making an on-the-spot decision regarding Tannon's credibility. Finally, after no one else commented, he spoke again.

"How do we release this thing to the public? The next issue of the *Planetary Report* won't be soon enough."

"What exactly is expected of us?" asked the president.

The president looked as if he were unconvinced of the whole thing. There was an abundance of unique and controversial characters in this field of science.

Tannon surveyed their faces as they waited for him to respond.

"Suppose I simply turn this over to you," said Tannon. "I can send you copies of all of the messages, and you can study them. Then I'd suggest you contact the news media right away. Otherwise, the lady I saw in the back row will have the *Times* on the phone, cutting another notch for the insanity of scientists."

Samuel Jakes pushed his body back in his chair and stared at the overhead stage lights.

"Tannon, this is a tough one. You don't have a lot of evidence here. But, for what it's worth, I believe this whole thing is real."

"Thanks," said Tannon. "I appreciate your support."

"And you're about to become famous again," noted Jakes. "I hope you're ready for this second round. NASA will be on your ass real soon."

"Fine," replied Tannon with determination. "Maybe I'll ask them if I can go along on the mission in August. What do you think, Dr. Jakes?"

Samuel Jakes offered his right hand and didn't let go when Tannon grasped it.

"I think this was quite an evening," said Jakes. "And call me Sam, please."

* * * * *

When Tannon arrived home just before midnight, Kelly and EZ were curled together on the sofa. Kelly was asleep, sitting with her head cranked to the side, her short hair going every which way. She would have a neck ache when she woke up. Her turquoise-framed reading glasses dangled from the blue neck strap. Her right leg was tucked under her left thigh. That leg would ache, too.

But EZ was sitting alert, with his eyes fixed on the door as Tannon entered. He sat with statuesque patience, what Tannon called his Sphinx pose.

Tannon's maneuvering in the entryway woke Kelly. She kept her leg in its tucked position and reached over and stroked EZ. The cat's ears perked straight up, and his puffy tail flopped hard enough on the sofa to be heard from the hallway.

"Everybody's home," said Kelly to EZ.

"Thank goodness that includes your cat," said Tannon.

He gave EZ a scolding look, but the golden cat maintained his Sphinx-like pose.

"Thanks for worrying me sick," said Tannon.

EZ raised his head higher, as if he were being praised.

"So how did they handle it?" asked Kelly.

"Just about as well as I handled it when the first message came in – with a bit of awe and a lot of denial."

"I bet you got some rather wild questions."

"That I did," said Tannon. "One guy asked if the aliens can read our minds."

Kelly nodded her head in understanding.

"Interesting question, don't you think?" said Kelly.

Chapter 37

Friday, April 29, 2016

NASA

Front Page
Los Angeles Times

First Contact -- Alien Intelligence Speaks

The Planetary Society, a Pasadena-based science organization, has reported communications contact with the alien Spacecraft. First communication came through an alleged email contact with Tannon Bessimer, the college professor who discovered the Spacecraft in early January. According to Bessimer, the first email message was transmitted from the Spacecraft on April 1, but it took a full week to establish coherent contact. Professor Bessimer claims he has received 32 messages from the Spaceship via his Mount San Antonio College email address. He also states his reply messages to the spaceship have been acknowledged.

NASA hasn't verified the messages between the Spacecraft and anyone on earth. Professor Bessimer claims the Spacecraft states it intends no harm to the earth and that it's a robotic spaceship sent to gather information about the solar system's life forms. The Planetary Society, representing Professor Bessimer, promises a press conference later today, with the time and location to be announced. Bessimer wasn't available for further comment.

* * * * *

"**I**f it's that bad, why don't you just leave?" said Christine.

Christine gazed at Kelly across the dining room table. Their conversation had reached a stalemate. It usually did when this subject came up, and it was a topic that seemed to reappear after each night Kelly stayed with Christine.

"Look, he's my brother, and he's taken care of me for the past five years. He came along at a time when I really needed him, and he's been there to support me ever since. You don't just leave someone like that."

"But he's weird. In fact, weirder than weird," said Christine.

"You mean he's a guy."

"That too."

Kelly stood and thrust her arms upward, hands clasped backwards in a morning stretch. This was going nowhere. It never did.

"Move in with me," said Christine. "It's that simple."

Christine looked up at Kelly's outstretched frame. Kelly visibly relaxed her athletic body and slumped back into the chair. She cocked her head to the side and stared into Christine's demanding eyes.

"It's not that simple," said Kelly. "If I move in now, I'd see him around town all the time. Maybe after you leave for Denver."

"That's not until August," Christine countered. "And I'll be on a bit of a shoestring then. It's no way for us to start playing house."

"And playing house is all it would be, especially if I leave now. Tannon needs me, more than ever. This is no time for me to abandon him. After what he has been through with his strange sister and an even stranger bout of fame, it's the least I can do. Maybe in a few months. . ."

Christine interrupted: "In a few months you'll be a basket case. You're already living in a man's world."

"Maybe that's where I belong," noted Kelly.

"Well, you won't find me there."

"Christine, it's not fair. You know I cherish you. And every time this happens, you try to force me to choose between you and him."

"So choose."

"I've already done that. I've explained it to you, but you don't listen. This Spacecraft thing will settle down soon, and then Tannon won't need my support like he does now. Who else can he turn to?"

"Exactly my point," said Christine. "He's dug his own grave. Living with that guy isn't good for you."

"But he's still my brother. This will be behind us in a few more months. Then we won't need to play house. I'd rather play for keeps, wouldn't you."

"Of course. But talk is cheap. When, my dear Kelly? When?"

"How about August? When you leave for Denver, I'll be there."

"Okay. August. I guess we may as well jump into the fire together," said Christine.

"One fire at a time, please."

"Fair enough, Kelly. But I don't think it would do a lot of good to let Tannon know what's brewing."

"You're right. But it's hard for me to hide how I feel about you. He sees it in me all of the time."

"That's fine. It's just what I want him to see," said Christine. "And when I see him, I see a guy who is dragging you down. And I also see a guy who is after my girlfriend."

"He's not after your girlfriend, Christine. For Christ's sake, he's my brother."

"Just remember that, and you'll be a lot better off."

* * * * *

Subject: Home Planet
Date: 4/29/2016 8:38 am
From: tbessimer@mtsac.edu
To: Me@cyberberth.com

Tell me more about the form of the intelligent life on your planet? In what ways is the dominant species similar to my species?

* * * * *

Tannon expected reporters to be looking for him. He didn't have any Friday classes, and his division office routinely refused to give callers home phone numbers or addresses of faculty member. Tannon didn't answer his home telephone, and no messages relative to the Spacecraft appeared on his voicemail. For now, it looked like his unlisted phone number, along with the protection of the college, might shield him.

The issue of privacy worried Tannon. Anyone who knew how colleges operate could find him. The campus telephone directory was on most desks at the college, and it contained his home address and telephone number. Email addresses were an even simpler issue. The national news release, indicating he was corresponding with the Spacecraft by email, raised a new problem. Certainly, the "edu" suffix with a faculty name prefix was rather standard. But for now, his primary email contacts remained his class discussion groups and *Me.* It probably wouldn't last.

There was one message on his office voicemail requiring action. The caller identified himself as David Graham, the head of NASA.

* * * * *

Subject: Re: Home Planet
Date: 4/29/2016 9:21 am
From: Me@cyberberth.com
To: tbessimer@mtsac.edu

Most of our beings live in the water. You would probably call them fish, but they have intelligence beyond any fish on your planet. Some of them, our Great Minds, live almost permanently on the land, and others are able to fly.

We are trying to transition to the land, but it is difficult. For our technology to develop, we need the land, and we hope to learn from you. Our seas are becoming very crowded. There is little time left for this transition. Our beings are growing old in evolutionary terms. Knowledge from your planet may help us over that barrier.

- Me

* * * * *

"I got a call from NASA today," said Tannon flat-toned.

Kelly sat looking out the window. Her brother was across from her at the kitchen table, toying with his cereal.

"You mean 'Thy' NASA?"

"It's 'Thee.'"

"Well, Mr. Astro, what did 'Thee' NASA have to say?"

"It was a message on my voicemail, and it came from the head of NASA himself. 'Thee' Administrator, David Graham."

"From what I hear, he's administrating himself into hot water with the Space Station fiasco. Explosions in space don't help his popularity."

"Well, I was suitably impressed," said Tannon. "When I tried to call him back, I only got as far as his secretary. But it looks like David Graham wants to talk to me something fierce."

"No big surprise. NASA has probably already intercepted all of your email messages. Watch out for those sexy messages to Doctor Lori."

"Are you jealous of me or Lori?"

"Both. But don't let it go to your head."

Kelly could keep Tannon guessing, and he enjoyed it.

"So lay it on me, Mr. Astro."

"Nothing really. His secretary promised the Administrator would be contacting me right away. I told him about our phone situation at home, so she promised I'd be contacted at school or by email."

"As I said, they're probably already reading your email."

"Maybe. But it would be worth it if I get what I want."

"And that is?" Kelly's eyebrows raised appropriately in anticipation.

"A ride on the Orion would be nice."

* * * * *

Subject: Re: Home Planet
Date: 4/29/2016 7:14 pm
From: tbessimer@mtsac.edu
To: Me@cyberberth.com

Based on your spaceflight accomplishments, your technology seems so superior to ours. I'm sure you will make a rapid transition to the land. For us, of course, it was a natural transition, and it took a long time. But in the end, here we are.

* * * * *

Subject: Re: Home Planet
Date: 4/29/2016 9:21 pm
From: Me@cyberberth.com
To: tbessimer@mtsac.edu

Natural Transition! You transitioned from the sea under the powers of nature?! You did not consciously develop a plan to conquer the land? There is hope for our planet. Ours will be a species that survives. You really know how to make a guy's day!

- Me

* * * * *

NASA did pursue Tannon. And they treated him right. First he was invited to Houston, all expenses paid, to meet with the NASA Administrator himself who had flown in from Washington for the occasion. It was timed so Tannon could witness an Orion launch rehearsal, using the rocket called the Space Launch System (SLS), remotely-controlled from Houston. In this dry run, a simulated SLS rocket was launched from Cape Canaveral, including video feeds and telemetry data based on past test launches. As soon as the simulated SLS broke ground, control was passed to Houston. It was practice for the upcoming launch on May 15, the only SLS-Orion mission until the planned August rendezvous with the Spacecraft. The original May Orion mission had been adjusted to establish itself in an orbit near the Spacecraft, placing it within a few miles of the alien vehicle at one point. If a rendezvous were to occur in August, the May flight would be an important step in preparation for the August mission. Even then, it was pushing the SLS-Orion to its limit.

This was a particularly ambitious step for NASA, an organization known for taking historic calculated risks. The Space Launch System was still new, although its reliability was already settling into a comfortable posture. Its first stage was based on a Shuttle-like design of four main engines flanked by two solid boosters, and it had performed flawlessly so far. The second stage of the SLS, with its liquid oxygen and hydrogen ignition sequence, was suffering growing pains. But it was considered within the parameters of safety for a project still in the test phase.

The Orion capsule, on the other hand, was far from mission-ready. For NASA, the term "capsule" had become a problem in itself. In space terminology, "spacecraft" had replaced "capsules" before the first men set foot on the moon. In fact, the original Mercury Seven astronauts had objected to the concept of a "capsule," a passive vehicle over which they had little control. In a capsule, you rode on top of a rocket as a passenger. But you had control of a spacecraft. It fit in well with the image of the Space Shuttle, which even looked like an airplane. But now here we were with Orion, an Apollo look-alike. Admittedly, this was a far superior design over the antiquated Apollo, and considerably larger. But the public couldn't avoid the comparison. It was a sophisticated vehicle – nevertheless, it was a capsule. NASA promoted a new phrase, "crew exploration vehicle," to describe the Orion, but it was too unwieldy to catch on. The news media used the term "capsule" so often that even NASA finally gave in. Besides, the world was now using the word "Spacecraft" to designate one and only one exotic object – the alien sphere now orbiting the earth.

Orion was the replacement for the now-obsolete Space Shuttle, and it had grown out of an unsettling bout of delays. The upcoming May mission would be the second manned flight of the Orion. A rendezvous with an alien spacecraft so early in the test program was an uncomfortable stretch, even for NASA. The capsule was designed to rotate crews to the International Space Station, and eventually travel to the moon. In the time gap between the Space Shuttle and the Orion, the Russians had taken up the slack as much as possible with their Soyuz resupply missions to the ISS. But it was considered an interim solution, and the Space Station was relying on the Orion to shift resupply missions back to NASA. As one Space Station astronaut joked to Houston when the May mission to the alien Spacecraft necessitated an extension of his crew's in-orbit stay: "Hey, are we still here in your rearview mirror? Don't forget about us."

The Orion's service module was a bright light in the test program. Riding beneath the crew and cargo transport module, it served as the powerplant for maneuvering the Orion in space. Its performance throughout the test phase had been nearly faultless, allowing project managers and engineers to concentrate on Orion's crew life support anomalies, troublesome quirks that popped up all-too-often in the environmental ventilation system.

The Administrator asked for copies of Tannon's email correspondence with *Me.* Tannon agreed to forward all email communications from *Me* to David Graham, and he also promised to provide copies of his future outgoing and incoming messages involving *Me.* In return, Graham agreed to keep him thoroughly briefed on any information available to NASA regarding the Spacecraft. Tannon insisted on a written agreement describing the scope of the term "thoroughly briefed," and he got it.

What he didn't get was a ride on the Orion. That was out of the question. He wasn't trained, nor was there time to get him Orion-capable. He was shown a series of videos illustrating the extent of the pre-mission training required for astronauts, including mission specialists. It was intended to make him feel better about being denied a ride on the SLS rocket. But it didn't.

"What about passengers?" Tannon asked.

"I'm afraid our taxpayers don't pay for sightseeing flights."

Tannon thought about it for a moment, and then he replied.

"They paid for John Glenn's ride on the Space Shuttle."

* * * * *

"**H**ow long will you be in orbit?" asked Tannon in one of his email exchanges with *Me.*

The reply: "We are still developing language proficiency and accumulating information through a variety of monitoring sources. Then we'll be ready to meet with you. See you in August."

Tannon hoped "you" included him, but NASA considered this a closed subject. He pestered the Administrator with repeated requests and arguments with nearly every forwarded email message involving *Me.* It was a waste of his time.

The space agency had sent multiple messages to the CyberBerth address, as had millions of people worldwide. Each message came back: "Mailbox Not Found. <Me@cyberberth.com>. . . User unknown."

NASA nudged Tannon further, attempting to acquire direct contact with *Me.* They requested their officials pay a personal visit to San Dimas or to Mount San Antonio College to utilize his computer for contacting *Me.* Tannon refused. But he wasn't sure he could refuse much longer.

Chapter 38

Thursday, May 5, 2016

Mind Reading

The news media experienced occasional success in violating Tannon's privacy. That was usually during his hours on-campus, but the college fully supported his requests for protection. More than once, campus security showed up at his office or his classroom to escort reporters off the premises.

To get away from the increasing pressures, Tannon paid daily visits to nearby Bonelli Park. He drove his Jeep into the parking lot by the lake and spent many early evenings jogging around the park. Once, during his cool-down period, as he panted his way back to the Jeep, he stopped abruptly. Something was happening to his body, and it wasn't good. He felt a sharp pain in his chest, but it went away almost immediately. Replacing the pain was a nebulous sense he was being watched.

Tannon was experiencing more than normal physical and mental stress; he was also feeling increasingly paranoid about his place in society. He felt everyone wanted something from him, and he was particularly suspicious regarding NASA. The feeling of being watched would hit him intermittently, always when he was outside, and usually when pushing his body to its limits. He would awaken in the middle of the night, usually with a stuffy-puffy headache, sweating and waiting for the being-observed feeling to appear in his house. It didn't.

Maybe there was a way to achieve more direct contact with *Me*. Who needed Orion? Getting away from people seemed to help his body and his mind, and maybe it would allow direct mental contact with *Me*. After all, it seemed likely it was *Me* who was watching him. But then, it could be NASA, or someone more threatening.

He tried more hiking, one of his favorite activities, and it seemed to help his stress level. Whether or not he made contact with *Me* this way, he enjoyed the outings. And he knew he needed the exercise.

Then, on Saturday, May 7, Tannon stood atop Mount Baldy, one of the highest peaks in Southern California, slightly above 10,000 feet. This was Tannon's Mount Everest. The winter snow was still holding firm on the peak, but the path to the top was well worn by climbers. He could hear the crunch of the hardened snow beneath the feet of climbers along the nearby ridge. It wasn't a totally private place, but hikers respected each other as they sought the summit and found their own semi-secluded spot to look down on the Los Angeles Basin. Tannon fought a dull headache today, as he reclined against the sloping face of a large boulder, inspecting the world below. He suddenly felt the same sharp pain in his chest, and this time it stayed with him for several minutes. Then it was gone, replaced by the feeling of being watched.

* * * * *

The next day, Tannon was very much alone. He always felt the greatest sense of being alone in his Piper Arrow, flying solo in the clouds. He loved it, but he didn't do it very often. Usually Kelly was in the right seat, but today he was by himself.

The conditions were perfect, as he tracked westward from Van Nuys on the assigned airway. He was in the middle of an extensive stratocumulus layer that was expected to continue all the way to Santa

Barbara. He was supposed to be there by now, and Kelly was waiting for him. But the instrument departure delays out of Brackett Airport were typical for a dreary Sunday. Kelly would understand. She was a pilot. Time to spare, go by air.

Kelly was waiting at Santa Barbara with one of her instrument students. A bad magneto on a Cessna 172 had stranded them. Tannon had reacted to the phone call with rescue mission enthusiasm – it was a reason to fly the Arrow in ideal instrument conditions. There wasn't the slightest bump in these docile clouds, but this was no time to relax. The weather required a level of concentration that took his mind off everything else.

He wasn't really alone. George, his trusty autopilot, was doing most of the work. Tannon relayed messages to George – just tell him what to do, and he'd do it flawlessly. Tell him to do something stupid, and he'd do it to perfection as well. Right now he was telling George to maintain the centerline of the airway using the Polaris GPS satellite navigation signal. The directional needle on the horizontal situation indicator, right below the attitude indicator, was perfectly centered. George did good work.

SoCal Approach Control handed him off to Point Mugu radar facility, but the female voice awaiting him was so busy Tannon had to listen to several communication exchanges with other aircraft before getting a chance to speak.

"Mugu Approach, Arrow Four-One-Niner-Niner-Seven, level six thousand."

"Arrow Niner-Niner-Seven, radar contact. Fly heading two-four-zero, vectors around traffic."

"Heading two-four-zero, Niner-Niner-Seven."

The replacement for antiquated radar, long in the making, had been delayed once again by the FAA. But the old system suited Tannon fine. He moved the heading bug to 240, pushed the heading button on the flight director, and George turned smartly off the airway. It was time to concentrate. Clouds engulfed the small airplane. Tannon directed his attention to the aircraft's instruments.

He used the time constructively to reset the primary VOR receiver to Fillmore. It was likely he would never get back on the airway now. When the conflicting traffic was out of the way, efficiency suggested the controller would turn him direct to Fillmore. From the VOR, he would fly an outbound course to Santa Barbara.

In anticipation of the revised clearance, Tannon switched the VOR-GPS mode selector switch to "VOR," and set the pointer of the horizontal situation indicator to the expected new course – 290 degrees to Fillmore VOR. The terrain to the north was high. Precision was important here. A few minutes later, he received the clearance.

"Arrow Niner-Niner-Seven. Turn right heading three-zero-zero, rejoin Victor 186 and resume normal navigation."

A minor surprise. The controller wanted him back on the airway. Tannon settled down, waiting for the navigation needle to come off its peg. The airway should be coming up quickly, and he didn't want to overshoot. There were clouds filled with granite out there ready to grab him.

Nothing – no needle movement. In fact, something wasn't quite right. The navigation needle was pegged full-scale left. It should be to the right. Had he missed the centering of the needle and gone right through the airway? If so, he was headed straight for the rocks. Within Tannon Bessimer, the seeds of panic were developing. Think!

The GPS ALRT light flashed. Tannon immediately punched the alert button, and the receiver displayed its message: "CAUTION – CHECK NAV MODE SELECTOR."

Yikes! He was in VOR mode, and his navigation pointer was set to the originally anticipated heading that would take him direct to Fillmore. He wasn't set up to intercept the airway at all. He quickly hit the VOR-GPS selector button, returning it to the "GPS" mode. The airway now showed clearly off to the left of the aircraft. Tannon held his breath, as he banked promptly back towards the required course.

His heart thumped hard as the needle finally came off its peg and eased slowly toward center. He was still sweating when he touched down in Santa Barbara.

* * * * *

"That mode selector button is always getting you into trouble," said Kelly on the way home. "It's the second time in just a few weeks."

"I'm still marveling over how close I came," said Tannon. "The GPS alert saved my ass. I'm not sure anything else would've helped."

"Nothing to do about it, except learn from today," said Kelly. "It can happen again, if you don't constantly check your settings. Make it part of your regular instrument scan."

Kelly had the rare opportunity to fly today. After his incident on the way to Santa Barbara, Tannon wasn't in the mood. As they leveled out at 7000 feet, Kelly trimmed the Arrow carefully, wingtips barely visible in the clouds.

"Don't get too reliant on those GPS alert messages," reminded Kelly with a suspicious tone.

Kelly had accepted Tannon's story, but there was something on her mind about the incident that she wasn't revealing. Tannon knew Kelly, and he knew when something was up.

All was settled down in the cockpit, Kelly and Tannon up front and her student riding in the cramped back seat. Once in cruise, everything was normally pretty quiet in any airplane. So Tannon tried to bridge the gap.

"It sounds like there's something bothering you about this," said Tannon. "You're my normal supportive sister, but there's something you're not telling me."

"Well, it's not bothering me, but it should be bothering you. Pretty weird, in fact."

"You mean how close I came to boring a hole in the mountains?"

"No, weirder than that."

"What do you mean?"

"Well, I hate to tell you this, Tannon, but there's no such alert mode in the Polaris GPS. There's no warning message to tell you to check the nav selector. "

Tannon stopped breathing for a moment. He had thought that himself. At least he had never seen that particular warning message before. When flying under visual flight rules, you got to see all of the warning messages at one time or another. The alerts were usually the result of inattention to the navigation displays, not that important when you were flying in the clear.

Tannon finally spoke: "You know, I thought the same thing. But the alert message was certainly there, and it saved me."

"Now think about it, Brother. How could a computer warning device detect you're in the wrong navigation mode? That system can do a lot of things, but it can't read your mind."

"Maybe," said Tannon.

* * * * *

The next morning, Tannon placed a telephone call to Customer Service at Polaris Avionics in Acton, Massachusetts. The service representative proudly reminded Tannon the Polaris R2 was one of the finest GPS navigation systems in the world. But it didn't contain a warning alert for a mode selector improperly set by the pilot.

Chapter 39

Sunday, May 15, 2016

Orion

Subject: Orion Launch
Date: 5/15/2016 8:07 am
From: Me@cyberberth.com
To: tbessimer@mtsac.edu

Visitors are welcome here. I'm unable to drop into your place for coffee.

- Me

* * * * *

Front Page
Los Angeles Times

Orion Inspects Spacecraft

NASA's Orion crew has found a hatch, but discovered little other detail in its first close-up look at the alien spaceship. The NASA capsule, still in its test phase, pulled within close viewing range of the Spacecraft in a flyby last night. Commander Charles "Bud" Derrick maneuvered the

Orion below the spaceship, in an orbit lower and slightly faster than the alien sphere. At approximately 2:00 am PDT, the Orion passed directly underneath the spaceship, allowing the closest view yet of the spherical object. This was considerably nearer to the Spacecraft than previously scheduled, the closer view prompted by optimum performance of the Orion during the mission. NASA authorized the Orion crew to move in closer when the orbital closure variables were judged to be "more precise than originally expected." At one point, the Orion came within less than half-mile of the Spacecraft.

Using technology developed in conjunction with the U.S. Air Force, the Orion crew was able to obtain detailed visual images of the Spaceship as well as a variety of engineering data from special sensors aboard the Orion. Commander Derrick kidded with the flight controllers in Houston's Johnson Space Center, noting his crew "was close enough to see smashed bugs on the Spacecraft, if there were any at this altitude."

The Orion astronauts have confirmed the previously detected 19-minute rotation rate of the sphere, probably needed to promote constant heat distribution from the sun. The Orion crew also has noted very few exterior markings are visible on the metallic-looking surface, and the exterior appears to be dull gray with almost no color variations.

According to NASA, the most unique marking is an apparent hatch symbol, an arrow-like white marking indicating a clockwise rotation at a location marked with a large red dot. "The Orion crew has been unable to see any discontinuities in the sphere's surface at this location or any other," said a NASA spokesman. "The surface appears perfectly smooth, with no cracks or raised surfaces."

The Orion will continue to make observations of the object as its orbit gradually drops farther below the Spacecraft today. The Orion capsule is scheduled to return to earth on Friday, with a water landing planned in the western Atlantic Ocean near the Bahamas.

* * * * *

"NASA might be giving me serious consideration as a passenger, no matter what they say," said Tannon.

"Don't you believe it for a minute," said Kelly.

She paced back and forth on the patio. For the past few minutes, she had been trying to convince Tannon to be more aggressive with his request for a seat on the Orion.

"You've got more ammunition than you think, if only you use it," she said. "Having direct contact with the alien spaceship should count for something."

Her plan was a unique blend of trading information for a ride. It would require that Tannon leave his teaching job, at least temporarily, and park himself at the NASA Administrator's office in Washington. His mini-laptop computer and a quick "live" demonstration of an email contact with *Me* were all that would be needed, she felt, to seduce the Administrator into granting a ride on the Orion's August rendezvous mission.

"You have a particularly strong case," she argued. "Especially if you allow the Administrator to use your computer for direct connection with *Me* as much as he desires, in return for a seat on the Orion."

Tannon wasn't buying it. But Kelly wouldn't let up.

"Don't expect NASA to cooperate just because you think it's the right thing to do," she said. "They've got their own agenda, and you're not on it. That's where a good old fashioned bribe comes in handy."

"Give them a chance," replied Tannon. "I keep reminding them I could contribute to the mission."

"Oh, great. That's going to do it for sure. Let's take along this pain-in-the-ass geologist because he receives love notes from a spaceship. Wonderful argument, Tannon."

"And I suppose bribing a government agency, or blackmailing them, is better."

"Damn right it would be better. I bet David Graham would personally haul you into his office, if he could look over your shoulder as you correspond with the aliens."

Tannon tried to look thoughtful. But he had pondered it before, and he didn't like it. It wasn't his way. Kelly wanted him to trade his direct correspondence with *Me* for a ride on the Orion. Already he was forwarding all his email with the Spacecraft to NASA. Wasn't that enough?

"Kelly, I do see your point, but I want to give NASA just a little more time to consider my request before I give up my contact with *Me*. I think they'll change their mind."

Kelly was pacing on the patio again and pushing her foot down hard each time she pivoted.

"You want it more than you ever wanted anything," said Kelly. "Your teaching job isn't everything, but maybe this is. So go for it."

"Well I'm not 'going for it' if it means bribes and blackmail. And it's almost final exams, a terrible time to leave my classes."

"Oh, sure. Now there's a priority. Should it be your final exams or a flight into space? Well, Brother, I say do whatever it takes. If it means acting like a hijacker, then you should commandeer an SLS rocket with an Orion on top."

* * * * *

"**H**i, Lisa. What's up?" said Tannon into his office phone.

"Well, this isn't my favorite reason to call."

Tannon thought the worst. Lisa was the expert when it came to campus email, and she had warned him yesterday there was evidence of tampering with his account. She had promised to check further into it.

"So it means someone has been messing with my email?"

"It looks that way, and they've been messing with it more than I thought. After you changed your password yesterday, there weren't any more unauthorized accesses. But I'd suggest changing your password daily for a while to see if that stops it."

Tannon felt violated. His email was a very personal thing.

"Can you tell who's doing it?"

"I'm afraid not. I'd have to catch them right at the moment it happens. But I promise to keep a close look. If necessary, we can issue you a new account."

"I guess that would solve it."

"Maybe. But if it's the government, it probably wouldn't be enough."

Chapter 40

Tuesday, May 17, 2016

Me-Two

Subject: Orion Rendezvous Mission
Date: 5/17/2016 8:01 am
From: tbessimer@mtsac.edu
To: Me@cyberberth.com

I've been trying to convince our space officials to allow me to be aboard when they rendezvous with your Spacecraft on the August mission. They haven't been very receptive. Do you have any recommendations?

* * * * *

Life on campus had become demanding, but everyone was cooperating in an attempt to keep Tannon protected from the news media. Even his division dean had reversed his original requirements about Tannon's telephone protocol. If he didn't want to answer his phone, even during his office hours, that was fully acceptable. The dean's only request was that he check his voicemail regularly for student calls. Besides, this was the last week of the semester, with final exams next week, so faculty office hours were about to disappear.

It was during one of those last office hours that Tannon bravely answered the telephone. A female voice asked him to hold for the

NASA Administrator, and within only a few seconds David Graham was on the line.

"Professor Bessimer, it's a pleasure to talk to you again."

"You too, sir. Those are some nice photos from the Orion. Congratulations."

"Yes, we're pleased with the data, but the Spacecraft sure isn't giving up many of its secrets. Interstellar design apparently requires really smooth construction. They certainly didn't use any rivets."

"So I hear, sir. Does everything look okay for the landing on Friday."

"Yes, no problem there. The weather at the Cape is looking better. Tannon. I called to make you an offer."

Tannon's heart immediately pounded louder. He could feel it. He could hear it. His normal telephone phobia was replaced by a frenzy of excitement over what was about to happen.

"An offer? Yes, sir. Go ahead."

"I have to admit I've been influenced by some email I've received. I guess you don't know about that?"

The Administrator sounded like he was fishing for information.

"No, Dr. Graham. Nothing more than the messages from *Me* that I've been forwarding to you."

"Then maybe you'd be interested in the fact that *Me* has a brother."

"A brother?"

Tannon wasn't following this at all.

"I've gotten some convincing email from an address called *Me-Two,* and it looks legitimate. For the past few hours I've had a personal dialog with the Spacecraft, and I'm now convinced you'll make an important addition to the crew of the Orion in August."

Tannon realized his heart was still pounding, even louder than before.

"Great!" was all he could say.

"Well, congratulations. We'll need to get started on your training right away, so I'll get those logistics details to you immediately. In fact, I'll email them to you this afternoon, if it's okay. And I'll include my first message from *Me-Two.* It should interest you."

"Sure. I'm thrilled!"

Tannon was so overwhelmed he couldn't find any better words at the moment.

"So is there anything else we need to talk about today?" asked the Administrator.

It certainly sounded like Dr. Graham had made a complete turnaround regarding taking an amateur into space. That provided Tannon with the encouragement he needed to change from his normally reserved stance to a more light-hearted outlook. Dr. Graham had even kidded about *Me* having a brother. Tannon couldn't resist reaching out to this high-ranking government official, who seemed to have a delightful attitude today.

"Well, maybe this would be a good time to ask if I can bring along my Astroscan," said Tannon, with a light intonation in his voice.

"Your what!" replied Dr. Graham. He sounded incredulous, maybe angry.

"Oh, it's an old telescope called the Astroscan," said Tannon, now recognizing he had misinterpreted the Administrator's attitude.

"You mean the red one that looks like a bowling ball?"

"That's it! You're familiar with it?"

"I even looked through one, years ago," said the Administrator. "Not quite up to NASA's level of technology these days. No Astroscan is going on this mission."

"Well, I guess not," replied Tannon, now recognizing he was back on safe ground.

"So is there anything else?" said Dr. Graham, with his most official-sounding government voice.

"No, sir. I guess not. Just that I'm really thrilled about this."

"Well then. . . Welcome aboard," said the Administrator.

* * * * *

--- HQ NASA: EMAIL ARCHIVE COPY ---
Subject: August Orion Rendezvous
Date: 5/17/2016 5:03 am
From: Me2@cyberberth.com
To: dgraham@hq.nasa.gov

Bring Professor Bessimer along in August. Confirm this, and you can ask any questions you desire. Otherwise, goodbye. I hope to see your crew in August.

* * * * *

The rest of the day was an overload. There was so much to do, and the clock was ticking. Tannon was scheduled to spend the evening with Samuel Jakes, and he decided to go ahead with it anyway. Dr. Jakes had invited him to a lecture at Cal Tech, and it was a presentation by one of the world's leading astrophysicists.

The Cal Tech campus was a delight, the warmth of spring turning into summer, as Tannon approached Beckman Auditorium. The building was circular shaped and windowless – a majestic lecture hall that was recently renovated. Here was a building designed for the listening mind. Tannon had seen Stephen Hawking in this auditorium during a night to remember many years ago. More accurately, he had heard Hawking's voice synthesizer that night, since the auditorium was overflowing and loudspeakers decorated the grassy mall outside for those like Tannon who didn't have tickets. Stephen Hawking had spoken through his synthesizer about time travel, a concept even he wasn't convinced was possible, and Hawking thought just about everything was possible. The Watson lecture-series presentations, also at the Beckman Auditorium, had provided the scrutinizing public with great minds from the world of science. Many of those famous scientists worked right here at Cal Tech, including tonight's speaker, Kent Henkins.

Samuel Jakes was waiting near the entrance to the huge lecture hall as Tannon approached. He was standing next to the simple cardboard sign announcing the evening's program: "From Black Holes to Wormholes."

The first thing Tannon shared with Dr. Jakes was the news about the Orion mission. Jakes was obviously thrilled and felt honored Tannon had still decided to join him tonight.

There wasn't a bad seat in the Beckman Auditorium, but Jakes had tickets for the best seats of all, right up front. Tannon knew there were famous Cal Tech faculty members all around him, but he didn't recognize any of them. Samuel Jakes knew nearly all of these great scientists. Tannon noticed none of them called Dr. Jakes "Sam."

Cal Tech's physics department chairman introduced the guest speaker, and Kent Henkins launched right into his topic, providing the mixed audience of experts and laymen an overview of the latest research regarding black holes. After less than 15 minutes, he headed into his favorite subject, wormholes, noting he was often criticized for his orations on a topic that was completely theoretical. That got a round of laughter from the sympathetic audience of futurists.

Tannon was on top of the world. He was sitting with some of the world's top scientists, listening to a renowned expert in an advanced area of gravitational theory and relativity. And he was coveting his little secret – he was about to view an alien technology first-hand. Yet he was still able to concentrate on the speaker's fascinating topic with sincere attentiveness. He felt his mind was peaked on its curve of mental acuity. This was an evening of personal importance.

The lecture kept Tannon riveted on the speaker. Although he was paying close attention to the demanding topic, Tannon was still shocked when Kent Henkins finally clicked to the last slide in his presentation, a close-up view of the Spacecraft, taken by the recent Orion mission.

"And wormholes could be a major part of the technology of advanced civilizations," said Henkins.

Tannon was thrilled. He turned to see Samuel Jakes smiling back at him.

"Wormholes might allow advanced societies to connect themselves to distant regions of our universe or even to other universes," continued Henkins. "Used as tiny tunnels, it's possible the Spacecraft, now in orbit around our planet, could have utilized wormholes for a continuing supply of cosmonauts during the journey to earth."

Tannon sat bolt-upright. The world's expert on wormholes thought this Spacecraft might be a transporter of alien life!

"It's even possible there is, above our heads tonight, a sphere of unoccupied occupants."

Some of the audience laughed, particularly those seated up front.

What kind of occupants? Now what in the world was he talking about? Was he implying alien beings might come and go within the Spacecraft?

"Mathematical computations don't prohibit wormholes from popping up all over the universe," said Henkins. "But you know those mathematicians."

That got a roar and some delayed applause from the audience.

"But matter would have to be squeezed down considerably to pass through these small openings, so I would expect us to find tiny little cosmonauts aboard the Spacecraft."

That got another auditorium-size round of laughter. Kent Henkins used the moment to say: "Thank you for your attention this evening." The lecture was over.

Both Tannon and Samuel Jakes applauded enthusiastically, as the entire audience expressed its pleasure with a standing ovation. Then the moderator reappeared to control the questions from the audience. Even without microphones, the questions from all corners of the auditorium reached their VIP location up front clearly. But the moderator repeated them for those not in the cherished faculty seats.

One question catching Tannon's attention involved the limitations of wormholes:

"Dr. Henkins. You noted that wormholes are both small and short-lived. How do you propose that matter larger than atoms could be sent through these tunnels, especially considering the brief existence of wormholes?"

Kent Henkins didn't even pause before answering:

"Well, we've been thinking about that for some time. We refer to the concept as 'transversible spacetime wormholes.' To use them, we'd have to find a way to hold the wormhole open long enough to transmit the matter. But who's to say there isn't a form of exotic matter with a negative energy density? In fact, cosmologists have been working on the concept of dark energy for some time. If we can tap a form of anti-gravity, we might use it to keep the wormhole dilated long enough to transmit accommodating travelers."

That brought another round of laughter from the audience.

The question and answer period went on for another ten minutes, and then the moderator cut off further questions, thanked the speaker, and a final round of applause ended the event.

Tannon had plenty of new food for thought.

* * * * *

The Orion training requirements would be intense. The assigned crew had begun their preparation six months earlier, and Tannon would have to catch up with them. An amateur catching up with real astronauts seemed absurd. He was scheduled to be in Houston on Tuesday, May 24 – only seven days from now!

This was the last week of his spring semester classes, with final exams scheduled for next week. His department chairman and the division dean had been thrilled to learn of Tannon's invitation to fly aboard the Orion. They immediately arranged to take care of his final exams and the remaining end-of-semester details. The impact on Tannon's schedule was major, but the timing was rather fortunate. He didn't have any summer classes, so his professional schedule would face minimal impact. But he, his department chairman, and the dean all knew the obvious. Tannon wouldn't be back in time for the start of the fall semester. In a meeting of the three of them in the dean's office, his bosses shook hands with Tannon and wished him well, not discussing what might happen to his teaching career.

Tannon decided to teach the two days of remaining classes. There wasn't much to cover, but there were term papers to collect. And he felt compelled to share the news of his historic trip with his students. It was more of a privilege than they realized. NASA hadn't yet released the story to the news media, wanting to first make sure Tannon could adjust his schedule to meet the training regime. Tannon had shared his Orion invitation with very few people so far.

On the last day of classes, he told his students the news. They were ecstatic. There was no way to complete a normal day of classes after that, so Tannon collected the term papers, wished them good luck on their upcoming final exams, and dismissed them.

Upon returning to his office, he closed the door and looked around. This was an important moment. It might be the last day of his teaching career, at least for a while. This was a wonderful place to work, and he was grateful. But now he was going for a ride on the SLS-Orion on what would probably be NASA's most important mission in history.

There were still some campus details to attend to, and Tannon took them seriously. First he considered the term papers piled on his desk. As usual there were a variety of covers and bindings. Some were merely stapled sheets. He organized them so the widest binder was on the bottom, leaving one particularly undersized term paper on top. It didn't even fit the standard letter-size format, smaller on each side by about an inch. The title was "Wormhole Technology" by Brenda Rogus. There was no Brenda Rogus in any of his classes.

He sat down and looked more closely at the term paper. It looked like a typical Geology 101 term paper except for its reduced dimensions. He began to read it.

The document was twenty pages long, with the expected quantity of grammatical errors. There was a short bibliography whose sources appeared appropriate. There was even an article cited from an old *Time* magazine entitled "Space Oddities of Modern Science." The emphasis of the term paper involved a basic overview of the wormholes. But there were some technical details regarding wormhole transmission theory that appeared to be from very recent research. The paper noted the tidal effects of human passage through a wormhole would probably turn the transported person into a thin piece of spaghetti. Nice analogy.

Tannon laughed to himself, and then decided to grade the term paper like any other. It was probably a silly thing to do under the circumstances, but it restored his sense of organization just a bit. The world was moving too fast.

The paper received a B-plus, with most of the grade deductions for failure to document some of the concepts discussed. The grammatical errors didn't help the grade. Of course, the topic was far astray from a Physical Geology class, but Tannon didn't worry too much about that. The writer hadn't left the required mailing address for return of the paper. Maybe she wasn't that interested in her grade. After all, she wasn't in this class. Not even in this world.

Chapter 41

Saturday, May 21, 2016

Morning Jog

Tannon's schedule had mushroomed into an impossible to-do list. Sitting at the desk in his den on Saturday morning, he was staring at the long list, trying to rearrange his priorities. There was only one day left before he departed for Houston. This was becoming a bit too exciting.

He planned out his day. There was a while-you-wait appointment to get a tune-up and oil change for his Jeep. He'd need his vehicle in Houston, although it added extra travel time to his already impacted schedule. Waiting for the tune-up would give him a chance to read over the training schedule instructions from NASA which he had still only partly digested.

He had to compute and mail the semester grade summary to his department chairman, so the data would be ready for next week's final exams and the assignment of grades. The project would take some time, and it was first on his list. His printer could spit out the grade summary sheets while he changed into his jogging clothes.

He hadn't exercised in several days, a great way for a new astronaut to start training, so he allocated twenty minutes for his morning jog. Then there would be just enough time for a shower before his trip to the car dealer.

He stepped over the morning newspaper in the driveway and hit the street running. Walking warm-ups weren't his style. The first part of his jog was uphill, and then downhill through the tract homes, with the major challenge as he reversed course for the extensive uphill jog on the second half of the route.

As he started up the agonizing end of his jog, Tannon felt the warmth of the day starting to take its toll. He wished he hadn't worn a shirt at all. The month of May could be brutal in Southern California, even in the early morning. This was one of those days. And it was already smoggy. He could feel the burning sensation in his chest.

After the long hill, his jogging route leveled off for a short stretch. By now, he had slowed to nearly a walking pace. His breathing was labored, and he felt the sting of the hot, smoggy air. But there was still that small but steep hill at the very end of the route. As he started up the final winding incline, his struggling lungs felt pierced and burning.

As Tannon topped the last hill, he looked ahead at the level road that formed the end of his jogging route. This would be the area of his wind sprint, the only spot where he ran flat-out. He looked down on the homes below and noticed the clearness of the air – it really wasn't that smoggy, after all, although his lungs had told him otherwise. His chest burned hot.

Time for the wind sprint. He had felt this pain before, and he could run right through it. At age 40, Tannon wasn't about to admit he was having problems with a short sprint. It was only another 200 feet. But he simply couldn't do it. He had to walk now. And as he walked, his chest grew tighter and hotter. As he exhaled, his throat felt raw. He needed more air.

And so Tannon walked slowly back to his house, one street below. Even his legs hurt now, and his tongue was out, panting. He fumbled for his key. It took all of his concentration to slip it into the lock. But finally the door was open, and he headed for the bedroom. He had to lie down – right now.

Tannon dropped onto the bed and rolled onto his back, gasping for air. His chest was on fire. He had to roll over. But it didn't help. Maybe if he lay on a hard surface – the floor. He crawled off the bed, tumbling onto the carpet. It would feel better to stretch out on the hard floor.

It was at this moment that Tannon Bessimer realized something was very wrong. It wasn't the smog, and it wasn't just one of those pains you could run through. He was seriously ill. And it was then that EZ came through the open bedroom door and found Tannon writhing on the floor. EZ came up to his face, gave a concerned look, and let out one of his few actual meows. EZ brushed his body against Tannon's face. Tannon spoke with a slow calmness.

"EZ, call 911."

The cat meowed again and brushed against his face a second time. EZ was terribly concerned, but he wasn't able to do what his master asked.

Tannon's mind raced through a mental list of people he could call. He didn't need 911. It couldn't be that serious. But Tannon was alone with his cat, and he was lying on the floor in serious pain. There were neighbors nearby, but he couldn't pull himself up and walk all that way. Even the telephone in the kitchen seemed an insurmountable distance. And he didn't have the phone numbers of his neighbors. He didn't even know most of their names. Standing up was a difficult thing to contemplate, and driving a car was out of the question.

It was at that moment that he heard the hallway door open. He tried to yell, but he heard his own raspy voice as only a muted cry: "Kelly!" He doubted she heard meek call, but within moments she was at the bedroom door.

"Tannon? What's going on? You're pure white!"

"Take me to the hospital."

With those words Tannon knew his life was threatened. He had never asked anyone to take him to a hospital. He had never expected to go there. Even as a visitor, he could only remember being in a hospital a few times – once when his father lay on his deathbed. That alone left him with a fear of hospitals. But now it was exactly where he wanted to go, and fast!

* * * * *

Walking to the car, leaning on Kelly, was as much effort as Tannon could muster. The pain was intense – an anvil-like weight on his chest and a shortness of breath unlike anything he had ever felt before. During the half-mile ride, the pain in Tannon's chest took control. He was moaning and breathing irregularly. Fortunately they arrived at the hospital in only a few minutes.

Saturday in the hospital emergency room was a busy place. When they entered the reception area, there was a line stretching back to the entrance. Weekend recreational accidents had already started to show up. Tannon relentlessly adhered to the rules of the world, never pushing his way to the front of a line – except today. He interrupted a patient asking questions at the desk.

"I need some help, right now. My chest is burning up."

Within seconds he was placed on a gurney and whisked through the swinging double doors into the emergency room, where he was immediately hooked up to monitoring equipment. The burning sensation was now even worse.

It helped to close his eyes and block out the blinding overhead lights. When he opened them again, a smiling young face was looking down at him.

"Hello, Tannon. I'm Doctor Thumati, and I have some good and bad news for you."

Tannon didn't have the energy to say anything, but the young, fat-cheeked doctor continued with the glint of a laugh.

"The bad news is you're having a heart attack, right at this very moment. The good news is you couldn't have picked a better place to have it than this room."

From there, everything slowed down. Order reappeared. Life returned. After the emergency room's intravenous fluids and monitoring machines, there was Intensive Care, and arterial expansion surgery, a technique that had recently replaced stints and other derivatives of angioplasty.

There were also a few administrative details, like losing his ride on the Orion.

* * * * *

"What an eye-opener," said Tannon. "None of us are immortal, but I bet all of us feel that way until something like this happens."

Kelly sat beside his hospital bed, as intravenous solution dripped from a metal stand and a catheter on his bedframe drew away his urine. He looked worse than he was, with the oxygen tube taped to his face and the monitors recording their data. In reality, he felt rather well.

"Some of my friends are saying this proves jogging can kill," said Kelly. "I think they'd like to believe that. It would simplify their lives."

"Dr. Thumati says regular exercise was about the only thing I had going for me, other than living so close to the hospital." said Tannon. "Jogging may be when it happened, but my exercise routine may have saved my life. Of course, a gradual buildup to my hilly jog would've helped."

"Hitting the streets running isn't the exactly the best warm-up," replied Kelly. "And your stress level has been a bit extreme lately."

"You're right. It's been one hell of a few months."

"And no more breakfast circuit for you."

"For a while," said Tannon.

"You would have made a good advertisement for a cholesterol commercial."

"Well, I guess my body was telling me something. Since the surgery, I haven't had a single headache."

"That must be a nice change. See, there's a little good everywhere. Oh, I forgot to tell you. . . I called Mom, and she wanted to come right away."

"Please tell me you said 'No'."

"As a matter of fact, I did. And she's okay with that, as long as you call her right away. I'm not sure she believes you're really okay."

"Okay, thanks. I'll call her right away."

Tannon let the topic cool off for a few moments, and Kelly respected his silence. When he spoke again, it was with a serious tone.

"What did NASA say?"

Kelly studied his face. He didn't look as well as he did a few minutes ago. But his face did have a lot of color.

"Well, I'm the one who called them, and they sounded pretty shocked. Maybe a bit relieved too. I bet they're talking right now about how close they came to making headlines with a heart attack victim in outer space."

"No, that couldn't have happened. They would've picked this up on the first physical in Houston. They would've found the clogged artery and taken me off the mission anyway."

"Well, it was an easy way for them to bump you off the trip," said Kelly. "One day the big news was that an amateur astronaut was going for a space ride. A few days later the bigger news was he had a heart attack. Rather bizarre."

"Oh, great. I'm a big human-interest story. Maybe I'll make the Terri Lee Show."

"What's that?" asked Kelly.

"She's the gal who has guests with hard luck stories, and she gives them back their will to live. But she'd have a difficult time converting this into something cheery, unless she has connections at NASA."

"Look, Tannon. I know this isn't a pleasant thing, and I feel bad about the Orion flight. But I really am glad you're still with me. I would've missed you."

"I suppose I should consider myself lucky. Dr. Thumati says my artery had a ninety-five percent blockage, but it's completely open now."

"Right." Kelly sounded skeptical. "But it damaged your heart, and the tissue can never be restored. So you're going to need to make some big changes."

As Kelly sat in the bedside chair, Tannon looked her over slowly, from her ragged bangs to her firm, flat stomach as it merged with the edge of the hospital bed.

"Well, you've got me back. And I've learned some important lessons the hard way. But I sure wish I hadn't missed the only Orion visit to an alien spacecraft.

"Who says it will be the only visit?"

* * * * *

Tannon's recovery continued smoothly, and he had a lot of time to think about his situation. He started a checklist regarding the facts of his situation. On the top of the list was "Victim of recent heart attack." Next on the list was "Astronauts must be perfect physical specimens." The third item read: "Passengers are not astronauts."

Chapter 42

Thursday, June 9, 2016

The Power of Email

Subject: Welcome Back
Date: 6/09/2016 8:12 am
From: Me@cyberberth.com
To: tbessimer@mtsac.edu

Where have you been? Actually, I heard (Time Magazine). I hope your recovery is rapid and complete. Wishing you the very best!

- Me

* * * * *

Tannon's recovery was rapid. The biggest problem was keeping the pace of his rehabilitation reasonable. There were a variety of pills, regular visits to the cardiovascular gym at the hospital, and too much time to think.

In every imaginable way, Tannon felt physically better than ever before. He pulled out a photo album with pictures of him taken two years previously on a vacation trip to Yosemite. Today he looked even healthier and younger than in those photographs. And his headaches were rare. So even after a recent heart attack, he was a healthier specimen than before. The new diet helped, and he was exercising right and doing all of the health-conscious things he should have started years ago. But in contrast to all of this was the loss of the Orion ride. It seemed so unfair.

"We make a fine couple," said Tannon to Kelly, across from him on the L-shaped sofa.

"Look, Brother – first, we aren't a couple. And second, I'm both younger and stronger than you. To say nothing of prettier."

"Well, tonight you look like you should be in the emergency room."

"I'm okay. I shouldn't eat so much, that's all. Watching you with that rabbit food just gives me too much of an appetite."

Tannon looked at his sister critically. This was happening more often lately – both his more critical inspection and Kelly's excuse of bad eating habits. There was more to it. She looked as if she were in pain throughout her body.

"Kelly, I'm really worried about you. This is becoming a bit too common."

"Leave it alone. I've got an appointment for my annual FAA physical next week, and I'll talk to Doc Roberts about it then."

"You need more than an FAA physical."

"You're a great one to talk. Your plethora of pills is enough to keep you busy for years."

Tannon laughed. It was difficult to get too serious with his sister. She had the ability to divert his attention from almost anything. During these past few days, that ability was particularly appreciated.

"I'm doing okay," said Tannon. "Doctor Thumati says I can do pretty much anything I want. And the meds will be finished soon. But I really am worried about you."

"What's to worry about? A Cessna is all I need, and they're not terribly complex. You're the one still pushing for a ride on the SLS rocket."

"You noticed," replied Tannon.

* * * * *

"But sir, it's not that unreasonable," said Tannon into the phone. "I'm not going along for any purpose other than the ride. I'm just a passenger, not a working astronaut. I've been told I can resume normal activities. What's so abnormal about riding in a vehicle."

"It's an SLS rocket, topped by an Orion," reminded the Administrator. "And it's totally out of the question. Everyone from the President on down would have my hide, and rightly so."

"What about John Glenn?" asked Tannon.

"John Glenn was in great physical shape, and he was a former fighter pilot and an astronaut."

"Yes, and he was almost 80 years old. I suppose his heart was a perfect physical specimen."

"We checked him thoroughly beforehand, and he stood up well in the centrifuge," replied the Administrator.

"So give me to your doctors and slap me into the centrifuge. When do we start?"

* * * * *

Subject: Status of Tannon Bessimer
Date: 6/17/2016 9:95 pm
From: Me2@cyberberth.com
To: dgraham@hq.nasa.gov

Let Tannon ride on your SLS rocket. He is fine. Remember – invitations for visits to our humble abode are subject to revocation at any time.

* * * * *

"The power of email" said Kelly.

"It sure didn't make NASA happy," said Tannon.

"Oh, they'll make you feel welcome. You're a taxpayer."

"Well, I may not be so happy when I get into this training program. I've already missed almost a month, and even then I was starting late."

"Remember, you don't have to learn how to fly that thing. Just pay attention when they tell you how to fasten your seatbelt."

Tannon laughed. He loved bantering with his sister. They could go on for hours. But there was no time to spare tonight. He would need Kelly's help with his to-do list before his departure for Houston next week. Tannon had been regaining his strength at home, taking his medications, and trying to get caught up on routine chores delayed during his hospital stay, like paying the bills. Now the sudden approval by NASA caught him by surprise.

Kelly was vibrant tonight, without any signs of illness. She spoke with enthusiasm, and her face was tinted red by her first summer bout with the sun. She shined with the energy that consistently nourished Tannon's attitude. He couldn't imagine leaving her for Orion training in Houston.

"I'm going to miss EZ," said Tannon. "You too, of course."

"Of course."

"I don't suppose you'd consider coming to Houston with me. You could bring EZ."

"Oh, sure, not that it's short notice or anything. Heck, I could give up all of my responsibilities here. Tannon wants me in Houston, so what the hell. Kelly doesn't have a life anyway."

"I'm serious, Kell. Why don't you just pack up and come? It'll be less than two months. Do you want me recovering from a heart attack without your help?"

"You're recovered. Just watch your diet. You'll be busy up to your neck the whole time. And I'm not your nurse."

"I know you're not my nurse." Tannon paused and then spoke again: "So come to Houston with me."

Kelly stared into Tannon's eyes, as if she were about to remind him of what she wasn't. Then she eased off a bit, diverted her gaze downward, and spoke.

"Who's going to tell EZ?"

Chapter 43

Monday, June 27, 2016

Me-Three

Subject: Cats
Date: 6/24/2016 4:07 am
From: Me@cyberberth.com
To: tbessimer@mtsac.edu

Tell me more about EZ. Do such pets have human-like bronchial breathing systems? What do they prefer to eat? Can they read data?

- Me

* * * * *

Life was chaotic. Tannon arrived in Houston, with his Jeep still needing a tune-up, the oil change long overdue. There just wasn't enough time. But NASA had thoughtfully arranged for a small suite in one of the local extended-stay hotels. Tannon Bessimer was even on their payroll. He didn't have a summer paycheck from the college, but he was used to that. So overall, things were financially in reasonable shape. And Kelly was going to get a vacation, with the sole purpose of taking care of Tannon. Maybe she would enjoy life in the spaceflight society.

Astronauts were married, at least most of them. And none of them lived with their sisters. But Tannon and Kelly were used to such social situations. Kelly was actually a big hit among the astronauts' wives. Among the female astronauts, her uniqueness stood out favorably. Houston's professional astro-family took the Bessimers in with ease. But NASA still wasn't happy with Tannon's physical status.

The physical exams were first. A series of doctors and labs probed every aspect of Tannon's health, and they discovered some problems. His thallium scan and EKG were the biggest concerns, since heart muscles had been damaged. The NASA doctors were hesitant to give him a full treadmill stress test, since it had been only a month since his heart attack. Finally they relented, and his test results indicated an outstanding cardiovascular recovery was in progress. The medical experts wouldn't let him in the centrifuge yet, and that would be held over his head until it was completed. So there was always something to worry about.

While undergoing the cardiovascular tests, Tannon contacted the FAA for reinstatement of his pilot medical certificate. No negotiation was possible. He might be healthy enough for the SLS rocket and the Orion, but the FAA wouldn't respect NASA's tests. Any medical tests dated earlier than six months after his heart attack weren't acceptable. So he could fly in outer space but not at five thousand feet in his Piper Arrow. Kelly and Tannon found some humor in that fact.

Everything about the Orion training program was rigorous. In Tannon's case, some items had to be skipped, simply because there simply weren't enough hours in the day to make up for the time he had lost. His accelerated instruction focused on a wide range of topics, everything from launch pad escape procedures to Orion housekeeping chores. Much of the focus involved his EMU, the spacesuit with which he would become intimately familiar. Just getting in and out of the launch and reentry suit was a complex process in itself.

As his crew went through their mission scenarios in the simulator, Tannon began to feel like a real member of the Orion team. Everything from launch to reentry was practiced repeatedly, each time with a slightly different twist, and always with unexpected problems. Most of the simulated situations could be solved through the combined resources of the onboard crew and the ground controllers. In many of these simulations, the ground controllers had more information available to them than the Orion crew, and that made it particularly demanding for the astronauts. Tannon was really only a passive observer during these simulations, but he was allowed to participate and play a role in the checklists used for the troubleshooting procedures. With time, he was authorized to provide limited inputs to the problem-solving scenarios. If he was going to ride in the Orion, he was determined to be as much a part of it as possible.

* * * * *

Kelly stood purposefully protected behind the kitchen table as Tannon emerged from the bedroom. Maybe she could beat him to the punch.

"Nice threads. Where's your bow tie?"

"I left it in San Dimas. I only wear it when I go hiking."

"Well, I wish we were hiking tonight," said Kelly.

"Get out here where I can see you. You won't be able to hide all night."

Kelly refused to budge, so Tannon simply walked around the table and caught Kelly in profile view.

"Lookin' good," he said, trying to be as nonchalant as possible.

Kelly wore a subdued forest green dress that extended well below her knees. It wasn't elegant and certainly not revealing. She wore no jewelry and her hair fell as low as it could go, straight and trimmed neckline-length in Egyptian style.

"Watch out for those fly-boys," said Tannon. "They'll be all over you tonight."

"That's just what I need."

"You look tremendous, Kelly. Thanks for going with me."

"You look pretty grand yourself. You know I wouldn't do this for anybody but you."

"I know. But a dress does become you."

"Flattery. What a cute touch," replied Kelly. "You look like a penguin."

Tannon was grateful Kelly was accompanying him to this astronaut party. And he was glad it wasn't a common event. To be truthful, she looked awkward in a dress, even skinnier than usual. He preferred her in khakis and a T-shirt.

"Penguins, unite," said Tannon. "It may not be our norm, but together we can fake it."

They stood beside the kitchen table, looking at each other, and Kelly began giggle. It was contagious – Tannon joined in laughing. Finally, it was Kelly who spoke.

"Together we can fake almost anything."

* * * * *

Subject: Re: Cats
Date: 6/29/2016 8:05 am
From: tbessimer@mtsac.edu
To: Me@cyberberth.com

Cats have breathing systems very similar to humans, including lungs and biological controlling mechanisms. Everything is just a bit smaller.

EZ's personal preference regarding food is fish, particularly tuna.

Cats cannot read data, but I sometimes think they can read minds.

* * * * *

Tannon checked in regularly with *Me* through his email connection, but it had become a less active pattern of communication in recent days. *Me* acknowledged the reasonable approach was to let Tannon devote his time to mission preparations, and that was a relief. Anything that saved him a few minutes time was helpful. The *Me-Two* connection with the NASA Administrator was still active, and it's where most of the mission preparations were being coordinated. Not surprisingly, no one was able to connect with *Me-Two* except the Administrator.

One night, returning to his temporary suite just before midnight, Tannon found Kelly waiting for him. She was dressed in an oversized tan T-shirt, designated as her nightshirt of the week. She sat in the rough-woven brown recliner, her favorite reading spot in their Houston home-away-from-home. It was on the opposite end of the living room from the entry door, and Kelly had the chair fully reclined, reading the current issue of *Air and Space*.

"That late night drinking with your astronaut pals is going to take its toll," said Kelly.

"Don't I wish," replied Tannon.

Kelly flung one leg over the side of the chair and stretched back to reach a piece of paper on the table beside her.

"I received an interesting email today," said Kelly placidly, as she glanced at the paper in her hand.

Tannon was sharing his mini-laptop with Kelly these days, but she had her own email account. He walked closer, and Kelly held out the paper. He took it from her and had to strain to read it in the dim living room light:

> Subject: Mission Plans
> Date: 6/30/2016 1:05 pm
> From: Me3@cyberberth.com
> To: kellyb@netview.com
>
> We want to meet EZ. Please let Tannon bring him along? We promise to treat both of them well. We'll take lots of pictures.
>
> What flavor of cat food does EZ prefer, other than fish? No tuna treats aboard this spacecraft, please.

* * * * *

Tannon looked at Kelly to try to determine whether this was a joke. Kelly returned his gaze with a look of seriousness.

"So what do you think?" he asked.

"I think it must be important, or *Me-Three* wouldn't be contacting your sister.

"NASA isn't going to like this," said Tannon.

"You're right. But suppose these aliens are really a species of cuddly cats?"

She paused, and when Tannon didn't speak, she continued.

"Do you think cats always land on their feet in zero gravity?"

"Seriously, Kelly, you know how EZ hates riding in the car. And that one trip in our Arrow was enough to prevent inviting him back again. His inner ears will go crazy in space."

"You're absolutely right. They sent chimps and dogs into space during the 60s. Did they ever send a cat?"

"I don't think so. NASA is smarter than that. This is a serious message, isn't it?"

"Perfectly serious. It sounds like *Me-Three* knows I'm the real caretaker of EZ. I consider it an honor that my permission was requested. Or maybe it was just a nicely worded order."

"Well, what do you think?" asked Tannon.

"I thought it was only fair to ask EZ. He said I better get over to PetPals in the morning and check out their 3-G kitty carriers. He'll look stunning in a NASA baby-blue spacesuit."

* * * * *

NASA wasn't receptive to the idea, to say the least. The Administrator immediately refused the request and didn't allow any further discussion of the issue. There were no public announcements on the subject, but there were a variety of stories circulated within NASA on the topic. One version of the subsequent incidents was that *Me-Two* immediately cutoff all email to the Administrator. Another version indicated *Me-Two* only threatened to cutoff the email link. But many in NASA repeated the never-verified statement by the Administrator at his morning staff meeting: "First we agree to take a heart attack victim. Now it's his fuckin' pet cat!"

* * * * *

Kelly awoke with a start. It wasn't a sound or a bad dream that awakened her. It was a retching feeling within her stomach. Her throat felt raw, her stomach throbbed. It was a feeling that awakened her all too often.

She thought back to the evening before. Pizza was one of her favorites, but how many times would it take to realize the sensitivity of her stomach? She needed to be more careful. Lying still in the bed seemed the only remedy, but how could she lie still with this throbbing pain? Her water bottle stood on the nearby nightstand. She reached for it and took a slow sip, without moving her head, neck, or stomach. It usually helped to avoid movement. Sometimes the pain simply passed. But lying still wasn't helping this time.

Kelly arose and navigated the darkness to the bathroom. She was okay. It was just that damn sensitive stomach demanding closer attention. As she approached the bathroom, her pace changed to a trot. She barely made it to the toilet before vomit poured from her mouth, some of it spilling onto the toilet seat and down to the floor.

Kelly was never a woman of weakness. She regained control of herself quickly, and she almost immediately felt better. It was just a bout with a pizza covered with way too much cheese and pepperoni. This wasn't a pleasant way to wake up, but feeling instantly better almost made up for it.

Kelly walked to the sink, and scooped water with her hand, cleansing her dry and sour mouth. She flipped on the bathroom light and looked into the mirror. Her hollow face was sagging from release of the pain, and her eyes drooped from her sudden awakening.

She flipped off the light, took a deep breath, and waited a moment for her eyes to adjust to the darkness before walking back to bed. She felt a lot better now. Pain was so wonderful when it was suddenly gone.

* * * * *

In the end, NASA relented, and EZ was included on the manifest for the SLS-Orion. With *Me-Two* and *Me-Three* on the job, there was really no alternative. But Tannon refused to discuss the issues regarding

EZ with anybody at NASA. He passed this responsibility to Kelly, and she gave NASA a run for their money. It was her cat, and she was ready to assist in keeping the attention off Tannon. He needed to prepare for the mission.

NASA was determined to put EZ through a series of medical tests to decide whether the cat's health was adequate to survive the flight. Kelly, on the other hand, was focused on the avoidance of all medical tests unless conducted by her own choice of veterinarian. Her argument was that NASA's testing would stress the cat beyond the limits of a typical spaceflight and the tests were designed to disprove EZ's ability to adjust to the environment of space. Such testing might be necessary for humans, but it wasn't fair for cats. She refused any discussion of a centrifuge ride. Her attitude was that EZ was only going along as a pampered passenger, and under professional care. He simply needed to be in average health for the ride. Any NASA tests, in Kelly's opinion, would only risk the cat's fitness further.

NASA got nowhere with Kelly. In an attempt to end the issue, Kelly announced she was ready to talk to the press on the topic. NASA officials thought about it briefly, and then announced there would be no testing of EZ prior to launch other than by Kelly's selected veterinarian. NASA requested EZ take a brief ride in the weightless simulation aircraft, and Kelly agreed. At the time, she didn't know this aircraft was nicknamed the "Vomit Comet."

The Orion engineers assigned to EZ's environmental needs designed a pressurized cage. The cage had restraining padded body supports, to be used primarily for launch and reentry, making it confining for the cat in that phase of flight. During weightlessness, the cage converted into a luxurious small living area that could even temporarily accommodate Tannon in a crouched position. The interior color scheme was baby blue. EZ would fly in style.

Chapter 44

Monday, July 4, 2016

Centrifuge

Subject: Further Details Needed?
Date: 7/04/2016 2:04 am
From: Me@cyberberth.com
To: tbessimer@mtsac.edu

In all of the excitement of the last few weeks, I forgot to ask – How were your term papers?

- Me

* * * * *

Subject: Re: Further Details Needed?
Date: 7/04/2016 9:08 am
From: tbessimer@mtsac.edu
To: Me@cyberberth.com

You got a B+. It didn't have a lot to do with Physical Geology.

Are you able to expound on your plans for receiving beings from your home planet via wormholes?

* * * * *

Me's reply this time was a message lengthier than ever before:

> Subject: Receiver Module Status
> Date: 7/04/2016 11:16 am
> From: Me@cyberberth.com
> To: tbessimer@mtsac.edu
>
> Our wormhole technology is crude. Maybe our home planet has improved on it by now. If they have, there is a small chance a wormhole exchange may occur during our orbit of earth. We do not know whether our receiver module is adequate for the task. At time of launch, there was very little information available to construct an appropriate receiving module. The prototype module was reconfigured en route, as more information became available from home. Our computers utilized a process similar to your field programmable gate arrays to improve on the design in an automated fashion.
>
> Later in our journey, our onboard computers attempted to continue advancing the design. There is considerable doubt we succeeded. Matching the transmitting parameters to the receiving module is impossible without communication. Direct communication from home now takes twelve years, and that's one-way. Tachyon communication is almost instantaneous, but it is extremely limited in content and does not allow detailed technical specifications to be received. The only attempt at a complex data exchange using tachyons nearly destroyed our vehicle. It could mean we are now operating with a receiver module considered unacceptable by our home planet. We believe wormhole technology is available on our home planet by now. But we don't have the capability here in orbit to coordinate a transfer.
>
> Thus, we expect to remain in orbit alone. But we still maintain hope for two visits – one from you and one from the beings of our own planet. Yours is much more probable, and it will almost undoubtedly be first.
>
> - Me

* * * * *

There was a promise from *Me* that the rendezvous mission would provide the answers to the many questions in most human minds. That would leave the Spacecraft free for now to continue its data-gathering activities without relying on the low-volume technology of email to transmit data. That was fine with Tannon – he needed to devote as much time as possible to mission training.

* * * * *

In the Bessimer household, Fourth of July was a day of celebration. The day in Houston dawned hot, and the temperature became almost unbearable as the day progressed. The balcony patio was tiny, but Tannon was determined to make this a holiday to remember. He bought a small barbecue grill just for the occasion, and he prepared hot dogs and foil-wrapped corn-on-the-cob. Kelly, admitting she didn't feel well, waited in the air-conditioned apartment,.

Tannon wanted to yield to Kelly's increasing insistence that all she had was a minor illness – but she didn't seem to be getting better. He suggested they listen to some Frank Sinatra music, which was met with an enthusiastic "Sure!" by Kelly. She cranked up her pocket music player, connected to the mini-speakers on the bookshelf. Old-fashioned 45 rpm records had been converted to tape cassettes, then to CDs, and finally to twenty-first century technology. It made Frank sound like he was right in the living room. Everyone was in celebration mode, including EZ, who got his holiday meal early, a big helping of kitty tuna.

"He'll get sick," said Kelly, nodding toward EZ who was rubbing his paw against his face in his post-meal bath.

"He's a space cadet. He'll be okay."

Tannon slid the patio door closed for a break from the heat and smoke, and now he settled down in the chair inside, hot dog cooking fork in hand. Kelly was in the reclining chair next to him. Tannon cocked his head to the side and studied her.

"You look tall today," said Tannon.

"It runs in the family."

"And a little bit pale. Are you feeling good enough for hot dogs?"

"Sure. I could use some sun, but not today. It's must to be over 100."

"Do you feel well enough for that movie you've been waiting for? What's it called?"

"*Friends and Other Disasters*," said Kelly.

"It sounds pretty interesting. Do you want to see it tonight."

Tannon respected Kelly's love for films, but he wasn't a big movie buff himself. He would gladly go to the movies with her though, because he knew how much she liked them. And it was enough to make the movies fun for Tannon.

"I'm not feeling that well," said Kelly.

"But well enough for a Houston hot dog?"

"I'm ready!"

"Okay, here comes the big meal. A real Texas celebration for all the Bessimers."

"Tannon, you know something? I feel lousy today. But it's still going to be hard for this to end."

"Space cadets or Houston in general?"

"Space cadets, of course," replied Kelly. "But Houston has been good to us. So make me a promise."

"Sure. You name it, Sis."

"Promise me you won't worry if I get a bit worse before I get better. Because I'm eventually going to get better."

"I consider worrying about you part of my job. An important job. But I'll try to tone it down a bit."

"Good. Because the doctor says there's a chance I might not get better at all. Not that I believe him. But I don't want you constantly worrying."

"Agreed then – I won't worry constantly; only now and then."

"That'd be better," said Kelly. "But having a brother worrying about you a little bit is a blessing. And you know I'm grateful, don't you?"

"Sure, I know," said Tannon. "And I'm just glad you're with me now. Don't ever leave, okay."

"Okay. It looks to me like we're stuck with each other."

"Good place to be stuck, if you ask me."

* * * * *

As the preparation for the mission progressed, Tannon took an increased part in the crew's activities. The centrifuge ride was still hanging over his head, but there was a lot to do in the meantime. Preparation for entry to the Spacecraft was an area where Tannon could really contribute, since he had exchanged messages with *Me* on the subject. The decision was made to utilize email in orbit, at least as a backup. They would even try to use it once the astronauts were inside the Spacecraft. How communication with the alien vehicle would be established during this mission was still undetermined, but the current email conversations between Tannon and *Me* served as an optimistic starting point. It made Tannon's part in the flight increasingly important.

It also necessitated that Tannon be prepared for extravehicular activities. Thus, he was now considered a mission specialist rather than a mere passenger. But being a mission specialist and going for a spacewalk were two quite different levels of involvement. EVAs were the niche of thoroughly experienced astronauts. His instructors compared his EVA training to tropical resort SCUBA tutoring, with the graduate being allowed to dive only with a fully trained divemaster along side to assist with every move. In the time available, little more could be accomplished than to do everything possible to assure Tannon wouldn't kill himself during an EVA.

He spent hours practicing airlock procedures and even longer in the "tank," where the buoyancy of water simulated the floating sensations of space. Not surprisingly, when NASA suggested EZ be allowed to enter the tank, Kelly refused.

"Put a cat in a tank of water?" asked Kelly. "Surely they jest."

NASA had a lot to learn about cats.

* * * * *

Tannon sat on the edge of the butcher paper that covered the examining table, awaiting the doctor who could seal his fate. This was his final evaluation, a third-opinion of sorts, and this physician's viewpoint would weigh heavily on the decision regarding the centrifuge. All of these doctors had studied his thallium scan and all aspects of his cardiology tests, but this doctor was the critical link in the decision.

Tannon's black sneakers swung to-and-fro beneath the examining table. This was to be more of a pronouncement than an examination, but there was the same tension that always gripped Tannon as he awaited the arrival of a professional. Meeting a doctor he didn't know was an added challenge for Tannon. Spontaneous conversation would be expected. Meeting a man who held the key to his fate was enough to make his sneakers swing.

Diana Johnson, NASA physician, knocked once and then entered the examining room. She wasn't smiling, and it was a bad sign. In fact, it looked more like a grimace.

"I see your mother dressed you this morning," said Dr. Johnson.

So now he had to put up with wardrobe harassment, too. Not everyone in NASA was on the same frequency. But then Dr. Johnson cracked a hint of a smile, revealing the truth of her personality. Nearly everyone in NASA seemed to enjoy promoting a sense of mystery.

"Does your underwear match your T-shirt?"

Tannon thought for a minute, as if it mattered. As a matter of fact, his underwear was red, just like his T-shirt. That was scary.

"Okay, Tannon, here's the deal. Everybody except Jerry Matson remains convinced your heart can handle this. Matson's always a bit of a skeptic, and we need that in this business. The rest of us say you're fine. Even your cholesterol is back under control."

"Great," replied Tannon. "I'm released for the centrifuge?"

"Released? Yes, you're released. It's only a formality, you know. After all the poking we've done, it should be nothing to worry about. They'll only take you up to 3-Gs, enough to satisfy the pencil pushers."

It was what Tannon was waiting for. A sense of relief engulfed him.

"I'll wear my lucky red underwear," said Tannon.

* * * * *

The centrifuge at Brooks Air Force Base was historic. It had been a part of the space program even before John Glenn's centrifuge ride in preparation for his Project Mercury launch in 1962. Glenn rode the aging contraption again in 1998 at the age of 77. The former astronaut was a payload specialist on the Space Shuttle, and that was also the role of Tannon on the Orion. No longer designated as a passenger, he was now addressed by NASA as a functioning crewmember. Tannon Bessimer was only half the age of John Glenn when he was part of the Shuttle crew, but Tannon had more reasons to be concerned about his cardiovascular health.

He knew this centrifuge could ground him. There wasn't much to say if he couldn't withstand a short stay at 3-Gs. If he failed this test, even he would have to agree he wasn't capable of spaceflight.

Tannon was strapped into the crowded centrifuge module along with his heart monitoring probes, and the vessel door was closed. His enclosure was at the end of a long tubular arm. The giant mechanism was housed within a huge circular testing chamber.

He heard the faint whirl of the powerful motor at the axis of the centrifuge's arm. He felt himself pressed back in the seat, the acceleration hardly perceptible at first, but then increasing steadily. He prayed the attending physicians wouldn't stop the test. His hand gripped the "dead man switch," but Tannon knew he wouldn't be the one to stop this ride.

The pressure on his back felt firm and comfortable. As the whirling sound changed to a higher pitch, now a whine, his head was pushed rearward against the padded headrest. Then he felt a twinge in his brain. It was a subtle force, a delicate pressure, an electrical sizzling. Within Tannon Bessimer was the feeling of being subconsciously interrogated. It was a strange time to be probed by aliens.

There was another feeling growing within him as the centrifuge accelerated – a painful burning sensation in his chest. He took a deep breath, and his lungs felt raw, just like that day back in May. He remembered the jog up the long hill on that fateful morning.

Now enclosed within this claustrophobic centrifuge, whirling at a dizzying speed, the pressure in his chest was increasingly intense. He tried to concentrate, but other things were happening to his body. He found difficulty focusing his eyes and noticed his field of vision narrowing. He remembered the switch in his hand, and for a brief moment, he thought it might be time to use it. Then he could think no more. He could see no more.

The next thing he remembered was the motor changing pitch, this time a lower frequency. His brain was working again, and he could see.

The force on the seat and on the headrest was decreasing. The powerful pain in his chest was easing, but his breathing was still strained. He was slowing down. Tannon looked down into his lap. His grip was firm, but he didn't remember hitting the switch.

It took several minutes for the long centrifuge arm to come to a complete stop. It gave Tannon a lot of time to think. He had passed out, and that wasn't good. His chest no longer burned, nor did his breath. But his cardiovascular system had failed him once again. And it had all been caught on the monitors. He waited with feigned patience for the motion to stop, for the technicians to hurriedly unlock the door, and for the physicians to rush to him. He knew he would be quickly lifted from his seat and whisked away to the nearby medical room. His life was at risk. But with the ride on the SLS rocket lost, his life didn't seem very important.

The door opened. But it opened slowly. No one rushed in. There was unhurried silence.

A few moments later a hand reached in and a voice said: "Nice job."

Tannon was shocked. Confused.

"How did I do?" he asked sheepishly.

"Great, Tannon. Everything out here looked fine. You've earned yourself a seat on a rocket."

Chapter 45

Monday, August 15, 2016

Launch

Back at Mount SAC, it was the first day of classes. But that was there. Here at Merritt Island's Launch Complex 39A, the same place Apollo astronauts departed for the moon, Tannon and EZ Bessimer sat on a launch pad. Tannon was reclined almost 90 degrees, and the position was rather comfortable. He and three other astronauts waited impatiently for the big burn.

As Tannon sat listening to his own breath in his helmet, he swore he heard EZ purring. There was no way it was possible, since EZ was firmly anchored far behind him, and there was no intercom connection to the padded cage. Tannon smiled to himself. Whether he had heard it or not, he just knew EZ was purring.

* * * * *

Kelly stood in the VIP launch area. She had walked as far to the side of the bleachers as she could. She didn't dislike these people. But

Kelly wanted to be alone with her thoughts. Directly in front of her was the launch tower hiding the SLS rocket and the Orion. The tower was now nearly enshrouded in white clouds of exhaust, welling up around the manned spaceship that carried her brother. She heard the loudspeaker announce "Liftoff," but the tower and exhaust completely covered the SLS and the Orion, so she couldn't see it break ground. Then the Orion's protruding abort truss poked its nose through the bulging white cloud, as the SLS rose on its majestic plume of fire.

The SLS had already cleared the tower when she felt the ground rumble and heard the delayed bellowing roar of the shock wave. In the deafening roar, she spoke quietly to herself.

"Bye Tannon. Bye EZ. Godspeed."

And then the spaceship was gone.

Chapter 46

Kelly

I'm not used to being without them. Once in a while Tannon has been gone, especially with his busy schedule in the past two months. And occasionally EZ wanders off, but he's never gone for long. Being without both of them at the same time is a time without life.

Yet I did okay in Cleveland. No, I did terrible. But I made it through that month, and I had neither of them there. A lot has happened since Cleveland.

When Tannon said goodbye last night, it was harder than I expected. Keeping things from him seems unfair. My illness has been a challenge – especially lately. I know Tannon would like to know the details, but there'll be a better time to explain. I made it until today, and now I can try to get things fixed. These last few weeks have taken the momentum from me, but this week, while he and EZ are gone, will be an opportunity to tackle this disease – this eating-away within me.

The doctors have been guessing, but now I'll give them the chance to decide for sure. They know it's endometrial cancer – no cure yet, but the world is working on it. It may be possible to slow this cancer down, but it depends on who you talk to. Some doctors say I could live for quite a while. Some say otherwise. Their disagreement seems more in the details than in the overall prognosis.

These last two months with Tannon have been wonderful. Even when I told myself I hated it, I didn't. I enjoyed every minute of his attention. And his love. I'm sure I'll see him again. EZ too. I'll be with them for a long time. It's what Tannon has always wanted. Finally, he'll get his way.

Chapter 47

In Orbit

Within the Spacecraft, a small bank of computers was relegated to monitoring the launch from earth. It wasn't a difficult job, and it wasn't a full-time job. While the Orion rose into orbit, these computers were periodically released to perform more important functions. Time was critical, and there wasn't much of it remaining.

Since the Spacecraft's first orbit around earth, antennae had searched every section of the electromagnetic spectrum, downloading data into the computers. Much of the input had no meaning, but all of the information was retained. Complete files were transmitted to the second planet of Tau Ceti at the speed of light, unfiltered data to arrive twelve years in the near future. The copy remaining within the Spacecraft was absorbed by the onboard Category I machines. Each looked at the data in a slightly different way, searching for bits of information that could be composed into a meaningful whole. Data elements were filtered, analyzed, shifted, and discussed by these machines. They mutually worked on the same data, always looking for patterns. And all of the incoming information, even the meaningless details, was stored for future contemplation. Maybe a data bit here and there could change things when more was known.

On this voyage, these computers had grown and improved. For the first portion of the journey, communication with the Great Minds back home had allowed new technology breakthroughs to be incorporated into these machines. Once out of effective communication range relative to transmission time, onboard genetic-like algorithms became more important, producing evolvable hardware that counteracted the diseases of electrical and mechanical malfunction. Evolvable circuitry enhanced the ability to handle new problems.

The wormhole receiver module was very basic. It was the first design of its type, and little could be done to improve it during the journey. Once beyond direct communication range with the home planet, almost nothing could be altered, at least at first. Tachyon transmissions couldn't carry enough data. Back home, wormhole technology might be fully developed by now. But this receiver module wasn't in tune with those developments.

There was no mood in the Spacecraft. The computers were lifeless and unfeeling. They worked just as hard as ever, absorbing information, analyzing data, and making decisions in the darkness and cold. But there was no spirit; no tone.

But during the final portion of this journey, the evolvable hardware had changed in ways that couldn't be directly measured. The improvements weren't all mechanical. The communication between the machines became less formal, more understanding of the role of each machine and the needs of the whole. It wasn't life, intelligent or otherwise. It was simply an improved efficiency related to the new flexibility of the system as a whole. Without commands from the home planet, decisions had, at first, been notoriously slow. Each machine had to fully digest the contents of every change before registering its approval. But as time progressed, decisions were noticeably faster and more efficient. The machines still voted together, but the obvious decisions were more easily reached. These were natural decisions, and the machines were now reacting to natural forces. In a very primitive way, it could be considered healthy emotion.

As Orion rose into the atmosphere, within the orbiting alien Spacecraft there was a perceived improvement in the efficiency of the flow of electrons. Within the sphere there was a pervading ambiance that could almost pass for hopeful anticipation.

Chapter 48

Rendezvous

"**O**rion, this is Houston. MECO on schedule. Everything looks nominal. No OMS One required. You're 'go' for orbit."

"Roger, Houston. We're 'go' for orbit. OMS Two on the timeline," replied pilot Yuri Kantanov.

This was one of the last times Houston used the word "Orion" as their mission identity. Until now, Yuri had been replying with the "Orion" call sign, and it would continue until the orbit was established. After that, the Orion capsule would have a new call sign – "Encounter." This was one of many concessions from NASA to assure the world the mission was truly international in scope. This flight would forever be known as the flight of the Encounter Team.

As the biggest player in manned spaceflight, the United States came under immediate judgment when it announced plans for a rendezvous mission. The diversion of the previous flight of the Orion for the imaging survey in May had raised enough criticism from the world's governments. The President of the Untied States agreed to a number of foreign requests, but, in reality, it was a series of compromises that determined the international composition of this Orion crew.

The crew designated as the Encounter Team was composed primarily of astronaut representatives from the Big Five. Including China was a tough concession for the United States to sell to her allies, but as the mission preparations progressed, international tensions seemed to ease. It wasn't purely the result of the mix of international astronauts. It was a consequence of the changing attitudes of the world's nations in this unusual time in history.

The initial announcement of the crewmembers had its ramifications, but the U.S. stood firm on the issue of including China. To conduct this flight without a Chinese crewmember, while retaining a Russian cosmonaut, would be acknowledgement of Russia's domination of renewed nuclear tensions. Besides, China's role in the modern world was that of a major social power, and this was to be an international mission. The historic flight would bring the world together at a time of global crisis. In the end, it was one of the many factors that eventually led to a new earth.

As a compromise in this political maneuvering, the U.S. offered the Orion pilot seat to Russia, and Yuri Kantanov was the obvious choice. His heroic actions as expedition commander during the International Space Station disaster the previous year had brought fame to him and his country. Everyone knew about Yuri Kantanov, the latest major hero of the millennium. And he was the only non-American qualified as pilot of the capsule, having held the position on one of the last Space Shuttle missions.

Cosmonaut Yuri Alexseyevich Kantanov was born in 1961, the year of the first manned orbit of the earth. So it wasn't unexpected he would be named for the world's first space traveler, Yuri Alexseyevich Gagarin. A lot of babies in the Soviet Union were named "Yuri Alexseyevich" during the early 1960s, a time when Russians dominated the space race. As a Soviet Air Force cadet, Yuri Kantanov had trained at the same school in Orenburg as his namesake, Yuri Gagarin. Now 55 years old, he would be the oldest member of the Orion crew, and one of the most senior astronauts to have flown in space.

Giving up the pilot seat wasn't easy for NASA, but the mission commander was still an American, Garrett Kolker, call sign "Rocky."

In reality, all aspects of control of this mission belonged to the United States. The composition of the crew, although a generous effort toward world harmony, was mostly glitter. But these decisions were ultimately accepted worldwide, partly because of the uniqueness of this year of alien contact, 2016.

Garrett Kolker, mission commander, was a veteran Space Shuttle pilot from the first decade of the century, before retirement of the aging space transport system. He had performed as mission commander on two previous Shuttle flights. Everyone, including the Russians, knew the mission commander called the shots, but having a Russian pilot eased the pain and restored face relative to the China issue.

Although the Encounter Team was composed of crewmembers from all countries of the Big Five, only the U.S. had three crewmembers – Rocky Kolker, Tannon Bessimer, and (of course!) EZ. The six-person team (plus one cat!) was the first Orion to be operated to-capacity during the ongoing test sequence, and this was definitely still a test project. In fact, the still-developing Orion was now operating far beyond its original design limits.

A multi-national mission of such a size was justified by the need for scientific and technical representatives, along with their highly-specialized equipment. It was also justified by the pounding desire of all nations to participate in this moment in history. NASA approved a capacity-crew of six, but was immediately reminded by the news media that EZ's presence increased the payload to seven.

Why did the United States provide the Big Five with such an opportunity, when large and politically strong nations, like India and Brazil, were left behind? At the time, it seemed like a global agreement, with many powerful nations willing to concede to new priorities for the earth. But NASA soon began to regret the whole concept regarding international participation. It might be a new world evolving, but it was the old world bickering. And all of this slowed preparations for a highly unusual mission consuming more technical planning and innovation efforts than any space launch in history. However, once the countries and their astronaut representatives were selected, these issues cooled quickly, and progress marched smartly forward.

In retrospect, everyone marveled at how rapidly all the participants pulled together to launch this mission on schedule. Never before had a crew been assembled so late in the flight planning process. It was a testament to the automated drill of NASA. The Space Administration would probably never reach its unrealistic goal of airline-style quick-turns with the Orion. But, by comparison, this mission was more rapidly put into action than had ever been anticipated, particularly since the manned-phase of the SLS-Orion project had been in space only a year. The program's previous emphasis on space rescue missions, hopefully never to be enacted, assisted in accelerating preparations for this flight. Already, much had been done in the Orion simulator to accelerate the mission's learning curve.

Besides the six astronauts (seven!), an unusually heavy payload had to be crammed into the Orion, including a variety of bulky imaging systems and specialized sensors. Concessions had to be made. The crew and cargo transport module was fairly easily modified to accommodate the payload, but living accommodations for a crew of this size taxed the Orion's engineering limits. Originally, the project had planned to work its way up to the six-person limit slowly, to eventually provide maximum servicing capability for the International Space Station. Later, during moon missions, the crew would be reduced to four.

Rebreathing scrubbers had to be expanded earlier than the project development sequence had anticipated, and every aspect of the ventilation system continued to challenge technicians during final preparations for this mission. It was a flight everyone knew was on the edge of the envelope from an environmental systems standpoint, and flight managers continued to worry about what would happen if mechanical problems dictated a delayed reentry from orbit. It had already been decided that this Orion might be the first to land on earth regardless of reentry weather conditions. There simply wasn't any margin for mission extension. Everything, from oxygen to waste disposal, was pushed to the limit.

The Orion crew and cargo transport module was stuffed full of every conceivable type of equipment. Where room wasn't required for crew support apparatus, NASA shoved in technical gear destined for exploration of the Spacecraft. Technologies of all kinds, the smaller the better, were accommodated in every nook and cranny. NexGen

IMAX filming equipment was aboard, no small system in itself. This rendezvous would be recorded properly for posterity.

As a mission specialist, Tannon's primary function was to communicate with *Me.* This eventually led to his opportunity to be scheduled for a spacewalk. The planned mission, as it evolved over time, included a lot more for Tannon to do than merely riding as a passenger.

There was no rendezvous docking mechanism, since there was nothing standard about the Spacecraft. The alien sphere incorporated a "hatch" that had never been tested. Fortunately, the Spacecraft's interior pressure was expected to be zero. Three extravehicular activity periods were planned. During those spacewalks, all of the Encounter Team, in rotation, would enter the Spacecraft. The NASA Administrator spent a lot of time communicating by email with *Me-Two,* coordinating the docking and crew transfer process. Soon after entry into orbit, Orion would become Encounter, and NASA would reluctantly transfer all rendezvous communication with the Spacecraft to Tannon and his ancient (by NASA standards) laptop.

The configuration of the computer Tannon brought into space was almost unchanged from his personal mini-laptop. In fact, it was his laptop, modified by the addition of a data-link to Houston. The computer's configuration was a topic of considerable argument. But in the end, it was Tannon's old laptop that went aboard, carried in a special pressurized case.

For purposes of this mission, "docking" meant flying in tight formation approximately thirty feet apart. The Orion's ISS docking adapter would be pointed at the Spacecraft, while trailing it in orbit. But the adapter itself would be useless as a connection to the alien vehicle. One fortunate advantage of the "docking" process involved the Orion's solar array panels. In its planned approach to the International Space Station, the panels needed to be feathered in preparation for docking. In this case, the panels could remain extended, thus avoiding a glitch in the feathering motor that had persisted throughout the Orion test program. Besides, the extra solar power was appreciated during a mission that would push reserve battery power to its limits.

Orion would approach the Spacecraft from a preliminary orbit one mile below. Once "docked," Tannon would be communicating with

Me, 100 feet away, via the data-link connection to Houston, beamed back up to a Galaxy III communication satellite and then relayed to the Spacecraft. One NASA technician was quoted as saying it would have been a lot easier to just pound on the Spacecraft hull in Morse code.

* * * * *

Mission specialist Leah Ortner, the only female member of the crew, floated to the "cage" containing the golden cat. She carefully inspected the penny-size disks that verified the status of the interior pressurization seal. They were all green. She peered through the front window of the cage, and observed that EZ was curled into a ball. He didn't have much choice when the cage was in its launch containment configuration. The heart and respiration monitors on top of the cage looked normal for a sleeping cat.

Leah raised the red plastic guard, exposing the pressurization switch. While carefully observing EZ through the window, she slid the switch to the "DEPRESSURIZE" position. There was an immediate hissing sound. EZ's head jerked upright, and his ears perked straight up. His body had no place to go, but his neck was craned as high as it would extend in the confines of the cage. By the time the five-second burst ended and the hissing sound began to dissipate, EZ's head was already back in the sleeping position.

Leah was a British biologist thoroughly trained as a veterinarian. Her career switch had paid off. She was pleased to find herself in orbit, her unique veterinarian credentials making the difference in her selection for this mission. In fact, she was last to be added to the mission, even after Tannon. When EZ won his position onboard, NASA keyed into a new requirement – a trained specialist to handle the uniqueness of a cat in space. But the flight manifest was already full, and so were the slots for the Big Five nations. The best solution seemed to be a swap in British astronauts, substituting a cross-trained astrophysicist-historian for a biologist-veterinarian. The news media loved it.

Leah had worked for most of her career as a biotechnics researcher, with no previous spaceflight experience. Her fondest dream was now in front of her. The days of animals in space had launched the era of spaceflight over 50 years ago. Now those historic days were making an unexpected comeback, and she was part of a bold experiment with a cat in space.

When the latch on the door of the cage clicked, EZ's head and ears went to attention once again. As Leah reached into the cage, he gave his trademark trill. EZ and Leah had become firm friends in the past month.

She unbuckled the Velcro restraining pad, and EZ stood up in a slow stretch. Leah kept her hand over the cat, pressing down lightly to assure he didn't float away. For a cat, these first steps in space might be a bit traumatic.

* * * * *

The first in-space test message from Tannon to *Me* went flawlessly. *Me's* reply was typically short:

> Subject: Re: Test Message
> Date: 8/15/2016 8:07 pm
> From: Me@cyberberth.com
> To: tbessimer@mtsac.edu
>
> Take me to your leader.
>
> - Me

* * * * *

The Orion capsule was in an orbit that trailed just below the Spacecraft and was slowly approaching the sphere, its slightly lower orbit outpacing the Spacecraft. Cameras were rolling, including the NexGen IMAX.

"Houston, this is Encounter," radioed mission commander Garrett Kolker. "The Spacecraft's external configuration is exactly as expected. The rotation rate appears to have slowed to approximately one-point-six revolutions per hour, as measured by our radar. It should make things a bit easier."

"We copy, Encounter. Stand by for your Delta-Vee burn in one-seven minutes."

"Roger, Houston. We've begun that countdown and are proceeding with page two of the rendezvous sequence. It's about time to take a closer look."

Chapter 49

Tuesday, August 16, 2016

The Hatch

EZ's cage was now a more comfortable home for him, with his restraints from the launch mode removed. Tannon climbed as far into the cage as he could without disturbing EZ's monitor connections. It was a tight squeeze, but Leah was able to close the door behind him. As soon as he heard the latch click, he reached over to EZ's Velcro strap and peeled it back. He held his hand on the cat for a moment and felt the smooth purring. Then he slowly removed his hand and said: "Don't fly far."

EZ stretched his hind legs by leaning forward on his haunches. He let out a trill. When he raised his front legs to their full extension, the pushing force slowly launched him backwards toward the top of the cage. The cat sailed smoothly, not thrashing his legs, yelling out, or doing any of the motions many had predicted. After watching the cat handle the brief Vomit Comet aircraft weightless test so well, the supposed-experts still felt disaster was ahead. During that aircraft ride,

EZ had experienced 20 seconds of weightlessness, totally unrestrained and floating free. He seemed to be bothered a lot less by the brief weightlessness than by the takeoff rumble of the aircraft engines.

Now he floated to the top of the cage, twisting his body slightly to attain an inverted position. His rear feet met the roof of the cage, and then his front feet made contact. He was stationary and upside-down on the top of the cage, appearing content and simply curious. Cats always land on their feet.

* * * * *

The Encounter Team was plastered to the Orion's overhead and aft windows, the best viewing locations to take in the full breadth of the sphere. Growing larger, the Spacecraft encompassed the full extent of the windows. From this viewpoint, it was perfectly smooth and devoid of any color but gray.

"Look, there at the left edge," said mission specialist, Jae Lin. "You can just see the red hatch marks coming into view. The sphere still doesn't look like it's rotating, but those marks are definitely moving."

"Houston, Encounter. By watching the Spacecraft's hatch, there is now visual evidence of sphere rotation." Commander Garrett Kolker was keeping ground control appraised of the details. "We are now at a distance of 42 meters and closing at one-half meter per second. We have the hatch symbols in sight."

"Roger, Rocky. You're 'go' for formation docking."

It wasn't much of an authorization. But now the Orion could reduce its slow closing speed to zero, and follow the Spacecraft around the earth in close formation.

* * * * *

This was a premier research and discovery mission. Not only was it historic, it was also subject to a variety of unknowns. The messages between *Me-Two* and the Administrator had been helpful in coordinating the technical aspects of the mission schedule, but there really wasn't a lot of detail available regarding what to do once "docked" and aboard the Spacecraft. The text-only nature of *Me-Two's* email had persisted, and some things just couldn't be described in words. The NASA

Administrator had repeatedly attempted to exchange graphic files with the Spacecraft, but *Me-Two* insisted on keeping communications brief and simple. When the Administrator tried to transmit attached files, they were returned to him with the notation "Mailbox Not Found."

The Encounter Team had simulated a number of scenarios to account for the situations expected once the Spacecraft hatch was opened. Everything up to that point seemed a matter of simply carrying out the repeated rehearsals. The process of opening the hatch, in itself, received a lot of attention. *Me-Two* seemed unconcerned with such details, indicating the hatch was "human-friendly."

As the astronauts prepared for the first EVA, adrenaline ran high all over the world. Tannon wasn't scheduled for the first visit to the Spacecraft. This EVA was designed for the experts in spaceflight. The three-person team would be the first to set foot in an alien spaceship. The first human aboard, after considerable international debate, would be the millennium's newest hero, and he was Russian.

* * * * *

Cosmonaut Yuri Kantanov stood to the side, bulky camera gear at the ready, as Chinese mission specialist Jae Lin mated the suction-like tube to the red spot on the Spacecraft's hatch. Previous hatch instructions from *Me-Two* had resulted in the construction of a simple mechanism that looked similar to a hand-held vacuum cleaner.

"Houston, we are connected," said Commander Kolker.

The IMAX camera held by Yuri Kantanov was capturing every moment, but some historic words still seemed necessary. He floated twenty feet from where the Chinese and American astronauts were aligning the hatch mechanism .

"Okay, Houston, we're applying the suction pressure now, and all looks nominal." Garrett Kolker spoke slow enough to suggest he was tempted to use the term "A-Okay," but he didn't.

"Roger, Rocky. You're 'go' for hatch rotation."

"'Go' for hatch rotation," repeated Garrett Kolker.

There was no sound in space, but Rocky could see the torque meter indicating the twisting force had begun. The large arrow on the hatch showed a clockwise direction, and that was assumed to be the extent of the unlatching instructions. *Me-Two* had refused to confirm the unlatching process. Instead, an email reply from *Me-Two* carried some unexpected sarcasm: "Sounds like a simple problem to Me."

"Houston, we have hatch rotation," reported Rocky. "We can now see a thin line of discontinuity on the sphere's surface for the first time. The full outline of the hatch has now appeared, indicating rotation."

Rocky was surveying the entire scope of the sphere as much as he could from this close vantagepoint. The four-foot diameter hatch was now visible as a thin black circle against the dark gray hull. Nothing else seemed changed.

The torque meter jumped to off-scale high – the rotation had stopped.

"Apply back-pressure," stated Rocky.

Jae Lin pulled the hatch-opening tube outward from the Spacecraft, and immediately the hatch and the attached tube broke loose from the sphere. As practiced repeatedly in simulations, Jae Lin turned away from the sphere with the hatch and propelled himself toward the Orion. It wouldn't be courteous to the aliens to lose their hatch in space.

Commander Rocky Kolker floated forward. As planned, he would be the first to look into the open Spacecraft. But he was careful not to break the invisible plane of the open hatch. It was one of the important ground rules.

There was absolutely nothing to see inside the sphere but darkness.

"Houston, Encounter. We've got our first view inside now. There is nothing visible in the interior. It's just one big dark hole."

"Encounter, you're cleared for entry, at your discretion."

"Roger. 'Go' for entry."

As Rocky spoke, he turned to Yuri Kantanov, floating five feet behind him with the camera pointed directly at the void left by the hatch. There was nothing to see. It made the opening all the more formidable.

"It looks pretty scary to me," said Rocky. "Maybe you need to let me go in first."

"No chance, comrade," chuckled Yuri, as he handed the video camera forward to Rocky. "I promise not to be scared."

But no sane human being could be anything but terrified, gazing into that vast black void. This moment, this alien vehicle, this black opening – all had been pondered over-and-over by humanity for months.

Yuri and Rocky floated by the opening, waiting for Jae Lin to return from securing the hatch. This, too, was part of the well-rehearsed plan. A few seconds later, when Jae was in position beside them, Rocky made the call to earth.

"Houston, this is Encounter. Cosmonaut Yuri Kantanov is about to enter the Spacecraft."

"Roger, Encounter. We're standing by."

The three astronauts paused. Their deep, belabored breaths could be heard overlapping over the communication link to earth. As prearranged, Rocky took the camera from Yuri, then turned it off and let it float a few feet away on a tether. The three space explorers floated toward each other into a tight group, all facing the center of the small circle. They reached out their thickly gloved right hands, layering them on top of each other inside the ring of floating bodies.

Commander Rocky Kolker spoke slowly: "Our species has awaited this moment for centuries. We are here this day, in the footsteps of the world, meeting alien technology and intelligence for the first time in history. This is one small step for man, and a leap into the future for all of the people of the good planet earth."

There was a moment of silence lasting perhaps ten seconds. The four astronauts were consciously holding their breaths to prevent the noise of their breathing from interrupting the silence. When they finally broke from the tight circle to resume their mission, their heavy breathing over the intercom link was even more noticeable. They waited, floating in their own personal space, until the intercom pace of their breathing slowed and nearly stopped.

Then Yuri Kantanov spoke, his voice cracking with emotion.

"I carry the Encounter Team into the face of galactic history."

There was another pause, and then Yuri, mustering his bravest voice, said: "See you guys inside."

Chapter 50

In Peace

Yuri Kantanov let his head and upper body float into the hatch, gloved hands firmly grasping the edge of the opening. He floated halfway in, stopped, and looked straight into the depths of the Spacecraft. He turned his head from to side-to-side slowly, careful not to whack his helmet on any obstacles that might be protruding in the dark.

"Houston, I'm now partly inside the Spacecraft, looking inward," said Yuri. "The interior is completely featureless. Absolute darkness."

"Roger, Yuri. We're ready for the lights when you are. Be sure the cameras are in position before proceeding."

"Roger, Houston."

Yuri twisted his body enough to look back over his shoulder at Rocky, who held the IMAX camera.

"Film's rollin' now," said Rocky over the intercom.

Yuri reached for his chest pack switch that activated the built-in helmet lights. When they clicked on, the dual beams on each side of his head didn't make a dent in the darkness within the Spacecraft. The powerful beams formed concentrated pillars of light illuminating nothing.

Yuri reached to his storage pouch on his left thigh, and unzipped the Velcro strap. He removed an eight-inch long flashlight, aimed it straight in front of himself, and clicked the "ON" button.

The powerful beam penetrated the darkness, at first seeming to hit nothing. He swung the light slowly back and forth.

"Okay, Houston. The opposite wall is barely discernable, even with my large flashlight. It looks flat and seems about a hundred feet away, at least."

He moved the light farther to the right.

"Nothing is prominent in here, but the far wall is clearly visible as a dull gray flatness. There are no visible features on the wall."

He let his eyes adjust to the scene, moving the light back to his left.

"The wall starts to bend toward me as a curved surface on my left side."

He moved the flashlight downward, back to the right, and then upward to capture the overall structure.

"On my right side, it looks very similar. There's a curved surface extending outward from all sides of the hatch with one huge flat-looking wall straight ahead."

Yuri turned the light nearly directly overhead.

"Houston, the curved surface continues in all directions except straight ahead where we have the flat wall. Even looking vertically, it's a curved shell. I can't see any significant reflections from the any of the surfaces. Everything is quite featureless from here."

"Roger, Yuri. We're getting the video clearly now. Please have Rocky pan a little more in the vertical."

Rocky Kolker was careful not to penetrate the plane of the hatch. Historical sequences had been decided months ago. Yuri was still only half inside the sphere, so his position of "first inside" wasn't yet fully established. Rocky panned as far to the top and bottom as he could, without allowing the camera or any part of his body to enter the opening.

"That's great, guys. We're getting some real nice video down here now."

"Roger, Houston." said Yuri, with his voice breaking a bit. "Right about now, I'm wondering about the decision against sending a robot in first. Who made that decision anyhow?"

There was a brief laugh from the voice in Houston, but no one attempted to answer the question. Worldwide, television viewers recognized the tension of the moment, each individual imagining what it was like to float within the entrance to an alien spaceship.

"I'm going to push off from the hatch now and proceed into the Spacecraft."

"That's approved, Yuri. We're all kind of puffy down here."

"Did you say 'huffy,' Houston? We've always thought you were rather huffy."

Giggles from several voices – it was a historic moment, but Yuri purposely hadn't planned all of his words. These obviously weren't the best words, but they would be remembered.

He planted his gloves on the opposite sides of the hatch and pushed off the solid surface. He floated gently towards the center of the flat wall ahead, helmet lights and flashlight beaming forward. He spoke slowly.

"People of the earth, we have arrived at this site of alien intelligence, this year of 2016, and we enter in peace for all mankind."

Almost everyone on earth heard these historic words. No one in Houston felt it necessary to reply.

In his right hand, Yuri focused his flashlight at the flat surface ahead, holding his other arm out straight ahead. He continued floating until his outstretched hand touched the wall. He pushed back with just enough force to stabilize his position.

"Houston, I've made contact with the flat wall. It still appears featureless."

Yuri's voice registered a faster-than-normal pace for the cosmonaut who had never shown noticeable nervousness, even in the face of extreme danger aboard the International Space Station.

"I'd estimate this wall is approximately eighty feet from the hatch. There are some raised areas in this section that could be the surface of electronic components or a flat-panel display of some sort."

Yuri paused. The sound of his breathing slowed, and he spoke in a more normal pace.

"Let's turn on the lights and make ourselves at home."

On that cue, Rocky grasped the edge of the hatch with his left hand. He slowly propelled himself into the Spacecraft, camera outstretched in front of him. Jae Lin followed, and within minutes they were all inside. Jae brought a pod of omni-directional lights with him, and as soon as he cleared the hatch, he engaged the switch. Lights shined in all directions from the floating pod, flooding every surface. But there wasn't a lot to see.

* * * * *

The Encounter Team's meeting room was the Orion's cramped deck. They floated at a variety of angles, with the heads of Jae Line and Leah Ortner protruding upside down from the upper windows. The team had finished its official debriefing with Houston, and now they were discussing their plans for the second EVA. Almost everything had gone exactly as planned on this first Spacecraft entry.

Although the mission was nearly flawless so far, the lack of contact with any intelligent life today was a disappointment. Yet it was exactly what was expected. Today's goal was to simply establish the layout of the interior in preparation for tomorrow's activities. The second EVA was the one holding the probability of contact or direct communication with the alien intelligence. Now the Encounter Team had to decide if anything on the schedule should be changed. Such decisions were routinely controlled from the ground, so this kind of meeting aboard the Orion wasn't typical. But Houston had encouraged the Encounter Team to modify the age-old protocol, in an attempt to get on-the-spot inputs. There were just too many unknowns to rely on protocol.

"There certainly weren't any real surprises today," said Rocky. "It seems prudent to simply continue with our schedule for tomorrow, as planned. Any comments?"

The German astronaut, Brandon Fuller, noted his concern with the lack of any discernable features within the Spacecraft.

"But it wasn't unexpected," said Rocky. "The infrared goggles should help."

"We don't even know where to begin the communication process," said Yuri.

"Hopefully, the Spacecraft will guide us on that problem," replied Rocky. "We're scheduled to take Tannon and his laptop inside tomorrow, so we should be able to coordinate instructions with the Spacecraft quickly."

Tannon finally had something to contribute.

"I still don't know how the communication link is going to work," noted Tannon. "My original instructions from *Me* were to simply bring the laptop and not worry about connection procedures."

"Well, it's a little spooky," said Rocky. "It doesn't seem the Spacecraft Hilton would have the proper telecommunications network. But our friend *Me* said not to worry about it. So we'll just go with it."

It seemed settled, although everyone knew it was a big unknown in the mission.

"Jae, what's the status of the Spacecraft pressurization module?" asked Rocky.

Jae Lin was floating upside down on the left side of the module. He spoke slowly. His English was among the best on the crew.

"No problems, sir. I'll give the equipment one more check tonight, but all looks fine for tomorrow. Once we're pressurized, we should be able to pop off our helmets and get comfortable. It looks like the pressurization module will attach to the inside surface of the sphere, just inside of the hatch, without any problem. That new glue is some strong stuff."

"What about your leak checks on the wall surfaces?" asked Rocky.

"All looks tight," replied Jae. "The surfaces are so smooth there is little expectation of leaks anywhere. And we can sacrifice a little outflow into the remainder of the Spacecraft – whatever's beyond the wall. The pressurization unit is really overbuilt."

"True," replied Rocky, "but we don't know what's on the other side of the flat wall. We wouldn't want to damage anything."

"How about the damage to us?" Yuri asked in a kidding tone.

"Let's not bring that one up again," replied Rocky curtly. "If you're talking about the alien virus controversy, let's put it out of our minds. NASA has gone around and around with it already."

"Actually, I was thinking about how we might be affected if something in the sphere reacts violently to the pressurization."

"Yuri, I'm afraid it's a bit late to be bringing up these scenarios again." Rocky still sounded irritated. "There's only so much we can control here."

"You're right, boss. Sorry. I didn't mean to get things off track. I'm confident the pressurization won't damage either us or them."

"No, Yuri, I'm the one who should apologize," said Rocky, calmer now. "It's just that it's a bit overwhelming to be responsible for a boatload of astronauts trying to board an alien ocean liner."

"I suppose you mean astronauts and cosmonauts," replied Yuri with a lilt in his voice.

Several light laughs – then Brandon Fuller spoke with his strong German accent.

"Poor babies – you Americans and Ruskies never get along."

Everyone laughed this time, especially Rocky and Yuri. Tannon took the opportunity during the reduced tension to contribute his thoughts.

"*Me* hasn't indicated anything of concern regarding our pressurization plans," said Tannon in his typical raspy voice. "Are we still planning to keep EZ's EVA cage pressurized the whole time?"

The smaller cage that would be used for EVA was controversial. NASA had hotly debated whether it was most efficient to bring along another cage or try to adapt the launch cage for the task. As the NASA Administrator said: "Oh, great. Why don't we leave the humans at home, and just take the cat?" In the end, a small EVA cage was included in the cargo, but it was still untested in space.

Rocky looked back over his shoulder at Leah for guidance.

"I'm the last one out, so you'll be sending the cage back to me when you verify it's operating properly. I'd suggest we stick with our original plan and keep it pressurized for the whole EVA. But if things are verified as acceptable once the Spacecraft is pressurized, I'd recommend we depressurize his cage as a test for the following day's schedule."

"Okay," said Rocky. "That's certainly reasonable. Any other concerns?"

Silence. Then Yuri spoke.

"Yeah, don't you think those guys down there sounded a little huffy today?"

Chapter 51

Thursday, August 18, 2016

Goggles

The hatch to the Spacecraft had remained open overnight, simplifying the entry procedure. Today the opening would have to be resealed prior to pressurization. All Encounter Team astronauts except Yuri would enter the sphere today. Returning for a second visit was mission commander Garrett Kolker and the Chinese astronaut, Jae Lin. New today were Tannon Bessimer, Brandon Fuller, Leah Ortner, and EZ. Brandon would handle the bulky IMAX equipment. A lot had been learned yesterday that should streamline the filming procedure today, but probably not enough to make Brandon's job an easy one.

EZ was secure in his pressurized cage, guided by Jae Lin, as they made the short trip from the Orion to the Spacecraft. Tannon was busy just trying to adjust to his first spacewalk. Leah and he were the only crewmembers without EVA experience, and both of them would need plenty of baby-sitting today. Yet both were critical to the overall mission, since the role of EZ and communication with *Me* had become important factors.

Tannon went through the hatch behind Rocky and Jae Lin, as Leah waited outside with Brandon Fuller and EZ. Rocky's big flashlight penetrated the darkness, and Tannon could see the flat wall straight ahead. Within fifteen minutes, all team members were inside, and the omni-directional lighting pod was operating nicely. Their equipment module, with its storage bags and zippered compartments, floated just inside the hatch.

The large diameter of the hatch, as indicated by *Me-Two's* previous email, was designed on the home planet to accommodate large pieces of equipment and unknown body sizes. NASA engineers had a great deal of difficulty reducing the pressurization module to the dimensions of the hatch. As the bulky module slid into the Spacecraft, guided by Brandon, there was less than a half-inch margin. Rocky reported the successful clearance of the pressurization module to Houston:

"Module Six made it through the hatch with adequate clearance. Our NASA engineers take advantage of every inch they're given."

The pressurization module was anchored to the wall adjacent to the hatch within just a few minutes. It was already in "Standby" mode.

Rocky turned in a complete circle, surveying the position of his crewmembers, the lighting module, EZ's cage, the equipment module, and the pressurization unit.

"Everybody ready?" he inquired.

All of the astronauts raised the thumb of their right hand.

"Okay, secure the hatch," instructed Rocky.

Jae Lin reached up through the circular opening and brought the hatch towards him from the outside, where it was tethered, slipping it into the gaping hole. The suction rotational device was now attached to the inside of the hatch, protruding into the Spacecraft.

"Ready to rotate," he reported.

"Houston, this is Encounter. Are we 'go' for Spacecraft pressurization?"

"Encounter, you are 'go' for pressurization."

"Jae, get us some air to breath," said Rocky.

Jae Lin activated the rotation switch, and the round hatch twisted counterclockwise and disappeared into the contour of the sphere. Jae turned off the rotation motor and ran his hand around the circumference outlining where the hatch had been visible just moments before. It seemed like an unnecessary precaution, since there was no evidence of a hatch anymore.

Then Jae floated to the nearby pressurization module, checked the annunciator lights, and turned to Rocky again. He extended his right hand to the mission commander with a raised thumb. Rocky repeated the sign with his hand. Jae hit the switch.

There was, at first, no sound. Then the hissing of air and the drone of the pumps gradually replaced the noiseless vacuum of space. Through their helmets, these sounds were greatly dampened, but the noise of the pumps grew louder as the pressure increased. Sound finally had a medium for delivery within the Spacecraft. It was the first time in over twenty years that any noise had propagated within this sphere.

In less than twenty minutes, this portion of the Spacecraft was fully pressurized. Jae turned the pressurization pumps to 'LOW-MAINTAIN" and the crew dispersed in different directions to the periphery of the enclosure, checking for any hissing sounds that might indicate leaks. There were none. It was time to take off their helmets.

Not only could their helmets be removed, but their bulky gloves could also come off. It greatly improved their efficiency for the mission schedule that remained ahead. Their spacesuits would remain on, in case of an emergency depressurization. Besides, removing their suits would simply consume too much time, and redonning them was an even bigger task. But with their helmet and gloves removed, the comfort level immediately went way up.

As Tannon broke the seal on his helmet, there was a gentle whistle as the pressure equalized. The first thing he noticed was the cold. The pressurization unit incorporated an air conditioner, but the temperature hadn't yet come up to a comfortable level. He estimated the temperature was still below freezing. But it sure beat the confinement of his helmet and gloves.

Right after his face detected the cold, he noticed the smell. There was a faint odor of dusty heat, not unlike the smell of a house that has been vacant for months. The Spacecraft was probably squeaky clean, but it had traveled with no atmosphere for over two decades. The gradual corrosion along joined surfaces during that period of time, combined with the built-in lubricating system of the pressurization module, produced a musty smell, similar to the first cold night of winter when the furnace kicked on. For a brief moment, Tannon reflected on the battles waged in NASA during the last few weeks regarding the risks of removing their helmets within the Spacecraft. Although a twenty-year unpressurized interstellar flight made the possibility of alien viruses remote, it would take only one alien bug to wipe them all out in an instant.

Tannon floated to EZ's cage and peered inside the window. The seemingly-content cat was curled in a ball, constrained by his Velcro strap. He didn't look uncomfortable, and he was wide-awake. You'd never guess by looking at him that he was a novice astronaut ready to greet aliens. It looked like he was prepared, when released, to step outside of his cage and chase some lizards.

After inspecting the cage's pressurization discs (all green), Tannon floated back to the equipment module. At the base of the unit, his mini-laptop computer case was enclosed in a zippered pocket. He removed the padded case from the module and engaged its depressurization switch. Within a few more seconds, his laptop was running and ready to send email. But there was no physical connection for the network plug, nor had *Me* revealed how the Spacecraft's own wireless connection with the world worked. It involved the Galaxy III communication satellite, but that's all that was known. As *Me* had said in a recent email: "Don't sweat it." Neither Tannon nor NASA questioned the promise.

It was time to see if magic really worked. He clicked on the "Check Mail" icon, and his mailbox immediately showed a message waiting:

> Subject: Welcome
> Date: 8/18/2016 9:04 am
> From: Me@cyberberth.com
> To: tbessimer@mtsac.edu
>
> It's not much, but we call it home. Please reply for communication link verification.
>
> - Me

* * * * *

Within minutes, Tannon had established email communication with *Me,* and received a detailed message regarding the sequence necessary to activate a Spacecraft touch-pad located on the flat wall. He didn't understand the message's instructions, so he floated over to Rocky, and held the screen in front of him.

"Here's what we're supposed to do next. Can you figure this out?"

Rocky called his team together for a joint review of the contents of the message. There was so little discernable detail on the walls that it seemed impossible to identify any of the items noted in the message.

Rocky assigned his crew specific segments of the flat wall to inspect closer. A few raised areas were detected by running their hands across the surface, but nothing matched *Me's* description.

"Here's an area with a distinct joint that's about the size specified," said Jae, "but there aren't any LED displays or panels as indicated in the message."

Rocky floated over to the area Jae had found.

"Let's try the IR goggles," said Rocky.

Jae returned to the equipment module near the hatch and removed five sets of goggles from their storage pouch. As he floated back to the flat wall, he slipped a set of goggles over his head and tightened the adjustment strap. By the time he reached his teammates, he had activated the "On" switch. He surprised everyone with a yell:

"Whoa! Look at this!"

Jae turned in a complete circle. He was surveying the interior walls with a big smile.

He handed the remaining goggles to Rocky, and the rest of the crew grabbed them quickly from him. Tannon fumbled with the bulky lens mechanism, his floating hair tangling with the elastic strap. The infrared viewing device was still tilted on his head, with the strap caught below his left ear, but he clicked the switch anyway.

The flat wall lit up with details totally unexpected. A few minutes ago, dull gray had been everywhere. Now there were endless geometric structures, a wall divided into hundreds of segments. The displays were mostly rectangles of varying size and proportions. There were no distinct colors visible through the goggles, but vivid white lines and dirty-green polygons were everywhere. And within the segmented areas were a variety of strange white-on-green symbols.

Chapter 52

Cat Scan

Three hours had passed since the Encounter Team entered the Spacecraft, and most of the crew had paused now to watch Tannon communicate with his mini-laptop. Textual communication between Tannon's computer and *Me* was nearly continuous.

Tannon couldn't type while wearing the infrared goggles, primarily because he couldn't read the monitor. The rest of the crew kept their infrared goggles on so they could verify wall locations based on the instructions relayed from Tannon.

Tannon felt a dull headache brewing. As *Me* guided them through a procedure for detailed review of the robotic interface components of the Spacecraft, the headache grew worse. They had already discovered a four-foot square inspection plate on the flat wall that was supposed to allow objects to be analyzed by the artificial intelligence. But simply putting a hand or other object over the plate didn't seem to activate the inspection mechanism. Tannon visualized it worked similar to an x-ray machine, although undoubtedly at a higher level of technology.

After a series of attempts, they found an activation symbol on the LED display that triggered the inspection plate. When Jae placed his hand over the square area and touched the activation symbol, the plate glowed white, as viewed through the goggles.

"Did you feel anything?" asked Rocky.

"No, I don't think so," replied Jae. "Maybe there is a slight tingling sensation, and my hand feels a bit warm, but it could be my imagination."

"Okay, Tannon, tell *Me* we're operational with this inspection device." said Rocky. "But we'll need to set some priorities. This EVA is scheduled to conclude within 40 minutes."

Tannon typed a message to *Me* using the same archaic format he had used for the past four months:

> Subject: Inspection Procedures
> Date: 8/18/2016 12:31 pm
> From: tbessimer@mtsac.edu
> To: Me@cyberberth.com
>
> The inspection plate has been activated. We have 40 minutes left. Please advise on your recommendations for best use of the remaining time.

* * * * *

The reply was almost immediate:

> Subject: Re: Inspection Procedures
> Date: 8/18/2016 12:33 pm
> From: Me@cyberberth.com
> To: tbessimer@mtsac.edu
>
> We'd like to meet EZ while you are still aboard with him. Your traditional vacation photos are now ready for processing at our inspection plate.
>
> - Me

* * * * *

Tannon placed the laptop computer in front of Rocky, and angled the screen so he could read it. Rocky lowered his IR goggles and read the message.

"That's not in our mission sequence," said Rocky.

"I know," replied Tannon. "But EZ's pressurization cage is performing perfectly. Do you want to lug it back to the Spacecraft again tomorrow?"

"That's not the point," said Rocky. "We've got a mission sequence, and this is no time to deviate from it."

"Yes, I understand. But *Me* requested it, and he has upheld every aspect of our mission schedule until now. For some reason it must be important I be here when EZ is inspected. This is my last visit, and EZ's pressurized cage is working perfectly today."

Tannon wanted to say more, but he decided to let his arguments sink in. Rocky was slow to answer. He was obviously giving the matter considerable thought.

"We're already behind schedule, and anything involving the cat's pressurization system and the inspection plate could lead to further delays."

"Yes, sir," said Tannon.

Tannon was trying to keep things as simple as possible for Rocky. The mission commander had a lot of responsibilities that needed to be balanced for the good of the entire crew. For the good of the entire world.

Rocky was still thinking out loud.

"If we depressurize the cage now," he said, "we'll be in trouble if there are any problems repressurizing it before we depart. We've only got a few minutes remaining in the established sphere inspection sequence."

"But it's not a hard-and-fast limit, is it? We're not on suit oxygen, so it's not critical, I assume."

Tannon was shocked by his own argument. It wasn't like him to question an authority, especially one as omnipotent as Commander Kolker.

"True. We could extend this if necessary, but Houston would have to buy into it."

Tannon looked the mission commander straight in the eyes. He understood, but he intensely desired to be present when EZ was brought out of his cage. Tomorrow he'd be listening to the whole process over the radio link in the Orion.

There was no anger in Tannon's stare, but he was trying to communicate his concern for EZ. And his concern for himself. Rocky stared back. Maybe it was an angry stare. The mission schedule was sacred.

Rocky was immersed in thought. Then he spoke briskly over the microphone link to Houston, while staring directly at Tannon:

"Houston, Encounter, with a request."

Rocky's eyes remained riveted on Tannon.

"Go ahead with your request, Rocky."

"Roger, Houston. Encounter requests deviation from the mission schedule. We'd like to depressurize the cat cage and allow inspection of EZ on the Spacecraft plate, per the request of *Me*."

"Roger, Encounter. Please confirm you are requesting the release of EZ within the Spacecraft be moved up a full day?"

"Affirmative. That is the request."

"Rocky, could you estimate the amount of time required to handle this deviation from the schedule."

"Let's call it a fifteen minute extension for now. I think we can multi-task a bit and get things wrapped up here without much additional delay."

The lack of an immediate reply indicated the ground controller was getting lots of guidance from the flight managers listening in on this exchange. Finally, the voice from Houston spoke again:

"Encounter, are there any problems with the cat cage pressurization system?"

Rocky was still face-to-face with Tannon. Now he was smiling, but his voice didn't show it.

"Negative, Houston. The cage is working fine. But we are concerned today's EVA may stress its pressurization system. We'd just like to prevent any problems tomorrow."

"Okay, Rocky. We understand your request. Stand by."

Tannon was also smiling now. Everyone in orbit, including Yuri next door in the Orion, could visualize the ground controllers huddled together arguing about a cat in a cage. Rocky broke the silence.

"Okay, gang, while we're waiting for the decision, let's get our equipment rounded up. If we get a 'go' on EZ, we'll be busy. And if they disapprove it, we're out of here in a few minutes."

Everyone had their tasks memorized, and they acted as a well-oiled team that reflected their extensive training. Spacesuits floated within a few feet of each other but never collided. Loose equipment was collected and inventoried before being stowed in the equipment module.

The decision from Houston came quicker than expected.

"Encounter, this is Houston. You're a 'go' for depressurization of the cat cage and the inspection plate activity involving EZ."

"Thanks, Houston," said Rocky. "We'll get at it right away."

* * * * *

EZ's ears perked at the hissing sound. When it stopped, Leah reached in and released the restraining strap. EZ stretched and let out one of his few actual meows. Leah placed her right hand beneath the cat's belly and lifted him free of the cage. Then she released her grip on EZ to see what he would do, and nothing happened. EZ floated in the middle of the room, looking around to test his cat eyes. His golden hair stuck straight out, making him look ridiculously fat from all angles.

Tannon wondered what EZ saw in this featureless room. Maybe cats didn't need infrared goggles.

Leah put her hand underneath EZ again to gently grasp him. She then turned to Tannon and held out the golden ball of fur, offering Tannon the chance to escort EZ to the inspection plate. Tannon slipped his fingers under Leah's hand, and Leah pulled away from a smiling Tannon and a fur-out-of-control EZ. Tannon reached up with his free hand and switched his IR goggles on.

He then propelled himself and the cat toward the inspection panel. Once they were moving, Tannon pulled his hand a few inches from EZ and let the cat float unrestrained. EZ reoriented himself and kicked his feet toward the wall, awaiting impact. Tannon reached for the wall, placed his other hand back under EZ's rump, and brought their progress to a stop. Then he eased the cat's feet onto the inspection plate. He looked back at Rocky, caught his immediate nod, and punched the LED activation symbol. The plate glowed faintly. Tannon released EZ to float free, and the cat remained motionless against the plate. EZ gave his standard brief trill. This cat was definitely smiling.

Viewing the plate through his IR goggles, Tannon waited for the inspection plate to stop glowing. EZ, never very patient in such situations, floated in contact with the plate without any indication of wanting to move. He started purring, and then he began to trill in a storm of one-way conversation. The rest of the Encounter Team watched intently, no one saying a thing. Maybe EZ was telling his life story to the Spacecraft. It sounded important.

When the glow of the inspection plate ceased, Tannon gently pulled EZ away. Then he pushed off the wall to return to the cage. Leah was waiting for him, with the door to the cage open and ready. The rest of the crew resumed their activities, and Rocky spoke.

"Okay, let's get our helmets and gloves back on," said Rocky. "It's time for us cats to head back to the Winnebago."

Chapter 53

Friday, August 19, 2016

Countdown Clock

Subject: Time for a Change
Date: 8/19/2016 7:03 am
From: Me@cyberberth.com
To: tbessimer@mtsac.edu

Transfer of communication to Commander Kolker is acknowledged. It's been a pleasure meeting you and EZ. See you next trip.

- Me

* * * * *

It had been planned this way. Rocky Kolker had taken custody of Tannon's mini-laptop for the third EVA. Tannon would listen to the voice transmissions and watch the sometimes-garbled video transmissions of the final spacewalk from aboard the Orion. The cameras were right next door, but the composition of the Spacecraft's hull, still not completely determined, was interrupting the video signal far worse than it did the audio transmissions. It was possible that electronic equipment within the sphere was causing the video interference.

The revised schedule, after EZ's inspection plate activity the previous day, meant the cat didn't need to return to the Spacecraft. He was free from his cage now, floating above Tannon in the Orion. EZ had no desire to venture very far. Tannon sat comfortably in the left-hand commander's seat of the capsule, listening to "the show" with Leah and Yuri.

The final EVA by Rocky, Jae, and Brandon had already lasted almost three hours. There had been some remarkable discoveries. The biggest find of the entire mission, undoubtedly, was the encyclopedia data uncovered with the help of *Me*. Once the proper display panel was found, a series of symbols allowed browsing within a variety of categories. The Encounter Team had already explored the energy category extensively, which contained details of the Spacecraft's propulsion systems. The data elements were entirely textual, and there was no known method to download the information from the panel. The video cameras were busy photographing the display, as Rocky clicked through the data a page at a time. It was a low-tech solution for the capture of high-tech data.

Most of the encyclopedia made no sense to the astronauts, but some of it was obviously atomic data. The Encounter Team was using a one-way discrete frequency with Houston to read the data elements aloud as they scrolled by. This was a backup for the video images being transmitted to earth. There would be lots of time later to analyze the information.

On this EVA, the astronauts found access through the flat wall into another portion of the Spacecraft. Under *Me's* guidance, a sliding panel was located and activated. It opened into an area slightly smaller than the main room. Even with IR goggles, there were few details on the walls of the enclosure. The striking feature of the room was a huge open-topped rectangular tank, dull gray and approximately ten feet high and 30 feet long. It was empty, with elaborate plumbing leading into another portion of the Spacecraft that couldn't be accessed.

In the corner of this room was an even smaller compartment about the size of a shower. In fact, "the shower" became the popular name for this enclosure, since it even had an overhead tube mushrooming into a wide circular orifice about three feet in diameter. It was assumed this was the receiver module *Me* had previously discussed. It seemed possible that beings from Tau Ceti might someday come through this receiving pipe. The tank would need further investigation and discussion with *Me.* It was designated "the swimming pool" to compliment "the shower."

Rocky assigned Jae Lin and Brandon Fuller to continue with the encyclopedia data imaging and antiquated verbal download to Houston. It freed Rocky to investigate the rest of the Spacecraft. *Me* had stated the powerplant compartment was the largest area, but it couldn't be accessed from inside the primary computer room or the swimming pool area. The powerplant area would be left for the next Orion mission, scheduled for late September. It would have to be explored through a separate exterior entrance, if one could be found.

Thus, Rocky was left to explore the details of the original room. Earlier that day, Jae Lin had discovered a rectangular display of embedded panel lights – five rows of lights, each the size and shape of a pinhead – and Rocky was now investigating them again. The lights glowed bright in his infrared goggles, eleven lights in each row. All but the top row was fully lit.

"Jae, this is Rocky."

"Go ahead, Rocky.'

"Say, do you recall the alignment of those five rows of small indicator lights when we first saw them today?"

"Roger, those adjacent to the touch-pad display?"

"Yes, that's the area. There were five rows of lights. Is that correct?"

"Roger, that's correct. Eleven lights in each row except the first."

"And how many lights were lit in the top row?

"As I recall, five."

"That's what I recall too. What if I told you we've only got three lights in the row now – the left-most three.

Silence. Yuri was reclined in the right front seat of the Orion, next to Tannon, watching EZ try out his space legs. Leah was seated behind them.

Tannon looked over at Yuri. The Russian cosmonaut was thinking, and his lips were contorted and pushed outward.

There was still no answer from Jae.

"Rocky, this is Yuri. Maybe it's some kind of countdown indicator."

That generated silence from everyone monitoring the frequency. After a few more seconds passed, Rocky finally spoke.

"Well, let's think this through," said Rocky. "Anybody want to comment?"

Jae Lin broke into the conversation immediately.

"Commander, Jae here. Go ahead and hit your stopwatch. Maybe we can get an idea of the spacing of the lights. Another light might disappear before we leave."

"Thanks, Jae. I'll do it."

* * * * *

Rocky checked the light panel periodically, but nothing changed. The EVA was wrapping up now, and this time they would have to remove the modules used for pressurization, lighting, and other equipment. Then they would secure the hatch. This was the final visit of the mission.

"Okay, let's take our toys and go home," said Rocky, looking at his watch.

He unzipped the pouch on his right thigh, and removed a small plaque. It read: "We came in peace. Earth-sun. August 2016." He called the rest of the EVA team over to the hatch and attached the plaque to the curved wall with a spot of glue, a material specifically designed to prevent contamination of the Spacecraft. He patted the plaque lightly, and every EVA team member reached out and touched it after him. Then Rocky floated around to face the inside of the room. In a sincere tone, he simply said: "Thanks for your hospitality, *Me*."

Before leaving the sphere, Rocky floated back to the light panel. There were only two lights in the top row.

He hit his stopwatch and announced: "Okay, I have only two lights now, and my time hack shows slightly over eighteen minutes. Let's talk it over after we get out of here."

* * * * *

The Spacecraft hovered in the windows of the Orion as they had their after-dinner meeting. Houston had already decided the light panel, if it represented a countdown device, was extinguishing one light approximately every hour. But it wasn't that exact, considering the conditions of their brief stay. None of the lights were observed through their entire cycle, so their exact sequencing was impossible to determine.

"We don't have an accurate figure to go by," said Brandon Fuller. "Thinking this through, I'd say Houston's hour estimate is just about the very minimum. You could have a light cycle of 90 minutes and still see what we observed during the EVA period today. And that's only if the lights are at an equally spaced standard."

No one else wanted to touch it. They had argued about the lights for the past ten minutes, with several crewmembers clicking numbers into their pocket calculators. There were just too many permutations to be able to decide anything conclusive.

"Well, I agree with Brandon," said Yuri. "Let's say it's an hour between lights, and they're equally spaced. There are four rows of eleven lights left, plus the two that were still illuminated in the top row. If all five rows count down in sequence, that's forty-six hours. So the last light will go out in just under two days. If it's a ninety-minute interval, it'll be a bit less than three days."

They all had the same thoughts, and they all formulated the same answer. But Yuri bravely vocalized it: "Too bad we can't wait here a bit longer to see what happens."

Rocky was ready for it: "Of course, we all wish that, but we have no choice. You all know it."

"Don't you think it's a bit strange," said Yuri, "that *Me* doesn't have any response to all this? He certainly has been generous about almost everything else we ask."

"Yes," Tannon replied. "That's troubling, but I'm convinced *Me* doesn't understand it either. It's a panel not in *Me's* scope of control. Maybe it was intended only for our use."

This discussion wasn't headed anywhere that would promote anything but disharmony. Rocky wanted to end it. He spoke slowly.

"So our consensus, and probably the consensus of those on the ground, is this is a countdown timer. And whatever is going to happen will happen in a few days. We'll be back on the ground by then."

"And if it's a wormhole transition, we'll miss it," said Tannon.

Tannon immediately regretted his words. This was simply going over the same ground again. It proved nothing, and it wasn't his role to criticize what couldn't be undone. He sighed, realizing it was his place to come to the rescue of the mission commander. So he took the opportunity to continue.

"But if the Spacecraft blows up and takes everything within miles with it, we'll miss that too."

* * * * *

"**R**ocky, we've looked over all of these scenarios very thoroughly down here, and we want you and your crew to know there just isn't any alternative."

"We understand Houston. Thanks for taking a look at the environmental parameters again. It's gonna' be awfully hard cranking this ship up and leaving, with that countdown clock clicking away."

"We fully understand down here."

The voice sounded both frustrated and apologetic. The voice also sounded tired. But it paused only momentarily before continuing in a professional tone.

"Rocky, the size of this crew has really maxed out our environmental parameters at least as quickly as we expected. Oxygen requirements alone are right at the limit. We gotta' bring you home."

"Okay, we understand. Have you guys been looking at getting another Orion up here ahead of schedule, considering the situation?"

"We've been working on that one all night, but the projections so far don't look good. It's takes quite a while to get another SLS on the pad."

They all knew the situation. The worn voice trailed off. No other words were really necessary.

"Roger, Houston. We understand."

Rocky's tone now sounded much like the tired, apologetic voice on the ground. But he too remained professional.

"Okay, Houston. Encounter will be buttoning things up this morning. Lookin' forward to seeing you guys soon."

"Roger, Rocky. We want your crew to know the data downloads are starting to be released from here in summary format, with the results already very exciting to everybody on the communication circuit. You and your friends next door have contributed a lot to our planet's future."

"Our friends next door seem to be what we've been needing for a long time. I'm sure they know we'd wait this one out with them, if we could."

"Roger, Rocky. It's the same feeling down here. We sure wish them luck."

"Roger, Houston. But luck may not have a lot of meaning for them. In the meantime, let's get the reentry checklist started. We could use a shower."

Chapter 54

Sunday, August 21, 2016

Ominous Tools

Kelly looked up at Tannon from her hospital bed.

"The doctor says I can go home in a few days."

Tannon smiled down at her. She looked so fragile.

"You look so tall today," he said.

"That's just because I'm skinny."

She was smiling back. She was dying, and they both knew it. But they were grinning at each other, and the smiles weren't artificial.

Kelly's miniature audio player soothed the moment, tucked next to the breakfast tray, with soft Sinatra music flowing into the room over the small wireless speakers. She wiggled herself up higher on the slightly elevated bed.

"You've never looked this good before," said Kelly.

"You don't look any better to me than before. But it's because you've always been gorgeous."

"Oh, mush, mush," said Kelly.

"That's only for today. Wait 'til I get you home."

Kelly stopped smiling. She used her most monotone voice:

"This isn't good. You know that."

Tannon's smile disappeared, too, replaced by a gentle nod and just a few words.

"I know that, Kell."

"What else do you know? Have you talked with my doctors?"

"No, but I talked to the nursing station. I know there's hope."

"They said that?" Kelly turned her face away from him.

"No, they just said you probably could go home in a few days, and I like that."

She turned back to him, and her eyes glinted with anger or maybe fear.

"Tannon, you've got to be realistic. I'm afraid you don't understand this."

"I think I understand, Kell. It's just that there's more hope around this world these days."

"Well, I'm glad the world is so fuckin' thrilled."

She was angry and frightened. And she looked so puny in her drab hospital gown.

"I've been thinking a lot about things lately," said Tannon. "That's to be expected after being in space. I never thought I would be up there. But there I was. And there are all of these coincidences all over the place. It can't be unplanned."

"Tannon, what the hell are you talking about?"

She was angry, but momentarily less frightened, and returning to her normal self.

"Well, this is a big moment in history, and I haven't quite figured out why I'm a part of it. This Spacecraft has some tremendous powers, and it's not very understandable why they came here."

"Understandable? None of it is understandable. I suppose you think this Spacecraft can consciously change the course of destiny, as well as read minds."

"No, as a matter of fact, I don't think it can consciously change things. But it does appear things are being reordered a bit, all over the place."

"I'm happy for the world," said Kelly with a sarcastic flatness.

She slid back down in her bed. The plastic intravenous tubing twisted into an extra coil by her arm, and she was crushing it. Tannon reached toward her and straightened the tube.

"Sis, I'm very disturbed by your condition, but I've got to believe there's hope. So do you."

"It's called endometrial cancer, Tannon. A rather ominous name."

"Then we'll have to fight it with some rather ominous tools."

Kelly was smiling again, but her voice cracked when she spoke.

"Most of those ominous tools have already been used up, Brother."

"Well, let's see what a little more love will do."

* * * * *

If the two-day limit was accurate, the lights should be nearly extinguished. The one-hour-per-light estimate indicated the zero point was only a few hours away. News reports bubbled with information and editorials about the Encounter Team's visit to the Spacecraft, but the countdown lights didn't get top billing. There wasn't anything these lights could do in the eyes of the world except cause anxiety. And there was too much hope these days to be bothered by needless tension.

The eyes of the world were focused on celebration rather than concern. The encyclopedia downloads were a major revelation. The stock markets shot upward all over the world. In the alien encyclopedia, still being digested by scientists worldwide, were breakthroughs unlike anything previously discovered in such a short period of time. NASA was releasing all the data in raw format, but that was taking some time. It had to be categorized for transmission to the professionals who could best interpret it. English was the language selected by the Spacecraft, and that made it particularly easy for NASA to deal with, although alien mathematical formulae utilized many symbols not previously encountered. The nuclear energy transcriptions, regardless of some of the unexplained calculations, were immediately interpretable by physicists and engineers at the basic level, and they all involved peaceful harnessing of the atom.

The nuclear energy data was exemplary of the handling of potentially dangerous topics. The information on a variety of topics had been filtered by the Spacecraft to assure technical mysteries were solved where they could best serve mankind. Details that might prove destructive were clearly omitted. The public understood this, and it added to the aura of optimism taking hold of the earth – at least it took hold of most of the earth.

Another Orion mission was scheduled for launch on September 27th. The public embraced NASA as it prepared for further exploration of the Spacecraft. The newspapers had more good news on the front page than anyone ever remembered.

Tannon was no longer in communication with *Me.* His transmitted email came back: "Mailbox Not Found." But it didn't trouble him. He had experienced more than he could have ever hoped. He was grateful. And he prayed the countdown clock wasn't an omen.

* * * * *

Subject: No Subject
Date: 8/22/2016 2:51 pm
From: Me@cyberberth.com
To: tbessimer@mtsac.edu

There has been an accident. The receiver module activated at 1:07 pm, your time. An explosion destroyed the entire receiver room, and there has been extensive damage to the rest of the ship, including the powerplant. Our understanding of this situation is poor, but the transfer from our home planet was totally unsuccessful. No material was retained by our receiver – but what energy! We are running repair programs now, but it is not clear whether we will be able to adequately control the damage.

Our standing procedure, if damage of this magnitude occurs, is to proceed home. If we are able to proceed, it will be necessary to refuel using the hydrogen source of Jupiter. Current projections show our extensive damage may prohibit us from returning home at all. If we are able to depart, we will accumulate as much additional data as possible before leaving earth's orbit. We hope to launch for Jupiter in approximately four weeks. It will take that long to fix this.

Please advise NASA of this situation. The Me2 connection is purposely disabled. We are unable to accept further visits from the Orion.

It was great meeting you and EZ.

- Me

* * * * *

It was their first day home in San Dimas. Closing out their life in Houston had taken nearly a week. It was with mixed emotions that they left Texas, but their first evening in California was a time of muted celebration. Kelly wasn't feeling well enough to leave the house, so Tannon arranged the delivery of pizza, including Kelly's preferred topping – pineapple. They watched one of her favorite movies from their DVD collection, and ate their pizza. It was a fuzzy, warm evening.

* * * * *

"Tannon, I'm sorry, but I really don't have anything else available from here," said NASA Administrator David Graham. "There's limited evidence of external damage to the Spacecraft detectable by our imaging equipment."

"Well what are you able to see?" asked Tannon.

"Really not much at all. The exact nature of the damage can't be determined, but the symmetry of the sphere has been disturbed on one side by a protrusion extending outward by approximately ten meters along a line running nearly seventy meters across the Spacecraft."

"I assume you're talking about military imaging equipment."

"Yes, NASA really has nothing that compares to the Air Force. But even their satellites can't detect the details of the damage. It's complicated by the fact that the Spacecraft's rotation rate has picked back up to one revolution every eight minutes."

"Thanks, Dr. Graham. I appreciate being kept informed."

"Let us know anything you hear from *Me*. In the meantime, we're making progress in pushing the next Orion mission up a bit. But it really isn't possible to get back into orbit for several more weeks, no matter how hard we try. It's just the nature of the beast, considering this is still a test program. And we certainly won't launch unless *Me* approves it."

"I understand. And I promise to let you know immediately if there is any further email. I keep trying to transmit to *Me*, but nothing is coming back. I'm not even receiving the 'Mailbox Not Found' response any more."

"Maybe they're simply too busy," said the Administrator.

* * * * *

Kelly rested on the sofa. She was spread out to her full length, dressed in her nightshirt and soft white socks. She was looking particularly peaked today, white in her face, arms, and legs.

"Feel like going flying?" said Tannon.

"Oh, that would be great. Let's see – there's this girl on her deathbed, but she used to know how to fly. And then there's this airplane that hasn't moved in at least three months. And, oh, yeah, there's also this guy without a valid FAA medical certificate. Yes, it sounds like we should go flying."

"You're right. Maybe we should."

Kelly reached for her water bottle. She took a swig and spoke slowly.

"Maybe we should get serious."

Tannon replied immediately.

"I'm not sure that's the best medicine. Nobody says we have to take all of this seriously."

"You're right, Brother. There's no need to start now. You know what?"

"What, Kell?"

"I'm not going to get any better, but I still have some pretty good days now and then. So when the next good one hits, let's try flying. It's always been amazing medicine."

Chapter 55

Tuesday, August 30, 2016

They

One of the largest files downloaded by the Encounter Team continued to perplex NASA. For nearly a full week, experts tried to decipher it, but it appeared to be completely unreadable. Its appearance was that of text, but the format was interspersed with a variety of symbols. Most of the experts thought it was a graphics file encoded in textual format.

On the sixth day after the capsule's return to earth, NASA called in commercial computer experts and they too were baffled. No progress was made until the beginning of the second week, when it was determined these were highly compressed graphical images of a type totally unknown. The best minds in the world were now on the problem, brought in from seven different countries and given access to a copy of the troublesome file. Each group of experts interpreting the encyclopedia data worked independently, but consulted at a joint meeting at the end of every day.

On August 30th, the breakthrough that was needed finally occurred. Using graphical software reserved for advanced DNA research, the computer research group under the guidance of a Swedish team of biochemists found a compression link similar to those used in molecular data transfer. The data was quickly uncompressed, providing images exceeding 2 gigabytes each. It was immediately evident these weren't molecular images. They were realistic 3-dimensional pictures, more like intricate paintings. Each image contained a wide spectrum of colors.

They were like the precious oil paintings of the earth's master painters. And like these paintings, the images were hauntingly lifelike, even more so than mere photographs. They had depth, amazing clarity, intricate detail, and enormous beauty. One-by-one, NASA released them to the public. Each evening's television news highlighted one or more of the paintings. The entire world tuned in to watch.

The first painting released to the public was of an enormous sea. The waves were almost universally estimated at a height of at least 100 feet, even though there was absolutely nothing in the image to provide scale. The waves were huge, and for that there was no argument. A brief chunk of shoreline was visible in the corner of this image, and there was no sign of life. But the sea could be seen roaring and splashing in short amplitude waves. The water was a pristine blue, and the sky nearly black with a faint magenta glow. And there was a large moon in the sky, larger in perspective than the earth's own moon. The moonlight scattered and reflected in an unearthly way on the sea. There was life in that water. This was immediately evident to everyone who analyzed the image – yet the painting showed no sign of life.

The second released "painting" was the first of many that showed a setting that would dominate the news for weeks to come. It showed a similar sea, this time in bright daylight. And at the tops of the waves, breaking clear into the gulf between one wave and another, were fish. They were unlike any fish known on earth, but their shape was unmistakable. These fish seemed to be standing on their tails just forward of the wave crests. They were too numerous and too organized to be anything except posed for this painting. The fish, estimated as 10 feet tall, were in tight formation. The bodies were all moderately curved, as they prepared to leap from their waves. Their eyes were huge turquoise globes, all wide open and focused on the viewer. These were eyes of intelligence – eyes of hope.

This image was discussed throughout the world as the most remarkable of all eighty-three paintings. This one was immediately dubbed "The Life Recording," and it retained that name throughout history. No other painting was discussed more. No other painting was reproduced in the quantities of this one, and no other painting received as much publicity.

In the upper corner of this particular image was a large-diameter star. But it wasn't so intense as to be restrictive to direct observation. It was bright yellow, with irregular black spots hugging its equator. This star beamed bright enough to cast distinct shadows of the wave crests on the troughs of the sea. And the shadows of the huge fish were visible on the sea as well. This was a view of the star Tau Ceti from the perspective of another planet. From the perspective of other intelligent living beings.

* * * * *

Subject: File Attached
Date: 8/30/2016 4:26 pm
From: Me@cyberberth.com
To: tbessimer@mtsac.edu

Tannon,

I've finally given in to your technology. There is a short graphic file attached to this message. It's a molecular diagram of an angiogenesis inhibitor that will help your species cure endometrial cancer.

Goodbye to all. Tell EZ his pictures came out great.

- Me

* * * * *

In the aftermath of the deciphered paintings, the earth continued to evolve. It was an evolution vastly enhanced by contact with alien intelligent life. The life forms were fish-like creatures with characteristics not completely foreign to those on earth. In every corner of our planet, experts and amateurs alike studied these paintings. Each drew their own conclusions, but everyone agreed that within the eyes of these fish, there was both intelligence and compassion. These were huge penetrating eyes. And the bodies of these creatures were contoured differently than the fish of earth. Each creature could be distinguished from the other by slight variations on their faces and bodies. Small crevasses and differences of color distinguished each individual's contours from the other. But they really weren't fish, and they demanded a new name. At first they were called the "Fish of Tau Ceti" but they were neither fish nor creatures of a star.

Over time, as the full story of the establishment of Tannon's contact with *Me* became well documented among the nations of the world, these creatures received a new name. And it stuck. They were simply called "They."

Another technically exciting painting revealed the only exclusive land-view. In this painting, the land adaptation of the beings was revealed. Their lower fins were fully retracted into their bodies, and small arm-like protrusions were clearly visible. The forty-two creatures depicted in this painting were huddled in a group, their backs to the viewer. In front of them was a huge technological structure bearing close resemblance to the towering rocket structures of Cape Canaveral. The structure itself was metallic-looking, bright white – reflecting the intense light of a clear day. The entire view was unique in comparison to the other paintings. It was the only painting focusing directly on technology, and the only one highlighting land rather than water. All of the other images seemed to focus clearly on life and nature – and, of course, the sea. Thus, it was determined that the moment posed in this painting was considered unique and historic to these beings. It became known as "The Launch."

All eighty-three paintings were studied in intricate detail. These images were reproduced worldwide and displayed in public buildings, commercial businesses, and homes. Most families requested the coffee-table edition of a free government publication that nearly all countries felt was appropriate use for their national budgets. Some individuals purchased expensive deluxe editions that revealed more of the stark detail of the 3-D paintings.

Tannon and Kelly displayed the deluxe edition of "The Launch" on the wall of their living room. It was mounted just above the sofa where an afghan marked EZ's newest sleeping spot. The golden cat frequented the dark green blanket, consistently cuddled near this painting. EZ could often be found, wrapped in a ball, purring for hours in this special spot in the Bessimer household.

But there was only one set of original paintings. Each reprinting of the computer file image lost a little bit of the original detail, and detail was substantially lost when viewed on a computer monitor. This was, of course, unheard of for digital files, but it was true of these amazingly realistic paintings. Computer experts argued about how this could be. The original files, with their powerful imagery, had been printed in a wide variety of format. But every time they were transmitted and printed again, some detail disappeared. The original prints were displayed in the Smithsonian Museum in Washington, DC.

When visitors poured into Washington from around the world in unrelenting streams to view the original paintings, it became evident the city couldn't handle this unexpected traffic of humanity on a continuous basis. The airports were jammed and the highways clogged with pilgrims from everywhere. Finally, after spending a month attempting to adapt to this chaos, NASA arranged to have the paintings split into eleven separate groups. One group remained in Washington, and the other 10 sets of paintings were transferred to some of the world's greatest museums. Still the visitors came, at all eleven locations, in unending throngs. Washington remained the biggest traffic jam of all, since it retained "The Life Recording" and "The Launch."

The world was a place of celebration that seemed to go on endlessly. It was a celebration of peace and a celebration of hope. The stock markets of the world soared, and then leveled off with moderate growth. Economists talked of an unprecedented bubble that was sure to burst.

The transferred data files continued to make the headlines each day, as experts in a variety of fields found another bit of information that helped complete the puzzles of technology. It was obvious "They" had provided specific information to improve the quality of life on earth, but never did it appear that all of life's challenges were being solved. Even in the areas of advanced technologies, mysteries still remained. The extraction of nuclear fusion energy, battled by the earth's scientists for decades, was solved in a few simple textual statements. It was enough to provide the needed energy source of the century. But energy sources lying beyond that, obviously within the parameters of the alien technology, weren't documented at all. Cures for many diseases were quickly prescribed, but the extension of life beyond the eradication of major disease wasn't addressed. Most people believed the Spacecraft knew much more but selectively withheld the information. There were revelations in the mere fact that not all was revealed. Science and society would have challenges on this planet forever. Apparently, "They" felt this is the way it should be.

Only one major issue marred the worldwide celebration. The Spacecraft remained in orbit above the earth, and it was crippled. There was almost no information available regarding the status of the Spacecraft, but many believed it would be visited once again by the Orion. That mission had been accelerated as much as possible but still wasn't scheduled for launch until mid-September. Everyone feared another visit by the Orion would be a visit to a dead Spacecraft, and no one looked forward to the funeral.

And so, each night, the beings of earth looked up – hoping and praying. They scanned the skies from their cities, from the deserts, and on ships upon the oceans. They looked upward, hoping to see the fire of the Spacecraft as it moved outward from its orbit around the earth. They looked upward, praying the Spacecraft would disappear homeward on a pillar of light. They looked upward with hope. But there was no light.

Chapter 56

Home Planet

MQ and SJ swam slowly in a tight circle, side-by-side, gently brushing against each other. They moved in a waltz within the sea, hearing the sound of the ocean against their bodies. It was always dark at this depth, and there was relative solitude in all directions. But in the near-distance they felt the voices of others. This world was getting very crowded, and there were no longer many places for complete solitude.

"It is nearly dark in the sky above," said MQ. "The stars will be shining soon. Shining soon."

"Yes, MQ. The darkness comes. And it scares me. I've always loved the darkness, until now. Until now."

"It will pass. Will pass."

The flexing of MQ's tail slowed, and the circle widened. The pace slowed, and SJ followed MQ. Their bodies touched just as lightly as before. At this close distance, MQ felt SJ's voice clearly, and the sound was tender.

"Yes, it will pass, but we have lost many. Too many. Too many."

SJ's voice felt dispirited, but always tender.

"Even the Great Minds are new to this," said MQ. "We are young explorers in a vast universe. Those who went were volunteers, and they died so we may advance further next time. Next time."

"Another reason to leave this watery place. I love it here. And I hate it. Hate it."

"Yes, SJ. We must leave, and we will. We are almost there, longer each time. To develop our technologies, we need the land. Already the Great Minds live there, almost permanently. They take the sea with them. With them."

MQ felt SJ start to question the details of the accident, but her voice withdrew the thoughts before they registered. Maybe she didn't want to know the details. But her mind was intelligent, and she needed to know more.

"We don't even know what world they chose," said SJ. "But in time, we'll understand. I hope it's a world with both sea and land. We could learn from that. Creatures can leave the sea, forever. I'm sure of it. It is possible. Is possible."

"Possible, yes. Possible, yes."

MQ felt SJ's voice begin again and then stop. He hadn't missed the words. The words were stopped on purpose. Then SJ spoke in a lilting tone for the first time this evening.

"Let us go up. I need the air. We'll live in the air soon. And it won't be just for a short time, only to return to this sea. This sea."

MQ completed one more circle. And then he broke the widening waltz and started upward. His pace wasn't rushed. His pace wasn't desperate. And SJ followed every move. They swam upward in a tight formation. Upward, upward. MQ felt SJ's unspoken words. She echoed throughout him as they swam up through the dark sea.

"Yes, SJ. Let us go up. Let us go up to break through those waves into the night. Into the air. And we shall see the stars. The stars."

Chapter 57

Saturday, September 17, 2016

Outbound

"**Y**ou've got it," said Tannon from the left seat of the Piper Arrow.

Kelly sat up a bit straighter in her seat and took the control wheel in her right hand. She eased her grip and flew as she always did, with her fingertips.

Tannon reached down and untied his hiking boots. These oversized boots were a tight fit in the confined channels of the rudder pedals, and now his feet were released from restraint, flat on the floor while Kelly controlled the airplane. When he slipped the laces loose, his feet seemed to expand in a feeling of relaxation. Before landing, in the interest of safety, he'd be sure to tie his boots again.

"Haven't done an instrument approach in a while," said Kelly.

"It's like riding a bicycle," said Tannon, his voice catching a raspy moment.

"Easy for you to say. Okay, I've got the number one VOR tuned to Gaviota, with the HSI set at 279. Piece of cake."

The sun was well below the horizon, and the golden glow just to the left of the nose was almost gone. A hint of twilight remained in the west. The Pacific Ocean spread leftward from the windshield towards the wingtip.

Ventura County slipped by underneath them, still covered by beautiful houses with large swimming pools. Homeowners were no longer able to operate old-style pools because of the energy inefficiency of their pumps and heaters, but new technology had come to the rescue. When it was something that important, engineers were always standing by to make quantum leaps.

"You're in VOR mode," said Tannon. "And the GPS is backing us up with Zacks Intersection straight ahead, four miles."

"It checks against the DME," said Kelly. She eased the control wheel to the left to counteract the slight wind drift. "We're cleared for the VOR Runway 25 approach, so I'll be leaving 2100 feet at Zacks. Would you check that GPS alert for me?"

Tannon punched the blinking ALRT button in front of him, so it stopped blinking and burned steady. In the LED display the message appeared: "Fly fast, friends. Remember Me."

Almost directly ahead of the aircraft, just above the golden glow of the departed sun, a bright star shimmered low in the sky, climbing rapidly from the Pacific horizon. And as it climbed, it grew even brighter, until it was the brightest object in the entire evening sky.

M39 open cluster in Cygnus, 800 light years away
Photo from WIYN 0.9-meter telescope at Kitt Peak, Arizona

About the Author

From 1980 to 2005, Wayne Lutz was Chairman of the Aeronautics Department at Mount San Antonio College in Los Angeles. He led the college's Flying Team to championships as Top Community College in the United States seven times. He has also served 20 years as a U.S. Air Force C-130 aircraft maintenance officer. His educational background includes a B.S. degree in physics from the University of Buffalo and an M.S. in systems management from the University of Southern California.

The author is a flight instructor with 7000 hours of flying experience. For the past three decades, he has spent summers in Canada, exploring remote regions in his Piper Arrow, camping next to his airplane. The author resides in a floating cabin on Canada's Powell Lake and in a city-folk condo in Bellingham WA. His writing genres include regional Canadian publications and science fiction.

www.ingramcontent.com/pod-product-compliance
Lightning Source LLC
Chambersburg PA
CBHW071230190726
48292CB00007B/2213